Day Star Rising

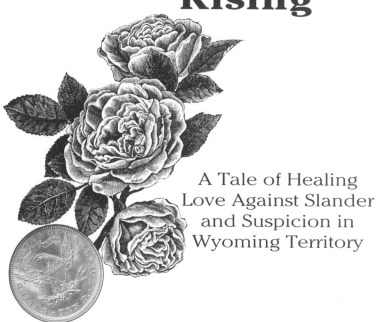

A Tale of Healing
Love Against Slander
and Suspicion in
Wyoming Territory

by Louise Lenahan Wallace

OGDEN PUBLICATIONS INC.
Topeka, Kansas

ISBN 0-941678-69-5
First printing, August 2001
Printed and bound in the United States of America

Fireside Library

Other books by OGDEN PUBLICATIONS

For more information about Ogden Publications titles,
or to place an order, please call:
(800) 678-4883

Dedication

To my daughters,
Dawn and Hope —
You were always there for me.
Love,
Mom

Day Star Rising

By Louise Lenahan Wallace

Take heed, as unto a light
*   that shineth in a dark place,*
Until the day dawn,
*   and the day star arise in your hearts*
*   — 2 Peter 1:19*

Prologue
1887

In the gray light of pre-dawn, Hannah Clayton stirred restlessly, her work-wearied body, even on the fringe of wakefulness, instinctively seeking the edge of the bed farthest away from Luke sprawled behind her. The sound that had penetrated her sleep came again. In the next room, 17-month-old Micah had started his baby murmurings — soft enough for the moment, but a firebell in full voice for his three brothers who shared the room with him.

A sigh started to escape her, but broke off before it had a chance to become reality. She had long ago learned that even such a small indulgence could attract Luke's attention. Slowly, carefully, soundlessly — all achieved from much practice — she slid out of bed. If she could get to Micah before he woke the others ...

In the act of reaching for her shawl to pull around her nightdress, her hand froze.

Luke's side of the bed was empty.

More puzzled than alarmed — Luke was not an "up before the sun" riser by any stretch of the imagination — Hannah drew the wrap around her tall, slender figure and

1

pulled free the hair caught between her nightdress and the shawl. Leaving the blue-black mass to cascade down her back, she started to open the bedroom door but paused as she saw the crack of light at the bottom. Weary resignation replaced the puzzlement in her green eyes. *Luke was in the kitchen, then. Probably drinking.* She hesitated, but Micah's murmurings were becoming insistent. She'd best get him before Luke became annoyed.

Flinching at the scraping sound, she pulled open the door. The light from the lamp on the kitchen worktable struck her squarely in the eyes, causing her to blink before she saw the room was empty, and that the note propped against the base of the lamp had her name scrawled across it in Luke's bold, unmistakable handwriting. She stared, motionless. Having lived with Luke long enough to know the only predictable thing about him was his unpredictability, she felt numbness creep into her veins.

She stared at the note propped against the lamp, and dreadful certainty began to replace the numbness. Slowly, she reached for the paper and unfolded it. The contents were brief. They were also brutally direct.

Dear Hannah,
I've left to find the men responsible for the raid on the ranch. I admit I talked in town that day, but I hadn't meant no harm. I just hoped that by spreadin' the word the Arrow A wasn't broke like every other place else, I'd find somebody interested in helpin' Pa build up the ranch like he'd always dreamed about.
I know you never really thought I was much of a man,

2

Day Star Rising

but when I return with the guilty men, maybe you'll see
how unfair you've been all this time and think a little
more kindly of me.

Luke

Ignoring Micah's clamoring, she yanked open the outside door. Dawn had not yet advanced beyond gray indistinctness. Heedless of her bare feet, she ran down the steps and across the dusty yard to the corrals. Luke's horse and saddle were gone.

Clutching her shawl against the tugging breeze, she stared wildly around at the gray-blurred outbuildings, frantically seeking a glimpse of his tall, shoulder-stooped figure, his red hair and beard.

"Luke," she whispered. "Oh, Luke ..." The dawn breeze caught her words and whisked them around the empty ranchyard.

As it stirred the edges of the note still clutched in her hand, the wind brought her the voices of her little boys — 5-year old Jeremy, the eldest, dark-haired as herself; the three youngest, Isaac, Sam and Micah as red-haired and freckled as their father. Tumbling down the steps, they called eagerly to her.

Still dazed by unreality, she instinctively started toward her sons, and the breeze again whipped at the edges of her shawl, flinging her hair behind her.

The last of the engulfing numbness receded as she crossed the lightening ranchyard, as barren of Luke's presence as if he had never been there before ... and would never be again, as their small sons, eager for breakfast, rushed to meet her.

3

One

Wind and rain had weathered the long, low-roofed ranch house to silver-gray. The front yard, bounded only by the porch and two hitchracks, reached westward to the limitless plains shimmering golden-green in the heat of the August day. To the rear of the house, a small creek fringed with willows and cottonwoods edged a grassy knoll. Three white-painted crosses crowned the low incline. The grave the smaller marker guarded was grass grown, but the earth of the other two mounds was raw and glaring. Cottonwoods and poplars bordered the house and outbuildings close enough to provide shade, but not close enough to conceal. Tied to porch post, hitching rail and tree, an assortment of horses stood heavy-eyed. They shifted stance only enough to stomp at flies that pestered beyond patience or to flick their ears as an occasional burst of laughter and voices raised in merriment floated out upon the windy morning air.

The front door of the house suddenly jerked open, startling the horses, shattering the calm. It jarred shut as Will Braden, wearing his Sunday best, jammed his wide-brimmed cowman's hat onto his coal-dark hair and strode across the porch. Every inch of his lean, six-foot frame stiff with anger, black eyes smoldering with resentment, he paused by the top step and abruptly slammed his open palm against the support post with such force that the wood shivered. Ignoring the pain shooting up his elbow, he leaned his arm against the pillar.

He stood thus, staring unseeing across the drying grassland until the horse nearest him sneezed in his face, effectively breaking his reverie.

"Why, you ... " Will's inaccurate, but heartfelt comment about the horse's ancestry didn't faze the gelding at all. He merely sneezed again.

The horse's aim had been uncannily exact both times. Because he refused to open his mouth and give the animal a third chance, Will's reply was mumbled, furious and short.

He began to sleeve the mess from his face, but stopped as he realized he had his good suit on. He blindly reached into his pocket for his bandanna. As he pulled it out, he heard a musical clink and opened his eyes in time to see his "lucky" ten-dollar gold piece roll off the step and into the waiting arms of the full-blooming rosebush beside the porch.

"Oh, f'r ... " Will's third, and most creative, comment snapped off as a murmur of voices and another burst of laughter from behind the front door caused him to start and cover the steps to the ground in one long-legged leap.

Abandoning his gold piece to the thorny clutches of the rosebush, he bolted around the south corner of the house as the front door opened. The voices, muffled before, drifted only too clearly to him.

"... nice weddin'. But you know, Catty, I sure never would of thought ol' Matt'd up and marry Eve."

"Now, Aaron, there's nothing wrong with them marrying, and you know it."

"Just seems kind of odd to think of, them bein' raised together all those years and Eve all set to marry Will Braden like she was. Then all of a sudden, she up and throws poor old Will over and marries Matt — his best friend and all."

"Aaron Grandler, Matt's my brother, and I won't have you talking against him and Eve." Catty's voice came sharply. "There's been hurt and sorrow enough. If they can find some happiness together, let them."

Aaron's voice mirrored his astonishment. "I wasn't talkin' against 'em, darlin'. I was just sayin' how it looks to other folks ..."

The voices faded as Will entered the passageway between the carriage house and the kitchen. But Aaron's words, shouting inside his head, echoed off the walls and kept impish pace with his pounding feet. Bitterness souring his throat, Will sought out his mount, Eagle, tied among several others at the rear hitchrack. In spite of his haste, he remembered to tighten the cinch before he flung himself into the saddle. *That would really put the cork in the bottle for today — to go sailing over my horse's tail, getting myself dusted fine as any greener.* Adept as he was at finding humor in unlikely situations, he found none in contemplating this prospect.

He urged the chestnut away from the house at a wild gallop, but the gelding's flying hooves could no more outrun Will's humiliation and resentment than his own feet had been able to earlier.

Aaron's voice fled with him, jeering with the rhythm of the hooves. "... kind of odd ... best friend and all ... poor old

Will! Set to marry him ... throws him over ... throws him over ... *throws him over ...*"

Will gritted his teeth against the burning lash of unasked-for pity and dug his heels into Eagle's sides. The chestnut's mane and tail streamed in the wind of their passing, but his speed could not put the truth of those blunt words out of reach.

The countryside whirled by. Trees, rocks and an indignant jackrabbit bounding away were only a blur. Will had sense enough, barely, to swerve to avoid the prairie dog town that lay ahead — not knowing or caring that its inhabitants scolded him shrilly until he was indistinct in the distance.

He would gladly have ridden on and on across the range into eternity if he could. But a sudden slap of lather across his cheek brought him to appalled realization of Eagle's heaving sides and sweat-soaked flanks.

Loosing a curse at his own thoughtlessness, he slowed the animal, giving him time to cool before he dismounted. The chestnut was trembling with exhaustion, head and tail drooping. Yanking off the saddle, Will rubbed him down with the blanket, walked him a bit more, and then rubbed him down again. All the time he spoke, apologizing, knowing his voice helped soothe his companion. "Sorry, ol' Boy. Shouldn't take it out on you. You'd of run yourself into the ground just 'cause I was sayin' to."

Anxiously, Will stroked the velvet muzzle, continuing to pet and praise him while rubbing him down with handfuls of yellowing grass. At last certain Eagle had come to no harm, he heaved a sigh of relief. Yanking off his hat, he pushed rope-callused fingers through his sweat-damped, dark hair.

He walked slowly across the plains, this time leading

Eagle. With no idea how long he wandered, he finally became aware that his feet, pinched by his tight Sunday boots, were rubbing painfully. Catching sight of a small creek to the west, he led the gelding over, off-saddled and let him drink, afterward ground-tying him so he could graze. Eagle snatched at the first mouthfuls with greedy haste before he settled to a contented chomping.

Sitting on the low bank, Will pulled off his boots and socks and thrust his burning feet into the sun-and-leaf dappled water. After the first, brain-numbing shock, he closed his eyes gratefully and let his mind go blessedly blank. But it would not stay so. Images intruded, taunting him. Restlessly fingering the stones beside him, he picked out a flat pebble, regarded it grimly, and shied it across the creek. It sank on the first bounce.

Unbelieving, he snatched up three more stones, snapped them in rapid succession and watched them sink. Furious, he stood to fling a fifth one, and belatedly realized how foolish he would look to a casual passerby — standing shin-deep in the creek, pant legs rolled to his knees, hairy legs and bare toes protruding below, venting his anger with a bunch of stupid pebbles! He'd already shown himself a master hand at playing the fool today; he couldn't believe he was chalking up a still bigger count.

Harmlessly tossing the remaining pebbles aside, he slowly resumed his seat. Elbows on knees, chin on fist, he sat long, brooding, staring across the little creek and the grassland stretching to the limitless horizon beyond.

Realization that his surroundings were familiar finally dawned.

He raised his head. The creek, sunk summer-dry shallow,

chuckled over its rocky bed. Wind, fanning his cheek and ear, flattened through the dying grass and whispered around the willows edging the water. All else, in all directions, was utter stillness.

Pulling his feet out of the water and shaking them dry, he gingerly drew on his socks and boots. Pushing up, he searched through the grass, working slowly away from the creek boundary.

He found them by the simple process of tripping over them.

The pile of stones, crumbling, was unrecognizable for the chimney it had once been. And only a few foundation rocks, weed-hidden, remained. He paused, and then paced a few steps eastward.

The graves were there, the crosses — like the foundation stones — grass grown.

Stephen Jamison   *Amanda Jamison*
1838–1865   *1840–1865*

A bouquet of daisies lay at the base of each marker. Someone — Matt or Catty most likely — had placed them there recently, for they were only slightly wilted.

Will gazed at the graves of Matt's parents. They had died in an Indian raid when Matt was three and Catty only a few months old. Ben Clayton, the Jamisons' nearest neighbor, had found the children huddled in the brush beside the creek and had taken them home to the Arrow A. For more than twenty years, Ben and Anne Clayton had reared Matt and Catty as and with their own children — Jason, Luke and Eve. Now Ben and Anne were two months dead, themselves victims of an outlaw raid on the Arrow A.

Will knew he should feel sympathy for Matt, for all of them. But for the first time in his lifelong association with the Clayton family, his heart refused.

Who could have foreseen that night of tragedy and violence 22 years before would so dismally affect his own life this day?

The wind blew around the crosses, ruffled the daisy petals and tugged past Will in its headlong rush across the grassy plains.

But it brought him no answer.

When Will finally turned homeward, remorse made him keep the gelding to a steady pace, but his torment had in no way lessened. All the way back, memory mocked him. Eve Clayton, her hair flame-bright above the green dress she wore, dancing in his arms last summer, the top of her head barely reaching his chin as they circled the floor ... in the fall, saying she'd be his wife ... telling him just before their April wedding day she couldn't marry him after all ... standing beside tall, dark-haired Matt a few hours ago, a wreath of creamy roses in her red-gold hair ... Matt, campfire-smoke gray eyes locked on her as he gave her his vows ... Eve's deep blue eyes raised to Matt alone, as she spoke the words that sealed her future to his forever, leaving Will ... *No!*

Will's fist clenched on the reins. Only by supreme effort, he kept from digging his heels into Eagle once more. *What use to dwell on it? It's over and done now, and best put behind quick.* Easy instructions to give himself ... impossible orders to follow.

The sun was setting in a glory of gold and crimson when, wearily, he turned Eagle into Jason and Becky Clayton's Jagged J corral. He would have gone straight to the bunkhouse, but Jason was hailing him from the back steps of the house.

Jason Clayton, oldest son of Ben and Anne, with auburn hair and brown eyes like his mother, broad shouldered like his father, had in these last weeks taken the burden of responsibility Ben Clayton had always before carried. The weight of it was plain in the new lines etched into his face, in the new gravity of his voice and eyes. Brother of Luke and Eve, he had been Will's boss since Will had come from Ben and Anne's Arrow A ranch to work here after Eve had told him she couldn't marry him. Much as he wanted to, Will could not ignore Jason's summons, so he turned toward him.

"Becky's got supper on the table. Been keepin' it hot till you got here." It was his only comment on Will's prolonged absence.

Will realized he had eaten nothing since the wedding breakfast that morning and had no clear recollection of having eaten much then. He wasn't hungry even now, but to refuse would only bring unwanted attention to his feelings. That he couldn't have stomached. He gestured to the washbasin. "I'd best clean up first." Jason nodded and returned to the house.

With the few moments' respite gained, Will made a fierce effort to get hold of himself. He straightened his tie and futilely tried to smooth the wrinkles and horse hairs from his wool suit. *Keep your pride*, he scolded himself sarcastically. *It's just about all you've got left*. Yanking off his hat, he thrust his head savagely into the washbasin and withdrew, sputtering and dripping, to reach for the flour-sack towel.

Day Star Rising

At the table, Will pulled out the chair he generally occupied between Jared and Reuben, Jason and Becky's two oldest boys. This meal the boys were out with the herd, waiting for their father and Will to finish eating and ride out to relieve them on watch. Shorthanded as the men were, the youngsters' filling in at odd times such as this was a large help.

The wedding today had disrupted the normal schedule. They were all going to have to work around Matt's temporary absence. That included Will and Jason pulling the 7 p.m.-to-midnight watch this night, and Aaron Grandler, who was married to Matt's sister, Catty, and Dan Mackley, Matt's foreman at the Arrow A, handling the midnight-to-5 shift.

Will dropped into his chair as Jason began to give thanks for the food they were about to eat. "Bless all our loved ones, both here present and those who are here in spirit and thought. Guide the work of our hands that it may be pleasin' unto You."

When he had finished, Becky thumped pieces of fried chicken onto the plates of Patience and Seth, the younger children. Short and rounded, with soft, brown hair, Becky, habitually rosy-cheeked, was now frankly flushed with indignation, her usually merry blue eyes shooting wrathful sparks. "I just don't understand how Luke could do such a thing!" she spat.

"He's my brother, but so help me God, if I ever lay eyes on him again, I'll kill him," Jason said fiercely. His eyes squarely met the sudden fear in Becky's. "I mean it, Beck. I swear to God."

Becky's grip tightened on the handle of the coffeepot as she stared at the flat determination on her husband's face. They had been married 12 years. She knew, as fear clutched at her with chilly fingers, that Jason meant every word. He would kill Luke, his own flesh and blood, if he ever saw him again.

Soul-sore as Will was, he felt numb relief that he didn't have their problem. Luke had been indirectly responsible for the murders of Ben and Anne Clayton, and had just this morning deserted his wife, Hannah, and their four small sons, supposedly to find the killers. Where he had gone, when he would be back — if ever — no one could say. Looking at Jason's furious face, Will thought, *It better be a long, long time before Luke shows himself around the family, seeing as Aaron and Matt share Jason's views.*

But glad as Will was he had no concern in that particular family matter, he soon found out different. He was vaguely aware of Jason and Becky discussing the events of the day, but he shut his mind to their words and the pain they caused.

"Will!"

Sunk as he was in his dreary thoughts, Jason had to call to him twice before he heard. "We have a problem with Hannah," he repeated impatiently. "She shouldn't be left on that ranch by herself. It's not safe."

The deaths of Anne and Ben had far-reaching effects. Before the raid, the women had been used to staying home, carrying the work of the ranch forward while their men were gone. Now, the men left them alone with great reluctance. Tragedy had struck swiftly and unexpectedly. It could do so again. Particularly in the case of Eve, who had been with her parents the night of the attack on the Arrow A and could identify the killers.

Eve again. Must my thoughts always return to her? She ...

"How 'bout it, Will?"

He looked up blankly.

"I said, will you go over to the Crescent C to help Hannah out? She shouldn't be left there with just the four boys." Jason was clearly angered with Will's lack of interest in a subject so vitally important.

With effort, Will focused on Jason's words. "I'm not so sure it's a good idea. She might not want an outsider stickin' his nose in her concerns."

"Good Lord, you're not an outsider. Besides, there ain't nobody else c'n go."

"It's family doin's. I'm not one of the family, you know."

"Oh, Lord," Jason muttered. "That business between you and Eve was weeks ago. She and Matt are married now, square and proper. You got any notions 'bout her, you better get 'em out of your head right now."

Will shoved his chair back so hard it crashed over.

The children, taught to be silent while their elders were speaking, looked with mute awe on this unexpected diversion as Becky cried, appalled, "Jason!"

Will cut in harshly. "It wouldn't do me no good if I had any notions, would it? Seems to me Eve's made her feelin's plain enough. Hannah's your problem. You take care of her." He spun on his heel and headed for the door.

"Will, wait!" Becky's cry halted him, hand on the doorknob. With a quick glance at Jason's fury, she rushed on. "Please. I understand your feelings, truly. But Hannah does need help. We can't just leave her and the boys there with no protection. What if someone else comes along ..." Her voice broke and she bit her lip hard.

Will stared at her, then glanced at Jason, who was still

15

glowering. His eyes swung back to Becky and he saw all her grief at the reopening of the wound. *But hang it all, I just can't! How can they even ask me?* He'd been planning on cutting out for good, had decided to tell Jason tonight he'd be going. They had no right to pressure him.

"Please, Will, just for a few days until she gets straightened around. That's all we're asking."

He set his jaw. "No, Becky, I'm pullin' out. I'll work my shift tonight, but that's it."

"Pulling out? You can't!"

"Jumpin' Jerusalem!" Jason exploded. "Not you, too. You can't leave here! What about the ranch? With Luke gone, we need you to help work it. You know that."

"That, like Hannah, is your problem," Will said grimly. "I'm under no obligation to stay, and I don't intend to."

"You walk out now, I'll see you never work another ranch in these parts." Jason's voice was as chill as spring water.

"Don't threaten me, Jason." Will's voice was even colder.

"Stop it!" Becky cried. "Stop and listen to yourselves. Do you hear what you're saying to each other?"

"Stay out of this, Becky," Jason said flatly. "I meant what I said. I'll have you blacklisted out of the Territory."

"That's up to you, but I'm still leavin'."

Jason gaped at him in disbelief, but Will said stubbornly, "I mean it. I'm pullin' out tomorrow." He pushed out the door, leaving Jason — but not Becky — staring dumfounded after him.

Day Star Rising

Seething, Will rode out to the herd. Jason — also still furious by the look on his face — arrived a few minutes later and ordered the puzzled boys home. Whether his boss, angry as he was, would have spoken or not, Will, keeping a healthy distance between them, didn't know. He kept this space all during the watch. Not out of fear, but simply because his mind was made up and he didn't want to argue about it.

Will consciously repressed his anger through the following hours, knowing the cattle could only too easily pick up on his mood and become uncontrollably restless. He didn't particularly relish the thought of a stampede tonight, and he assumed Jason had reached the same conclusion. Fortunately, it was a night of quiet and starlight, the herd giving no trouble as the men rimmed them at a slow, even pace.

At the end of the shift, when stoop-shouldered Dan Mackley, Matt's friend from the LB ranching days up north, and blond, lanky Aaron rode up to relieve them, still with no word between them, Will and Jason took their separate paths back to the Jagged J.

Long after the lights had been extinguished in the main house, Will tossed restlessly on his cot in the bunkhouse. It was a small consolation, at least, that he had the room to himself. All the other hands had been let go after the bad winter and spring just past, so there were no prying eyes to see as he forced himself to face up to the events of that bitter day.

Eve and Matt. His childhood friends. Wed today in the house where they had grown up as brother and sister after Matt had been orphaned in the Indian raid.

Eve and Matt. Sharing supper tonight. Alone together in the warm, lamp-lit kitchen of the house left to them after

Ben and Anne had died so tragically.

Eve and Matt! He drawing her close. She, smiling, accepting his embraces — lying in his arms at this very moment. Violently, Will flung back his blanket. Cursing his over-active imagination, he grabbed his boots and jammed them on — a grave mistake because his feet, rubbed raw from his journey across the plains that afternoon, promptly screamed their protest. One more grievance to add to the day's tally.

At the corrals, Eagle greeted him with a low whuff and a moistly thrusting muzzle. Will saddled up and led him a safe distance from the darkened house before he swung into the saddle. Coldly telling himself he had no particular destination in mind, he let Eagle have his head, and for a long space of time, paid scant attention to his direction. Doggedly forcing his mind to pursue a safe path, he turned his thoughts to Jason's proposal earlier that evening.

Why in God's name should I agree to wet nurse Hannah? He had been planning to get away, to shed all connections with the Arrow A and the entire Clayton clan. *I sure as fire have no reason to hang around. And they were mad because I refused to agree to their dumb-fool plan!*

He had nothing against Hannah. She was a nice enough young woman. Everyone was entitled to one mistake in life, and she had sure enough cashed in on hers by marrying Luke. But that had been by her choice. Why should he, Will, now have to assume responsibilities that belonged to her husband? True, Hannah was going to have a rough trail to ride, trying to provide for four little boys and oversee a rundown ranch in a time of economic scarcity, tasks daunting enough for an experienced cowman. For a lone woman ... *Let the Claytons take care of their own! They pride themselves on that.*

He pulled Eagle to a halt and sat gazing at the Arrow A below. Usually honest about his feelings, he now insisted to himself the only reason he had come was to retrieve his gold piece from under the rosebush. Before Caleb Braden had ridden off forever, he had given the coin to his small son and had told him to keep it carefully, and Will had for all these years. So it was perfectly logical to go get it now, when no one was around to ask prying questions. But instead of starting Eagle down the slope, he merely sat and looked bitterly at the ranch swimming in the moonlight.

The house was dark and quiet. How long he stared, he couldn't have told, for he was lost in remembering: Eve laughing up at him, hurrying to meet him when he rode in, beat after a grueling day's work out on the range. Was it really only a few short months ago? A shudder shook him from head to foot, and he gasped a strangling breath, trying to force air into lungs that suddenly would not open.

Cursing himself for a complete fool, flailing himself for his idiocy in deliberately inflicting pain, he slid off Eagle, dropping the reins to ground-tie him. He approached the house cautiously. All he needed was for Matt to hear him. He'd blow Will's head off first and ask questions later. He knew a moment of sharp gratitude that Matt had not yet brought their new watchdog home from Catty and Aaron's to take the place of Lass, who had died a few months earlier.

The passageway from the back to the front of the house was ink-black, and Will emerged from it with a sigh of relief that he had made no undue noise. He could get his coin, be out of there, and no one the wiser. Rounding the front corner of the house, he crouched near the window he knew opened onto the bedroom.

He bent over the rosebush, and highly respectful of the lavish display of thorns, pushed the foliage carefully back. Moonlight glinted on gold — but it was farther back than he could reach his arm. With an inward groan — wasn't anything going to go right this day? — he leaned into the bush, felt the thorns poking at him, stretched his arm until he thought it would come out of its socket and got his fingers around the coin. Just as he was triumphantly pulling back, Eve's voice, scarcely more than a whispered moan, floated to him out of the moonlight. "No, no-o-o."

Caught completely off guard, still precariously balanced, he tipped forward, instinctively putting out his hand to break his fall. By the time he extricated himself, his lips tightly clamped to keep from yelping out loud. Eve was sobbing quietly. Matt's voice, demanding enough at first, dropped to a mumble so that all Will heard was "... again."

Crouched beside the rosebush, he forgot the pain in his hand in his first, instinctive "you should have chosen me" satisfaction. Yet, even as he savored it, this triumph washed away in the swift, stark realization that all Eve's joyful marriage expectations in choosing Matt over himself had come to bitter tears this night. Everything in him wanted to break inside, to smash his fist into Matt's face and yank him away from Eve.

You don't know why she's cryin', he told himself fiercely, not the least bit convinced. Neither could he evade the harsh truth that, because Eve had made her marriage choice, he had no right to be here. That knowledge — and the fleeting vision of himself bursting into their bedroom like a wild fool, with the casual explanation that he had come to rescue Eve from Matt's evil clutches after eavesdropping on them on their wedding night — held him rooted to the spot.

Eve's sobbing was easing into racking breaths. But it was a long while before she quieted completely. It was a much longer time before Will crept away from the window, back to Eagle waiting patiently on the slope.

Speculation without answers hammered at him long after he lay stretched out on his bunk, staring at the ceiling. *Sure showed how little one person really knew another ... Who would have believed that perfect Matt, of all people, wasn't so perfect after all. But what of Eve? She's the one who matters. Where does this leave her?*

Will clenched his fists. In that moment, he knew he would not go away as he had planned.

He couldn't, not if there was the slightest chance he could be here for Eve. Married or not, she still needed him. He'd stay — stay and help Hannah — and Eve.

Two

Will told his decision at breakfast. He had fallen into uneasy sleep only a short while before it was time to get up, dozing just long enough that, when he woke, those pre-dawn events had taken on the unreal quality of a nightmare.

Heavy-eyed from lack of sleep, heart-sore for Eve, he didn't even remember his argument with Jason until he pulled out his chair at the breakfast table and his automatic morning greeting to the latter produced only a resentful stare. His plan to stay was so much a part of him already that he felt swift shock at realizing he alone knew of it.

Jason's mouth was a hard line; Becky's eyes were shadowed as she dished up the children's plates. Will, instead of sitting down, gripped the back of his chair with tense fingers. "Got somethin' to tell you."

Total silence — and Jason's continued icy glare.

Will cleared his throat. "Been turnin' over in my mind what you asked me to do last night. I wasn't really thinkin' clear when I told you I was plannin' on leavin'. I was kind of upset. But I did some figurin' on it. If you still want me to, I'll stay and help Hannah out."

23

Quick gratefulness washed all the shadows from Becky's eyes, and she turned to Jason. He didn't trouble to hide his surprise — and suspicion. "You was determined enough last night to light out. Any particular reason f'r the change of heart?"

Will shrugged even as he felt himself redden. "None particular. Except your family's been good to me. Now's my chance to do somethin' in return." *Which, at least if it doesn't tell the full truth, certainly isn't a lie.* But he didn't want them prying further, so he said curtly, "Don't have to be a real reason, does there? I just want to help."

Becky put in quickly, "Of course you don't have to explain. We're just glad you changed your mind. Aren't we, Jason?" she said pointedly.

He shrugged. "Sure. It takes a load off my shoulders, I'll tell you." And he looked and acted considerably more cheerful for the rest of the meal.

As they rode out to the herd a little later, Jason, good humor apparently fully restored, spoke up. "Luke'll prob'ly show up home before long, anyway. But your stayin' will sure ease things all the way 'round." He said no more about his threat of the evening before to do Luke in if he did return, and Will didn't feel any pressing need to remind him.

Jason's mind was obviously on more immediate matters. "I wonder if Matt'll join us f'r work today?" If he saw Will tense, he gave no sign. "I told him to take a couple days before comin' back, that Jared and Reuben could fill in f'r him, but he didn't say if he would. Figured it was the least we could do f'r 'em, seein' they ain't havin' a weddin' trip."

Will spoke through stiff lips. "I heard Matt say they just

24

wanted to settle down to normal livin' without a bunch of fuss beforehand."

"Can't say as I blame 'em. They've had mighty little peace and quiet up to now. Guess they deserve some." Jason said nothing more. Will, too, was silent as they rode on toward the meeting place where Aaron and Dan were waiting. Finishing up their shift of guard duty, they would get no rest until the day's work was completed.

Aaron, with all the bounce-back of youth taking the lack of sleep in stride, greeted the newcomers cheerfully. Dan's nearly 60 years were obviously feeling the loss much more keenly. His only comment, however, was to mumble something about his "danged stiff joints" as he eased to a sitting position on a boulder near where the others had begun planning the day's activities. Will had pulled out his pocket knife and was examining Eagle's hoof for a suspected stone when he heard Dan exclaim, "Here comes Matt!"

He glanced up as Matt swung off Tumbleweed, but as ribald teasing began to fly about how Matt had "got himself roped and branded proper," and "the advantages of married life," Will's mouth tightened. Matt grinned at their joshing, and Dan grasped his hand warmly. Jason and Aaron thumped him on the back.

Will continued to seek the pebble in Eagle's shoe, devoting all his attention to the painstaking task. Then, abruptly, the choice to ignore was no longer his, for Matt strolled over to where he was bending over the chestnut. "Mornin'."

Will glanced up and returned his attention to his work.

Matt waited a moment. Thrusting his hands into his pockets, he said levelly, "Jason says you're goin' to help

25

Hannah out. I appreciate that. We all do. But it means you and me are goin' to be workin' together every day. I'd like f'r us to at least be able to get along."

Will slowly straightened, his black eyes hard as flint. "That's easy f'r you to say." Matt opened his mouth, but Will rushed on. "If you think you c'n come struttin' 'round me, high and mighty because you won her, you c'n just think again. All right, you married her; she's yours now. There's nothin' I c'n do. But I'll be damned if I'll go lickin' your boots."

Matt broke through the rush of words. "Wait a minute, Will. I have no intention of lordin' it over you. Remember, the choice was Eve's, not mine — or yours. God knows I understand how you feel."

Will broke in with a sneer. "No, Matt, you don't know how I feel."

Will couldn't know Matt was remembering the night he thought Eve had married Will, and Matt would not speak of it. Some things must never be put into words. So he said quietly, "Will, listen to me. I do know what I'm talkin' 'bout. If you and me can't be good friends any more, so be it. We've been close since we was both knee-high to a bull calf. Granted, you can't force somethin' that ain't there. But f'r Eve's sake, let's at least tolerate each other. She's been through more hell in the last few months than some people see in a whole lifetime. I won't have her hurt now. Not while there's one breath left in me to stop it!" He spoke so fiercely, Will stared.

But, remembering those heartbroken sobs of the night before, Will snorted. "You're a great one to speak of that." And now the fierceness in his voice matched Matt's, and it was Matt's turn to stare. "She'd of had no cause to come to grief over anythin' if she'd married me. But she just had to go and marry you instead. I warned you yesterday you better take damned good care of her. I meant it. And I swear to God you'll answer to me if I ever prove you're treatin' her bad." He bent over Eagle's hoof, flicked out the offending pebble, pocketed his knife, and strode off to join the others, who had removed their hats for the prayer with which they began every morning's work. Will, too, bowed his head.

"Heavenly Father, we ask You to bless the work of our hands this day, that what we do may prove pleasin' in Your sight. And may each of our words and deeds be worthy of the goodness and love You have so abundantly given. F'r all Your blessin's, we now thank You."

Jason paused to let each man give private thanks before their voices joined.

"Our Father, Who art in heaven ... f'r thine is the kingdom, and the power, and the glory, f'r ever. Amen."

The final words were borne away on the breath of the wind, leaving a hushed moment that each man would carry through his day's duties. Only then did they begin discussing how to divide the work, and Will concentrated as doggedly as though it mattered who would tend the herd grazing in Bush Valley, and who would dig postholes.

Before the bad winter and spring, the cattle had been allowed to graze freely on the range as long as they stayed reasonably within the ranch boundaries. Of course, they had drifted to some extent, but the fall and spring roundups had returned them to their home territory, just as the cowhands had removed cattle wearing other brands to their proper feeding grounds. Thus it had been, year after year, since

27

ranching had begun. Until this past year.

A dry summer, followed by a devastating winter during which some herds were completely wiped out, and others had their count reduced by as much as 90 percent, changed the rules of ranching forever. The cattle were no longer allowed to roam free and unprotected. Ben Clayton, of the old school who saw good neither in sodbusters nor in fences, had argued to the last ditch against such a move. But, choking on the bitterness of the decision, he had finally been forced to agree with his sons and son-in-law that the open-range method of ranching was a part of the past.

Because of the shortage of readily available timber for rock and rail fencing, they decided to go with post and barbed wire, and they had begun the — to Ben at least — degrading task of digging holes and cutting, hauling and setting fenceposts. They had no money to buy the barbed wire for stringing, but they had to start somewhere.

Ben had managed to salvage more of his herd than the others had — about 30 percent. Jason and Aaron had between them about fifty head. Luke had lost his herd to the last cow. Matt had never "owned" any cattle to begin with because, until his departure up north last fall to work on the LB, he had been right-hand man to Ben. So the families had agreed to combine the remains of their herds, work the cattle together and share the results — good or bad. They had let all the cowhands go. There was no money with which to pay them or feed them — except for Will, who could scarcely be called a hired hand when he and Eve were to be married so soon.

Thus had been their situation in the early spring. All of them, not just Ben, had to adjust to this new way of life. The rules had indeed changed, and no one was really sure just what the new ones were. They were feeling their way, learning by trial and error. At times only one knowledge kept them going — they must not fail. They must not!

Then the Claytons' world, always self-sufficient before and secure in its family ties, rocking now on its foundations, had been shattered. Ben and Anne had died so abruptly, so tragically. Matt had returned from up north to marry Eve. Luke had run off. And nothing would ever — could ever — be the same again. For any of them.

Nor for me either, Will thought morosely, watching Matt and Dan ride off toward Bush Valley. Only when they were far in the distance did he turn, with Aaron and Jason, to put his back and sweat into digging the postholes.

Will's bad mood persisted through all that interminably hot, dry day. Still feeling wrung out emotionally, tired and sticky from those hours of physical effort, he was definitely not in an agreeable frame of mind when he and Jason rode over to Hannah's after supper.

The Crescent C, Luke's spread, bore all the earmarks of an indifferent owner's slack care. Paint-peeling buildings, makeshift patching and tumbled-down corral railings spoke volumes. Three-year-old Sam and little Micah, both barefoot and dirt-grimed, squatted in the dusty houseyard, solemnly pouring dirt over each other's heads. Five-year-old Jeremy was pulling weeds in the garden, trying to supervise his younger brothers at the same time. This latter task was a full-fledged job in itself. Isaac was treating his authority as a joke and doing his best to annoy Jeremy by tickling the back of his neck with a long, feathery weed, then scampering out of his outraged reach to tease baby Micah until he squalled in indignation.

"Cut it out, or I'll wallop you!" Even at that distance Jeremy's bellow carried clearly to the two men on horseback. Red-headed Isaac thrust the offending weed under his older brother's nose once more. This time, however, Jeremy lunged, tackling him, and they both went down in a dusty, furious heap. Jason and Will pulled their horses into the yard as Hannah Clayton appeared at the door and flew down the steps.

"Boys! Boys, stop it now!" Heedless of flying fists and heels, she swooped and brought each of the boys up by the back of his collar, shaking them as they continued to make futile stabs at each other. "I said stop it!"

Four-year-old Isaac's initial whimper turned to a loud wail. Jeremy, face streaked with dirt and indignation, pushed his black hair out of his eyes and tried to explain between gulps of air. Hannah cut him off with another sharp shake. "You know better than to fight. You're supposed to be watching your brothers, not picking on them. Now, into the house, all of you, and to bed!"

"But Ma ..."

"I said, into the house. Now!"

His face a furious mask at the injustice of it all, green eyes shooting wrathful sparks, Jeremy twisted away from her. "Come on, Isaac," he said sullenly. "You, too, Sam."

Isaac, quickly perceiving that Jeremy, not he, was to receive all the blame for the fight, changed his crying to a sneer of triumph and stuck his tongue out at his brother. Jeremy grabbed him by the shoulder and gave him a disgusted shove. Isaac started to return the gesture, caught his mother's eye on him, and in light of his earlier victory, thought better of it. On the way to the house, Jeremy collected freckle-faced Sam, who had been standing to one side watching, his blue eyes big as saucers at Isaac's defiance. Jeremy hauled both of them, Isaac kicking and squirming, up the steps.

Hannah watched them disappear through the doorway before turning to her visitors. As she faced them, her motherly anger faded, leaving only an inexpressibly weary sadness. Even glum as he was feeling, Will was struck by the sorrow in her eyes.

For no reason, his mind flashed a sudden, clear picture of her impish smile, her droll sense of humor before six years of marriage to Luke stilled her laughter and made her retreat inside herself. Before poverty, hard work and four children in five years had taken the joy of living from her. She was only 24, but her eyes were those of an old woman.

She put a hand to her hair and set her fingers to tucking a loose pin more securely. Her smile was bright and stiff, accenting the grief in her eyes. "Jason, Will, come on in. How about some coffee?" She picked up Micah and led the way toward the house, inquiring about Becky and the children.

The room into which she led them combined kitchen and living areas. To the right of the doorway, a window over the sink looked south to the backyard and the yellowing plains beyond. Against the facing wall, a pot of coffee bubbled on the stove, rich, warm fragrance filling the air. In the center of the room a table holding a cut-glass lamp served both eating and working purposes. Two doors broke the line of the back wall. A rocking chair, bright with calico covering, was positioned to the left of the doors. Beside the chair, a small table held some sewing. A three-tiered shelf fit neatly into the nearby corner, on it a Seth Thomas clock, a Bible, and a McGuffey reader. A fern, fronds sweeping the floor, perched in a wooden stand in front of the west window. Crocheted rugs dotted the white-scrubbed wood floor, and curtains of the same blue-and-white calico as the rocker cushions hung at each window. The room was small but spotlessly clean, no mean feat to accomplish with four lively boys racketing through it. The furnishings were of the plainest materials, but obvious thought and hard work — the crisply starched curtains, the hand-stitched cushions, the colorful rugs — had gone into making this crudely built shelter a true home.

Hannah plunked the baby down on the floor and gave him a stuffed toy. As she poured steaming cups, she kept an ear on the thumps and occasional howls that issued from the boys' bedroom. Smoothing her apron, she finally sat at the table. "I'm sorry you had to witness such a disgraceful scene. I just can't seem to keep them from fighting." Again that pinned-on smile.

Jason and Will, settling in their chairs, glanced at each other, and Will nodded once, briefly. Jason spread his hands, palms down, on the table. He studied them intently for a moment before he looked directly at her. "Hannah, that fight wasn't Jeremy's fault. Will and me seen what happened. Isaac started it. If I'd been in Jeremy's boots, I'd of punched Isaac out a whole lot sooner."

Hannah started a quick protest, but it died as she caught Will's eye and he slowly nodded. She bit her lip. "I suspected as much. I shouldn't have been so quick to blame Jeremy. My own temper's been pretty short lately." She glanced at the bedroom door and stood hastily. "I'll be right back. Help yourselves to more coffee."

She shut the door behind her, and they heard a low murmuring — hers and Jeremy's. Micah had watched her go, and after a curious glance at Will and Jason, began an animated conversation with his rabbit. The two men looked at each other as Jason shuffled his feet uneasily. Will fiddled his hat in sunburned hands, wondering how he had ever been brainless enough to get himself involved in what was none of his business. He had opened his mouth to tell Jason he'd changed his mind when Hannah came back.

She paused beside the closed door and squared her shoulders. "Well, now." Briskly she picked up the pot, pouring more coffee before she sat down. "You were saying about Becky?" Micah hoisted to his feet, toddled over and plopped his rabbit onto her lap. She lifted him, cuddling him in her arms.

"Hannah." Jason's voice was unexpectedly gentle. "We didn't come to talk 'bout Becky. We came 'bout you."

Again that surface-only smile. "You don't have to worry about me. I'm doing fine here, and of course Luke will be back in just a day or two ..."

"Hannah," Jason cut into the flow of words, "just what did Luke say in his note 'bout comin' back?"

She dropped her eyes, refusing to answer.

Jason went on, patiently. "We come to see 'bout helpin' you out. But we have to know where we stand. If we c'n get an idea where he went, maybe we have a chance of gettin' him back here sooner."

"You mean go after him? No!" she burst out. "I won't have you dragging him back here like a — a runaway school boy. I won't, Jason. I can't tell you where he was going because he didn't say. Just that he was heading after the men

who raided the Arrow A. He was going to show everyone by
being the one to bring them back here. I don't know any
more than that. Don't you understand? I don't know."

"In that case," Jason said, still patiently, "we have to be
realistic. We don't know when Luke is comin' back." He
almost said "if," but changed it in time. "It might be a while.
You have to face that. Until he does, you should have someone here on the ranch to help you out."

As she shook her head, his patience fled. "Don't be a
fool. A woman alone out here, with just four little boys. Do
I have to spell it out? We've had one attack on our family
already. We sure don't need to invite another."

"But I'm not your family. You don't owe me anything."

Jason stared at her, speechless for a moment. "Of course
you're our family," he exploded. "You're Luke's wife.
Whatever he's done don't lessen our responsibility to you or
the boys."

"Is that what we are? A responsibility?" she cried in a
sudden flash of fury. Micah, who had been nodding in her
arms, jerked and dozed again. "No, thank you. You've all
suffered enough because of ..." She swallowed and went on
more quietly. "You've all suffered enough. Let's just let it be."

"But Hannah ..."

"Wait." Will cut across Jason's outraged sputter reluctantly,
but the other two were obviously getting nowhere fast, and he
didn't feel up to sitting all night listening to them trade insults.
"Hannah, will you just hear us out? That can't hurt, c'n it?"

The wariness back in her eyes, she didn't answer, but he
plowed on anyway, cursing the fate that had shoved him into
this rotten position. *If Eve didn't need me so much ...* "The

main thing is, you need a man 'round. Now, just listen to me f'r a minute," he snapped as she tried to break in. "If you had a man here, you wouldn't be such an easy target. You have to admit that. You're leavin' yourself wide-open like you are."

Her laugh was quick and bitter. "What's there to take? The ranch? It's so run-down nobody in his right mind would give two cents for anything on it!" She clapped a hand over her mouth and turned red at having voiced aloud disloyalty to her husband.

"Hang the ranch!" Jason's fist slammed the table, waking Micah, who began to whimper. "It's not the ranch. It's you! Can't you see it?"

She stared at him and the high color slowly drained from her cheeks. She started to speak, shaking her head instead as she set her hands to patting the baby's back. Reassured, Micah drowsed again.

Will put in brusquely, "It's a fact you got to face. We just want what's best f'r you, and right now that means acceptin' the fact that you'd be better off with a man 'round."

"But Luke ..."

"Hannah." Will's tone was flat. It was also unyielding.

She glanced at Jason and swallowed. "Who do you have in mind if I decide to go along with your dumb-fool scheme?"

"Me."

Her eyes swiveled back to Will. With cold amusement, he saw her shock as she stared at him. She wet her lips. "Why?"

Now it was his turn to feel surprise. "Why what?"

"Just that. Why? Why should you bother yourself about me?" She flung it, her challenge, into his face.

35

He felt his own resentment rising once more. *Wouldn't you like to know the truth about that one?* he thought sourly. It was bad enough he didn't want to come. But to learn that she didn't want him ...

He would have stalked out then and there, had actually started to rise, when Jason cut in. "Hang it all, Hannah," he snapped, "Will's just tryin' to help out. We all are. Now he's gonna stay so you might as well get used to it. Quit bein' so prickly."

She glared at Jason, all her resentment plain in her eyes. She turned back to Will sitting with clenched fists, looking ready to blow up.

"I guess I don't have any choice," she said bitterly. "But that doesn't mean I like your interfering!"

Three

Will lay stretched on a cot in the bunkhouse, arms locked behind his head. What a fine mess! His fury and resentment matched Hannah's. She'd let him know plain enough he was doing her no favor, that he was not there by her choice.

Well, it certainly wasn't all his choosing either. But he sure seemed to have a talent for pushing himself in where he wasn't wanted. He remembered Hannah's resentful surrender, her decided coolness after Jason rode away to relieve Jared and Reuben on evening watch, Will to follow as soon as he got squared away at the Crescent C. Carrying Micah, she had stalked into her bedroom, banging the door shut without a word or a look for Will, leaving him standing flat-footed in the middle of the kitchen.

He had stared at the closed panel and turned on his heel to leave the house. But as he reached to open the back door, she reappeared with a blanket and pillow. Thrusting them out so he had to grab to keep them from dropping, she said stonily, "You can use the bunkhouse, same as any other hired hand. The roof leaks, but that's your problem." She had turned away to pick up the used coffee cups as if he didn't even exist.

Louise Lenahan Wallace

So that was the way it going to be. Well, it was a game two could play. He had jerked open the door, closed it — not gently — behind him, and felt a perverse satisfaction.

But his triumph was short-lived. He open the bunkhouse door to such a dismal scene that even he — inured to lack of comforts as he was — felt chill. Groping along the shelf to the right of the door, he found matches for the Angle lamp. In the flare of light, he saw a half-dozen bunks scattered along the walls, a rough-made table and chairs, a rusted stove, a fly-specked mirror, and a wobbly stand with cracked pitcher and basin. The chill was real enough, he discovered. The evening breeze, considerably cooler since sunset, was pushing through the open window. It rustled the litter of castoff papers on the warped board floor and caught at the edges of patent medicine ads pasted to the walls in the vain hope of covering the cracks. As he contemplated the dreary reality in front of him, a long-tailed, furry body scurried past his boots into the night.

She had been right about the roof, he thought now, gazing upward. It had probably seen neither hammer nor nails since the day it had been put on. The whole ranch was in dire need of repairs. *A little paint here and there wouldn't hurt, either.* There was enough to do to fill his hours away from the herd for quite a while — or until Luke showed his face again — that he could avoid Hannah under pretense of being busy. It was a rotten shame, a waste to let a place fall apart like this one had. He would not acknowledge, even deep inside, his relief at the prospect of being able to stay out of Hannah's way.

... It is better to dwell in the corner of the housetop, than with a brawling woman and in a wide house ...

38

He grinned in sympathy. *Old Solomon must have faced a woman sharp-tongued as Hannah to come up with that truth!* His momentary lightness faded. The knowledge that he would be able to keep his hands busy was a definite reprieve. The less time he had free to dwell on Eve, the better.

She had cried again tonight.

He knew, because he had heard her.

After their midnight watch was up, he had made a vague excuse to Jason for not returning to the ranch with him. Instead, compelled by a gut-deep need, he had ridden over to the Arrow A. And arrived in time to hear the trail-off of her muffled sobs.

Powerless to go to her aid, sick with frustration at his own helplessness, he had turned away. Not because of any legal or moral restraints. Neither of those would have mattered a whit when it came to helping her. But because the choice she, herself, had made tied his hands more effectively than any rope could have. Matt was her husband; the law would certainly side with him over any vague complaint Will could issue against his behavior. Will had to consider, too, that any action on his part might only make it worse for Eve. Whatever "it" was. All the might, then, was on Matt's side. And where did that leave Will? And Eve?

Eve. He groaned and rolled over. Eve ...

He was shaving the next morning — staring gloomily at the wavering reflection of dark, straight hair and coal-black eyes — and wondering what he was supposed to do about breakfast. Little Spit-fire hadn't bothered to mention such a trifling detail last night. Maybe, like the roof, it was his problem.

As he reached for the flour-sack towel, a hesitant tap sounded on the door. "Come in," he called, wondering whether it was Hannah and if she would do so. The door creaked open and a dark head cautiously poked around the edge. Catching sight of Will clad only in work pants and boots, it backed hastily out again.

"Jeremy?" Will tossed the towel aside and crossed to pull open the door. The little boy looked up at him fearfully.

"I didn't mean to," he blurted. "Don't tell Ma!"

"Hold on a minute." Will drew him inside. "Didn't mean to what?"

"See you without your clothes on. Pa always said we shouldn't ... that it's bad!"

Will hunkered down so his face was on a level with the boy's scared one. "Your Pa told you that?"

At the child's nod, he felt a swift rush of anger. *If that wasn't Luke all over.* Putting his hand on the boy's shoulder, he pulled at his own lower lip and appeared to think deeply. "Well, now, if your Pa meant we shouldn't run 'round without anythin' at all on, f'r folks to see us, he was right. But that's not what happened. I called you in, and you saw me without my shirt on because I was shavin'. Nothin' shameful in that. Matter of fact, I go without my shirt lots of times when it's hot and I'm workin' 'round the place. Don't you and your Pa ever do that?"

The little boy shook his head, wide-eyed at the very thought. Again anger flashed in Will. *For Luke to smear dirt on such a natural happening.* Once more Will appeared to think hard.

"I'll tell you what, Jeremy. We wouldn't want to go

against a direct order of your Pa's, would we?" Again the head shake, most emphatically. "But since your Pa's not here and your Ma is, why don't we ask her what she thinks?"

Uncertainty wavered in the green eyes. "We have to tell her," Will said gently. "It's not right to keep things she should know from her, is it?"

"No, sir." Very low and dejected, Jeremy hung his head. Will put his hand under the small chin and raised the boy's head. "You've done nothin' wrong. But a man always faces up to his responsibilities."

Jeremy studied him. "Is that what you do?"

"I try. One thing I know, waitin' don't make it any easier."

"I'll tell her. But I hope she don't strap me like Pa would!" His voice trembled.

Will stood and reached for his shirt. "Long as you tell the truth, I don't see why she should."

Jeremy looked doubtful at this adult reasoning, but tried to match his stride to Will's on the way to the house. As they reached the bottom step, he jerked to a halt and stared up, stricken. "I f'rgot! I was supposed to tell you breakfast is 'bout ready."

Will grinned. "I'm glad to hear that. I'm so hungry, my belly's rubbin' my backbone!"

Jeremy grinned back as they entered the kitchen, but catching sight of his mother at the stove, stirring a pan of oatmeal, he remembered and the smile disappeared. He looked at Will imploringly, but Will gave him a gentle push. "Go on, son."

Hannah's face flashed concern. "What's wrong?" Anxiety sharpened her tone, and Jeremy hung his head in anticipation of the scolding to come. She glanced at Will, standing with thumbs jammed into his pockets.

His look indicated she should ask the boy, so she dropped to her knees in front of her son. "Jeremy," her tone was unexpectedly mild, "tell me what's wrong."

His eyes slid up to her face. "It was an accident, Ma. I didn't mean to look at him."

Plainly bewildered, her eyes sought Will's.

"He saw me without my shirt. He said his Pa wouldn't approve of that, and he wanted to tell you so he wouldn't be hidin' anythin'."

"I'm sorry, Ma, but he said he didn't mind. He says he takes his shirt off lots of times when he's workin'!"

Hannah stood. "It's all right, Jeremy. Why don't you go finish helping your brothers dress?"

"You ain't goin' to strap me?"

"Of course not. You didn't mean any harm. Now go and help your brothers."

Flashing Will a relieved grin, Jeremy scurried to obey.

Hannah clasped her hands in her apron. "Luke had a rule about the boys not seeing each other, too. But I already talked to them about that. With so much to do, I've needed Jeremy's help. I suppose I should thank you," she began stiffly.

Will shrugged. "Not if you don't want to."

She flushed. "I didn't mean that. I do thank you."

He glanced at the closed bedroom door. "He's a good boy."

"I ... thank you." She turned to the stove. "Breakfast is ready. Sit down and I'll dish up. By the way, thank you for milking and taking care of the other chores."

He waved a hand in dismissal. "That's what I'm here f'r.

To help. You don't have to thank me f'r every little thing."

She flushed again. "I just meant I appreciate it."

This futile circling was interrupted by the thumping arrival of the four boys. Sam and Isaac were scuffling and giggling. Jeremy had baby Micah by the hand.

"Wash up, boys, and sit down."

After much horseplay at the basin, including a water fight started by Isaac and ended by Hannah pulling him and Sam apart, they grouped around the table.

Hannah asked Will to say the blessing, and he managed to get as far as, "Heavenly Father, we thank you f'r this bounty ..." before Isaac punched Jeremy in the ribs with an active elbow.

"O-w-w-h, cut it out, Isaac," he protested.

Hannah's "Hush, boys, let Mr. Braden say the blessing," was met with a smug grin from Isaac and a furious beginning objection from Jeremy. Hannah cut him off, signaling Will to continue.

"... May we prove worthy of it and of your blessings. Amen." He finished hastily before Isaac could start again. Apparently the boy was satisfied with his success, for he fell to with the others, eating quickly and with no pretense of manners.

Will had been ravenous. His appetite, however, ebbed with the increasing under-the-table kicks and punches, the howls of protest, and Hannah's distracted rejoinders for them to behave. He forced himself to eat, calmly and with no appearance of even noticing the bedlam. Until Jeremy's cup of milk landed in the middle of Will's plate of fried eggs and toast, effectively squelching the rest of his desire to eat.

Isaac giggled and poked Jeremy. "You're gonna get it

now," he hissed triumphantly.

Jeremy's eyes widened with horror. "I'm sorry, Mr. Braden, I ..."

Hannah, feeding Micah, hadn't seen the cause. She turned in time only to see the mess in Will's plate and Jeremy's obvious guilt. "Jeremy Clayton, how could you!"

Will had had enough. He pushed back his chair, the thought flicking through him that maybe Luke wasn't so dumb after all, taking off like he had ...

"I got to be gettin' out to the herd." He spun on his heel and snatched his hat off the peg by the door. He had reached the bottom step when Hannah spoke behind him.

"Will, please, I'm sorry."

He halted and thought carefully before he slowly faced her. At the stricken look in her eyes, his jaw tightened. He just shook his head once and turned away.

He loped Eagle out to the herd, telling himself the whole way that he was a fool. *If I had the brains of a goat, I'd never of fallen into this trap.* But even as he railed, conscience nagged. Luke had already walked out on her. However unwilling Will might to be to stay, he had given his word.

His resolve wavered as he cantered Eagle toward the men gathered at the appointed place, where Matt had arrived just ahead of him. He pulled up to the side, dismounting away from the cheery morning greetings. He would have stayed apart had Jason not caught sight of him and strolled over. "Will, how's it goin'? Hannah all right?"

Abruptly, Will became busy as he stooped to loosen Eagle's girth. "She's fine. So are the boys."

Jason felt his shortness and frowned. "You sure there ain't no problem? Hannah takin' more kindly to you bein' there than she did last night?"

Will shrugged. "We didn't leave her much choice, did we? It'll take some gettin' used to f'r all of us."

"You're right, sure. It's not an easy situation. If I c'n help, if any of us c'n, just let us know." He seemed on the point of saying more, but Aaron hailed him and he moved away to answer.

The day's work had begun.

All through the morning's duties, Will kept his mind strictly on his job. Their pile of cut posts was dwindling and they would soon have to go for more, so Jason had sent him on a scouting trip for a fresh supply. The Medicine Bow Mountains to the west were the usual source of timber for corral railings and railroad ties, but he figured he'd have a look to see if he could spot anything closer to home.

As he rode out across the sun-soaked plains, the dying grass crackled under his mount's hooves, and the heat drenched his shoulder blades. Grasshoppers thumped and chirred. Overhead, a hawk soared lazily, a black dot against blue sky. To his right, a prairie dog chattered angrily at this intrusion, popping into his hole, appearing only after horse and rider had passed.

Will couldn't help comparing the grass today with the way it had been just a year ago. Seeing, in memory, the acres blackened by fire and those baked brown by blistering drought, he knew deep gratitude that Nature's temper tantrum had ceased and that she was once more smiling upon them.

He covered a lot of territory that day but tried to stay reasonably near where they were digging. No sense having to drag the poles extra miles.

In late afternoon, he headed Eagle back toward the morning meeting place. Hot and only half awake, he didn't realize until he pulled up in front of the fire that Matt was already hunkered there. Matt, reaching for the coffeepot, glanced over his shoulder to identify the incoming rider. Seeing Will, he calmly poured a cup and set the pot back on the coals as casually as though Will didn't even exist, totally ignoring the fact that, for the first time since the wedding, they were alone.

Will, dismounting, eyed Matt grimly, wanting nothing so much in that moment as to punch him out, exulting that his chance had come at last. He could face Matt down, get some answers from him without anyone else around to hear. But Matt, staring moodily into his coffee, didn't see Will's anger. Refusing to be put off, not bothering to curb his temper, Will asked harshly, "How's Eve?"

"She's fine," Matt said briefly, not so much refusing Will's challenge as relegating it to a lower level of importance than the thoughts that occupied him. For sure Matt didn't look so set up and jaunty today as yesterday.

Will, doing some ignoring of his own, hardened his resolve. Eve wasn't fine. And Will knew it.

A hundred questions hammered at him, demanding utterance — all those things Will had seethed to confront Matt with during those bitter, sleepless hours. But somehow, even as he opened his mouth, the words wouldn't form. How in hell's name could he bring up a subject he was supposed to know nothing about? What excuse could he possibly give?

Only the truth ... He hadn't considered, in those hours of staring at the ceiling, how he was going to berate Matt into a confession of the facts, only that he was going to do it. Even as that certain knowledge knifed into him, Will stalked over to Matt, grabbed his shoulder and crunched his clenched fist into Matt's jaw. Caught totally off guard by the swiftness of the attack, Matt, who had started to rise, went over backward, pulling Will with him. Veterans of many a boyhood "just for the fun of it" wrestling match with each other, each knowing the other's tricks, neither could get a telling hold. They rolled on the ground, Matt bewildered but game, Will deadly determined, until a cascade of water drenched them both. Choking, Will rolled aside. Blinking water out of his eyes, staring up, he saw Jason silhouetted above him, holding the empty bucket, looking as if he would like to use it against Will's head.

"Of all the knothead-fool things to be doin'," Jason roared. "What in the blue blazes has gotten into you?"

Matt, who had rolled the other direction to escape the flood of water, now surged to his feet, holding his jaw. Gray eyes cold as ice, he faced Will. "I ain't f'rgot how I punched you once when you didn't deserve it. I reckon you owed me one. But the tally's even now. You ever try that again, it'll be your last time, I promise you." The chill of his voice left no doubt of his sincerity.

Jason eyed Matt, then Will. "Don't know how it got started, but there'll be an end to it. Now!" he said furiously. "Personal grudges got no room here. We can't be havin' carryin's on like this or we'll all end up throwin' in our hands. So don't let it happen again!" He flung the bucket down hard.

Matt, fingering his jaw, eyed Will coolly. "Suits me just fine, Jason. If there's trouble, it won't come from me."

Jason glared at Will. "Well?"

Will glared back before turning a hard stare to Matt. Feeling their unity against him, he said bitterly, "You talkin' 'bout causes, ask Matt how Eve really is. See what he tells you 'bout how fine a husband he's turnin' out to be. Then ask Eve." He stalked off, feeling their shocked glances following him as he gathered up Eagle's reins, swung aboard, and wheeled away.

... the race is not to the swift, nor the battle to the strong ... nor yet favour to men of skill; but time and chance happeneth to them all.

Time ... and chance ... Will had lost.

But, obviously, so had Eve.

Matt, staring a long way off, lost in his own dark thoughts, seemed unaware of Will's departure.

Dog-tired, Will let Eagle set his own pace on the ride back to the Crescent C that evening. All his frustration and anger, all the tension of keeping his emotions under tight rein, had somehow seeped away in the fight with Matt, so that now, combined with the cumulation of sleepless nights, he felt so weary he could scarcely stay upright in the saddle.

Exhausted as he was, the last thing he wanted to face was another meal like breakfast. In his present state, he wasn't certain that, if there was a repeat performance, he wouldn't open his mouth and say a lot of things that were none of his business. So he took his time, enjoying the coolness that descended with the dark. Reining in, he gazed moodily at the house, warm with lamplight, before he motioned Eagle on in.

At sound of his boots heavy on the porch steps, the door flung open and Hannah stood silhouetted against the light. "Will."

He heard the relief in her voice and wondered briefly if she'd thought he wasn't coming back.

He paused, taking a deep breath to arm himself against the chaos waiting behind her. "Sorry. We didn't mean to keep goin' so late."

She saw his utter weariness. "You're exhausted. Come on in. Supper's keeping hot, and I've warm water for you to wash." Standing aside, she let him enter the kitchen.

He removed his hat and walked in cautiously, prepared for anything. The lamp glowed warmly. On the table lay a single place setting, and the aromas of bubbling stew and fresh-baked bread filled the air. The room was peaceful and quiet, a far cry from the disaster he had fled that morning. There was neither sign nor sound of the four boys.

He stared from the orderly room to Hannah, and she smiled faintly. "We're not always as disorganized as we were this morning." The smile faded. "I'll dish up while you wash." She moved past him to the stove.

She didn't speak again, but busied herself straining the evening milk while he appeased his appetite. After his third helping of stew, while he leaned back with a contented sigh and reached for his pipe, she pulled out the chair across from him.

"Do you mind?" He gestured with the pipe.

"Of course not. My Pa smoked a pipe. It's always seemed a homey, comfortable thing to me." She hesitated, looking down at her hands clasped on the table. "Will."

At the gravity of her tone, he eyed her sharply.

"I'm sorry about this morning and last night, too. It was Jason's idea for you to come here, wasn't it?"

When he nodded, she flushed. "I thought so. He's right, of course. But having you here, well, it just seems like admitting Luke won't be back. I can't do that. I have to keep believing he will come. Not just for me, but for the boys. Because how ..." She stopped, blushing again. "How can I tell my sons their father might never return?" She looked up at Will as though he could answer that question any better than she could.

He tamped the tobacco into his pipe, considering his words carefully before he spoke. "But, Hannah, you and me both know he might not come back. Just wait now," he said as she started a sharp protest. "It's a fact you got to face, like it or not. That's the way Luke is."

Quick anger lit her eyes but was suddenly washed away by a great sadness. "I know, but if he doesn't come, what will happen to the boys? I'm so worried for them." Her voice was dry with her fear. Looking at her clenched hands, she didn't see the softening in his eyes — a softening he quickly masked by drawing on his pipe. She didn't need pity, she needed commonsense help.

"Seems to me you've done all right tonight." His gesture took in the peaceful kitchen and the bedroom door behind which, presumably, the boys were sleeping.

She raised her head and saw that he wasn't laughing at her, but totally serious. "The boys and I had a discussion today. I talked and they listened. They'll apologize to you in the morning."

Will, with a pretty fair idea of what the "discussion" had consisted, seeing its obvious results, did some mental revising of his estimate of Hannah's backbone. She, reading his thoughts, said dryly, "I'm not in the habit of letting them get away with behavior like that. It's just these last few days ..." She stopped, embarrassed again, but plunged on. "And Isaac. I can handle him now, but he's getting big and strong. And he's so stubborn. It's like he makes it a contest between him and me to see who can hold out longer. He's only 4, but he's so, so ..."

So like his father. The unspoken words hung between them. Will's fingers curved around the bowl of his pipe. "He's his father's son," he said quietly. "I remember how Luke used to be. Always wantin' to be first, best at ever'thin'. Just like Isaac is now."

She closed her eyes as if in pain, pressing her lips tightly together. When she spoke, her voice was surprisingly firm. "I'll manage him. Somehow. I have to. I know he causes a lot of the trouble. He thinks of mischief and leads Sam into it, and I'm not going to have it!"

Will smothered a grin. Isaac Clayton was about to receive his comeuppance. Aside from what he had been handed out today. He spoke soberly. "It's your concern, not mine. But if you need a hand, I'll be here."

She sighed. "If they were girls ..."

"That's an advantage I have over you. I was one of the critters once, myself. I know how a young boy's mind works. Devious, usually."

She laughed, and it occurred to him it was one of the few times since her marriage to Luke that he had heard her laugh outright. It was a pleasing sound. "Did you get Jeremy straightened out on the shirt business?"

She nodded. "That was Luke's doing. I could never understand it. A boy has to feel healthy about himself, not be ashamed." Her eyes met his. "You said if I needed help, you'd be here. You mean it? You are staying?"

His eyes held hers a long moment. "Long as you want me to be here, I'll stay."

He had committed himself. Irrevocably. Suddenly the prospect didn't seem nearly so dreadful as it had only a short time ago.

Four

It wasn't all still waters and green pastures, of course.

They had come too fast from total resentment to begrudging admission of necessity, and they had to find a level at which both could feel comfortable — a difficult goal in an awkward situation.

Regretting her brief lapse into amiability, Hannah drew a shield of reserve around herself. Whenever their lives met unavoidably at mealtimes or in some discussion of ranch work, she was carefully polite to Will. *As she would have been to a stray skunk come sniffing around*, he thought dourly. At all other times she kept as distinct a distance from him as though she had drawn an invisible line over which she would not cross, nor let him.

A few evenings after his arrival, Will rode into the house yard — and smack into total bedlam. His first awareness of the situation was a screeching fit to wake the dead. His second was Sam, pelting full-tilt past Eagle and yelling like a banshee. His third and last, as he dismounted, was something slamming him in the back of the head.

When he opened his eyes, all he could see was a blur. All

he could hear was a tremendous roaring. All he could feel was that his head must for sure be knocked off its hinges. Then the pain struck. And he wished it had been knocked off. *Sure as fire it couldn't of hurt more.*

From a great distance he heard his name being called by a frantic voice. He thought for a moment it was Eve. He tried to speak her name, to assure her he wasn't dead, he only felt like it. But his tongue seemed too thick in his mouth to let the words by, and he wasn't certain whether he actually spoke or only imagined it.

He blinked, hard. The blur cleared enough for him to see — not Eve, but Hannah bending over him. Unyielding ground below. Summer sunset tilted at a crazy angle beyond Hannah's face. His head pillowed in her lap. "Will, say something!"

He groaned. "Can you hear me?" she asked sharply.

He groaned again and struggled to sit up. "I c'n hear you."

With this reassurance, her anxiety promptly gave way to exasperation. "What were you doing, anyway?"

"Me? I don't even know what happened," he mumbled. "Feels like somebody hit me with a brick."

"A rock. Isaac threw it."

Will shook his head in disbelief — a large mistake. "Where'd he learn to pitch like that?"

"Luke taught him."

Naturally. Will struggled to his feet, almost losing his balance. He closed his eyes against a wave of dizziness and reached blindly for the porch railing. After an initial whirling, his head started to clear.

"Maybe you should sit down for a while longer," Hannah suggested shortly. "I'd still like to know what you think you were going to gain by getting in the middle of the boys' fight."

As the world tilted again, Will unintentionally took her advice by swaying with a skull-splitting thump onto the porch step. "I wasn't plannin' on gainin' nothin'. Especially not this." He touched careful fingers to the still-swelling knot on the back of his head. "Instead of raggin' me, why don't you find out what Isaac was up to?"

She inspected the lump with quick, impersonal fingers. "Don't worry. I intend to," she snapped. As he watched her disappear around the corner of the house, Will felt relief her temper wasn't aimed in his direction. His head felt like a mule had kicked it. Two mules, to be exact. He closed his eyes against a whirl of nausea, opening them as a furious Hannah reappeared from around the side of the house. She had a kicking, screaming Isaac in tow and she hauled him up the steps past Will into the kitchen. The door slammed shut, but the boy's howls carried plainly on the evening air. Will held his throbbing head as Isaac's yells beat against it.

The door finally jerked open and Hannah stuck her head out. "Supper's ready if you feel like eating. And from now on, I'd appreciate it if you'd stay out of the boys' fights. Nobody asked you to interfere." She thumped the door shut on his dumfounded expression.

It was just as well, for he couldn't think of a single answer he dared repeat to her.

Will had a wicked headache for the next few days, but whether it was from the rock, which left an admirable lump — the little beast had terrific throwing power — or from lack of sleep because of his midnight rides to the Arrow A, he didn't know. He felt drugged, half-asleep on his feet. Like the aftermath of a three-day drinking binge, only worse. And he hadn't even had the actual pleasure.

During these days he came to hard realization. He couldn't possibly keep up the killing schedule he had of working all day and half the night, and keeping watch at the Arrow A, too. Opportunities for sleep were scarce enough. If he kept going like he had been, he'd be falling asleep in the middle of his job. He had actually caught himself dozing a time or two before the others had become aware of it.

He would not have the others pulling his share of the load, he vowed grimly. One Luke was enough. No one, including himself, had any use for another. So, reluctantly, he ceased his nightly rides. But not his sense of anxiety, of frustration at not being able to help Eve.

He had considered and rejected all kinds of wild plans, including riding openly to the Arrow A and confronting her. *With what?* he asked himself bitterly. *What are you going to say? That you stand night after night and listen to her cry her heart out, and you'd sure like to know why she's doing it? Or will you just tell her you've come like some grand hero to take her away forever from whatever it is?*

But sarcasm brought him no closer to a solution.

He wrestled fiercely and vainly, until the morning the answer hit him with about the same force as Isaac's rock. *Becky! If anyone knew what was troubling Eve, Becky would.* Of course, he couldn't ask her direct, any more than he could Eve, but there were indirect ways. And use them he would.

He could go over on the excuse that he had left something in the bunkhouse. He fell to planning, knowing that, above all, he must be careful, for it was his one chance.

And now that his way was open, Luck, that lady of the cards, dealt him an ace — and a joker. Days and nights he had agonized. And not two hours after his brainstorm hit, the means fell, as it were, at his feet.

He, Jason and Aaron had been digging postholes all morning. Aaron had just switched his shovel with Will's posthole digger, commenting that he, for one, would be almighty glad when they could afford a couple more and not have to depend on the shovels. Will absently agreed, since his thoughts were not upon his work but several miles away, envisioning his meeting with Becky.

He stepped off the proper distance and began a new hole. But after a few shovelfuls, he struck rock. Still preoccupied, he poked around with the blade and found the edge. Vaguely thinking to dislodge it by force, he positioned the shovel, stepped on the top of the blade and pushed. A crack, sharp as a rifle shot, snapped in his ears.

Falling, he tried to go limp. He hadn't parted sudden, complete company with more than one horse for nothing, he thought inanely. He tried to get up and couldn't.

He crouched, staring stupidly at the shaft of the broken shovel sticking in his leg just below the knee, the blade still embedded in the ground. His mind noted these details with detached curiosity, as though leg and shovel were a part of someone else.

Then his body exploded into pain.

He became dimly aware of hands, a voice. Aaron, working a few steps off, had heard the crack of the breaking handle and came at a run when he saw Will couldn't get up. "Take it easy, Will. Just stay still."

More hands, more voices. And all the time, pain searing his leg as though he had dipped it in fire.

His head cleared a little. Jason knelt beside him, talking anxiously. With effort, Will focused on his words. They gave him something to think about besides legs and shovels. He grinned crookedly at the thought. Jason, not understanding this logical show of amusement, thought Will had gone clean out of his head and clapped a worried hand on his shoulder.

"Will, c'n you hear me? We're goin' to take you to the Arrow A. It's closer than Hannah's. Aaron'll get you there. I'm goin' f'r the Doc. We'll come fast as we c'n."

Will nodded to show he understood, but the words were unreal. Only the pain was real.

On his horse, the shaft no longer sticking in his leg, but still feeling like it was. A neckerchief, Jason's, tied around his leg. Something warm and sticky trickling down his shin, into his boot.

The Arrow A. Eve running toward them, face white — with shock? Hands helping him off the horse, into the house, to a chair. Eve's hands. Cool, deft, gentle, probing the pain. A blaze of sudden anguish, so sharp it cleared his head of dream-like fuzziness, brought him to the reality of his surroundings.

Aaron stood by anxiously, ready to hand Eve whatever she needed. And Eve! Eve knelt before him, trying to staunch the bright flow down his leg. Her hands, the towel she was using, the water in the basin beside her, were all crimson. With his blood, he realized finally. *How could there be so much of it?*

He groaned. Aaron and Eve both jumped, for this was the first sound he had uttered. Aaron put his hand on Will's shoulder, pressing hard, reassuring him everything would be all right. Eve stood to the side, apologizing for hurting him. "How bad is it?" Will asked.

Aaron's hand pressed harder. "Doc's comin'. He'll take care of it."

Will gritted his teeth. "How bad?"

Eve, blue eyes wide and dark with distress, spoke quietly. "We can't tell, Will. We'll just have to wait."

They waited. The irony of the situation was not lost on Will, pain-drugged as he was. What a picture he must make with his pants leg slit up past his knee, boot and sock off, his leg white and bare except for its furry dark covering of hair — and bright blood — propped in the air like a belly-sick calf! The moment he had worked and schemed and prayed for — to be with Eve! And it was doing him as much good as ... The only comparison he could think of was unworthy of her.

Through the shifting pain-haze, Will became aware of Eve sinking down into a kitchen chair, covering her still-white face with her hands and of Aaron bending above her, pressing his hands to her shoulders. Her words came disjointedly to Will across the gulf of room-space. "All the blood ... Ma and Pa ... over again ..." He tried to grasp her meaning, sensed a pain as large as his own, but felt himself drifting once more.

Doc came, finally, to bend over Will's leg. To poke and prod until Will was sure he was taking it off at the knee without benefit of chloroform.

At last it was done, his leg wrapped and the pain, incredibly, easing a little. Doc talked to him bluntly. That was one thing about old Doc Fergus, he gave straight facts. "You're lucky. Near as I can tell, there'll be no permanent damage. You've lost a lot of blood, but you can get that back. How you missed hitting a nerve, I'll never know. You must have had an angel riding on your shoulder."

Will grinned, and Doc said crabbily, "Just don't go pressing your luck like that too often. The angels of my acquaintance got better things to do than keep foolish folks out of trouble. And even if they got the time, I don't."

"C'n I go back to work, Doc?"

Fergus looked disgusted. "Now what did I just say? I tell you to be careful and the first thing you want to do is get up on a horse and ruin all my nice work by falling off or getting dirt in it or something. You need to rest. In bed. For at least a week. If you don't, I can't be responsible for the consequences."

"I'll be responsible, Doc." The idea of a week of bed rest at the mercy — or unmercy — of Hannah was not exactly a joyful one. He'd rather take his chances with the horse.

Doc slammed his bag shut. "You a praying man?"

At Will's nod, he said roughly, "Then you better start saying all the ones you know, because you'll need 'em." He slapped on his hat and stomped out.

In spite of everyone's protests, Will went back to the herd. If he doubted the right of his decision, all he had to think of was Hannah's reaction to Isaac hitting him with the rock. What would she do with this happy situation? *Probably shoot me to put me out of her misery*, he thought gloomily.

Hannah, removing diapers from the clothesline, caught sight of Will, accompanied by Aaron, riding in late that afternoon. Her impulse, to ignore him — and Aaron, too — was overpoweringly tempting. She had just put in an exhausting day washing and ironing. She had made countless trips between the house and the clothesline. Her back ached from bending over the steamy tub. Her hands were raw and sore from the washboard and strong suds. Her feet hurt. Her always simmering temper flared. What right had Will, bouncing and chipper, to bring company home tonight — or any other night? Promising herself she would deal with him later, she pushed a sweat-damp lock of hair back from her forehead. As she faced the two men, however, swift shock overrode her anger at sight of Will's bloody pantleg and white bandage. Before she could react, Aaron blurted out the whole story.

She listened in total silence until Aaron stumbled to a stop, both of them obviously waiting for her to say something, and squirming when she didn't. *This is just what I need — to add nursing to everything else I'm doing! How could Will? Look at him standing there, balanced on one foot, silly smile on his face as if he's just been caught with his hand in the cookie jar!*

Her lips tightened. "Please help him to the house, Aaron."

"I c'n make it," Will insisted, even as he swayed.

"Aaron." The word was clipped and precise. Aaron, after one swift glance at her set face, handed Will a crude crutch and helped him limp up the back steps. Once Will was safely in the kitchen, Aaron wisely beat a hasty retreat from her wrath. "I'll do up your horse," he promised, backing out the door. "See you tomorrow."

He made good his escape before Will could cajole him into staying and before Hannah could deliver her scorching opinion. Tomorrow! Both of them had to be insane.

Insane or not, Will stuck to it, refusing to burden Hannah beyond the supper she had already prepared for him. When he had finished eating, she offered, not very graciously but nonetheless sincerely, "I'll help you out to the bunkhouse."

"No need f'r that." His tone was as stiff as hers had been. "I'll manage." He demonstrated by hobbling off on his own. *Fine! I tried to be nice. Let him take care of himself. He just better not come running when his leg falls off from lack of care — or when his pants need sewing up!*

After that first tight-lipped evening, Hannah was non-committal on the whole subject, figuring that if Will needed help, he'd ask for it. Will, figuring sourly that she was as relieved not to have to nurse him as he was not to have her do it, kept his offensive self out of her sight as much as possible.

In spite of Doc's dire predictions, no evil befell Will for his foolish disregard of medical orders. He took it easy, and the wound healed without complication. Doc shook his head when he inspected it several days later. "By all rights you ought not even to have a leg, and here it is healing clean," he muttered in disgust, as though by defying him Will had upset all the accepted medical theories.

"You think you're so smart about it all, maybe I should turn my bag over to you. You be the doctor and I'll be the cow nurse!"

Will grinned, not the least bit discomfited by this outburst, and Doc knew it. He stamped out, but not before Will glimpsed the pleased expression he tried hard to hide.

The only permanent scars Will bore were the jagged one on his leg and the equally vivid one that gave him a healthy respect for shovels.

As for his quandary about Eve, he was no closer to a solution than before. His one chance to see her, and he'd been in no shape to judge. He hoped Lady Luck was fond of a good joke. This one ought to keep her in stitches for a long time to come.

Short-fused as he was over this failure, Hannah's continued touchiness swiftly became a large irritation to Will. *It keeps cropping up at the most unlooked-for moments*, he thought, irked. He had no intention of breaching the barrier between them, but he did wish she'd act a little less like he was a bull with hoof-and-mouth disease.

If he had any doubts about what she meant, she set him straight the morning he rode in unexpectedly and found her hoeing in the garden. When he offered to take over for her, she drew away, telling him tartly, "I'm used to doing this. You certainly don't need to baby me."

It was a rebuff of the first water, and Will reddened. "Just tryin' to help out," he said with a coolness matching hers. "I figured there was no sense you breakin' your back when I'm here to lend a hand. But if that's the way you want it, fine. I'll try to remember next time." He stamped off, seething, feeling a total fool.

Isaac wasn't much help, either.

For a reason known only to himself, the child continued to be possessed of the desire to make life as miserable as possible for everyone around him, including Will. *As if I needed any help*, Will thought gloomily.

He had to admit that after the rock-throwing spree, Hannah did her best to handle Isaac, meting out severe enough punishment that, in her presence at least, he did no more than glower at Will or answer sullenly. Out of his mother's sight, he wasn't so discreet. It wasn't the frog in his bunk, the snake down his boot or the worms in his water bucket that bothered Will. He could put them down to boyish mischief and laugh them off, except for the obvious childish desire behind them to hurt.

He said nothing to Hannah, not wanting to make either Isaac's or her resentment worse, hoping the boy would tire of his pranks and come, if not to accept Will, at least to tolerate him. But as the days passed, it seemed a forlorn hope at best.

As if all these personal trials were not enough, Fate's friend Circumstance stepped in to show him that no matter how bad things are, they can always be made worse. Out at the herd, they were preparing to call it a day, and a backbreaking one it had been as they worked feverishly to set the last of the fence posts before winter should clamp down over the country.

Aaron, preparing to mount, stumbled as his boot caught in the stirrup. With a disgusted curse, he pulled at the loose piece of leather that had caused the slip and the whole sole came off in his hand. "Patches on top of patches!" he grumbled. "I'll sure be glad when we make our roundup sale so we'll have a little money. The first thing I'm goin' to buy is a pair of boots — brand new with no patches, holes or cracks!"

"None?" Dan teased. "I didn't know there was any!" He lifted his own ill-shod foot. "Sure you c'n handle somethin' like that?"

"I know I'd sure like the chance to try! But you're right. It'll be downright strange to feel a whole piece of leather underfoot instead of the ground."

"I know what you mean," Matt agreed. "When we get our share we plan to ..."

"You might just as well quit plannin'," Jason broke in sharply.

They turned to stare. "What do you mean?" Aaron finally asked for all of them.

"I mean," Jason said tiredly, "that if we sell off even part of our herd now, we'll be back worse than we was in the spring."

"But ..."

"No buts," he said flatly. "I'm the one's been keepin' the books, and I'm tellin' you straight out. We can't sell any cows this fall and come out ahead. We can't even break even because the expense of gettin' 'em there would outweigh the profit we'd make."

"Are you sayin' ..." Will cut in.

"That's exactly what I'm sayin'. We'll lose, even go bust, if we try to make a drive now." Defiantly, he faced their stares. "Don't look at me like that! I don't like it any more'n you do. But if you don't believe me, you c'n take a look at the books f'r yourselves."

This was not necessary and they all knew it. Jason kept the account books as scrupulously as Ben Clayton ever had. If he said it was so, it was. "Why didn't you tell us sooner," Matt demanded, "instead of lettin' us count on it?"

"I've been huntin' the words to tell you," Jason snapped. "My God, you think it's any easier f'r me than you? Don't f'rget, my family'll be just as hungry as yours come winter. I've been hopin', prayin', somethin'd happen to change things. But I just don't see any way out."

A thoroughly disheartened group split to go their separate ways home. They had all been counting on that money, putting days of grueling work behind them because each one gotten through was a step nearer the time they would be paid for their efforts. But now ...

Will rode slowly into the ranchyard, wondering how he was going to break the news to Hannah. That cash was to have seen them through the winter. In a household with four hungry, growing boys, there could not help but be money going out, no matter how carefully she might manage.

Unsavory as the idea was, Will knew he could not stall letting her know. So that evening, standing awkwardly, arms crossed, he told her bluntly. Clutching her dishtowel, she listened in silence, her expression unreadable.

"Is Jason sure?"

"He's sure. We'll prob'ly be able to sell a few head in the spring, but right now there's no way. We'll just have to be patient, let them rebuild a little so when we do sell, we won't deplete our stock."

She carefully set down the plate she had been drying. "It's a blow for sure. I am sorry for them."

He blinked. "Sorry f'r them? It's us, too, you know."

"But it isn't. Luke — we — didn't have any cattle left, so we aren't entitled to a share of the profits."

His mouth fell open. "Not entitled? What in God's name are you talkin' 'bout?"

"It's the simple truth," she said stonily. "I'm not about to take from the others when I don't have a share coming."

He stared at her set face. "Just what do you think I been bustin' my back out there f'r all this time? My own health? You better think again, lady."

Her cheeks flamed. "We — my sons and I — don't need your charity. And we will not take what isn't ours!" She turned in flat finality, leaving him fuming.

He glared at her rigid back, opened his mouth to say what he really thought, then closed it with a snap. What good would it do, anyway? If there was anything she didn't want to hear, it was his opinion. Frustrated, he turned away and almost tripped over Jeremy, standing close behind him, eyes wide and scared.

"Mr. Braden ..."

Hannah whirled. "It's bedtime."

"Ma, I ..."

"I said it's bedtime. Now go!"

Jeremy, not daring to argue, went. She gathered up the other boys, all but shoved them into their room, slamming the door shut behind her.

Will's frustration turned to total disgust. *So she wouldn't even finish an argument once she'd begun it!* He jerked on his coat and did a little door-slamming of his own.

He should have known that wouldn't be the end of it.

The next morning he shoved open the barn door and hauled out the milking stool. As he set to work on Daisy, he saw out of the corner of his eye a flash of fur and heard the terrified squeak — abruptly stilled — of the barn cat's luckless mouse-victim. In a few moments, the calico appeared out of the shadows and sat just out of Will's reach to commence a thorough washing.

"Good breakfast?" he muttered. "Here's somethin' to wash it down with." He aimed a healthy squirt, and the unsuspecting cat caught the stream full in the face. She jumped, spat and began a vigorous washing. Her expression when she discovered the taste of what she had considered an indignity was enough to make Will chuckle. "Not so bad after all, was it?"

From behind, he heard a giggle, quickly stifled, and turned just in time to see a dark head pop out of sight around the door. Lips twitching, Will turned back to Daisy's business end and let fly another blue-white stream at the amazed cat. Jeremy giggled again and sidled through the doorway. The cat, torn between her desire for more of the great stuff that had appeared so magically and her half-wild instinct to flee Jeremy's approach, compromised by hissing and retreating into the shadows where she watched Will hopefully.

Jeremy didn't say anything, just followed Will's every movement with Daisy. When he let go with one last squirt and the cat opened her mouth and actually caught it, the little boy howled in glee. "She's a smart one all right, ain't she?"

"Jeremy!"

Hannah's voice, unmistakably angry, made the boy jump guiltily. His eyes filled with horror as he saw his mother advancing upon him wrathfully. "Get in the house right now, young man!"

"But Ma ..."

"Go!"

He slid past her and bolted out the door.

Will had watched and listened in silence, but as Hannah started to follow her son, he knew he had to speak up despite the consequences. "He wasn't hurtin' nothin'."

She whirled. "What?"

"I said he wasn't hurtin' nothin'. He was just watchin.' Is that so big a crime?"

It was the wrong thing to say, of course. If he had thought her angry before, she was undeniably furious now, her mouth a tight line. "I didn't send him out here to watch you waste food. I sent him here to tell you breakfast is ready. Did he do that?"

"No," Will admitted, "but he didn't hardly have time. He just got here when you hollered at him. Why don't you ease up a little? Seems like all you do is yell at him without givin' him a chance to explain. Or are you afraid I'll corrupt his morals if he so much as speaks to me?"

A snowball thrust down the back of his neck would have been far warmer than her eyes or voice. "He is my son. I will raise him as I see fit." Each word was distinctly spaced. "When I want your help, I will ask for it. Until then, I would appreciate it if you would keep your opinions to yourself!" She spun around and stalked out the door, leaving him standing in a fury equal to her own.

As he canted Eagle out to the herd a little later, he was still steaming. *Just exactly what right does she have to treat me like the lowest type of snake? If that's the way she got along with Luke, no wonder he took off. Her own husband felt no obligation to stay, so why should I?* After all, a "hired hand" was entitled to leave any time he pleased. And her treatment of him was fast becoming even less than normal courtesy asked.

He swung down as Jason, catching sight of him, strolled over. "Will, how's it goin' with you and ..." His voice trailed off. "Not so good, I take it."

"You take it right. And I'm strongly tempted to tell you — and her — just where you c'n take it."

"That bad? I was hopin' she'd calm down after a while."

"Well, she hasn't. And I'm gettin' god-awful tired of bein' treated like I'm a no-good skunk. There's a limit, Jason, and I've more'n reached it!"

The other men stared curiously, and Jason signaled for Will to lower his voice. "I don't blame you f'r bein' upset ..."

"Upset?" Will hissed. "That's puttin' it mild. She don't want me there. Fine. You c'n either find some other sucker or leave her alone like she wants. It's up to you. But I'm through."

"Now hold on, Will ..."

"No! I'm done puttin' up with it. I told you she was your problem before. That's the way it should of stayed. Well, she's your problem again." He started to shove off, but Jason grabbed his arm, dropping it hastily as Will's eyes turned to ice.

"Wait. We can't just up and leave her — all right, maybe that's what she is askin' f'r. I don't know what's been goin' on. Up to now a stump's been more talkative than you. But I do know we can't leave her alone like she will be if you take off."

"Why not? She'd be in no danger. Her tongue's sharp enough to do in anybody fool enough to tangle with her." Seeing Jason's shock, he said impatiently, "All right, all right. But I mean it. I'm through."

"Can't you try talkin' to her?"

"You ain't been listenin', Jason. Talkin' to Hannah's like — like talkin' to one of those fence posts out there. Except the post'd prob'ly be a lot more friendly."

Jason turned up his palm in a gesture of pleading. "I'm askin' you, Will, as a friend, don't give up on her yet."

Will set his jaw. "I'd be a fool to keep on tryin'."

"No, you wouldn't. Maybe Becky could talk to her and get her straightened out. She does have a way with words!"

"So does Hannah," Will said grimly. "And I don't fancy hidin' behind Becky's skirts while she does my fightin' f'r me." He sighed. "I'll handle it. Or try, at any rate." He refused to acknowledge Jason's relieved grin and shoved crossly past him.

He was still feeling disagreeable when he rode back to the ranch that evening. It had been a long, hard day, and he was in no frame of mind for either argument or a cold shoulder. He wondered, without humor, which she'd dish out tonight.

Neither, as it turned out. All during supper she was so preoccupied she answered him and the boys briefly or not at all. Which left him, when he had been all set to do battle, without an opponent. Women! He didn't reckon he'd ever be able to figure 'em out.

When Sam approached her after the meal was over and held out his well-worn fairy tale book for her to read a story, she shook her head. "Not tonight. I have a headache."

Will, on his way out the door, paused. *So that's the reason for her distraction.* He realized unsympathetically that she did look green around the mouth. He didn't know whether to be relieved or annoyed. Lady Luck was sure playing games with him. And he was ending up the loser no matter what he did.

The next morning Jason hailed Will straight off. "Did you talk to Hannah?"

"Didn't get the chance. She wasn't in a talkin' mood."

Jason cuffed back his hat. "Just like Becky. Can't get her to shut up one time, can't get her to open her mouth the next!"

"She said she had a headache."

"If that ain't typical. They c'n come up with a headache at the most inconvenient times. I guess you c'n just be glad you ain't married to her." Will's deadly glare caused him to clear his throat and finish hastily, "Let's get to it. Daylight's burnin'." Swinging up on his horse, he pulled away before Will could answer.

But even the thump of his mount's hooves could not obliterate the one-word reply Will hurtled after him.

Five

Because he had not spoken to Hannah right away, Will found it difficult to do so at all. That first, high flame of temper had, inevitably, wavered so the words that had burned in his throat now stuck there. It wasn't simply an aversion to arguing — he had held his own in more than one fight during his growing-up years. Those, however, had been matches settled with fists, not voices. He had never been much of a hand at verbal scrapping. The words, some-how, never seemed to come out like he wanted.

More than that, though, Will kept seeing Jeremy's scared, white face the night of that last blow-up with Hannah. How many times had the boy witnessed a similar scene between his parents? More than a few, he was ready to wager. Memory tugged so that, for a few moments, he heard other parental voices raised in anger, saw another small boy huddled under his covers, trying desperately, futilely to drown out those scorching tones. *Strange how the words and the fear could echo even after so many years.*

The next few days Will withdrew into himself, resolving to keep every inch of the distance Hannah set between them.

Unexpectedly, this became increasingly difficult because he, doggedly determined to remain the dutiful hired hand, found himself drawn more and more into the concerns of this family.

In spite of his mother's efforts, Jeremy persisted in trailing after Will as he went around the place doing chores and badly needed repairs while keeping strictly out of Hannah's way. The child was gravely silent at first, standing well back, looking ready to leap and run like a scared rabbit should the tall, brooding man express the least annoyance at his presence.

Having no desire to incur a repeat performance of Hannah's ire, either for Jeremy or for himself, Will let him be, but presently, curiosity overcame shyness and fear of maternal wrath, and he crept closer.

"What'cha doin'?"

"Eagle threw a shoe last night. I'm goin' to make him a new one."

"How do you do that?"

As seriously as if he were discussing the cattle market, Will explained, showing him the various steps involved.

When Will trimmed the hoof, Jeremy flinched. "Don't that hurt?"

"No more than your Ma cuttin' your toenails. I have to be careful, though, not to go too deep, just like she does."

The boy watched every step, fascinated. Only after it was all done, he looked aghast. "I f'rgot!" He started to back away. "Ma said we weren't to bother you *at all*." Innocently, he pronounced the last words with telling mimicry.

"Hold on," Will put in before the child could flee. "What makes you think you been botherin' me?"

"Ma said not to be a nu-nusi-"

"A nuisance?"

The dark head bobbed miserably.

"Well, now." Will wiped his hands on a rag. "How c'n you be a nuisance when you been helpin' me?"

Jeremy looked uncertain.

"You handed me the nails when I needed 'em, and you kept the fire goin', didn't you? If that's not helpin', I don't know what is."

A great light sparked in the green eyes.

"Didn't you ever help your Pa like this?" Will asked curiously.

The light faded. "No, Pa always said I asked too many questions and made double work f'r him. He always said to go away and not bother him. How come I bothered him but not you?"

Will felt a quick stab of anger. Tossing the rag aside, he reached over and tousled the boy's already rumpled dark hair — Hannah's hair — and looked into the wistful green eyes — Hannah's eyes. *Would Luke have deliberately ... ?* He snapped the question off before his mind even completed it. Only too obviously, Luke had. "I guess it's all in the way you look at it, son. The way I see it, how's a man goin' to learn if he don't ask questions? How's he goin' to find out anythin' if he don't do f'r himself?"

"Did you learn by askin' your Pa questions?"

"I sure did. I still ask when I don't know. No shame in that. The only shame is not askin' if you don't know."

Jeremy digested this information silently. Will could almost see the wheels turning in his head. "You mean my Pa was wrong?" he asked earnestly, puzzled by such a possibility.

Will put his hand on the child's thin shoulder. "Come here." Sitting down in the barn doorway, he drew the boy down beside him. "It's this way," he said slowly, "every man has his own way of thinkin', his own way of doin' things." Jeremy was staring at him.

"If everybody did ever'thin' exactly the same, it'd be a pretty borin' world. Take eatin', f'r instance. What hand do you hold your fork in?"

Jeremy thought. "This one." He wiggled his arm.

"That's right. Your right hand. Now me, I eat with this one." Will raised his left. "But that don't mean either of us is right or wrong. We just use different ways to get the same job done. Same with your Pa and me. He does a job one way, I do it another. Makin' your choice of how to do it is part of bein' a man."

Jeremy studied a large scab on his bare toe, and Will wondered whether he understood. Finally he said slowly, "Pa got awful mad at me sometimes. I like your way of doin' things lots better."

"Jeremy, where are you?" They looked up, startled, as Hannah hurried around the corner and caught sight of them. "There you are! What did I tell you about bothering Mr. Braden?" she began sharply.

Jeremy cringed, but Will spoke quickly. "He's not bein' a bother. He was helpin' me shoe Eagle. We just finished and sat down to catch our breath."

Some of the frost melted from her voice as she looked uncertainly from her son's suddenly bright face to Will's matter-of-fact one. "By all means, if he's making himself useful."

"He is," Will assured her, wondering at the totally

unexpected softening of her mood. "He did a good job. Did you want him f'r somethin'?"

"It's time to water the garden. I want you to get started now, Jeremy."

The child sighed and looked hopefully at Will, who tipped his head in the direction of the vegetable patch and smiled as if they, alone, knew a secret. Jeremy sighed again and dutifully trudged off.

The two adults watched him make his reluctant way to the well and reach for the bucket.

"He really was helping? You're sure you don't mind his being around you?"

"I'm sure. He learns quick, and he's definitely not a nuisance."

Her mouth tightened. "He learns quicker than he should, sometimes." She started to walk away but turned back hesitantly, obviously searching for words. "Thank you," she finally said bluntly.

"F'r what?"

"For bringing a happiness to my son's face that I've never seen there before."

She turned away before he could answer.

By becoming friends with Jeremy, by giving him an adult male he could respect and emulate without fear of scorn, Will was drawn more closely into the circle that formed this family. Unlike Isaac, the littlest boys, Sam and Micah, accepted him as very young children will — simply because he was there.

One evening Will, leaning against the cleared supper table, discussed with Hannah the means of re-roofing the bunkhouse. Thought of this conversation did not exactly overwhelm him with eagerness and he had, consequently, put it off as long as he dared. But autumn was coming on. If he didn't get the job done soon, he'd be flooded out by the heavy rains. Such a repair would be costly, however, and where were they to get the money now?

She had acknowledged his need, impatiently to be sure, but at least she hadn't brushed him off completely.

Even as they debated the hopeless question, Sam dashed past, giggling. Micah toddled at his heels, frantically trying to catch up, for Sam had his stuffed rabbit and he wanted it back. As Micah passed the table, he stumbled over Will's boot and would have fallen headlong had the man not caught him. Without thinking, he swung the baby up in the air.

"Hey, little Polecat, that was my foot you tromped on! Where's the stampede?"

Micah's initial cry changed to a giggle as he caught the teasing behind the words, if not their meaning. Will swung him again, tickling his belly. Sam, deciding after an open-mouthed second of hesitation that he wasn't going to be left out, charged in.

"Not two of you! Help!" Will yelped in terror as he allowed them to pull him to the floor. Jeremy, laughing, dove for his ankles, and the battle was on. With Micah tugging on his hair and Sam sitting on his legs and tickling his stomach, all of them shrieking with glee, the din was deafening.

Hannah looked on in amazement and consternation as her sons delightedly accepted the mauling that, among themselves, would have produced tattling and indignation. Will, wincing at the pain in his leg, suddenly heaved to a sitting position, scattering his attackers. Breathless, he fended them off as they came back for more. "Enough!" he gasped. "I give up!" He stood and their jubilant shouts changed to whining protest. Hannah started to speak sharply, but decided instead to let Will get out of it by himself, just like he'd gotten into it.

"You want to do it again tomorrow night, don't you?" Will gazed at the three pleading faces upturned to his. "If you beat me up tonight, we won't be able to."

Reluctantly they untwined themselves from his knees.

"And it's bedtime, anyway," Hannah put in firmly.

"Aw, Ma!"

Will cut through their pouting. "If you don't go to bed now, how c'n tomorrow night come so we c'n do it again?"

Knowing there was a hole somewhere in this adult question, but unsure just where it was, they disappeared reluctantly into the bedroom. Only then did Will catch sight of Isaac glowering from the corner. Hannah saw him at the same time. "You, too, Isaac. Off with you."

Isaac glared at his mother, pointedly ignored Will, and ambled into the bedroom.

Will glimpsed worry in Hannah's tired eyes and wondered whether he should say anything. He had no desire to be put in his place yet again by either icy looks or words. And she had proved herself a top hand at both. Probably the best thing to do was keep his nose out of it. But that look in her eyes ... "He'll be all right, Hannah, you'll see." Remembering the wildlife that had taken up residence in the bunkhouse, not to mention the still-tender spot on the back of his head, he tried to speak with conviction. A chill voice seemed to whisper, *Would he?* Luke had lived all his life with the same attitude Isaac showed now.

His attempt at sympathy was a mistake. She stiffened, the pain in her eyes becoming swift resentment. "I don't need you to judge the good and bad in my sons. They're my responsibility, not yours, and I'll take care of them."

His own face hardened. "You really are somethin' else," he blurted. "What's with you, anyway? It's not my fault you're in this mess. It's not your boys' fault, either, but you're sure actin' like it is."

She tried to break in as he rushed on. "You been carryin' a burr under your saddle ever since I got here. Well, let me tell you that you've made it plain enough you don't want me here. But have I made it plain enough to you that I don't want to be here, either? If I haven't, maybe this'll say it: I am disgusted." He all but spat the words out. "I've had it. With you. With the work I been doin' f'r you. With the whole rotten mess. I don't need your bitterness. I don't need your anger. And I don't need your resentment. I got enough of my own to keep me supplied f'r a long, long time."

He stomped out the door, leaving her staring shocked after him. As he tramped across the moonlit yard toward the bunkhouse, he tried to get a grip on his temper. He probably shouldn't have spoken like he had, but he felt absolutely no regret. Truth to tell, he felt better than he had in days. For once he'd gotten to slam the door first! He grinned at memory of her shock. She just might think twice before giving him the sharp edge of her tongue again!

Why had he bothered to give her sympathy at all? He sat on the edge of his bunk to pull off his boots and the question struck him. Why, indeed? Except that in that one moment with her guard down because she was worried about her son, he had glimpsed a measure of Hannah's suffering.

He had no desire to become enmeshed in Clayton family troubles. He was too involved already, the way he saw it. He'd just have to put a halt to it. He had problems enough of his own, and he sure didn't need to add someone else's to them.

He fell back onto the bunk, hands locked behind his head. Was it ever going to get easier — the thought, the knowledge of Eve and Matt together? If he wasn't awake thinking of her, he was asleep dreaming of her. Which was worse, he couldn't decide. Always now, waking or sleeping, was memory of the touch of her hands — cool, deft, gentle — as she worked over his hurt leg. *How had life suddenly become so complicated?*

Only a few months ago all the future had been his and Eve's. They had dreamed and planned, and nothing had been impossible. The memory of his confident strength, his fearless willingness to face whatever might come, was only a mocking echo now. All the world had been theirs and then, abruptly, there was nothing. Eve had told him she couldn't marry him, that she didn't love him after all. Anne and Ben Clayton, close to him as his own parents, had been murdered, with Luke, their own son, the indirect cause of their deaths. Matt, his childhood companion and trusted friend had returned suddenly out of the night to claim Eve as his own so that Will was faced with the bitter truth of why she had changed her heart toward him. Love, family and friend — all irrevocably gone. Only the pain remained to remind him what had been. The pain ... and the memory. One as futile as the other. One as impossible as the other to stop dwelling on in spite of what he might tell himself.

Louise Lenahan Wallace

On a mellow September Sunday, with the trees and bushes beginning to hint of autumn, Will hitched up the wagon. *Summer weather'll linger awhile longer*, he thought gratefully, *but it'll be without the oven-heat of the past weeks.* He shook his head. Here he was, grouching about a little warm weather when only last winter he had been certain he would be chilled forever through to his bones! He finished buckling the team and led them closer to the back door.

In the house, Hannah was struggling to get, and keep, all four boys presentable at one time. From the indignant squeals issuing from the kitchen, she was having a difficult time. At least the howls belonged to the boys, not her, although to judge from her face as she finally emerged with all of them in tow, her thoughts would probably not bear repeating in church.

Wisely, he smothered a chuckle. She had been almost human since the night he had blown up at her, and he couldn't see taking a foolish chance on sparking her temper. Lifting the older boys into the wagon box, he assisted her over the high wheel and handed Micah up, all in a most tactful silence. She adjusted her bonnet, twitched the skirt of her gray Sunday dress aside, and moved the baby to a more comfortable position on her lap. Will climbed up beside her. "Ready?" he asked pleasantly.

She whirled to face the wagon bed. "Sam Clayton, sit down before you fall out! Isaac and Jeremy, hang on to him." Giggling, the two boys dove enthusiastically for their brother, firmly pinning him down. Ignoring his protesting squalls, Hannah turned back to Will. "Ready," she said briefly. As he shook out the lines, he heard her mumble something distinctly like, "Lord, help me!" as she raised her eyes heavenward.

With effort he kept his voice sober. "Prayin' before you even get to church?"

She shot him a startled look and started to frown, but smiled sheepishly. "I admit it. Between them and me, one of us needs all the help we can get, and I have a feeling it's me!"

"Never hurts to ask, anyway," he agreed cheerfully and urged the horses along, for they were late starting.

Pulling in front of the church, he eased himself down on his still-sore leg and reached to lift Hannah out. She swung lightly in his firm grasp, but her knee inadvertently knocked against his injured leg. He caught his breath in pain and lurched, sending her backward. He managed to grab her before she tumbled, and for a moment she was close in his arms. Laughing apologetically at her own clumsiness, she pulled away as he released her. "Is your knee all right?" she asked anxiously.

He managed a weak smile. "It's still there, no doubt 'bout it!"

She started to protest worriedly, but he had already turned to hand the boys down, so she reached for Micah, neither of them aware of the curious, interested glances that had followed their innocent movements.

The bell was ringing as they hurried up the steps, and they had time for no more than a hasty greeting or two to friends as they found their places and the opening hymn began.

A mighty fortress is our God,
a bulwark never failing ...

Micah started squiggling and Will reached to take him. Rubbing her aching arms, Hannah smiled her relief, as her voice rose clear and true.

... and armed with cruel hate,
on earth is not His equal.

Reverend Wardley motioned them to be seated and stepped to his pulpit. Fresh out of divinity school when he had been called to this church, he had at once set about reforming the building and the congregation. Now, after five years, the building conformed to his standards. The congregation had proved less cooperative, but he was still working on it. Tall, and lean to the point of boniness, he had lost none of his youthful zeal. This morning he surveyed his flock in total silence. " 'Know therefore that the Lord thy God, He is God, the faithful God, which keepeth covenant and mercy with them that love Him and keep His commandments to a thousand generations, and repayeth them that hate Him to their face, to destroy them: He will not be slack to him that hateth Him; He will repay him to his face.' " He paused to draw breath, his eyes grim. "The sermon this morning is on the Tenth Commandment."

Will, startled by this particular choice, looked up from handing Micah his battered pocketknife and found Wardley's glare pinned on him. In spite of himself, Will felt a stab of guilt.

But he found his discomfort was only beginning.

" 'Thou shalt not covet thy neighbor's house, thou shalt not covet thy neighbor's wife, nor his man-servant, nor his maid-servant, nor his ox, nor his ass, nor anything that is thy neighbor's.' " Wardley rendered the ancient words in tones solemn as death. "This commandment, given by God to Moses, means exactly what it says. 'Thou shalt not covet thy neighbor's wife.' It doesn't say it's all right some of the time or if it happens to be one person instead of another, that you can't do this thing but it's all right for me to because God understands my reasons. 'Ye shall not turn aside to the right hand or the left.' To desire even in thought is just as wrong, just as damnable as to actually achieve."

By now Will, red to the ears, was certain every eye in the church besides Wardley's was on him. He would have slid down in his seat, sunk through the floor if possible, but pride held him glued upright.

"You understand, of course, that this commandment, this law, works the other way as well. It is just as wrong for a woman married before God to desire, even in her heart, a man other than her husband."

Will had been concentrating his gaze on Micah, who was puzzling over how to open the knife. At those words he raised his head and caught the sidelong stares of his neighbors, their eyes quickly dropping as he glanced up. *What was this all about, anyway?* Indignation seeped into his puzzlement and embarrassment. Wardley had no reason to make insinuations about him and Eve. As Jason had pointed out so bluntly, in the eyes of their friends what they had had was over and done. Since the wedding, he hadn't even seen, let alone talked to Eve, except for that one miserable morning. If there had been something romantic about that meeting with his blood all over the place and him half out of his head with pain, he had missed it.

For that matter, he hadn't talked to the minister, either. So how could Wardley know Will's private thoughts and feelings?

Deciding it must be coincidence or shrewd warning at best, he shrugged the Reverend's words off and held his head high. *Let Wardley suggest; let them stare!* What did he care if they had nothing better to do with their minds and their time?

He focused his attention on the bonnet three rows ahead and almost directly in front of him. Eve and Matt were sitting close together and were, he suspected, holding hands. If the sermon disturbed her, she gave no sign.

After services the congregation mingled, greeting friends seldom seen except at church. Will, guiding Hannah and the boys out the door, again became aware of curious scrutiny. Again he tried to shake it off, but the sense of it persisted.

Jason and Becky, chuckling over the antics of Aaron and Catty's 10-month-old daughter Eden, greeted Will and Hannah warmly, but the smiles of the rest of their friends held a subtle — what? *Nothin'*, he told himself, exasperated, determined to ignore it. He would not let them shame him with their sneaking suspicions and their smugness.

"Hello, Will, how's your knee?"

He stiffened at sound of the soft voice at his elbow. Turning slowly, he looked straight into Eve's clear blue eyes. "Hello, Eve," he managed to say quietly. "How are you doin'?" His voice caught as memory of her terrified wails echoed in his ears.

The faintest of shadows darkened her eyes for a split second and was gone so quickly a casual observer would not have seen. But Will was not a casual observer and he had seen. "Eve ..." he began, but a cool voice cut across his words.

"Will." Matt had turned from chatting with Catty in time to halt his anxious question. His gray eyes held no warmth for his old friend, but Will saw only too plainly Eve's glow of joy as her gaze met Matt's. It was only an instant as the answering light leaped in his eyes, but far too long for the man watching. Defeated, he turned away. He had been cherishing his secret suspicion that something was wrong between Eve and Matt. Something was wrong, to be sure, but obviously not between them.

"Will?" He hadn't even noticed Hannah standing beside him. "Are you ready to go?"

"All set." He put his hand under her elbow and steered her out of the crowd toward the wagon. Turning, she caught a glimpse over his shoulder of Eve and Matt, accepting well-wishes from enthusiastic friends. Hannah glanced at the man striding so grimly beside her. Then away, knowing that no one — she least of all — had the right to intrude on his pain.

As Will lifted Hannah to the wagon seat, she looked back. Hand in hand, Matt and Eve were strolling toward their buggy. God forgive her, she would never be deliberately jealous of another's happiness — she was truly glad for Eve — but how came it that Eve should be so blessed in love while she, Hannah ... Blindly she flung the thought aside, not daring even in her heart to complete it.

Except for the innocent chattering of the boys in the wagon box, the ride back to the ranch was a silent one because neither Will nor Hannah, each immersed in private pain, made any effort to talk.

Six

Will was so sunk in self-pain that he never gave another thought to the curious glances or Reverend Wardley's sermon. Back at the ranch, he changed clothes and plunged into the waiting repairs, hoping that if he worked hard enough, he could drive from his mind the memory of that shadow in Eve's eyes. And even more so the joyous glow of love that had lit them as she looked at Matt. As if he could forget, ever!

Jeremy, by now his faithful shadow, helped clean out the chicken house. The day had turned hot after all, and the little wooden building seemed to have trapped all the sun's rays. The task had been put off much longer than it should, and along with stifling heat, the henhouse had stored all the unpleasant odors of its inhabitants' leavings. A job perfectly suited to his present mood, Will mocked himself.

He had no particular scruples against working on Sunday. With so much to be done and so little time to fit it all in, he felt it would be more of a sin to waste the day in idleness than to spend it working at urgently necessary tasks. He hoped, however, the Lord would forgive him for choosing this particular chore this day, and decided that since He had created chickens and their odorous habits, He would, indeed, understand.

Because it was a messy, unpleasant chore in a cramped, stuffy space, Will removed his shirt. Jeremy, trying very hard to be casual as though it were not the most daring thing in the world, followed suit, wistfully eyeing Will's muscular build and deep tan.

Seeing the youngster's skinny ribs and white skin, Will said solemnly, "Workin' out in this sun'll put muscles on you and brown you up, too, before you know it. We'll just have to be careful you don't burn. Your Ma'd skin us both."

Jeremy glanced cautiously over at the house. "She sure would!"

They were well into their unsavory task when the rattle of wheels warned them someone was coming. Jeremy scooted backward and poked his head out the door. "It's Uncle Jason and Aunt Becky!"

Will groaned. What a time they'd picked to come. A few minutes more and the blasted job'd be done. On the other hand, what was their arrival to him when they'd come to see Hannah and the boys?

Hannah had come hurrying out to greet them, and Will saw her gesture toward the henhouse. She and Becky started inside as Jason turned in his direction. The cousins had scattered to play. "Afternoon, Will, Jeremy. Looks like you latched onto a fun chore."

Will leaned on the shovel. "A regular laugh a minute. Want to help?" he asked politely.

Jason grinned and backed off. "Not me. And don't let Becky catch you doin' that. She'll be after me to do ours next!" He glanced down at his nephew. "I see you have a helper."

"I do, and a good one." Will smiled at the boy.

"I been helpin' Mr. Braden shoe horses and clean the barn and fix the side of the house and ..."

As he paused for breath, Jason put in, "Sounds like you been busy. Your Ma and Mr. Braden must be proud of you. But you know, the other fellas are down by the creek. I bet Mr. Braden wouldn't mind if you took a break and joined 'em."

Jeremy looked up at Will, who nodded. "Sure, son, go ahead and take a breather. I'll call you when it's time to start workin' again."

As the little boy trotted off, Will called him back. "Hold on just a minute. Even if you are goin' to play in the creek, you are a mite ... unsightly. Think we better do somethin' 'bout it, first?"

Jeremy looked down at his grime-encrusted body. "Gee whiz, you mean I gotta take a bath?"

Will smothered a smile. "Now I wouldn't say you have to go that far, but a little dousin' off wouldn't hurt. You don't want the others to smell you comin' before you get there. Come on. Grab your shirt and let's see what we c'n do."

Reluctantly, Jeremy obeyed, and Jason strolled curiously along behind. They rounded the corner of the barn, out of sight of the house, and Will gestured for the boy to stand away from the horse trough. Picking up the bucket that stood nearby, he dunked it into the water. "Take a deep breath and hold it."

Jeremy obeyed, taking a breath that would have filled a moose. As Will poured the bucket of water over his shoulders, he gasped and let out a shriek.

"Quiet! Your Ma hears you, she'll hog-tie us f'r sure. Permanently." He dunked the bucket, and Jeremy giggled.

"Ready?" Another lung-bursting breath promptly exploded as he giggled again. "Here it comes!" Will warned, pouring carefully. "That should do it. What do you think, Uncle Jason?"

Jason, who had been watching in amused silence, studied him carefully. "I'd say that's a heap better. Least a body c'n be downwind of you now."

"C'n I take all my baths this way, Mr. Braden, please?"

Will chuckled. "I don't think so. This is between us men, alone. Women, particularly Mas, just don't understand this kind of thing."

Solemn-eyed, Jeremy agreed.

"Here, dry yourself with my shirt, then off with you. The others are waitin'!"

Jeremy toweled hastily and scampered off.

The two men watched him out of sight before they turned back to the chicken house. "Might as well finish the job, if you don't mind," Will said.

"Sure, go ahead. You know, I never seen such a change in such a short time."

"What do you mean?" Will stooped to pick up the shovel.

"Jeremy. He used to be so quiet you couldn't get two words out of him. Now he'd be a match f'r my boys, and that's goin' some."

"Guess he just needed a chance, is all."

"I suppose. You've sure done a lot with the place, too. Looks better'n I've seen it in quite a spell."

"I've managed to keep busy," Will said wryly.

Jason tugged at his lip. "Got somethin' to say, but don't know quite how."

Will looked up warily at the sober note in his voice. "I

always figured the best way to say anythin' was straight out."

"Maybe you're right. Beatin' 'round the barn won't do it. It's 'bout all the buzzin' that was goin' on at church this mornin'."

So he hadn't imagined it. Apparently he couldn't even say two words to Eve on a crowded church step. "What 'bout it?" he asked coldly.

Jason thrust out his hand as if to ward off Will's anger. "Now mind, Becky and me don't put no stock in it, we just feel you ought to know what's bein' said. If you don't already."

"Just what is bein' said?"

"Nothin' in so many words, just hints 'bout you and Hannah."

Will gaped. "Me and Hannah?"

"That you and her have it pretty cozy here, just the two of you, and Luke gone off God knows where."

Will's jaw dropped. "Hannah? And me? My God, you got to be jokin'! Luke may be gone, but she's still married to him. Have you f'rgotten that? Or do you place so little trust in her sense of values and mine?"

"Wait a minute, Will. I said Becky and me don't hold with what they're sayin'. We been tellin' that flat out to anybody who's even hinted."

Will's smile was grim. "Don't you know the surest way to make a rumor fact is to deny it? You've prob'ly convinced them one and all that we are beddin' together."

"Will ..."

"No, let me finish. Have you f'rgotten whose idea it was f'r me to come here in the first place? It wasn't Hannah's. Or mine. If you'll think back just a bit, you'll recall that neither of us was exactly wildly in favor of this — this — scheme. But you really didn't leave us much choice, did you? We've made do the best we could. And we've done nothin' — nothin' — to be ashamed of!" Jason had never seen him so angry.

"Will, calm down. I told you how we feel, and I meant it. But you can't fight what's bein' said by gettin' all hot under the collar. You said denyin' it's a sure way to prove it true. Well, so is gettin' all mad. That'll only show you think you have somethin' to hide."

"What do you want me to do?" he asked furiously. "Pack up and leave? And what'll that prove? Only that I have somethin' to run from. Well, I don't. And neither does Hannah. And that's all there is to it."

Jason was silent for a long minute. Then he said slowly, "I'm glad you're goin' to stay. You'll prove 'em wrong in the end. I know you will."

Will smiled sourly. "Thanks f'r the vote of confidence."

"I mean it. I'm glad you're stayin'. None of this changes the basic fact that Hannah needs someone here. Now maybe more than ever."

Will's temper flared again. "I don't take kindly to bein' used, Jason. Sure, Hannah has to be protected. That was the whole idea to start with, wasn't it? But I have feelin's, too. How do you think it makes me feel to know people are snickerin' behind my back? I've done more'n a few things in my life that I was embarrassed 'bout. But mighty few that I'm downright ashamed of. And I don't intend to start now. You c'n go tell that to your 'Christian' friends who go snoopin' and carryin' tales."

Jason reddened. "That's hittin' below the belt, and you know it. I didn't come here to be carryin' tales. I came because I thought you should know. And tearin' at each other's throats ain't goin' to solve nothin'."

They glared at each other until Will slowly let out his breath, his anger flattened. "Sorry, Jason. You're right. I'll talk to Hannah, tell her what's goin' on so she c'n be prepared."

"I'll tell her if you don't want to."

Will shook his head. "It's her and me. I'd just as soon tell her in my own way."

Jason stood silent a moment. "I got to get goin'. I'm sure sorry 'bout all this."

In a daze of unreality, Will watched Jason walk slowly back to the house as the children, wet and muddy, came running to pile into the wagon. With numb detachment, he saw Jason help Becky up, heard them call their farewells as the wagon rattled away.

Hannah stood waving until the wagon disappeared around the corner of the barn before, shoulders drooping, she turned to go inside.

Stooping to pick up the shovel, he began wielding it furiously.

"Mr. Braden, you want me to help you some more?"

He jumped. He had been so lost in his own dark thoughts he hadn't heard Jeremy come up.

Will looked at the bright, trusting little face, and his stern expression softened. "Sure, take off your shirt, grab your shovel, and let's get to it!"

They plowed in and were just finishing when Hannah came up with a jug and two cups. She glanced at Will's chest, bare except for its covering of curly, dark hair, and her gaze lingered a moment before she realized she was staring and lowered her eyes in acute embarrassment. Flustered, trying to cover it, she asked lightly, "Do you know any hardworking men who might be able to use a drink of ginger water?"

Jeremy whooped. Will, in light of Jason's revelation sharply aware of her reaction, reached self-consciously for his shirt and used it to wipe his sweaty, dirty forehead, then stood clutching it awkwardly.

"I would, Ma!" her son said eagerly in answer to her question. Unaware of the adults' discomfort, he was childishly pleased when they both laughed so heartily.

"Jeremy, you look like you've been dumped head first into that pile," Hannah protested, handing him a cup.

"Aw, Ma, I been workin' real hard. Ask Mr. Braden."

She looked up at Will, and he said soberly, "He sure has been, Ma."

"You two!" But she was laughing. "One thing's certain, before either of you set foot in my clean house, you're going to have to take a bath!"

"Aw, Ma," Jeremy objected again. But he brightened. "Mr. Braden, c'n we ..."

"No," Will said hastily, and smiled innocently at Hannah. Jeremy looked painfully guilty.

"Something's going on," she said suspiciously.

"Of course not," Will assured her cheerily. "We wouldn't hide anythin' from you that you should know."

"What about something I shouldn't know?" But she was laughing. "Will you be much longer? I've started supper."

"Just finishin', and I'm starved with all this hard work. How 'bout you, Jeremy?"

"Yeah, Ma, I'm starved!"

"I can believe that. You always are, lately."

"All this outdoor work gives a fella an appetite," Will put in. "But before we eat, I think we'd best heed your Ma's warnin' and clean ourselves up a little."

"How we goin' to do that without goin' in the house?"

"I'll show you. Come on."

Hannah watched as Will led the boy over to the well and drew up the bucket. Jeremy promptly giggled and flashed a hasty look at his mother. Will just as promptly shushed him by telling him to start rinsing off as he poured a careful portion over the child's shoulders.

Hannah, shocked into speechlessness, watched in dismay as Jeremy, crowing with laughter, scrubbed vigorously under the flow of cool water. "Do it again!" he yelled.

Will, refilling the bucket, shook his head. "My turn, this time. I don't know how it's possible, but I'm even dirtier than you. Wait till I get my boots off, though!" He sat down to tug them off. "Come give me a hand, boy."

Pressing his ample boot to Jeremy's backside, he let the boy tug it off. Jeremy went sprawling but sat up, waved the foot gear triumphantly, and returned gleefully for the other one. Will drew his knees up to his chest, ducked his head and closed his eyes. "Ready," he declared. "Just pour it over my shoulders."

Jeremy reached for the full bucket, but couldn't lift it. Hannah shook her head. Putting a finger to her lips, she tiptoed forward, picked up the pail and dumped it full over Will's head.

He yelled and jumped at the shock of the chilly water. Swiveling around, pushing hair and water out of his eyes, he saw Hannah holding the empty bucket and Jeremy doubled up with laughter.

"Your hair needed washing, too," she said innocently.

All he could do for a moment was sit and gape foolishly, before his roar of laughter joined theirs.

The littlest boys came tumbling down the steps. "Me, too, Ma," Sam pleaded.

"Too, too," Micah chorused.

"I don't ..." she began, but Will cut in.

"Why not?"

Hannah looked doubtful. "Will, are you sure?"

"Won't hurt 'em a bit, you'll see." And he carefully poured water over them until they, too, were dripping wet and squealing with laughter. It wound up a merry battle royal as Jeremy dumped more water over Will, who tackled him in mock fury. Soon there was only a tangle of arms, legs, shrieks and mud. Hannah stood well back and watched in amused dismay as the four of them disappeared in a covering of grime.

Finally, breathless, Will emerged. "That's enough, fellas," he gasped. They continued to pull at him, but he said firmly, "Line up and get ready f'r one last dunkin'. Here it comes!" He sluiced each of them in turn, then eyed them ruefully. "Guess that won't quite do it," he said apologetically to Hannah.

She surveyed her three muddy, dripping sons before she turned to look him up and down. "Someone," she said, speaking distinctly, "will have to give these boys a bath and wash their hair. I have to finish supper. Any suggestions as to who will help them?"

Will grinned like a small boy caught in mischief. "I think I've just been volunteered."

"I think you have, thank you. Supper will be in half an hour. I want them at the table, clean, then." She looked him over from head to foot once again. "You have mud in your ears."

Daintily lifting her skirts away from the muck, she turned to flounce into the house, but stopped as she caught sight of the figure standing on the top step. "Isaac, you should have joined in the fun, too. Why didn't you?"

He simply stared at her with open hostility, jerked past her outstretched hand, and fled down the steps around the corner.

"Isaac!" But he neither paused nor looked back.

Will had been watching silently. Now he stepped toward her. "It's my fault. I should of included him."

She shook her head, looking where the boy had disappeared. "I'd better go after him."

"I will if you want, Hannah."

"No, I'll go."

He watched her follow her son's path around the house and turned back to the wide-eyed youngsters. "Come on, fellas. Let's get washed up."

Supper was a subdued affair. Hannah had returned with Isaac in tow as the others were dressing. She tried to make light of it, inspecting the boys' hair and fingernails with mock sternness and finally pronouncing them passable. Then, hands on hips, she turned to Will. "Bend your head down." He blinked blankly. "Right now. Put your head down so I can inspect your ears. You're not coming to my table covered with mud."

Lips twitching, he said meekly, "Yes, Ma'am," and bent for her inspection.

She peered at his ears, his hair, and lastly his nails. "Guess you'll do," she said finally. "Come along, Boys," she said briskly to her awed sons.

Those, however, were the only moments of levity. Will

didn't know what she had said to Isaac, but every time he glanced up the child was glowering at him. Such a fixed stare was not conducive to an appetite. But even more than that, Will had remembered Jason's visit and all it had revealed. He had to tell Hannah, but how?

They had shared a level of companionship today unfelt before — an acceptance, as it were, of themselves and their circumstances with neither strain nor suspicion. To tell the truth, it had been a position comfortable as an old boot and quite a relief after all the past tensions. What he must tell her could only destroy that peace, and he dreaded the freeze-up of her face and voice and eyes. But he had no choice.

She, unaware of his mental turmoil, chatted about her visit with Becky, but finally even her comments ran out against the wall of his preoccupation.

He waited, dawdling over a cup of coffee he didn't really want, until she came out from putting the boys to bed. Giving him a frankly startled glance at this break in his routine of always leaving right after supper, she turned her attention to the bowl of bread dough raising on the back of the stove. Removing the towel, she tested the mixture and reached for a handful of flour to sprinkle on the board. He watched as if fascinated by the process and said reluctantly, "Hannah, I've got to talk to you."

She dumped the dough onto the board and began kneading the springy mass. "I thought as much. You seem worried."

He watched her hands work the dough. "Did Becky have anythin' special to say to you this afternoon?"

"Becky? No, like I said, we just talked about this and that, same as always. Why?"

He sighed, wishing heartily that he could avoid the whole unpleasant subject. But wishing wouldn't make it go away.

"Will, what's wrong?"

He looked directly into her eyes. "Jason says there's talk goin' 'round."

Her hands stilled on the dough. "What kind of talk? About ... about Luke?" Her voice was tight, and she closed her eyes to hide the pain in them.

"No, not Luke. It's you and me, Hannah."

She looked blank. "Us? What about ..." She stopped, stricken, and turned red. "Will, no." She gave a bitter laugh. "They have to be joking." The insult rang against sudden, total silence, and she drew a sharp breath. "I didn't mean it that way."

He smiled thinly. "If it's any help, I had the same thought when Jason told me."

"I didn't ask you to come here," she retorted, stung. "If you want to leave, then go!"

The stare they exchanged was mutually resentful before she dropped down onto the chair across from him. "Will, I'm sorry. Sniping at each other isn't going to help. But what are we going to do?"

"I don't know f'r sure. I don't know there's all that much we c'n do. We're not up to anythin' we couldn't tell the whole world 'bout, if they asked."

"That's the trouble. They haven't asked. They're just assuming. Why do people do that?" she burst out. "Why? I heard the whispers in church, but I thought they were about Luke." Her eyes grew wide with horror. "That sermon! He was ... It was about ..." She choked.

"I was a little slow gettin' that, myself. He covered the subject pretty thoroughly, didn't he?"

"It's unfair! You've been good to me — and to the boys. Only Isaac — "

"Isaac hasn't exactly taken to me," he admitted.

"I don't think it's you, really. Luke spent more time with him, paid more attention to him than to the other boys. Anyway, he told me tonight he wishes his Pa would come back. I guess he just misses him so much and resents the fact you're here and Luke isn't."

"You could be right 'bout that. It would explain a lot." Remembering dark-haired, green-eyed Jeremy's wistful question, when they had been shoeing Eagle, about why Luke had considered him a bother and Will didn't, Will hoped fervently that neither Hannah nor Jeremy would ever see the full explanation.

"What are we going to do about the other?"

Her question brought his thoughts back and he considered gravely for several moments. "Seems to me we have two choices. I c'n leave. Or we c'n keep on just like we have been and ignore all the looks and comments. We know we have nothin' to be ashamed of."

She studied his face. "Do you want to leave?"

"I want to do what's best," he said carefully. "I gave Jason my word I'd help you out. But that was only if you agreed to have me here. We have to decide between us what's best f'r us and go on from there."

She bit her lip and avoided his gaze. "I know I haven't been very nice to you. I guess I've been blaming you for everything, same as Isaac. And that's not fair, either. I am

102

glad you've been here. I want you to know that. It's been a relief to me in so many ways. But I don't want to hold you if you don't want to stay."

He studied his hands. "The idea of walkin' off just don't sit right with me. I'd much rather face up to people, let them see the truth f'r themselves. They'll have to, eventually. All the suspicions in the world can't make a truth when that truth is somethin' else. So if you're willin', " he looked at her questioningly, "I think I'll just stick it out here awhile longer."

Relief flooded her face. "Thank you, Will. I'm glad," she said simply.

"It won't be easy," he warned. "How high c'n you hold your head?"

She smiled grimly. "With all the practice I've had lately? As high as need be."

Seven

They were to find out over the next days just how high they had to hold their heads. Will, being away all day, was spared much of the ensuing unpleasantness, for at the herd the men treated him much as they always had, and for that he was silently grateful. But that only put the brunt of it on Hannah.

The Monday following their tense visit to church dawned heavy and sultry. Hannah, who had planned a day of canning fruits and vegetables, quailed inwardly at the thought of being trapped in a steamy kitchen. Laughing, she groused to Will about it at breakfast. "Why don't you put it off f'r a day or two?" he asked with masculine impracticality.

Hiding her shock at the very suggestion, she shook her head. "Everything's ripening at the same time. The jars won't fill themselves. Which means if I put it off till tomorrow, that'll be just that much more to catch up on." She sighed. "I don't mind the doing of it. At least it means food this winter. I just wish it could be done in, say, January or February, when a warm kitchen is a treat. Things get kind of backward, sometimes, don't they?"

Will pondered the problem. "Maybe someday somebody'll

come up with a way of doin' it where you don't have to get the whole house heated up. Think 'bout just walkin' into the Clark's Valley Store and takin' your whole winter's supply of peas, that's already been canned up f'r you, right off the shelf."

Hannah shook her head over his fanciful musing. "It'll never happen. I can't imagine trusting a perfect stranger to cook and seal my vegetables properly." She rose and started to gather the used plates. "But wouldn't it be nice?" she added wistfully.

At mid-morning Hannah was washing jars at the sink, preparatory to finishing the second round of her day's canning. A kettle of cherries and a pan of water for sterilizing the jars bubbled on the stove, the steam from the two pots and the heat from the range adding to the temperature of the already warm room. A line of jars filled with string beans gleamed triumphantly from the corner of the worktable, but behind her, tomatoes waited their turn for processing.

She paused to push her damp hair back out of her eyes with her sleeve, and sudsy water promptly ran down her elbow to the floor. With a decidedly unlady-like exclamation, she reached for a cloth to blot up the mess. As she straightened, she glimpsed movement out the window. The boys were playing in the yard; their yells and squeals had assured her all morning that they were all right. She realized now that their noise had suddenly stopped. Lifting aside the curtain, she saw a horse and buggy drawing up to the door. The boys were staring at the occupants in total and uncharacteristic silence.

Hannah recognized her visitors — and rendered her second, even more heartfelt, unlady-like opinion of the day. With a despairing glance at the disorder rampant in her kitchen, and with the sinking knowledge that she probably resembled the cloth she had just used to mop up the floor, she turned to the door that was standing wide open in a vain attempt to lower the temperature of the room. Her third unlady-like thought of the day was a wish that she could slam it shut, but her visitors were already peering interestedly at her through the opening. She glimpsed the plump, frankly curious faces of the mother and daughter who were the two worst gossips in the community, and it was at that moment that her "imp of mischief" took over. *Why not?* jeered the small voice inside her. *Do you have a better way of getting through this?*

"Pearl Gilby and Miss Mabel!" she said hastily. "What a surprise! As you can see, I wasn't expecting visitors, but do come in." *To my sweltering kitchen that's steamy enough to uncurl the feathers on your fancy hats*, the imp added.

"Oh, dear, maybe we shouldn't," Pearl said, with every intention of doing so, anyway. Hannah stepped aside to let them precede her to the table, where she pulled out chairs for them and pushed aside the waiting vegetables.

"Would you like some coffee?" she asked graciously, only too well aware that every movement she made and every detail of her cluttered kitchen were being carefully catalogued for future discussion.

"We don't want to interrupt your work, dear," Pearl assured her. "We just came to pay a neighborly visit, since it seems we never see you in town any more. Don't you go to town any more?"

Hannah pondered the best answer to this innocent-seeming, barb-loaded question. Not for the world would she have admitted to these two that there was no reason to go to town when one had no money to spend. The imp, of course, had an immediate, to-the-point response that she reluctantly rejected. "I've been busy here," she said carefully, "as you can see. I'm looking forward to finishing my canning. Maybe when it's done I'll have more time for visiting." The polite hint was too subtle. It went right over the heads of Mabel and Pearl.

"I believe I will have some coffee, dear," Pearl volunteered. "How about you, Mabel?"

Mabel, who rarely said much — she just listened avidly and caught the finer details that Pearl missed — shook her head. "I believe not, thank you. It is a bit warm in here for coffee," she explained graciously, lapsing into silence once more.

"You are right, dear. I don't believe I'll have any, either, although I'm sure it would be delicious. I wouldn't want to put you to the trouble of making a fresh pot, even though I'm sure what you have left over from breakfast would be very good."

Hannah, refusing to get tangled in that one, stepped to the stove to set the kettle aside. As she turned back to her visitors, she caught the furtive glances they were giving the room. *I didn't invite you here*, the imp shouted indignantly. *What gives you the right ...*

"And how is Will, dear?" Pearl cut across the imp's tirade.

Somehow unsurprised by the introduction of this subject, Hannah lifted her chin. "He's just fine. I'll tell him you were asking about him."

Mabel and Pearl exchanged knowing smiles. "You do that, dear," Pearl urged her. "Such a hardworking man, and so good of him to take on looking after you and the ranch here, now that Luke's gone." Mabel nodded sympathetic agreement. "There are so many duties we look to men to handle. You are fortunate, indeed, to have his services here."

Hannah's response to this sledgehammer subtleness was, fortunately, never made. The moment she had her mouth open and the words formed, Sam charged through the open door, his bloodcurdling screams overriding lesser sounds. He dodged past Pearl and Mabel and took refuge on Hannah's far side.

Before any of the shocked women could question his panic, Isaac had torn into the room after him, brandishing some object between his cupped hands. Sam was shivering and clutching frantically at Hannah, and she was trying to calm him and stop Isaac, so she honestly had no way of preventing Isaac's next movement. He braked to a stop between Mabel and Pearl. "See my frog?" he asked proudly and thrust it first toward Pearl's shocked face, then Mabel's. The screams of the two women would have done a torture victim proud.

Hannah reached out to snatch Isaac, but missed because Sam, with a screech that paled his first ones into insignificance, chose that moment to let go of her and race out the door. Isaac reversed direction and was after him like an arrow. At the door, he paused long enough to face the hysterical women. "Bye," he said politely, and seeing Hannah start after him, wheeled out the door and was gone, presumably after the luckless Sam.

Hannah took a step or two after him, but realized she couldn't leave her frantic guests. Abandoning him to a later court hearing, she made an honest attempt to soothe the various ruffled feathers that had promptly turned their indignation upon her. "Well, never in all my life ..." Pearl sputtered.

Mabel, too, had been scandalized into speech. "... have I been treated this way!" she finished for her mother. "That child ought to be whipped ..."

"... within an inch of his life!" Pearl took her turn to finish for her daughter.

"But we shouldn't have expected anything else, considering everything!" they finished in perfect chorus.

Hannah tried to apologize, but they were beyond being soothed. Gathering their indignation about them, they fled the kitchen. By the time Hannah reached the bottom step, their buggy was halfway out of the yard and gathering speed. She managed to contain herself as long as they were in sight, but as soon as they disappeared, she sank onto the bottom step and completely gave herself up to the whoops of merriment that she had, from sheer force of will, been holding in.

After she had laughed herself into a sideache, she went, with a properly grim face, in search of her errant son.

Unfortunately, Mabel and Pearl were only the first of a parade of well-meaning neighbors who began to drop casually by "to see how you're getting along."

In spite of Pearl and Mabel, she accepted the next visitors at face value. As the list lengthened, however, she began to wonder. Martha Wardley, the Reverend's wife, yesterday; Elsa Parker and Caroline Sloan today. It was a busy season, and not one in which friends made unnecessary visits. Deep in her own canning and preserving, she couldn't understand how all the other housewives could take so much time off, especially the ones she was in the habit of seeing only at church or while on a shopping trip to town.

She made light of it as she told Will each evening of the latest callers and how each woman had tried to be casual. "But they all sneak glances around as if expecting to find something wicked. If they catch me looking at them looking, they get all flustered and try to pretend they weren't snooping at all. I don't know just what they're hoping to find. You hiding in the cupboard or your boots under the bed at the very least!"

Such a bald statement from proper Hannah shocked Will, but he laughed with her at the absurdity of it. "It'll all blow over pretty soon. You know how folks are. All upset and nosy 'bout somethin' until a new sensation comes along and grabs all the attention. We'll just have to wait 'em out, like we agreed."

"I just wish they'd hurry up and find a new victim. All this visiting's making a wreck of my canning schedule!"

The men, too, kept busy from "can't see to can't see" and beyond, preparing for the coming winter. The mellow autumn weather would not last forever. Jason, Matt, Aaron and Will felt an urgency to do as much as possible. Memory of the previous winter was too fresh a scar on their souls to take the coming time casually.

They had decided to try Matt's plan, borrowed from Lafe Bardlow up north, to keep the herd together and accounted for during the winter. Bardlow had used the idea the year before with his own herd, and it had worked. By riding day and night, keeping track of the cattle instead of letting them just drift, his men had kept losses far below average in one of the worst winters in memory.

Lack of vigilance had not destroyed Bardlow in the end, but simply forces beyond his control. A savage blizzard hitting the tail-end of February had cost the lives of a large percentage of the herd. A Chinook, a warm southwest wind that melted the snow too rapidly, caused the river to rise too fast and drowned many of the remaining cows. The flooding had proved the final undoing of Lafe Bardlow's LB — and countless other ranches from Canada to Texas. Many stock owners were never to recover. Others, including the Claytons and the Grandlers, were forced to begin again with a pitifully small number of cattle that had once been but the edge of great herds.

That was why, with a new respect for Nature branded into them, the men did everything possible and looked for more ways to lessen the coming assault. They put up tons of hay and kept constant check on the waterholes across the range, digging them out if necessary, shifting the cattle as needed.

Most important, the cattle had been nursed along as if worth their weight in gold — which they were, when it came right down to it. Such a bad winter had depleted the supply of cattle available for shipping East and to the rest of the country. Beef was scarce and the nation was clamoring for it.

Jason and the others had been working all summer on the grass near their homes. Ordinarily they would have moved the herds to summer grazing grounds in the mountains. But this year the men had been of no mind to do so and leave their families home, unprotected, after the raid on Ben and Anne.

Having decided early on to make do with what was readily available, they had combined all the herds into one and were using the grass and water on all the ranches. Over and over during the summer they told themselves and one another: If we can just hang on till spring, just until then ...

But the plain truth was, with no money coming in because they hadn't had a fall shipment, it was going to be a long, difficult trail through winter. They all knew it, but all the worrying in the world wouldn't change a thing. They could only vow to do their best and trust to God for the rest.

On a clear, crisp evening, Will galloped Eagle into the ranchyard, shouting for Hannah. He slid to the ground and leaped up the porch steps. "Hannah, where are you?" he yelled again even before he reached the door. She came running out, so fast she almost collided with him.

"Will, what's wrong?" He saw the fear in her eyes.

He grabbed her by the arms, grinning down at her. "Ever'thin's right! Word just come in there'll be a fella in Laramie in two days. Hannah, he'll be buyin' cattle! You know what that means?"

She stared at him, unbelieving. "A cattle buyer! But, we can't ..."

"We have to. It's our one chance of cash money f'r this winter. We can't pass it up. Even though, splittin' it between all of us like we will, nobody's goin' to get exactly rich, it's sure goin' to help out."

"But dividing it like that when Luke — we — lost all our cattle and we don't have any to send. It's not fair to the others, taking from their share to give us when they won't get that much anyway." He saw bitter disappointment replace her joyous excitement.

"Now just hold on. Jason figured you'd get some such notion in your head, and he told me to tell you to get it out right now because that's not the way it works. All of us have been workin' the herd and all of us are goin' in on it together. So we'll pick the most likely from all of 'em and share the profit. It won't be much, true, but it will bring hard cash f'r groceries and shoes f'r the boys."

With cold weather coming on, she had been deeply concerned about this last item. Now she struggled visibly between pride and harsh necessity. "Are they in good enough shape?" she asked, finally.

He let out his breath in sharp relief. "Some are more prime than others, to be honest. But sellin' even a few'll make a difference in the way we eat this winter."

"Cash money," she repeated wonderingly. "I can't believe it!"

They had only two days, but by working beyond even their own capacities, Jason, Aaron, Matt and Will scraped together a drive. A pitiful shadow of the former days' gathers, the rather motley group of critters was, at least, a step toward the future — a promise of financial recovery. The cattle would be inspected, of course, but from covert comparison of neighboring herds, these cows would match up, maybe come out a little ahead. Each man thought of the devastation of the winter and spring before and knew they were far luckier than many other ranchers who had been destroyed to the last cow.

Hannah waited in suspenseful agony while Will was gone. Every unexpected noise took her to the door to see if he was returning, even when she knew it was too early. When she finally heard the thump of his horse's hooves, she flung open the door to meet him. He ran up the steps, grinning jubilantly and thrust an envelope into her hands. "Go ahead, open it," he urged as she stared at it. With trembling fingers, she did so, cautiously touching the bills inside as though they might disappear.

"Oh, Will," she whispered. He could not know that as much of her wonder was for the fact he had brought her the money as the fact he had gotten it at all. Luke had always kept a tight fist around any cash that had come in, and she had rarely even seen it. But Will had brought it home, handing it to her — all of it. Her eyes were very bright, and he felt a surge of gladness for being able to put that happiness there, never suspecting the true reason for it.

Will was sitting on the back steps the next evening, enjoying the last of the golden October twilight. Enjoying, too, the break from riding herd. Jason had decided that after working so hard, the men were entitled to an extra rest. Tonight was Matt and Will's turn to be off while Jason and Aaron worked with Dan Mackley as fill-in. Tomorrow night they would switch, and then again to give Dan his time off.

Hannah, behind Will in the kitchen, was finishing up her chores, singing softly as she worked.

Soft as the voice of an angel
breathing a lesson unheard;
hope with a gentle persuasion
whispers her comforting word.

It put Will in mind of his Ma, singing as she carried out her household duties. His mind canted the backtrail of years, and he was, for a few moments, a small boy again in a world with the warmth and security of a child deeply loved by his parents

— his tall, dark-haired mother and his barrel-chested, bearded and mustached father. Both strong-willed, he realized now.

Caleb Braden had been constantly hatching new schemes that would bring untold wealth to the family, always waiting for one big turn of luck to make them rich. Phebe Braden, more realistic, had tried to instill in their son the necessity for living in the present, of making do while looking to the future. She had tried to teach him not to lose the small joys of today in the bigger, bolder dream of tomorrow.

His father's dream — and the world of the wife and son — had come to a crashing close when Will was 9. He still remembered the bitter quarrel between his parents, although he hadn't understood it completely at the time. For years his mother had refused to speak of it, and only after Will was grown did he comprehend her grief that the last words she and her husband had shared had been bitter ones.

For Caleb Braden had finally stumbled onto the one scheme that would bring them their pot of gold — and more. He would go to Texas, round up a herd from the longhorns running wild there, and drive it to Abilene. Once arrived, he would be able to sell the cattle for enough to realize a fabulous profit. Phebe Braden had argued fiercely that it wouldn't work, that it was a wild, dangerous plan and a fool's dream.

But Caleb, fired with his Great Dream, had refused to listen, telling his wife he knew what he was doing and she'd see when they were rich that she should have had more confidence in him. He rode away with jingling spurs and high hopes, thrusting aside her anger with furious words of his own.

And he had failed as he had so many times before. A blinding thunderstorm, a frantic stampede and a desperate, useless attempt to turn the panicked animals from a cliff. His horse had stumbled, throwing him over the drop-off. A thousand flailing bodies had smashed him to nothing as the cows, too, plunged heedlessly over the edge.

Weeks later, Phebe Braden learned the full extent of the tragedy. Caleb, sure that his wild scheme couldn't fail, had mortgaged the ranch to the hilt, without informing his wife. Unable to even begin to pay off the other debts from the loans he had finagled, she watched the bank foreclose on her home, the only home Will had known — the home she had fought to keep through all the years of her husband's ups and downs.

It was a tribute to her personal courage that she never once faulted his father to Will for the disaster he had heaped upon them. Tight-lipped, dry-eyed, she watched her home go under the block. Then she gathered up her pitifully few remaining personal possessions and her son, and moved into town. She found work in a millinery shop and sat day after day for the rest of her life making hats for other women to look fashionable, putting every penny she earned, except for those spent on the barest necessities, into paying back her husband's debts.

Only after countless hours of furious protestation that he was a man and should be helping out, did she allow Will to take a job on the Diamond L Ranch, two hours' ride from town. Of course she worried, he knew now. But it was also a tribute to her courage that, once she had agreed, she had kept hidden from him her terrible fears and let him go his way doing what he must.

Every Saturday night he had made the long ride home to hand her his pay. Sundays after church, at her insistence, they had gone over his lessons. It was the one request she had made of him after he began earning his way, that he not give up on his schooling. Although feeling it totally unnecessary to his way of life, a waste of time, he couldn't refuse her. He knew now this had been one of the bright spots of her week, that it gave her joy and pleasure in a world turned frighteningly dark.

Working day and night, scrimping and denying herself, she had paid the enormous debts. Then, just when she was free to begin to live for herself, she had sickened. She refused, however, to admit to Will that she was ill with anything more than a "female complaint." In his own ignorance of such things, he had taken her at her word. Believing she was of an age for "that kind of thing," he had asked no more questions until it became obvious she was dying, and by then it was too late. The doctor told him there was nothing that could be done, anyway, except to try to make her last days peaceful ones.

Against all the conventions, he had quit his job at the ranch to care for her, giving back all she had taught him of courage and love. She had died, writhing in pain, during the early morning hours of what would have been a bright April day. Three years ago, now. And he was not yet done missing her.

He had wandered blindly from ranch to ranch for a time after that, seeking he knew not what, until Matt Jamison had asked him to take his place on the Arrow A, the Clayton ranch, while Matt went riding hell-bent off up north. And in the presence of Eve Clayton's warmth and joy, he had no longer wandered lost.

As the old pain welled, he reached, fumbling, for pipe and tobacco. His pockets were empty and he remembered filling his pipe at the table after supper. Micah had toddled past on unsteady feet and tripped, striking his head hard against the sharp corner of the chair seat. Thrusting pipe and tobacco aside, Will had leaped to catch the baby at the same time as Hannah. While she cradled him on her lap, Will brought cold, wet cloths to put over the swelling dangerously close to his eye. They had finally agreed he would have nothing more than a bad bruise, but he was still frightened. Hannah decided to cuddle him in the rocking chair. Will had volunteered to see the other boys to bed, and after doing so had told her good night and gone out, completely forgetting his pipe and tobacco until now.

He turned his head to look back at the kitchen. He hadn't been conscious of any sounds of Hannah moving around for quite a while, and when he saw the light gleaming yellow in the window, he understood. After the boys were safely in bed, she often sat at the table reading. Her "quiet time" she called it. Well, surely he wouldn't disturb her by running in to get his pipe. So thinking, he bounded up the steps and pushed open the door, saying, "Hannah, I just ..." And stopped, dumfounded.

She was not sitting at the table reading. She had been taking a bath in the tin tub and had just stood, reaching for the towel on the wall peg. As he, all unaware, burst into the room, she froze in shock, arms still upraised. Lamplight glowing behind her etched too clearly the curving lines of cheek and breast and hip — and the definite, undeniable swelling of her abdomen. Only a second, but far too long a time as she stood, trapped, while his eyes swept over her, burning her with the blazing intensity of his seeking.

Only a second — that seemed to go crashing on forever as he slowly raised his eyes — and read in hers all her confused amazement and horrified shame. Until he spun on his heel and flung out the door, slamming it behind him. Even as it thumped shut, he heard a strangled sob.

Fleeing across the yard to the bunkhouse, he threw himself down on his cot, breathing as heavily as though just finishing an exhausting race.

In the weeks he had been staying at the Crescent C, he had kept his relationship with Hannah as impersonal as possible. Even had Luke's invisible presence not been always between them, there was also Will's intangible remembrance of Eve. He had loved her too deeply and sincerely to turn so quickly and easily to another woman. This mutual knowledge of Luke and Eve had raised a barrier between Will and Hannah even stronger than her original one of resentment or his of reserve.

He had been aware, of course, that she was a comely woman. Her face was care-worn from grief and too-heavy responsibilities, and her eyes held sorrow she would never put into actual words. But he had also, in these past weeks, glimpsed the depths of her dignity, courage and strength — attributes that gave her beauty far beyond the realm of the mere physical. Now, unchecked by moral restraints, without even a pretense of attempting to do otherwise, he had stood and stared upon her. And knew that she was, indeed, totally desirable.

And she was going to have a baby. He groaned, clutching at the fact as a drowning man would seize at any floating leaf-scrap to hold himself up. He didn't know much about women being in such a state, it was true, but he had worked with cow-critters most of his life, and he knew the signs in them.

The full-skirted dresses and loose aprons she wore around the house had effectively disguised her secret. Until tonight. The unconcealed rounding of her stomach had been too plain to be missed. She hadn't told him. Not one word or hint the whole time he had been here. *And why should she tell me*, he wondered sarcastically. *After all, it was none of my doing.*

Will slept little through the long hours that night. When he finally dozed, his dreams were such a chaotic jumble that he woke exhausted. Dawn brought for him no cheer, no gladness of a new day begun. How could it when he must soon face Hannah with the memory of those final moments between them? He could accept the fact of the baby, and even the fact she hadn't told him. What choice did he have when it came right down to it?

But how could he face her with this other awareness that even all the night's fierce tirade had not washed away? Argue as he might — as he had done all these last, long hours — that she was Luke's wife and therefore it was totally impossible to allow such a thing to happen, he knew he had begun to see her, not as a millstone around his neck, but as a woman.

How had it happened? Somehow, somewhere during these last weeks she had — and him all unaware — crumbled his shell of bitterness and resentment. He had known other women these past years and had left them with no regrets. Not until Eve had he felt such a compelling, deep attraction that he had wanted it to go on forever.

Eve would always be a part of him, but her rejection of him, her marriage to Matt, had slammed the door forever on that sharing of their lives. Rather, she had slammed it, and he must never, ever seek to open it.

He walked slowly toward the house for breakfast and paused at the door. What should he do now, he wondered. Knock? And call attention to last night? Walk in since he could hear her talking to the boys? He was going to feel the master fool no matter which way he chose. Gritting his teeth against a sudden, unnerving wave of panic, he pushed open the kitchen door, feeling rather like the condemned man who has just caught his first glimpse of the scaffold.

Hannah, putting a platter of eggs on the table, glanced quickly up, then down again, at his entrance. Her eyes were deeply shadowed as though she, too, had spent much of the night sleepless. They held an expression he couldn't identify, but at least he was sure it wasn't the shamed dismay that had jolted him so badly last night.

Cheeks red, she said with only the smallest hesitation, "Breakfast is ready. Sit down and I'll dish up."

He eased into his chair. "Is Micah all right?" he asked after a moment. The child had a magnificent shiner, but he seemed oblivious of it as he ate with gusto.

"He seems just fine. He's hungry as a horse, so I guess he can't be too bad off."

"They say that's a good sign," he agreed matter-of-factly. "Hey, pardner," he put in to Micah, "that must of been some scrap you was in. I'd sure hate to see what the other fella looks like!"

The baby chuckled, not understanding the words but at least the fun they were spoken in. As Will reached over to tickle Micah under the chin, he caught a flicker in Hannah's eyes. This time there was no mistaking it.

It was relief.

Eight

Will went about his necessary duties, but all day his reaction to last night troubled him. Why hadn't he turned and gone out immediately? Why had he stayed and stared at her?

It had been enough this morning to know Hannah didn't hate him for his blunder, but he realized, unhappily, that he was going to have to talk to her or else it would stand between them, an embarrassment whenever they came together. There had been enough coldness already — he could only pray fervently this wouldn't set it all off again.

The boys were playing in the yard when he rode up. All of them — except Isaac — dashed over to greet him as he dismounted. He rumpled the hair of the two older boys and picked up little Micah to toss him, squealing, into the air.

As he entered the kitchen, the good smells of meat frying and of fresh-ground coffee assailed his nose. Hannah turned from the stove where she was stirring a pan of potatoes. She smiled, but there was something of hesitation about it. He had seen her smile so at Luke when she wasn't sure how he was going to take something she'd said, and Will felt a stab of pain to realize she was so uncertain of him.

He greeted her cheerfully and kept up a light-hearted conversation on the day's activities while he washed up. Supper was the usual noisy meal, although the boys' table manners showed marked improvement over that first, disastrous breakfast he had eaten here. Hannah had little to say, but she answered readily enough whenever he mentioned something that required a response.

After supper and a wrestling match with the boys, Will volunteered to see them to bed while Hannah finished up the dishes. When he came out of the bedroom she was bringing out her broom, ready to sweep the floor. He shook his head. "Hannah, I'd like f'r us to talk before I leave. C'n you sit at the table a minute?"

She glanced at him and back to the floor before silently leaning the broom aside. With a calm he suspected she was far from feeling, she took the chair across from him, lacing her fingers tightly in front of her.

"I think you know what I want to talk 'bout." She reddened, dropping her glance to her clenched fingers.

"Hannah, look at me." She slowly raised her eyes to meet his, her blush deepening. "I'm not any more comfortable than you are, talkin' 'bout this, but if we don't get it out in the open, it'll always be between us. And that's no good." He paused to give her a chance to speak, but she only gazed at him mutely. He plunged on, sounding awkward to his own ears.

" 'Bout last night — well, I owe you an apology. I shouldn't of come bustin' in like that. I thought you was sittin' at the table readin'. It never entered my head you was takin' a bath." He stumbled to a stop.

Her lips twitched. "You shouldn't have been so shocked.

I do bathe sometimes, just like everybody else."

It was his turn to color. "I didn't mean you don't never take a bath," he said helplessly, "I just meant ..."

Her lightness died. "I know. I thought you'd gone to the bunkhouse and wouldn't be back until morning. Just like always," she said ruefully.

"Looks like we both thought wrong, but my mistake was the biggest. I should of knocked or somethin'. I'm sorry."

She nodded wordlessly.

"Hannah, you're goin' to have a baby, aren't you?" He said it as gently as he could, but it still came out sounding blunt.

Her cheeks flamed. "How did you ..." She bit her lip and would not meet his eyes. "You saw."

It was his turn to redden again. "I didn't realize till last night."

"I just didn't know how to tell you," she said miserably.

"It's not somethin' you go shoutin' from the housetop," he admitted.

"But you had a right to know, Will, involved as you are around here."

He had no light reply to that, for she could not know just how involved he was. "I'm sorry," she went on, so low he could barely hear. "I should have spoken up, but I kept expecting Luke to come home. He didn't know about the baby, and I just couldn't bear to tell anyone else when he left like he did. There've been enough whispers and pitying stares over that. If they knew he'd left me with a baby coming ..." She turned a deep, painful red and buried her face in her hands.

He reached over and touched the fingers hiding her face. "Hannah, look at me." It was a long moment before her hands slid down. Seeing the misery in her green eyes, swift anger kindled in him at the callousness of people. "You mustn't ever feel ashamed, you hear? You've done nothin' to merit shame and neither has your baby. If anybody is cruel enough to say anythin', well, we'll just face 'em down together." He finished in a rush that left her staring at him in amazement.

"I mean it, Hannah. You won't have to face it alone. I'll be right here beside you."

She smiled wanly. "I've sure messed up your life, haven't I? You didn't ask for any of this. I don't know why you stay. But I'm very glad you do. What we would have done all these past weeks ..." She stopped, embarrassed again.

"You didn't ask f'r it, either," he reminded her. "You and the boys would of managed. I know that now, because you're a damned brave woman, Hannah Clayton. And don't you ever f'rget it. But," he smiled as his hand closed over hers for a bare second, "I'm glad if I've made things a little easier f'r you."

Gossip or not, since they now had a little money to spend, Will and Hannah decided a trip to town was a must. The boys needed shoes for the coming winter. Will could also pick up the materials to repair the bunkhouse, and Hannah had to replenish her food supplies. "Just maybe there'll be enough left over for four peppermint sticks," she said to her sons. The boys whooped in anticipation of the rare treat.

Saturday dawned clear and crisp — a perfect Indian summer day. Breathing the air that morning was like taking a draught of heady wine. The trees and bushes displayed every shade from deepest red to crimson, from butter yellow to molten gold. Here and there, a lodgepole pine or Douglas fir retaining its vivid green only accentuated the pattern of beauty. The Laramie Mountains lay in the distance, their peaks snow capped beneath the cloudless, lake-blue sky. Frequently during that ride to town, Will and Hannah spoke of it: the rare-jewel quality of the morning and how they'd best enjoy it while they could before the snow started to fly.

In town, once the boys had been fitted for their new shoes, Will left Hannah and the youngest ones in the Clark's Valley Store, and with Jeremy — proud beyond words of his copper-toed boots that squeaked — set off in the wagon to buy the re-roofing materials.

As they approached Brown's Saddle Shop, the local lounging spot for those men who always seemed to have ample time on their hands for tobacco-spitting contests, Will saw the usual motley assortment gathered. Only when he got closer did he realize they were grinning at some huge joke.

Intent on his errand, he didn't slow the horses, but passed with a nod of greeting and heard a snicker that promptly spread throughout the group. Rad Marks, the acknowledged leader — Will privately suspected he held the office because he could go longer without a bath or shave than any of the others — always had some new joke to offer, and the more off-color, the better it was received. As he and Jeremy rode past, Will wondered vaguely where Rad got his stories. Surely he couldn't dream them up himself. That would take brains and energy, and Rad seemed on no more than a nodding acquaintance with either one. He forgot the thought and the man as he and Jeremy entered the store.

Evan Kilian, the owner and Will's friend from the old Diamond L ranching days, stepped from behind the counter to greet them cheerfully. When Will stated his errand, Evan nodded. "I heard you was stayin' out on the Crescent C and that you was fixin' up the place. I guess Luke wasn't much of one f'r makin' repairs."

The jangling of the bell over the front door interrupted him. Will, bending over the barrel of roofing nails, saw Evan glance up and heard him swear under his breath. Before Will could frame the question, he had the answer. Rad Marks' voice, piercing enough at the best of times, bugled behind him.

"Well, now, look here, boys! It's Will! The way he passed us on the street a few minutes ago without even speakin', I was sure it was somebody else. But you was right, Harp. It sure enough was Will, as I live and breathe. How come you didn't speak at us, Will?"

Will straightened, his eyes meeting Evan's, and he clearly read the flicker of disgust in his friend's expression. Taking his time, he turned to meet Rad's gleeful smirk. His pals, crowded close behind, were also grinning. "Mornin', Rad," he said calmly and returned his attention to Evan. "I'll take a pound of these." He indicated the nail barrel. But Rad wouldn't let it go.

"Guess he's just too busy, all that needs to be taken care of out on ol' Luke's spread, to have time to chat with old friends."

Mort Haley, Rad's shadow and straightman — and second in the running for Worst Body Odor — gave his high-pitched laugh. "From what I hear, Luke left a lot of unfinished business when he high-tailed it out of there. But I hear Will, now, is takin' care of ever'thin' that needs doin'."

Rad hooted. "I heard that, too, that he's workin' day and

night to get ever 'thin' done. 'Course some chores Luke left
is much more pleasant to get done than others!"

With much shoving of elbows into neighboring ribs and
more bellows of laughter, the group backed out the door.
Rad was the last to leave. "'Bye, Will," he said in honeyed
tones and banged the door shut. Their shouts of hilarity
echoed as they sauntered down the street.

Will's eyes met Evan's once more, and he slowly let out
his breath. Only then did he even realize he'd been holding
it. Fists clenched, he took a step toward the door, but his
friend's hand on his arm halted him. "Don't give him the
satisfaction, Will. Everyone knows if he'd just stop talkin',
there wouldn't be any wind left in the whole Territory."

Will continued to stand rigid, staring at the door, before
he relaxed. "You're right, sure. But I'd still like to rearrange
his face f'r him!"

Evan chuckled in understanding and began weighing out
the nails.

Will glanced down at Jeremy and saw his attention had
been held by a kitten that had come frisking from behind the
counter. "Has anyone else been talkin' like that?" he asked
uneasily, remembering Jason's warning.

Evan shrugged. "I wouldn't take him seriously. They're
just tryin' to rile you. I always hate to see 'em come in. They
leave such a stink behind. And I don't mean just 'cause they
don't waste any water bathin'! Too bad they don't take as
much interest in their own families. Me, I've had other things
to think 'bout the last few days." He shot Will a sudden
smile. "Lettie's goin' to have a baby!"

Will's congratulations for Evan were warm and sincere. He

knew the couple had been awaiting this event through five childless years of marriage. But knowledge that hints and remarks about him and Hannah — ones too vague to be objected to but nevertheless there — were being nudged about town as well as at church, was galling. How did one fight such a thing? For, in actual fact, Rad had said nothing that wasn't the total truth. And Will's going after him would only lend fuel to the deeper meaning of Rad's "innocent remarks."

Don't give him the satisfaction, Will repeated grimly to himself as he collected the rest of the roofing materials. *Just don't give him the satisfaction.*

He had almost worked himself into this shrugging-it-off mood when he and Jeremy re-entered Clark's Store in time to catch the middle of the conversation Pearl Gilby and her daughter Mabel were having with Hannah.

Fresh from his own experience with the male counterpart of this gossip fest, Will grimly motioned Jeremy to silence and stood rooted, none of the three women aware of his presence. Hannah had told him of Pearl and Mabel's introduction to Isaac's frog, and he wondered warily if they had chosen this moment to exact revenge. If so, he was ready to go to Hannah's aid, but from what he could see and hear, she was managing just fine. Remembering her way with words, he wondered whether he should feel sorry for Pearl, and decided not to waste the effort.

"... and you never said a word when we were there the other day, Hannah!" Pearl was scolding. "Maybe it'll be a sweet little girl this time. That'd be so nice after three — no, four boys, wouldn't it?"

Pregnancy was spoken of discreetly or not at all in public,

preferably the latter. But Pearl hadn't bothered to keep her voice down, and heads turned curiously as her words carried plainly to the other customers. There are many ways to seek revenge, and Pearl was evidently skilled at the task.

Because her clothes had become uncomfortably tight, for the trip to town Hannah had chosen to wear the only maternity outfit she had, saved from her time with Micah. Neat and becoming as she looked, the high-waisted dress made her state obvious.

Clearly embarrassed at this brazen attention to her condition, Hannah ignored Pearl's slur on the size of her family and answered sturdily, "Of course, a daughter would be nice, but sons are very special, too."

"Of course they are, dear," Pearl purred. "You should certainly know that if anyone does."

Will, facing Hannah, saw her lips tighten, a sure sign she was losing her temper. But she only said crisply, "Whichever God sends, we'll welcome it with love."

"We'll welcome — but you meant you and Luke, didn't you, dear? I'm sure he'll be back by then, from wherever he is, and so surprised."

"I'm sure he will be back by then." Hannah spaced each word distinctly — danger signal number two, as Will knew only too well.

Pearl continued, unheeding. "He'll be pleasantly surprised, too, to see how well you've managed without him." She gave a tinkling laugh. "Men always think we women are so helpless without them. You'll be able to show him a thing or two." She tittered again, her eyes fastening on Hannah's waistline. "A thing or two, indeed!"

131

Hannah, now fiery red, drew herself up to her full height and opened her mouth. Pearl had all the earmarks of prime-grade dumb, but it didn't mean Will had to be, too. The sight of blood — his own or anyone else's — always made him squeamish. So he prudently decided it was time to make his presence known. Before Hannah could say something she would surely regret, he sauntered forward. "All done with your shoppin'?" He asked casually. But his gaze, holding hers, was not casual.

"Will." Hannah's eyes were shooting green sparks. "Almost done. Mrs. Gilby and Miss Mabel stopped to talk."

"It's always good to talk to friends." He touched his hat brim to the suddenly simpering ladies. Hannah heard his emphasis on the last word and understood his unspoken support. It tromped right over the heads of Mabel and Pearl.

"We were just telling Hannah how brave she is to face all her troubles alone. Of course, she's not really alone since you're with her all the time. I dare say it's been such a comfort to her having a strong young man like yourself around." Again Pearl's eyes flicked to Hannah's stomach before she beamed up at Will. "And so handsome, too. Mabel and I haven't been so blessed since our own dear husbands passed on during the Civil War," she added tearfully.

The departures of the "dear husbands" had occurred more than twenty years earlier between the cessation of the hostilities between North and South and the return home of the erstwhile soldiers. Will, along with most of the rest of the community, had his suspicions about the nature of the "passing on."

Will honestly didn't know whether to laugh or cuss. Hannah was so furious she was speechless.

"Blessings do come most unexpectedly," he agreed.

"Oh, they do! Anyone can see you've been a blessing for Hannah, and we do want her to be well taken care of. Especially now."

"She is," Will assured her.

"Seeing Hannah today, like this, we have no doubt about that." She seemingly wasn't seeing the whole of Hannah — that the sparks in her green eyes had become a full-fledged grass fire. Or perhaps she was. As Hannah opened her mouth and Will tried frantically to think of something to beat the unvarnished retort that was about to descend on the head of the luckless Pearl, the lady switched tactics. "Come, Mabel, we must be going." She swooped grandly out the door, her daughter, like a dutiful calf, dogging her steps.

Will took one look at Hannah's livid expression and decided, wisely, that silence was, indeed, golden. He had a sudden, unholy memory of someone else standing with a mouthful of words and no one to spit them at. Having no desire to be the recipient of her wrath, he gathered up the supplies and the boys and installed them in the wagon. When he returned to the counter, she was paying the bill. He couldn't help seeing Clark glance curiously his way as he stood waiting for her to finish. Silently they walked out, silently climbed into the wagon, and silently began the drive home.

He dared not say anything. She looked mad enough to spit nails. After perhaps twenty minutes, during which time the only sound was the rattling of the wagon and the contented slurping of the boys on their peppermint sticks, she began to tremble. He pulled the team to a halt and turned to give her all the moral support he could. "Hannah ..."

She sputtered, strangled, and burst out laughing. He stared,

133

totally shocked, as she tried to speak. "I don't believe it," she gasped. "Of all the dirty-minded ..."

He personally didn't see that much humor in the situation. "Are you all right?" he asked anxiously.

She spluttered again and managed to nod. "If they only knew how rotten I really was to you, how ... how ..." Words failed her.

He realized what she was saying, thought of all those days and nights when she had been so distrustful of him and he so resentful of being there at all, and the full absurdity of the accusations, veiled though they had been, struck him.

He, too, started to shake, then roar, with mirth. He laughed so hard his sides ached. Tears streamed down her cheeks, and still they couldn't stop. The boys, excited by this most unusual display of hilarity from their elders, stared as though Will and Hannah had become unhinged, and began wrestling in the wagon bed in whole-hearted support of the adults' levity. They knew something was different for sure when their mother didn't even bother to correct them, but let them plow into one another with abandon.

With effort, she finally sobered and ordered them to stop. But the rest of the way home, all she or Will had to do was look at the other for both to begin again.

When they arrived at the ranch, Will jumped from the wagon and reached to lift her down. She swung in his arms, light as always in spite of the baby. He looked down into her green eyes, so full of merriment, and smiled to see the difference the release of tension had made in her. Freed from the shame and misery that had enveloped her these past days, she had become young again and strikingly pretty, with a bloom about her that had not been there before.

Will watched her shepherd the boys into the house, glad for her and for himself that they could face their troubles cheerfully. Nothing could be that bad as long as they could laugh about it together.

But the time came when they could not joke, could not cover the hurt with cheerful good humor.

The men were working the herd on the Crescent C range, and on Monday morning Will told Hannah that if there was time, he would ride back to the house when they made the noon break.

Just before noon, as Hannah was folding diapers and wondering if Micah would be out of diapers by the time the new baby arrived, she heard a buggy drive up. She hurried to the window and felt her heart sink to her toes. Reverend Wardley was already climbing out of the rig. The minister stopped by at irregular intervals as he made the rounds of his congregation, but he hadn't called on Hannah since delivering his scorching sermon.

With a heart-thumping she refused to identify as panic, she patted her hair into place and ran off a mental checklist — boys napping, house clean, no frogs in the vicinity, no suds dripping down her dress front. Taking a deep breath, she pulled open the door to the Reverend's knock.

Minutes later, Will canted Eagle into the yard and frowned at the horse and buggy tied to the railing. Another visitor — He started up the steps and halted as he recognized — how could he possibly forget Reverend Wardley's voice? The minister was finishing a query to which Hannah murmured in response.

The next question came distinctly. "Are you sure, my child?"

Hannah's reply was clear, and so was her indignation. "Of course I'm sure. How could I not be?"

Will thrust the door open to abrupt silence. They stared as his quick glance took in Hannah's high color and Reverend Wardley's sudden discomfort. He strode to the table. "You all right, Hannah?"

Relief was plain upon her. "I'm fine. Reverend Wardley and I were just having a ... discussion."

"So I heard."

"It was a private talk between a parishioner and minister," Wardley said stiffly. "But since you're here, I'd like to talk to you, too."

"Is this to be a 'private talk' or is Hannah allowed to listen?"

Wardley's mouth became a thin line. "This is not a joking matter. But, since you put it that way, yes, it does have to do with both of you, so you both should hear what I have to say."

Will dropped into the chair beside Hannah. He murmured, "Chin up," and smiled reassuringly at her before he turned to face Wardley head on. He was glad to see her smile, small as it was, in return. The shadow in her eyes remained, however, and he understood. Hints and suspicion from neighbors were one thing, but if the minister didn't trust them either ...

Quick anger spurted in him, but a shadow in Hannah's eyes curbed it. They must keep calm. As Jason had pointed out, a show of temper would put them in the wrong. So, instead of

136

jumping in with protests and explanations, Will looked straight at the minister and said nothing. Simply sat, and waited.

Wardley had expected protests and explanations. This silent attack threw him off. Flustered, he glanced at Hannah, who, equally silent, waited, too. He reddened. "No use beating around the bush. I suppose you know there's been talk going around about the 'arrangement' you two have here. And now," he gestured to Hannah, "you've really added fuel to it by parading your ..." he hesitated "... condition in town."

"But I wasn't 'parading' anything," Hannah burst out. "We had to go to town. The boys needed shoes. I didn't have any choice."

"Be that as it may," he said, unmoved, "as your minister of God I have a right to know just what the truth is about you two."

Hannah drew in her breath sharply. Will stiffened in his chair. Clenching her fists, she forced herself to speak quietly. "As our 'minister of God,' you know Will, and you know me. Just what do you think is the truth?"

Wardley eyed them in silence, first Will, then Hannah, a long, measuring look for each. "It's not for me to say what I think you're doing. It's for you to tell me one way or the other."

Hannah moaned, so faintly that Wardley, sitting across from her, didn't hear. But Will did. He shoved back his chair, but before he could get to his feet, she reached to put a restraining hand on his arm — a gesture Wardley didn't miss. His eyes narrowed but neither one noticed.

"No, Will, you mustn't!"

Will saw the sudden fear in her eyes and felt sick to his

stomach. Sinking back into his chair, he faced Wardley, who was still watching them intently.

"You think the same as all the others," he said, unbelieving. "Just what kind of truth will make you and everyone else happy? To hear I been takin' Hannah to bed mornin', noon and night since I got here? Well, I won't confess any such thing because it's not true."

Wardley, beet red, chose to ignore Will's crudeness. "I heard all about the conversation in Clark's. How you, Will, all but admitted you're the father of Hannah's child."

Hannah gasped. Will surged to his feet. She made no effort to stop him this time and couldn't have, anyway. "I never said any such thing," he exploded. "But you don't believe us, either!"

"Will, I can't help you if you insist on losing your temper."

Will shook his head, dazed. "Help us? By accusing us of ..."

"I haven't 'accused' you of anything," Wardley pointed out coldly. "I'm telling you what I've heard, and I'm giving you the chance to clear yourselves."

Will laughed bitterly. "That's very generous of you, Reverend."

Wardley flushed at the sarcasm.

"Will, please!" He turned to look at Hannah and felt sick all over again. Her green eyes were enormous with agony. The raw pain in them was like a knife slicing into his heart. What were they — he and Wardley both — doing to her?

He reached out and covered her hand with his, another gesture the minister promptly added to his "list." Will slumped into his chair. "Hannah, I'm so sorry." Their eyes held for a long, long, moment while Wardley had the grace to look confused.

"All right," Will said quietly, his hand still covering hers, his eyes still holding hers. "This is the way it is, once and f'r all. You and everyone else seem to have f'rgotten the little matter that Hannah has a husband. I have a lot of respect f'r her, too much to take her lightly. And that includes any way you care to define it. I think she's one hell of a lady caught in one hell of a situation, and you and all the rest of your 'Christian' congregation ought to be ashamed of yourselves." With effort, he controlled his rising tone.

"I happen to have a little pride, too. I do have moral standards that I try to live up to, believe it or not. Beddin' another man's wife isn't exactly in my line." By now Hannah looked ready to cry, and Wardley ready to explode, but Will wasn't finished.

"Even aside from all that, have you f'rgotten Hannah has four sons? Do you really think we'd do anythin' to hurt them or make them ashamed — now or later?" For the first time since he had begun speaking, Will took his eyes from Hannah's and looked straight into Wardley's.

"There's a line in the Bible maybe you never heard. It's a good one. It goes, 'Judge not, that ye be not judged.' Maybe you ought to preach a sermon on that to your sinless congregation before you go passin' out stones."

Wardley sat as if turned to ice. As Will halted, his expression became like the wrath of God. He regarded Will in cold, deadly silence before he turned to Hannah. Her eyes, on Will, were no longer filled with that terrible agony, but with a soft joy. Wardly stood slowly. When he spoke, his voice was frigid.

"I am quite familiar with the quotation, William Braden. But perhaps there's one you haven't heard: 'If a man be found lying with a woman married to a husband, then they shall both of them die, both the man that lay with the woman, and the woman: so shalt thou put away evil from Israel.'

"I know my Bible, too, and I'll not stay here and listen to blasphemy. I came to help, but apparently you don't want or care to be helped." His eyes swiveled back to Hannah. "As for you, Hannah Clayton, I'm warning you. Your very soul is in dread danger. There's talk all over town about you and Will — and your child. You haven't been attending services regularly, either. It seems strange that you can make it into town to shop but not to go to church.

"I can't refuse to allow you in church. I have no proof of your indiscretion. I wouldn't turn you away, anyway. You clearly need all the help you can get. But I warn you — both of you — watch your step." He stomped out the door.

Hannah had sat paralyzed during this tirade. Now she stumbled to her feet, all the light wiped from her face as though it had never been. "Reverend Wardley!"

She pushed past Will and ran to the door. But Wardley had already shaken the dust of the ranch from his feet and was disappearing in a cloud of indignation.

Will hurried out after her. Together they watched as the buggy out rode of sight. Then she turned blindly and stumbled up the steps. After a moment he heard her bedroom door shut. But the one quick glimpse he had had of her face gave a wicked twist to the knife in his heart.

Nine

After Hannah fled past him up the steps, Will stood stunned. Turning abruptly, he bolted for the bunkhouse, slammed the door open and shut it with a crash. Lurching over to his bunk, he sat with a thump on the narrow edge, grabbed a bridle he had been mending and thrust it savagely aside. Slamming fists against knees, he jerked to his feet and began pacing, his rage all-consuming.

"Tell the truth." As if they had been telling anything else! The gall of the man. Judging — yes, judging! — him and Hannah and refusing to listen when they tried to explain.

In his fury he failed to hear the first tapping at the door. He heeded only when it became a frantic pounding. He snatched the door open to find Jeremy looking up pleadingly. "Mr. Braden, you gotta come help Ma. She's hurt. She's cryin'!"

Will stared into the tear-streaked little face. She was hurt, yes. More deeply than this child could begin to understand. "Jeremy, I think your Ma just wants to be left alone," he said heavily. "Sometimes it happens that way with older people."

"But I'm scared! I never heard her cry so hard. Please come help her."

141

Will stared past Jeremy to the wall of the house as though he would find the answer painted in scarlet there. But there was no answer.

"Come on!" The little boy grabbed his hand and began to tug him across the yard. He kept pulling as they went up the steps. In the doorway he stopped. "See, she must be hurt."

Will listened as her shuddering sighs wrenched his already bruised heart. "Where are the other boys?"

Jeremy pointed to his own room.

"You go keep an eye on them. I'll see if I c'n help your Ma." Jeremy trotted obediently into his bedroom. Hating the whole awful mess, Will paused for a long second outside Hannah's door before he pushed inside.

It was the first time he had seen Hannah's room. His swift glance noted the bareness of the furnishings. What would Wardley and all the others say if they saw him now, he wondered sourly. All their worst suspicions confirmed. Yet they were the very cause ... He crossed to the bed where she lay face downward, breathing in racking moans. He sat beside her, reaching his hand to her shoulder. "Hannah."

She jumped and whirled to face him, eyes wide with misery and fear. "Will, what ... You shouldn't ..." Then she saw and recognized the stark unhappiness in his face and knew it equaled her own.

"Oh, Will." She flung herself into his arms.

His first instinct was to hold her close, trying only to soothe her, not even remembering that he had no right. Only later would he look back and wonder.

He held her, murmuring wordlessly, trying to comfort her as she would have comforted one of her own sons who was deeply hurt. He stroked her hair, letting her cry it out until finally her sobs eased a little.

She pulled away from him. "I'm sorry. I didn't mean to. It just all at once ..."

His mouth twisted. "I know. That was quite an earful we got from our understandin' minister. I don't blame you a bit."

"It was just everything, all of a sudden ..." She wiped at her eyes with her fist.

"Here." He pushed his bandanna into her hand. "It's prob'ly a little dusty and sweaty and a whole lot smelly, but it'll do the job."

She gave him the smallest of smiles, but at least it was a try. He waited while she wiped her eyes and blew her nose. "You haven't let loose since Luke left, have you?"

She shook her head. "I just couldn't, somehow, until now. Then it all just lumped together, and I couldn't stand it any longer. I'm sorry."

"Don't be. You've held it all inside way too long. Prob'ly was the best thing in the world f'r you to bust loose. Feel better, now?"

"I ... I think so."

"Good. Jeremy was pretty upset when he heard you. If you feel up to it, maybe you could talk to him."

"I never even thought of him or the other boys. Where are they?"

"In their room. I'll get 'em."

He found the little boys huddled on one of the beds. They all stared with wide, frightened eyes as he paused in the doorway. "Your Ma wants to see you," he said matter-of-factly.

They remained frozen for another instant, then piled off the bed and tore past Will as though a spring had released them. Little Micah couldn't figure out how to get off the bed without going head-first, so Will picked him up and carried him to the doorway. He watched him toddle, swaybacked and diaper drooping, arms outstretched, to the bed where the boys were trying at the same time to climb into Hannah's lap. She reached over and pulled the baby up, cuddling him close. Over his carroty curls she looked at Will. "Thank you," she murmured.

He smiled, the most gentle smile she had ever seen, before he strode quickly away. She could not know the turmoil of his thoughts as he pushed open the bunkhouse door. Ignoring the fact he was already past due back at the herd, he stretched out wearily on his cot. Such a tangle of emotions churned within him that he felt dazed.

Anger and resentment at Wardley's callous attitude were uppermost for a time. How could the man have been so unfeeling? Youthful or not, it wasn't as if he didn't know Will and Hannah well, didn't have a good idea by this time of their moral standards. If he didn't believe them, who would?

Hannah's storm of grief had at least given her an outlet for her unbearable stress. Will was glad she had been able to let it out, but for him there was no such release. Even after his first fury had spent itself, the pain and helpless frustration remained.

Without willing them, his thoughts slipped back to those moments when he had held Hannah in his arms. She had been bewildered and hurt, and his only instinct had been to comfort her. He had not held — had not wanted to hold — any other woman since Eve had last been in his arms. His arms, and his heart, remembered how it had been ... would never be again. He surged to his feet, despair a strangling thing in his throat as all the old bitterness and hurt came flooding back.

He pushed unseeing out the door, leaping to Eagle's saddle as though all the demons of the underworld pursued him. As he started the horse out of the yard at a quick run, he felt they were, indeed, after him.

Back at the herd, Jason looked askance at him for his delayed return, but seeing the forbidding look on his face, wisely asked no questions. Will just felt too weary to cope with either explanations or answers when he couldn't begin to explain and there were no answers.

Now they must begin all over to achieve a comfortable footing with each other. Hannah was shy and stiff in his presence, not unlike their first days together. She had given too much of her private self to a man not her husband, had turned for solace to one who had no right to comfort her, and had found that comfort in his arms.

For Will's part, he understood her embarrassment but was helpless to combat it. He was struggling with his own torment, trying to make some common sense out of the impossibility that he was in love with one woman, yet had held another in his arms. It was a devil of a note, he thought morosely, that all his heart and strength were bound up in caring for other men's wives when nothing could ever come of that caring.

But, as before, daily contact served to crumble the barrier as no forced effort could have, perhaps because neither one asked anything from their peculiar relationship, but just let it be. Although neither could have put it into so many words, mutual dignity and respect — intangible but nonetheless there — were slowly cementing a bond between them stronger than any barrier of discomfort.

So they went on as normally as they could, for their own sakes and the sake of the boys. A part of this normalcy, they decided after careful discussion, was church attendance on Sunday. Neither one was especially enthusiastic about appearing in public, or in front of Reverend Wardley, but they had little choice. As Wardley had said, he couldn't forbid them attendance at services. As Hannah pointed out, their failure to show up would only be an admission they had something to hide.

Will figured if Hannah was game, he could hardly be less so. Wardley's claim they hadn't been attending church regularly wasn't true. The men, aware winter could blast down onto them at any time, had decided a 24-hour vigil on the herd was vital. Spooky as the cattle were normally, a sudden snowstorm would be a prime-grade guarantee to set them off. The men must be there to control them and avert a total stampede. So they had been working and sleeping in shifts.

Toiling early and late, overlapping their own watches, they had yet attempted to make up for the lack of their physical presence in church by taking extra moments for prayer before beginning the day's work. After all, God was everywhere, wasn't He? They were every bit as aware of His presence out on the range as in the church building. Perhaps even more so because He was such a vital element in their chosen job. Without His presence all their work was as nothing.

True, Will and Hannah hadn't made it to services the Sunday before Wardley's visit. Will had been with the herd, and he had advised Hannah not to make the long trip to town without him, for the same reason they were guarding the cattle so carefully. If the weather broke unexpectedly, as it had been known to, she and the boys would be caught out in the open without shelter. It was simply common sense, they reasoned, to stay home and hold their own services, which Hannah and the boys had done. Wardley, evidently, hadn't seen it that way.

They decided, though, they could only do their best and trust God to understand.

"Do you think God understands, Will?" Hannah asked one evening after the boys were in bed. She was seated in her rocker, sewing a baby shirt, and he was relaxing at the table with his pipe.

He considered carefully. "I think He'd be pretty narrow-minded if He didn't. Maybe I'm wrong, but I've just never been able to see God as some jealous, angry old man sittin' on a cloud, pointin' His finger to 'destroy thee from off the face of the earth' just at His whim." He paused to light his pipe.

"How do you see Him?" she asked curiously.

"Maybe workin' outdoors so much has somethin' to do with it, but to me God isn't perched up somewhere on a cloud. He's everywhere, and He's with me even when I'm not con-sciously thinkin' 'bout it. He's there just as much in the bad times as in the good. I might not agree with how He's handlin' things at a particular time, but that don't mean He's not there. I don't think He makes things either good or bad — people do. He gives us a choice, and we c'n do right or not. It's up to us."

"But what about when something happens to a totally innocent person? My brother was only 6 when he died. Surely he couldn't have done anything so bad he had to die for it."

"I don't pretend to know all the answers. Maybe sometimes things happen that we won't know the reason f'r a long time, if ever. But there has to be a reason. Why did my Ma have to suf-fer so? Maybe her purpose — and your brother's — was to give happiness we aren't even aware of. And when they'd given, their task on earth was finished so God took them home."

"My Ma would have liked your way of thinking," Hannah said softly. "It would have given her a lot of joy to know."

"How do you feel?" he asked, equally curious.

"I understand how you mean about God being everywhere and always with you, even outdoors. I feel so, myself, when I'm gardening. There's just something about digging in the dirt that gives such a satisfying, close-to-God feeling."

She understands, he thought, surprised. *She really does.*

She threaded her needle. "I guess God, to me, is kind of like the lilac plant Luke's Ma gave me from her yard when we got married. It sits quiet through most of the year, not demanding — just there. Even during the winter when everything's so cold and dark, it's alive even though it doesn't seem so. Then, just when it feels as though winter won't ever end, but just plod on forever, spring comes and the lilac bursts into bloom, showing it was there the whole time no matter how stormy or dreary things got." She blushed. "Sounds kind of silly, I guess. But that's how I feel about God. In the dark times and the glorious ones, too, He's there."

"Reverend Wardley'd cull us both out of the herd f'r sure, if he knew how we really feel," Will said recklessly.

"I guess we better not tell him. We're already treading on thin ice."

"Thin water, you mean. We've already melted the ice!"

During those last Sundays before winter set in, Will and

148

Hannah, with the boys, attended church services when they could. Feeling that when folks could manufacture no new rumors to fan the flames, the suspicions would die a natural death, they held their heads high, meeting the eyes of their neighbors squarely. They found, with no small amount of triumph, that the eyes of their friends fell first. It didn't right itself in one Sunday, or two, but they persisted. Wardley continued to eye them balefully, but he gave no more such obvious sermons.

The snow began falling in the early afternoon — large, soft flakes that clung to bush and corral railing and porch post. When Will left that morning, he warned Hannah if it started snowing not to look for him until she saw him coming. The herd, sensing the change of weather, would more than likely be panicky and the cowhands would have to stay out with them until they settled down.

But all that afternoon as the temperature dropped and the blanket on the ground deepened, bringing with it an early twilight, Hannah felt a strange unease. Several times she paused in her work to glance out the window, hoping to see Will riding in. After the fourth such pause in the space of a half hour, she shook her head disgustedly, telling herself she was being ridiculous. Will knew perfectly well how to handle himself in bad weather. This snowfall was nothing compared to some of the storms of last winter. If he came in and caught her glooming around with her work undone, he'd be amazed.

The baby fluttered. She smiled, placing her hands gently over her stomach. "Scolding me are you, little one, for being so foolish? You're right, I'll quit!" But as she busied herself making a stew that would keep hot no matter when he came in, she paused more than once to listen. The wind was rising, blowing the snow against the windows with a sharp hissing.

Long after dark she heard his heavy tread on the steps. Pulling her shawl more closely about her, she flung open the door and peered into the night. "Will, come in and get warm. Is everything all right?"

He hastily shut the door against the biting cold, going at once to warm himself in front of the glowing stove.

"I've hot coffee ready. You look like you could use some." She poured him a steaming cup even as she spoke.

He peeled off his gloves and gratefully accepted the cup, curling his hands around its welcome warmth. "Careful, it's hot," she warned as he took a gulp.

"That's good," he admitted. "Been waitin' hours f'r a cup of your coffee."

She felt a ridiculous twinge of pleasure. "There's plenty more, and hot stew waiting, too."

"I knew I smelled somethin' good cookin' at least ten minutes back. I just followed my nose and it led me right here."

"Is it so bad out? I'm sure glad you're home."

He paused in taking off his heavy coat and glanced around the room. Outside, snow pelted against the windows, driven there by the keening wind, but inside, the room was warm, clean and glowing with lamplight. Mouthwatering aromas of hot coffee and bubbling stew filled the air. Hannah was at the stove dishing up meat and vegetables for him, her face alight with gladness at his return. Home. He had been so long homeless. How could one simple room such as this hold so much contentment when so many other rooms he had been in had been nothing more than four walls that kept out the weather?

He hated to snap the thread of the moment's warmth, but

he had no choice. "I can't stay. I got to get back soon as I finish eatin'."

"Will, no, you must be exhausted."

He smiled thinly. "Can't be helped. They're still edgy. They haven't spooked yet, but we're not takin' no chances. I got to get back so Aaron c'n go home and eat. We're takin' shifts so they aren't left alone."

She said no more, knowing he would do what he must, glad he was so, and knowing if it had been Luke ... She set the bowl hastily on the table and began cutting thick slices from a loaf of bread as though activity would turn away disloyal thoughts. Will ate quickly, hungrily, and she kept refilling bowl and cup until at last, with a sigh of repletion, he pushed back his chair.

"That was great, Hannah. I feel like a new man." He reached for his coat and hat.

"Any idea when you'll be back in?" She did her best to keep the anxiety out of her voice, but he caught it anyway.

He shrugged. "Can't say. It all depends on the storm."

"When you get in, be sure to come back to the house. I'll have coffee and stew keeping hot for you." She spoke calmly, but her eyes were dark with anxiety that wouldn't be concealed.

In a sudden, rare gesture, he reached out, touching her cheek. "I'll be fine. Don't worry." Then he left into the night.

She leaned her forehead against the door, listening, but the storm blotted out all other sounds. "Please, God, keep him safe," she whispered. Taking up her knitting, she pulled her rocker closer to the fire and sat down to wait out the long hours, until once again she heard his step on the stairs and knew with gratitude that — this time, anyway — her prayer had been answered.

Days of sunshine followed that first blast of winter. Nights were cold, starlit and clear. The men were kept busy shoveling snow off the grass so the cattle could graze more easily. They had put tons of hay into stacks during the summer. But always remembering the bitter scarcity of the previous winter and its consequent tragic results, they were determined to save as much of the stacked hay as possible for later when they might not be able to let the animals forage for themselves.

Will, working day after day alongside Matt, had come to accept, grudgingly, the necessity for his presence. He avoided his old friend as much as possible, and when it wasn't possible, said as little as he could. Matt, for his part, seemed willing to let it go at that. They were all doing the work of two men, and there was little time or energy left for quarreling.

But Will had not forgotten Eve's trouble. Nor could he miss the shadow in Matt's eyes even when he was speaking with pride and happiness of her to the other men. *What was it?* Will wondered endlessly even as he wondered what he could do about it if he knew.

He had not seen her except briefly. He hadn't spoken to her except a few hurried words. He knew her too well, however. He sensed something was troubling her deeply even while she laughed and beamed with joy equal to Matt's. Always his thoughts came to ground with the same end: Even if he knew what was wrong, what could he do? Then his brain would begin circling again, endlessly seeking answers that weren't there.

On a morning of silent cold with the glittering sun striking eye-burning sparks off the snow, Will stomped up the porch steps. Hand at the door, he paused. He heard Jeremy's voice, then Hannah's, and Jeremy again, earnestly. Pushing open the panel into the glad warmth of the room, he took in the scene before him of Hannah sitting in her rocker, mending and listening to Jeremy's halting reading, helping when he stumbled over a word.

Micah, Isaac and Sam were playing a game of wagon train on the floor, pushing chunks of wood along a danger-fraught trail. Micah didn't fully understand, but he was "gee-up"-ing lustily with an occasional "bang-bang" thrown in for good measure, proud of the additions to his vocabulary.

When Will entered, Hannah smiled and put a finger to her lips. Jeremy came to the end of his sentence and looked at her hopefully. "That was just fine, son. I'm really proud of you."

He blew out a gust of relief that would have been comical if Will hadn't remembered only too clearly the pain of those Sunday afternoon lessons endured at his own mother's knee. Jeremy placed the McGuffey's reader carefully on its shelf before he knelt to join his brothers in play. As he did so, Isaac retreated to a corner near the stove and sat watching the others balefully.

Hannah put aside her mending and turned to the stove. From the reservoir she added hot water to the coffeepot. "Didn't expect you for a while yet. I'm afraid you caught us playing, so dinner will be a bit late. How soon do you have to get back?"

"No great rush. Things are pretty quiet this mornin'. That's why we broke early. Jeremy's sure doin' good on his readin', isn't he?"

Her face lit up. "He's really come a long way just these past couple of weeks. He'll be ready for school next year, for sure. I just wish I had more time to listen to him. Seems as though he just gets started and something interrupts."

Will grinned guiltily. "Guess it was me this time. Sorry."

She reddened. "I didn't mean you. It's the other boys. They always seem to need something just at the wrong time."

He glanced over to where Isaac still sulked near the stove. Her eyes followed his. "I try so hard to be fair, but somehow it just doesn't seem to work out."

He saw her discouragement. "Tell you what, since I was the cause of the interruption just now, tonight after supper I'll take care of the little fellas and you and Jeremy c'n have a good readin' session without bein' disturbed. Then maybe tomorrow night you c'n give one of the others a turn. You know, switch off so each of 'em gets a chance to be with you by himself."

Her first reaction was a pleased smile, but her face fell. "That would be great, but it's not fair to you."

"I sure don't see why not," he said indignantly.

She hesitated another long moment and gave in gratefully. "If you're sure you don't mind."

"I'm sure." He grinned. "The roof's nailed on secure, ain't it?"

She looked startled. "I hope so. Why?" Then she realized and laughed. She wondered, as she turned back to the stove, at the fleeting, pleased look that crossed his face and vanished. She smiled secretly, wondering if he would feel so smug *after* the evening session with three active little boys.

While they were eating a little later, Will spoke up. "I almost f'rgot. Jason said to tell you Becky's plannin' on havin' ever'body to Christmas dinner at their place."

He saw her dismay. "Will, I'm not sure ..."

"You're goin' to have to face 'em all sometime," he pointed out with more assurance than he felt. "Seems to me this is as good a time as any."

"I just can't face all of them. Not all together like that after Luke ..." She stopped, suddenly aware of Jeremy staring at her.

"Hannah, you got to stop floggin' yourself f'r Luke." Will, too, was acutely aware of the child's wide-eyed gaze. "He's your husband, sure, but he's also their brother. Why should you shoulder any more blame than anyone else?"

"My head knows that. My heart just feels so responsible."

"You're not," Will said firmly. "So there's no use you thinkin' you got to heft the whole load. You've got to face them, chin up, and let 'em know you had nothin' to do with it. They know it, anyway, but show 'em you know it, too."

Jeremy, following this conversation, had understood only a small part. Now he asked with awful solemnity, "Is Pa bad?" He looked from his mother to Will and back.

Hannah's voice caught painfully. "No, son, not bad. Only confused and unhappy."

Confused, Jeremy wasn't sure about. *Unhappy*, he was only too familiar with. "Did he get scolded f'r bein' bad?"

Hannah, close to tears, shook her head. "No, no one scolded him."

"Why did Pa go away?" His innocent question dropped like a rock in pond water.

Distress tightened her voice. "I explained to you, son. Pa went away because he was unhappy. He thought he had to be alone to think about things."

"What things?"

"Jeremy," she said helplessly, "only your Pa can really answer that. Just like you get unhappy sometimes and don't really know why. Everybody does."

But not everyone runs away. The accusation hung in the air, unspoken but very real. Jeremy, however, apparently didn't hear. Too young to read the full meaning of his mother's anguish, he accepted her explanation as children will, knowing instinctively that here, once again, was adult reasoning and as such, not to be understood.

The rest of the meal passed rather silently except for the irrepressible chatter of the children. Hannah said nothing when Will pushed back his chair and reached for his hat and coat. Only when he had his hand on the door, she spoke. "Will."

He turned, waiting.

"You can tell Jason we'll be there for Christmas." Her eyes met his for a long moment and he saw her grief.

"I'll tell him," he said gently, and hurried out.

Ten

That evening after supper, as he had promised, Will took the three younger boys in hand while Jeremy read to Hannah. At least he took over Sam and Micah. Isaac, as usual refusing to have anything to do with him, hunched in a corner, lower lip stuck out. Will didn't want to leave him out deliberately, but he wasn't about to force the boy, either. After an initial attempt to get him to join in, which was coldly rebuffed, he let him be, giving his attention to Sam and Micah, who were only too glad to wrestle. Jeremy cast longing looks their way, but Hannah was adamant, keeping him at the book a good 20 minutes before she relented.

Will had to hide his smile at Jeremy's relief when it was over, but he could sympathize, too. He remembered so well.

Hannah continued her knitting as Jeremy joined the three on the floor, but her eyes went often to Isaac. *What am I going to do with him?*

She knew he was terribly unhappy, but he refused any sympathy or understanding, even from her. Did constant rejection give her the right to quit trying? She knew it didn't, but it hurt so when he turned away from her efforts. She loved him as she

157

loved all her sons, and she didn't want him to hurt as she knew he was hurting. She put aside her yarn and needles to kneel beside him where he still crouched in the corner. "Isaac."

He glanced up at her and back to the four tumbling on the floor. "Why don't you go join them, son?"

"Don't want to."

"Why not?"

"Just don't want to." Putting his chin on his drawn-up knees, he glared at Will.

"I'm sure they'd like to have you play. Five'd be much more fun than four."

"Nope."

Hannah held back a sigh and said with forced calm, "That's up to you. Would you like to sit on my lap while they're playing?"

This time his look was pure scorn. "That's f'r babies. I ain't a baby!"

"I didn't say you were. And it's not just for babies. Everyone needs to know he's loved, and a mother's lap is a good place to find it." When he continued to sit and scowl, she put an arm around him to draw him near, but he squirmed away. Not noisily, but with a calm disinterest more chilling to her mother's heart than anger would have been. Helpless to combat his isolation, she stood and put her hand on his head for just a second, taking it away before he could wriggle out from under. She retreated to her chair and picked up her knitting. Although she worked furiously, she had no idea what she was doing.

After the boys were in bed and Will was reaching for his coat, he said, "F'rgot to mention it earlier. I told Jason we'd

be at their place f'r Christmas. He seemed real pleased."
When she didn't answer, he glanced back at her. "Hannah?"
She jumped, dropping her knitting. "What?" She fumbled
with the needles, trying to cover her abstraction.
He repeated what he'd said, and she nodded. "I'm glad
they won't mind having us."
"Of course they won't mind." He watched her trying to
straighten out her work, and frowned. "Hannah?" She raised
her head, and he saw her unhappiness before she ducked
again. "What's wrong? You really that nervous 'bout facin'
'em at Christmas?"
Head still bent, she shook it slowly. Puzzled, he stood
holding his coat as concern pricked him. "Is it somethin'
I've done?"
She looked at him, then. "Oh, Will, no. Really. You
haven't ... It's not you."
He dumped his coat on the table and walked slowly to
her chair. "What is it, then? I know somethin's botherin'
you. Sometimes talkin' things out helps."
She hesitated. He dropped to his heels beside her chair.
"Keepin' it in won't do you no good."
She bit her lip. "It's Isaac," she said finally, so low he
could barely hear.
"I kinda thought so. I saw you talkin' to him earlier and
he pretty much ignored you, didn't he?"
"I just don't know what to do," she burst out. "I love him
as much as any of the others, but he just won't respond. And
he's getting worse. I thought maybe if I gave him time, he'd
snap out of it. But he's not. And I feel like such a failure!"
She broke off, pressing the back of her hand to her mouth.

He reached out, covered her other hand with his own big one and squeezed, hard. "Hannah, you're not a failure. You hear me? I won't have you cuttin' yourself down like that. And I mean it!" He spoke so fiercely that she stared at him. He went on, unheeding. "You've been dealt a mighty rough hand, it's true. I don't know what I'd of done, if I'd been in your boots. Nobody c'n answer f'r another, and I sure don't aim to try. You gotta do what you think best. The way I see it, you've been doin' just that and makin' a good job of it, too." She started to speak but he rushed on.

"Isaac's a tough little bronc, no denyin'. But from what I c'n see, you're handlin' him pretty good."

She looked down at his big hand still covering hers, moved her fingers so they tightened around his for just an instant before she pulled her hand away. He released his own hold immediately, and she picked up the mess in her lap. With her head bent again, he couldn't see her expression. But neither could she see his.

He set his jaw. "Hannah." It came out more sternly than he intended, for she raised her head, startled. More gently, he began again. "Maybe I'm interferin' where I shouldn't, and if I am, you just tell me to keep my nose in my own business. But have you given thought to why Isaac acts the way he does?"

Her eyes shadowed. "I've thought and thought. I know he misses Luke. I told you Luke was closer to him than any of the others. I've tried to make up his being gone by giving Isaac extra attention, but as you saw tonight, he won't have any of it."

"I saw."

"So," she spread her hands, "I can't truly feel it's lack of attention and affection."

A thought nudged the back of his mind. *How to put it into words?* He had enough trouble trying to express his own emotions, let alone attempt to speak for someone else.

"Will, what is it?"

He saw the anxiety in her green eyes, knew he had to try. "That could be the problem."

She looked puzzled. "Too much attention?"

"No, wait. He was close to Luke, right? Luke paid more attention to him than to the others."

"But I don't ..."

"And Luke went away."

She flushed. "He wrote that note and left in the middle of the night without even telling any of us goodbye," she said bitterly.

He fumbled with the words. "That could be it, Hannah. Don't you see? He gave his love to Luke, trusted him ..."

Her eyes widened. "And Luke ran out on him. So now he's afraid to show anybody affection because he thinks ..."

"That they'll leave him, too. Especially you."

Relief flooded her face. "Do you really think that's it?"

"I'm not guaranteein' it, but it's an idea to think on."

"Poor Isaac." Her heart was in her words. "How afraid he must be as well as unhappy." She blinked rapidly and bent over the snarl of knitting in her lap. "I'll talk to him, try to make him understand and believe that it won't happen again just because it happened once." Her eyes were wet as she raised them to Will, and he felt his own throat tighten.

He poked his finger at the mass of yarn in her lap. "What is it?" he asked, to cover his unwonted emotion.

She laughed, shakily. "It was a sweater for Micah for

Christmas. I'm doing one with a squirrel on the front for each of the boys. I'm not sure what to call it now, though."

"How 'bout a holy mess, f'r starters?"

She heard the teasing in his voice and smiled up at him in return.

In a gesture inexpressibly comforting to her, he reached out and touched her cheek with a work-hardened hand. Rising abruptly, he grabbed his coat and strode out the door.

Long after Will had gone, Hannah sat, her thoughts as jumbled as the yarn in her lap. Isaac. Her heart ached for her small son, carrying a burden he probably couldn't even fully understand. But how to help him? Words alone wouldn't give him the reassurance he needed. As tonight had emphasized, he stubbornly refused all gestures of affection. What, then? For a long while she wrestled with the question, finding no answer.

She felt deep relief that Will had seen the problem, as she hadn't, and gratitude for his perception. She remembered that first evening he had come, insisting she needed to be protected and informing her he was going to do it whether she liked it or not. How she had hated him that night! Her cheeks grew hot as she thought of her rudeness and how she'd wished he would leave. For if there was anything she hadn't needed at the moment, it was another man underfoot forever and ever making demands on her time and patience and responsibilities.

How she had burned those next days under knowledge of his resentment that she was not Eve. Oh, she had seen, to be sure. How could she not have? She had watched Eve and

Will together all those months before, had seen, in spite of her own misery, his white face and hard-set mouth at the wedding, had known he was a man who, having once loved, would not easily give up that love.

No, she hadn't been Eve, blessed with the love of two men. She had been simply herself, Hannah, who had so little. And that given so grudgingly.

So she had built that wall about herself and silently dared Will to breach it. But he never had, except with the boys. In the end it had been she who, finally acknowledging that he was no more happy with their circumstances than she, had come to realize she was being a fool to be so vengeful. No, she was not Eve, but then neither was he Luke.

What if Will had gone that night? She felt a chill. He had said, once, that she and the boys would have managed just fine without him, but would they have? Not just for the work he was doing around the place, but for his physical presence. Now that she thought about it, she realized how much, quietly, he had helped her cope these past months. Unobtrusively sharing the care of the boys, relieving her of some of the burden of unceasing responsibility, she hadn't heeded until now. What comfort she had come to draw, just from his presence. A comfort that had never been there with Luke.

Her cheeks grew hot again. But it was true, she thought rebelliously. She wasn't just glorifying Will and cutting Luke down. The fact was there, plain as could be — only she must not, for her sake and Will's, put it into words. No matter what he had done, where he was, Luke was still her husband.

Her thoughts turned back to her 16th year. Her mother had just died of fever, leaving Hannah to keep house for her father, whose heart had gone out of him with his wife's death. A year later he, too, was dead, leaving Hannah to get along as best she might, alone.

She remembered the months of hiring out to harried housewives, the menial wages — sometimes only room and board in exchange for hours of exhausting labor — the sense of never truly belonging, the unutterable loneliness. Until Luke had come riding into her life. Literally. She had been crossing the street in town and he had almost run her down, his horse having spooked at a piglet that had run squealing in front of his hooves.

Luke got his mount under control at last and returned to see if she was hurt. The charm he had had, when he chose to use it! And he had chosen. Though now again, as she had so many times, she wondered, *Why?* She had known him before, though not well, and in her joy at being accepted for herself, in the release from the terrible loneliness that had been hers for so many months, she had closed her eyes to his roughness, his bragging insistence that he was second to no man. He would change after they were married, surely, and anyway, his behavior toward others had nothing to do with the way he treated her. So she had told herself. And so they had married.

Disillusionment had not been long in coming, she thought now, wryly. But she had refused to admit to Luke's family the shame and disgrace that had all too quickly become a part of her life with him. His family was one of the few blessings that had come to her from their union.

Anne and Ben Clayton had accepted her as a daughter, asking no questions, giving freely all the love and warmth she had missed so sorely since the loss of her own family.

And now she had lost them, too, because of Luke. He had given them to her and he had taken them away. She pressed her lips tightly together as the pain of loss welled up in her yet again, the hurt of knowing Luke was responsible for the deaths of Ben and Anne, and that, instead of facing up to his responsibility, he had run out with no thought of what his desertion would mean to her or to his sons.

The baby punched her with an active foot. What would Luke have had to say about this coming child? She had a pretty fair idea, remembering his comments before — and after — Micah's birth. Tears stung her eyes, and she blinked them away furiously. Bawling wouldn't help. This baby must not be brought into the world drenched in its mother's tears. She must do for it as she was doing for the others. Thank God Will was here to help her cope.

Thus, full circle, her thoughts came to the dark-eyed man who, in these few short months, had come to mean so much to her and her sons. He was more of a companion to her, more of a father to them than Luke had ever been. And he could never be more to them, and to her, than that. Because of Luke, who had brought Will here. Because of Luke, to whom she was married until death. And she didn't even know, at this moment, whether he was alive — or dead.

Will, totally unaware of Hannah's agitation, tromped through the deepening snow to the bunkhouse, his thoughts in those first moments curiously close to her own. Isaac. He shook his head. *For all the world like his father, the little devil was.*

Luke'd probably split his sides laughing, did he know.

He pushed open the door to chill darkness and shivered. Memory of the warmth and brightness he had just left made this bleak room all the less welcoming. Used to physical hardships and lack of comfort, he wondered at himself. Then he shrugged. Must be getting soft if he let a little cold and quiet get to him! He'd have to remedy that.

Stretched out in his bunk, so empty-frigid, his thoughts turned to the coming Christmas gathering. The Claytons had not gotten together for Thanksgiving because, still deeply mourning their parents, they didn't have the heart for a day of joyous celebration. Thankful as they all were that their financial outlook had brightened, tenuously, over the last months, the thought of a family get-together without Ben and Anne had been unendurable. By mutual consent, each family had given thanks quietly at home for the good that had come to them and tried desperately not to dwell on the family's tragedy.

They could not, however, mourn forever. Nor would Anne and Ben want them to. Becky had determined that, for the sake of the children, Christmas must be a joyous day. Christmas — a time of birth and a time of new beginning.

Will knew Eve would be at the gathering. He scarcely dared admit, even to himself, how much he wanted to see her, calling himself every kind of fool for such lunacy.

With grim determination, he wrenched his thoughts away. Christmas. That was better. Christmas was coming, and four little boys deserved some kind of present. Hannah, too. But he had no money, no idea even of what they would like. Most anything, probably. They had few toys. He thought of Sam and Micah pushing rough chunks of wood around on the floor, calling them their "wagon train." An idea struck him. There wasn't a lot of time, and he would need Hannah's help.

The next evening, the boys asleep, Will put his plan to Hannah: A wagon that could also double as a sled by changing the wheels for runners. But big enough for all four of them to pile into. She was sitting in her rocker, the remains of Micah's sweater in her lap. She bent over the pile of yarn. "That's a fine idea. Thank you for thinking of them." She became very busy, still with her head bowed so he couldn't see her face.

"Hannah?" he asked, puzzled and also a shade doubtful. "If you'd rather not ... I just thought ..."

She raised her head, then, and he saw that her eyes were suspiciously moist. She blinked rapidly and smiled. "It's a wonderful idea. The boys will be so happy. To think you'd go to all that trouble for them."

He laughed, relieved. "Not just me goin' to trouble, don't f'rget. You're bein' roped into this, too."

"I don't mind. When shall we start?"

"How 'bout now?"

They did, drawing up the plans, figuring how they could use the scraps left from repairing the bunkhouse. Every evening thereafter that Will was free, the boys in bed, they worked on it, sometimes commenting on their progress, more often in a companionable silence.

Christmas Eve 1887. Outdoors, snow was falling steadily. Inside, all was warmth and light and joyful anticipation. The boys in their nightshirts sat in a row on the floor, listening to

Louise Lenahan Wallace

Hannah read the story of Christ's birth. Will, seated at the table, was engaged in a task at which they could only guess, although they cast swift, secret glances at him whenever they figured they could get away with it.

> *And they came with haste, and found Mary,*
> *   and Joseph, and the babe lying in a manger.*
> *And when they had seen it, they made known*
> *   abroad the saying which was told them*
> *   concerning this child.*
> *And all they that heard it wondered at*
> *   those things which were told them by the*
> *   shepherds.*
> *But Mary kept all these things, and pondered*
> *   them in her heart.*

Hannah closed the Book and laid it carefully aside. Reaching out, she enfolded each of her sons in a warm hug, smoothed the hair back from each face, and whispered to each something for his ears alone. Thus did she give of her love to her sons, individually so that they never became lost in the group. These last days, she had been spending extra time with Isaac, talking to him, Will knew — though not about what, beyond that she was trying to reassure him she wouldn't leave suddenly. Whatever she had told him, however he might feel, now on this night, Isaac did not draw away.

Afterward, with a notable decrease of pushing, shoving and giggling, the boys disappeared into their bedroom. After the thumps and whispers finally subsided, Will and Hannah set to work. He brought in the small tree he had hidden in the bunkhouse. She popped corn for stringing and brought out the box of decorations kept carefully back on a high shelf all the year, safe from exploring fingers.

She began to place the ornaments on the branches while he put the finishing touches to the wagon-sled. "They were my Ma's," she explained. "She got them the year we had our first tree. I can still remember that Christmas, plain as plain. Pa wasn't much for such a 'heathen' idea. He said it'd take away from the true meaning of Christmas, but Ma stood up to him. Said it wouldn't take away, couldn't when the idea was giving and thinking of others.

"And she got her way. When Jonah, my little brother, and I saw the tree that morning ... Well, it was a sight I've carried with me all these years. Ma so happy because we were happy and Pa, kind of uncertain at first, but finally admitting Ma was right and enjoying it more than the rest of us put together." Hannah laughed.

"Ma always said she was glad we'd had such a Christmas to remember. Jonah talked about it for weeks. He died that spring, and it gave Ma comfort, she said, to know he'd been happy and had such a good memory to carry with him." Her voice trailed off. Seldom did she speak so freely. Now she had given Will a glimpse of her heart.

"So," she went on quickly, embarrassed by her revelation, "that's one reason Christmas means so much to me and why I want so much for the boys to remember it as a special time." She stepped back to survey the tree now festooned with popcorn strings, paper chains the boys had made, and the precious ornaments. "What do you think?"

He put down his brush and studied her handiwork. After

Caleb Braden's death, Will and Phebe had exchanged handmade presents at Christmas, but there had been no trees for them. His mother had emphasized that the birth of Christ, not ornaments, made the day important. He remembered how hopelessly he had wished, the first couple of years after his father's death, that they could have a tree, however small. Then he had grown up and away from the idea, had forgotten it. Until now, looking at the tree Hannah had decorated so lovingly, he realized with a start that, quite unexpectedly, his old yearning had been fulfilled.

To cover his foolish emotion, Will walked around to view the tiny fir from all angles. "Hannah," he said huskily, "it looks just great. You really have a knack with your hands f'r fixin' things up. Now if I'd tried ..."

She laughed at his rueful expression. "There is one thing you can do." She handed him the star to fasten to the top. After it was in place they stood a moment more, admiring the results of their labor, before he remembered the wagonsled. Together they arranged it under the tree, in sled form at present, with the wheels nearby.

"Oh, Will, it turned out so nice. It'll mean so much to the boys. How can I ever thank you?"

He glanced sideways. All her weariness had vanished, leaving her young and pretty, excited over Christmas. He smiled slowly, unaware that the evening's happiness had brought a glow to his own eyes. "No need to thank me, Hannah. You did more'n a fair share yourself, paintin' and makin' the wagon cover and harness. Tell you what, let's take equal credit."

She laughed, her low, rippling laugh so pleasing to his ears. "It's a deal!"

Day Star Rising

Christmas morning Will stepped from the bunkhouse into a world of dazzling white. The snow had stopped during the night and an unbroken blanket lay over everything. Even the paths he had so carefully shoveled were no more. Tucking the bundle he carried more snugly under his coat, pulling his hat down to shield his eyes from the glare, he proceeded to make his own path by plowing straight through to the porch. Breathless, stamping snow from his boots, he was only too glad to enter the welcome warmth of the kitchen.

Hannah looked up from slicing bacon. "Will, Merry Christmas!"

"Merry Christmas to you, Hannah. You're up early. I couldn't beat you gettin' a fire started even today."

"So sorry to disappoint you. Want me to put it out so you can do it yourself?"

"I'll pass this time, I guess," he grumbled. "The boys up yet?"

As if in answer came the thump of four pairs of feet hitting the floor and a stampede behind the closed bedroom door. "I think the boys are up," she said wryly as the door jerked open and they piled out, Sam and Isaac in the lead, Jeremy holding Micah's hand, following close behind.

Micah was still rubbing the sleep from his eyes with his free fist when his brothers spied the tree — and the sled in front of it. With shouts of delight they charged forward, Jeremy now dragging Micah. Will and Hannah, standing well back and listening to their cries of pleasure, knew they were being amply rewarded for their efforts.

Will stepped forward to show them the mysteries of the sled and how it could be changed into a covered wagon when the snow was gone.

"C'n we take it outside and try it, Ma?" Jeremy asked eagerly.

"Your breakfast ..." Hannah objected.

"Aw, please, Ma, just f'r a little bit?"

"All right," she relented with a smile, "but just for a few minutes. You help the others dress warmly." She had to call the last words, for with the first the boys had already headed for the bedroom.

Will was grinning openly. "I declare! I believe you want to go out there with them," she said, astonished.

His grin widened. "I might at that."

She just shook her head.

He brought the small bundle from under his coat. "Merry Christmas, Hannah."

Her eyes widened. For a moment, she only stared.

"Go on, take it," he urged against her silence. "It ain't much," he added as casually as he could and thrust it into her hands.

She drew it slowly out of the paper and caught her breath.

"You said you needed a box to keep your thread in," he explained, still against her silence. "I hope it'll do."

She turned it over and over in her hands, touching the birds and flowers he had etched into the sides, smoothing her fingers over the "H" carved on the lid. She raised her face and her eyes were full of wonder. "Will, thank you. It's beautiful. I just don't know what to say. I never dreamed you were making it. I thought all that carving you were doing was for the boys."

He laughed, relieved she obviously liked it. For a minute he hadn't been sure. "I'm a pretty sly fella," he agreed as the boys charged out of their room and began tugging at the sled. He carried it outside and showed them how to work it. Yelling enthusiastically, they piled on and he drew them at a gallop around the yard. As he panted past the porch, Hannah hailed him from the doorway where she'd been watching with barely suppressed amusement.

Ignoring the boys' howls of protest at his desertion, he bounded up the steps and followed her inside. "Is somethin' wrong?" he asked anxiously, for she looked upset.

"You left too soon," she complained in the same tone she would have used to scold one of the boys.

He blinked, feeling ridiculously guilty as though he had actually been caught in mischief, but she was turning to her sewing basket, drawing out a parcel to hand him. Now it was his turn to stammer, hers to smile.

When he finally, clumsily, got it unwrapped, he found a new shirt, made with tiny, even stitches and hours of work. She chuckled at his astonishment. "You're not the only sly one," she said wickedly, and he grinned.

"I have been in need of one," he admitted, "but I didn't know it showed quite that much."

"It did. I can't have you running around looking like a refugee from a ragbag. What would the neighbors say?" she asked in mock horror.

Remembering some of the things that had already been said, they eyed each other ruefully and suddenly laughed. For abruptly, on this morning, the old hurt didn't seem to matter quite as much as it had.

"I'll try this on." He gestured with the shirt.

"Go ahead into the boys' room. I'll finish up here." She

turned back to the stove and the sadly neglected breakfast. She was setting plates on the table when he came out, and straightening, she surveyed him critically. "Turn around." She inspected the shirt minutely as he obeyed. "Guess it'll do," she pronounced finally.

"Now, Hannah, it fits great and you know it," he said sternly, "so you might as well admit it. I'm proud of it, I'll tell you!"

She almost managed to hide her smile of pleasure. "Don't get so proud you split the seams," she warned. "I'd hate to have to put all those stitches back!"

"Yes, ma'am," he said meekly and they both laughed. She was doing a lot of laughing this morning, she thought, surprised. But it was all so warm and right and good, how could she help it?

The warmth lasted through dragging the boys, snow-covered, rosy-cheeked, and laughter-filled into the house for breakfast, and through the meal itself. As she listened to Will give thanks, she closed her eyes, breathing her own heart-deep gratitude for a happiness she would never forget.

Only after the dishes were done, she felt a chill as she remembered she had to face the assembled Clayton relatives, and soon. She didn't mind individually, but the whole clan together ...

"What's the matter?" Will had caught her panic.

She turned quickly and straightened on its rack the dishtowel that didn't need straightening. "Nothing," she said in a small voice.

He moved behind her. "Hannah, turn 'round."

After a long moment she did so, but with her head bowed so he couldn't see her face. He reached out a big hand, tipping her chin up so she had to look at him. He saw the misery in her eyes.

"Hey," he said sternly, "don't let 'em pole-ax you. You hear me?"

"How did you ..."

He smiled grimly. "Remember I have to face all of 'em today, too. And I'm no more thrilled 'bout it than you are."

Rarely did he make even such an indirect reference to the hurt he still felt about Eve, and Hannah bit her lip. "I guess I just wasn't thinking."

"Just don't let 'em spook you. Remember, chin up and face 'em down, no matter what. And if you need me, I'll be there. Just whoop — or cuss — whichever comes to you first."

She had to smile a little at that, but he said gravely, "I mean it. You need backin' up, you let me know. Promise?"

Her eyes met his and he saw the shadow in hers lift. "I promise," she said softly.

Eleven

The boys rushed outside, heedless of the perils of snow and ice-covered steps to their new squirrel sweaters — or to their necks. Hannah, no longer sure-footed with the increased weight of the baby pulling at her, hesitated in the doorway. Will, carrying Micah to the wagon box, now on runners, saw her uncertainty. "Wait till I get these coyotes stowed away," he said over his shoulder. "I'll come back and help you down." He tossed Micah into the straw-filled bed and piled the other boys in after. Giggling and shoving, they burrowed into the waiting blankets. "Cover up good, now," he warned. "Jeremy, you keep an eye on ever'body."

As he turned back up the steps to Hannah, she gave him an embarrassed smile. "I feel like an overloaded mule, and foolish, being so helpless."

"Don't you dare," he said sternly. "You're only bein' sensible. You slip on this ice, you'd hurt yourself and the baby f'r sure."

To her disgust, she felt herself blushing at this rare mention of her pregnancy.

Putting one arm firmly around her, he extended the other

for her to grasp. Warning her to go slow, they descended the slippery steps.

Feeling his steady, solid dependability, breathing his pleasing masculine smells of leather, shaving soap, and pipe tobacco, and aware, most acutely, of his warm, hard body so comfortingly close to her own, something stabbed Hannah deep inside. She had to fight a sudden, fierce longing to lean against him, to relax in the shelter of his strength. Relax, and know how it could be in the arms of a man who ... Stunned, she jerked her errant thoughts back. *Foolish!* Frightened that she might actually do this wild thing, she berated herself fiercely. *Foolish! And useless, this dwelling on something that could never be.* Except in her heart ...

Careless in her agitation, she put her foot down on an icy patch and promptly skidded. Will's grip tightened instantly, protecting her from tumbling. In that moment she was held close in his arms, his head bent above hers. His arms tightened, drawing her hard against him, and his breath came faster. Her face raised to his, she clearly saw all the desire kindled his eyes.

Terrified, exultant, she knew. He was going to kiss her and she wanted him to. Oh, she wanted him to! Her lips parted as the world teetered crazily. Her eyes closed. His mouth touched hers as the baby, perhaps in protest at being locked so tightly between them, flailed out with furious fist and foot. Then Will, white-faced, stepped back, releasing her, his breath ragged as he reached to touch her cheek and let his hand fall.

"My God," he said, and his voice seemed strangely far away. "It must be a boy. He packs a wallop, don't he?"

And she was trying to laugh, so she wouldn't cry, while the world righted itself with an echoing crash.

"Shall we try this again?" He circled his arm around her once more. If there was the faintest hesitation on either of their parts, both chose to ignore it. "Nothin' like tryin' to take two trips in one day," he teased. "You almost went f'r a ride f'r sure."

They navigated the steps safely this time, and he assisted her carefully onto the seat. As he climbed in beside her and spoke to the horses, she arranged her wraps casually.

But her heart was echoing her earlier, silent cry. *Fool! Dreamer! Wanting what could never be.* Thus she chastised herself, trying to drown out the cry of her heart that had just become a keening wail.

Will pulled the horses to a halt near Jason's back door and cast a quick glance at Hannah. She hadn't spoken at all on the ride over, except to comment to the excitedly chattering boys. But, after all, what could she — or he — say? Mere words could never express what had passed between them.

He cleared his throat, tipping his head toward the house. "Ready f'r 'em?"

Shock at the total gladness with which she had turned to Will had driven from her mind all her earlier fears about facing the Clayton clan. Now, at his words, they came swamping back. "Chin up," she said sturdily, suiting action to words. The flash in his eyes this time was one of admiration.

"I'll get the boys out, then come back," he said quickly. "You just sit tight."

He lifted the squirming youngsters down, saw them

safely on their way up the steps before he turned back to Hannah. He reached to lift her down. "Scared?"

"Terribly!"

"Me, too!"

The thought of Will, so strong and sure and masculine, being scared of anything startled her. Their eyes met and she saw his crinkle humorously. Something seemed to lift from her heart, and her own eyes twinkled.

"Come on. Let's go face 'em, together!"

As he helped her up the steps, being extremely cautious where she placed her feet this trip — Becky came bustling out the door. "Hannah, Will, Merry Christmas! Here, let me help you," she added, slipping a capable arm around Hannah and thus nudging Will aside. "These steps are slick, so be careful."

"Time to unload the mule," Hannah murmured.

Naturally disbelieving her ears, Becky looked confused, and Will, behind her, rolled his eyes up. "She's just bein' a sassy sister-in-law," he explained.

Such impertinence from Will was so unexpected that Becky's mouth fell open. Seeing her shock, Hannah began to shake with silent mirth.

"What in the name of heaven has come over ..." But, looking from Will's wide-eyed innocence to Hannah's poor-suppressed merriment, Becky had the good sense to know when to give up and the grace not to finish saying what she was so obviously thinking about the state of their minds. Instead she merely said, "Come along, sassy sister-in-law," and ignoring the new fit of amusement these words produced, helped Hannah up another step. Not, however, before Will caught a glimpse of her own quick-concealed smile.

Effectively ousted, Will was left to retrieve from the wagon the mince pies that were Hannah's contribution to the day's festivities. Following behind into the kitchen, he found that Catty and Eve had already greeted the children and were helping them take off their coats. As the new sweaters with their brown-and-white squirrel pattern appeared, the two women murmured admiringly and bade Becky to come see. When Sam turned proudly to show the rear view of the squirrel scampering across the back of his sweater, their murmurs became chuckles of delight. Becky bent and examined the stitching carefully. "Hannah, you're incredible! Wherever did you find the time and the pattern?"

As Hannah responded and the feminine talk began swirling around the kitchen, Will, assured that she was indeed welcome, set the pies on the worktable, mumbled something about seeing to the horses, and beat a hasty retreat.

Safely outside, his footsteps slowed. What kind of man was he, he wondered bitterly, that he could swing so between two women? Tell himself what he would about forgetting Eve, how hopeless it was to carry her in his heart — that first glimpse of her red-gold hair and sound of her low voice had brought back all the old yearning.

And Hannah? Hannah was becoming dearer to him every day, whether he was willing for that to happen or not. He had been ready to risk everything those earlier moments when he had nearly kissed her. She had wanted him to as much as he had wanted it. He was certain. There is no mistaking such knowledge between a man and a woman. But — she was Luke's wife. How could he have forgotten even for a second?

He had flat-out meant it when he told Jason and Reverend

Wardley that he did not chase after other men's wives. But what else could he call his actions? Frustrated, angry with himself for such weakness, he circled frantically, uselessly, trying to make some meaning out of that which made no sense.

At last, though, he could find no excuse for delaying his return to the house. Reluctantly, he pushed open the kitchen door — to such a commotion of female busyness he heartily wished he had stalled longer.

Becky was basting the turkey, Cat and Eve were peeling potatoes and onions, and Hannah, seated at the table, was shaping bread dough into rolls. They chatted away a mile a minute until he entered, when sudden silence dropped heavy as a boulder off a cliff. He awkwardly took off his coat and hat, feeling like he had suddenly grown hide, horns and a tail, and wishing fervently he were a thousand miles away.

Finally, Becky spoke. "Will, Jason was just asking about you. I think he's getting ready to go see if you got stuck in a drift."

"Sorry, I got sidetracked out at the barn."

"No mules there," Becky said wickedly, threatening to set Hannah off again while Catty and Eve looked totally bewildered.

"None?" he asked in dismay. "I wouldn't of spent so much time lookin' if I'd known that!"

Becky pretended to throw her basting spoon at him. He fended it off with mock terror and winked. Crossing to the table, he murmured to Hannah, "How's your chin doin'?"

"Just fine."

"You sure?" he asked anxiously.

She smiled happily. "I'm sure!"

Relieved for her, glad that she had slain this particular rattlesnake, he straightened — and saw Becky, Eve and Catty all watching with avid curiosity. When he caught them, they turned hurriedly back to their tasks, pretending they hadn't been paying any attention. Seized by some unknown imp of mischief, he turned back to Hannah, bent and whispered for her ear, alone, "Glad you're havin' such a good trip!"

She blinked, hesitating for the merest fraction of a second while their eyes met. Then she laughed, the low, rippling sound of it carrying to the three listening women. Ridiculously pleased, he straightened, gave a general silly grin to the others, and sauntered out of the room. Behind him the murmuring broke out again, but right then he was past caring. Let them gossip! For sure, he'd given them something to think about.

Jason, Aaron, Matt and Dan Mackley were gathered in the sitting room when he wandered in. "Will, come on in and sit!" Jason greeted him. "We was wonderin' where you made off to."

"Becky already scolded me," he confessed. "I got sidetracked at the barn." He moved to drop into a comfortable chair near Jason, speaking to Aaron and Dan as he passed, nodding stiffly to Matt, who seemed about to say something, but didn't.

Jason grinned. "Becky's a good one f'r helpin' folks spot the error of their ways. You got any ears left at all?"

Will touched them gingerly. "They're still a mite warm," he admitted.

"Glad it was you and not me. She's a peppery one, all right." He chuckled, but every man of them knew that, "peppery" or not, Jason wouldn't have traded her for any other woman on earth.

They picked up the discussion where they'd dropped it —

the comparative ease of this winter to last — and started laying plans for spring roundup. "It shouldn't be all that bad this year," Jason pointed out. "We've kept close track of our own critters, so they shouldn't be very scattered. I haven't noticed but a few brands mixed in with ours. So we c'n get to the calf brandin' pretty straight off. And — the best f'r last — it does look as if we might just get a good-sized calf crop stacked up against our cows! Wouldn't that be somethin'!"

This optimism lightened their hearts and loosened their tongues, and made them deeply grateful they'd stuck it out all those harsh days and nights of the past year. If they'd given up — as it had been so tempting to do so many times ... It was Aaron who said for all of them, "Thank God."

Finally Jason sniffed the air, audibly. "Don't know 'bout the rest of you, but I'm gettin' downright hungry. Think I'll mosey in and see how long before we c'n eat."

Aaron called after him, "Careful they don't rope you with an apron and make you help!"

Jason, twirling an imaginary ruffle, gave a few mincing steps. "Wouldn't I be a sight?" he smirked. Hoots of laughter followed him into the kitchen. He was back in just a couple of minutes, interrupting a tale of Dan's about trail herding in the early days.

"Matt Jamison, you sly dog! Why didn't you tell us? Sittin' here all this time and never sayin' a word," he complained.

Matt smiled broadly, Dan chuckled, and Aaron asked, "What's up?"

"Becky just told me." Jason clapped his brother-in-law on the shoulder. "Ol' Matt here's goin' to be a Papa. How 'bout that!"

Day Star Rising

Matt's smile by now threatened to split his face. Aaron joined in the congratulations and friendly teasing that followed, but Will sat frozen. So Matt had that, too. The bandying words flowed past him unheeded. Pain ripped him, overwhelming the numbness in a nauseating tide.

Vaguely hearing Becky announce dinner, he realized the others were milling toward the laden table. He stood as Matt passed and the eyes of the two men met in a long, direct look. Again Matt seemed about to speak, but didn't.

Will's jaw clenched, but whatever Matt might have said was lost by the sound of Eve's voice. "Matt, are you coming?"

Both men swung to face her as she waited, hand reaching out to Matt. "Sure thing, Eve. Right now." Leveling one more look at Will watching so grimly, Matt pushed past him. Taking Eve's outstretched hand, he pulled her close, brushing a kiss against her burnished hair. She laughed up at him as, his arm still circling her waist, they joined the group at the table.

Eating was the last thing Will felt like doing, but he could hardly stand like a mired cow to the one spot all afternoon, so he followed in the wake of the merry crowd. Hannah was standing between two empty chairs. As he moved to her side, she gave him a warm smile and he forced himself to return it.

Careful, now, he thought sarcastically. *Remember your pride*. Pride! It was a poor substitute.

He bowed his head as Jason asked the blessing on all their loved ones, "Those here and those we carry always in our hearts." It was the only reference, direct or indirect, to Anne and Ben. Spoken or silent, however, not one of them could forget or fail to compare last year's joyous Christmas Day celebration with this. One short year for so much to happen:

the terrible winter, Matt and Eve married, Ben and Anne dead. And no gathering of the family could ever be the same.

Luke ... Will glanced at Hannah. She sat with head bowed and eyes shut for the blessing, but she had gone white. He wondered for a second if she was going to faint, but she murmured "Amen" with the others, raised her head, and he saw a definite lift to her chin.

Sensing his glance, she turned. Neither one in the depths of their pain could give the other a reassuring smile, but the look that passed between them was a mutual transfer of courage and encouragement. *Chin up!* hers said. *I understand,* his said.

The rest of the meal was a blur. Ever after, Will's only clear memory was of Eve sitting almost directly across from him and next to Matt. A baby — so that was why she seemed so lighted up. Hers was the rich glow of a woman who has been deeply blessed with happiness.

The interminable meal finally ended, and the men decided to stretch their legs by a ride out to check on the herd. Will followed along, since it beat doing nothing. As he was hauling on his outdoor clothing, Jeremy came sidling up. Will reached to tousle his hair. "How you doin', son?"

"All right, I guess." Shyly, he asked, "Mr. Braden, can't I go out with you? I'll be good, I promise." He looked so pleading Will hadn't the heart to refuse out right. "Please? Jared and Reuben are goin' out, and I'd sure like to go, too!"

"The other fellas are goin' along, are they? That does change the picture a mite. You'll have to ask your Ma. If she says so, you c'n come."

Jeremy dashed off, but soon returned with Hannah in tow. "Will, do you really think ..."

He reached for his hat. "Boy's got to find out what it's all 'bout sometime. Seems now's a good a time as any to start." The doubt didn't leave her eyes.

"He'll be fine, Hannah. I give you my word."

She hesitated another long instant as she glanced down at her son's eager young face and back to Will's steady, grave one. "All right," she relented, "if you do exactly like Mr. Braden says, Jeremy."

The boy let out a whoop and raced for his coat. As Will turned from Hannah, he saw the speculative looks — quickly concealed — of Jason, Aaron and Matt. He felt a flash of real annoyance. *Not them, too! Couldn't a man even have a family discussion without it being pried into?*

At the door he turned to Hannah. "We'll be careful," he assured her. "You be, too." She raised her hand in silent farewell, standing at the window long after they disappeared from sight.

Jeremy, excited beyond measure, had the time of his young life. Perched up front on Will's horse, he asked a thousand questions, all of which Will answered as directly and simply as he could. Back at the house, half frozen though he was, he immediately reported to his mother and aunts about searching for cattle and following their tracks to the draw where they had drifted for shelter. "Then we had to check their noses and mouths f'r ice and break the waterhole open so they could drink. If they got ice in their mouths and noses, they couldn't drink water. Or breathe," he explained as an afterthought. "And some of the Ma cows are goin' to have babies," he announced importantly. "Uncle Jason showed me how to tell. He said you have to look at their ..."

"Say, Jeremy," Jason broke in upon his nephew's explanation, "the other fellas are playin' marbles in the sittin' room. Why don't you go join 'em?"

As Jeremy, puzzled by his uncle's fiery red face, obeyed, Jason tried to apologize to Hannah. Not very successfully because Matt and Aaron were also red-faced from holding in their laughter until Jeremy was safely out of hearing. Jason finally gave up, glared at his brothers-in-law and stomped outside. They promptly nudged each other and followed him.

Will had been listening to Jeremy's version and now he told Hannah, "He did a good job tellin' you just now. He's got a sharp eye and he remembers."

Her embarrassment faded into a wistful smile. "He's hooked, isn't he? It's in his blood now, and it'll never leave."

Will, startled, realized she was speaking the truth as he remembered how it had been with himself.

They wandered into the sitting room where Becky, Cat and Eve had tactfully withdrawn and were now chatting comfortably. The Christmas tree caught Will's eye, and because he didn't feel up to joining their female discussion, he sauntered over to it, Hannah still beside him. She noticed first. "Look, Becky made ornaments for everyone, just like ..." her voice caught.

It had been one of Anne Clayton's Christmas traditions that she make an ornament — usually a cookie — each family member getting one with his name on it to hang on the tree. She had continued the custom even after her own family was grown and scattered to their own homes because, she had said, it was one way for the family always to be together, no matter what.

"Here's yours, Hannah." Will pointed to a cut-out stocking.

"And here's Anne's — and Ben's." It was his turn to falter.

"Luke ..." He barely heard her strangled cry, turned quickly to find her clutching a brightly-colored sleigh. Before he could say anything, Becky spoke behind him.

"Hannah, I ... Ma always said everyone gets one whether they're here or not. Luke's still family, just like Pa and Ma. Just like you are and always will be." Her voice broke.

Hannah stood rigid, her lids tight shut, her lashes wet. When she opened her eyes, the tears spilled unheeded down her cheeks. "Oh, Becky." The two women reached out to each other.

Will prudently decided it was time for his second hasty retreat of the day. He backed off into the kitchen, his heart rejoicing for Hannah. And came face to face with Eve washing her hands at the pump.

Twelve

Will, catching sight of Eve would have turned back but ...

"Hello, Will." At sound of her voice all his yearning welled up and it was too late to leave.

"Eve," he said huskily. "How are you?" He didn't need to ask. The answer was plain in her radiance. She had gained a sweet maturity these past months. Or perhaps it was only the faint shadow of grief that lingered in her eyes, that would be there ever after, the only visible scar of that night last summer.

"I'm just fine, Will. And you?"

Something hard-held in Will snapped, and he fought a sudden impulse to laugh bitterly. "Oh, I'm just dandy. Why shouldn't I be? Carin' f'r another man's wife and young ones, carryin' all the responsibility that's supposed to be Luke's, workin' his cattle and acres instead of my own. Oh, yes, I'm just where I've wanted to be all my life. It's my deepest ambition fulfilled!"

She flushed. "Will ..."

"Eve." And the bitterness was gone. "How do you think I've been all these months, rememberin' what you and me had, knowin' what we could have ..."

"No!" she said sharply. "Stop it, Will. You mustn't! I'm married to Matt, and I never knew, never dreamed, such happiness could be possible. I ..."

"Happiness!" The bitterness was back, full force. "How c'n you be happy with a man who makes you cry at night fit to melt a body's heart? What does he ..."

"What do you mean?" The flush had dropped from her cheeks, leaving her white and shaken. "How did you know about that?"

It was his turn to redden, but he refused to take his eyes from hers. "I heard ... talk. It don't matter how I know. Eve, we were goin' to be married. Don't you think by that I should know you well enough to tell when you're unhappy? By God, when I think of him hurtin' you at night, I could kill him with my bare hands!"

"Will, stop it! You must not think that way!"

"How am I supposed to think?" His fierceness matched hers. "What does he do to you?" He reached out to grasp her arms but she shrank from his hands. He saw, and the look on his face was as if she had slapped him.

"He doesn't do anything to me except love me like I never knew it was possible to be loved." The flush was back as she stared straight into his eyes, challenging him. He saw she told the truth, and his gaze dropped first.

She hesitated, then, seeming to search for words. "Will, I don't know how you found out about my nightmares."

Startled, his eyes swiveled back to hers. She smiled bitterly. "Yes, nightmares. I don't owe you an explanation, but I won't have you thinking hard of Matt when he's been so good to me."

Will stared numbly. "These dreams," she said haltingly, "I keep going back to the night of the ... the raid." Unaware, she gripped her hands tightly together. "It was so ... awful. I keep seeing Ma and Pa. And then I'm running, running from those terrible men. They keep chasing me, and I can hear them laughing. I trip and one grabs for me. I can't see his face." Her voice was a choked, desperate whisper. If her terror was such in a sunlit kitchen, what must it be in the dark of night? Will kept his hands rigid at his sides, lest he betray himself again by reaching out to her.

She closed her eyes, shuddering. "I scream and scream, but I always wake up before I can see his face." She raised her head, her eyes full of remembered agony he could not share. Then, incredibly, she laughed shakily. "But it's all right now, because I know. Matt and I hadn't talked about it. He didn't want to upset me more. But Becky told him maybe we should. And he said when he found me that morning, I ... I didn't know him right away. I fought him until I realized it was him. I don't remember." Head up, she looked full into Will's dazed eyes.

"That's just it. It was Matt that morning, and it was Matt in my nightmares. Just as it's been him every night I've awakened so terrified and not knowing. He's there with me. So steady and comforting and good to me, always. Which is the way I want it to be every day and night of my life."

"He's tied you to him," Will insisted, refusing to accept her verdict.

"If he has, I'm only glad. I want that more than anything else in the world." Lightly, her hands brushed her stomach.

He saw the gesture and knew sudden, total defeat. "Yes," he said heavily, "there's that, now, too. Matt ..."

"What's goin' on here?" Matt's voice, cutting from behind, made both of them jump. "You all right, Eve?" His eyes flashed concern first, last, and always for her.

She reached to him, her smile once more joyous. "I'm fine. Will and I were just talking. I wanted to tell him I hope with all my heart someday he'll be as happy as I am."

Matt turned to Will but kept hold of Eve's hands. His expression hardened, but he said nothing. Will, too, held stubborn silence as the eyes of the two men clashed. Then Matt was turning back to Eve, dismissing Will as though, knowing he had won, he didn't have to bother saying anything. The same silence, Will realized now, that he had held all these past months whenever the two men came into contact.

"Time to go," Matt told her. "You 'bout ready?" They walked past him, Matt's arm circling Eve, leaving Will suddenly chilled and totally alone in the middle of the floor.

How long he stood motionless, listening to the echoing silence, he could not have told, nor how long he would have stood had not Hannah's voice, calling, returned him to reality.

"Will, where ... There you are," she said from the doorway. "Everyone's leav — " She broke off as she caught sight of his face. "Will, what's wrong?"

He shook himself, shuddering, as a dog shakes water after emerging from a creek. He couldn't hide his misery. But this was Hannah, and somehow he couldn't mind if she saw what the rest of the world must never know.

She stood in front of him, not touching him, although the effort it cost made her voice tremble. "If you can't tell me, I understand, but if there's any way I can help, let me know. There's nothing more lonely than hurting by yourself."

Day Star Rising

He drew a shaky breath, let it out in a soul-deep sigh, but his glazed look cleared a little as he gazed into her eyes and saw the warmth, the hurting because he was hurt.

"Remember," she said softly, "all you have to do is whoop — or cuss."

He could not smile, but the flicker in his eyes told her he understood. "Everyone's leaving," she pointed out. "I've got the boys all ready."

"You're right," he said finally. "We should be goin', too."

The ride home was a silent one. The boys, exhausted by all the long day, dozed limply among the straw and blankets. Will was sunk deep in his own pain. Hannah, turning to catch his grimness, her own thoughts in chaos, said nothing either. *Not now*, her heart whispered. *Later, but not now.*

He pulled the horses up near the back porch, but merely sat, holding the lines slack. He finally glanced at Hannah, sitting tall and straight, hands clasped in her lap. He wrapped the lines around the whip socket and jumped to the ground. "Sit tight. I'll get the boys."

Carrying them one by one up the steps, he piled them on their beds. After helping Hannah into the house, during which moments she dared not look at him for remembering the morning, he assisted her in getting the sleepy youngsters ready and tucked under the covers. Through it all, except for that one comment of his outside, neither spoke a word.

Back out in the kitchen with its brightly decorated Christmas tree and its fragrant pine scent and the cold silence, she watched him trudge to the door. His hand closed over the knob before she spoke into that silence. "Will."

He turned slowly, wearily.

She found she was gripping the back of her rocking chair so hard her fingers were numb. Forcing herself to a show of serenity she was far from feeling, she unclenched her hands and moved to sit in the rocker.

"What is it, Hannah?" Even his voice was tired.

"Will, I know you're hurting. It's Eve, isn't it?" Resentment burned in his eyes. "Will, I'm not trying to pry. Please believe me."

His anger faded, leaving, once again, only the weariness. "Yes." His voice was flat.

"I thought it must be. I saw her leave the kitchen with Matt before I went in. She must have said something awful to hurt you this deeply."

Why not? What did it matter now? In a tight voice he said, "She rejected me f'r once and all. Told me flat out it's Matt she loves, and that's the way it'll always be. Period."

"Will, I'm sorry. What will you do now?"

He stared at her blankly. How could he think of the future when the future had suddenly ceased to exist? "I don't know."

Her fingers were clenched again. Realizing, she firmly straightened them, letting them lie clasped loose in her lap.

Misunderstanding her silence, he said wryly, "Don't worry. I won't leave you and the boys high and dry."

She shook her head. "I'm not worried about that. But I am worried about you. You're so lost."

He gave a short, harsh laugh. "No need to concern yourself 'bout me. I'll make out."

With supreme effort she kept her voice steady. "Of course I'm concerned. How can I not be when I care about what happens to you? I do care, Will." She drew a deep breath.

"Sometimes when a person is hurting, another person can help by being there. I told you this afternoon if there was any way I could help you, I would. I meant it then, and I mean it now. I'm here, Will. Any way at all," she repeated slowly, clearly.

Stunned, he stared at her. "Hannah, what are you sayin'?"

She laughed, shakily. "I'm not very good at this. I've never offered myself to a man before. I know I'm not Eve, and I know I'm not in the best shape ..." her hands touched her swollen stomach "... but, well, there it is. I'm here if you want me, no strings attached on either side."

Her voice was suddenly calm and steady, her shakiness stilled. Her green eyes held no evasion, only total honesty as they met his in a long, long look. Dazed, he couldn't take his gaze from hers. She was offering herself as simply and directly as that.

No, not simply. She was a God-fearing, loyal woman who would never easily break her marriage vows. Yet she was willing to give herself to him to ease his hurt, "no strings attached."

"Hannah," he said brokenly.

"Will, this isn't just a favor to you or out of pity. I know what I'm saying. I want to help if I can."

"Hannah," he said huskily, "come here."

Her eyes still on his, she rose from the rocker, a little heavily because of the child, but not awkwardly. It struck him in that moment how much grace there was about all her movements, always. She crossed to where he stood and paused in front of him.

He reached out, cupping her face with his hands.

"Hannah," he breathed, bent to her. As their lips met in a merging pressure, she gave a sighing moan and reached up to pull his head down closer yet to hers. Feeling the wild passion of her response, he drew her tightly into his arms while the world rocked.

Only after timeless seconds did he slowly raise his head. Her eyes were closed, but in the instant before she buried her face against his shoulder, he glimpsed her expression. It was one of total joy.

He held her close for a long, long minute, trying to absorb for a lifetime the feel of her, the clean, soap-scented smell of her, the warmth and joy and dearness of her. Then, gently, he stood her back, looking deep into her eyes once again. She saw his gravity and her own eyes questioned.

"Hannah, we can't," he said huskily. "We can't," he repeated fiercely and released her, turning quickly to the door.

"Will, why?" All but inaudible, it seared his heart. "You truly don't want to?"

His heart ripping to shreds, he looked back at her standing so bewildered. "Not because I don't want to. Never that. Rather that I do want you, so much. But I could only hurt you, and I can't risk that. Do you understand?"

She shook her head slowly, her eyes glistening with unshed tears.

"You're one hell of a woman, Hannah Clayton," he said fiercely. "Luke is the biggest fool God ever saw fit to let walk this earth." He turned, rushing blindly out the door.

In wordless agony she watched him go. Turning numbly, she picked up the thread box he had fashioned so carefully and pressed it tight to her breast. She moaned, a cry from the depths of her soul. She stood clutching the box, all the tears she had refused to let fall before spilling unheeded down her cheeks.

Thirteen

January 1888. The first month of the new year proved dismal, cold and raw, even as Will himself felt dismal, cold and raw. He did his best to carry on as though the very ground beneath his feet hadn't been blasted to pieces.

Whether it was pride or stubbornness that kept him going, he did not know, did not bother to ask. He merely accepted the sustaining power in blind relief. He tended the cattle, did the home chores, played with the boys as he had done all those days before — only now his motions were mechanical, and many times he carried out a necessary task with no memory later of having done it at all.

Hannah, too, went her round of work — caring for the house and the boys, cooking, baking and sewing. She was cheerful enough to the casual eye, but seldom did she laugh that month, and not once did she sing. Her attitude toward Will was the same as it had been since those first awkward days. She treated him with friendly courtesy as though Christmas Night — and his rejection of her — had never been.

What she was feeling on the inside, he could only guess, but he thought he understood her outward behavior. To acknowledge by word or gesture what had passed between them that night — and what had not — would have shattered the last remnants of dignity. He was just as glad she chose to ignore, for it meant he, too, could do so. Ignore, but not forget, ever, the selflessness, the joy of her offer.

Only the boys, too young to grasp the unease of their elders, racketed through the month with all their customary enthusiasm. There were snowstorms, but none was of great duration, only enough to provide a convenient fresh blanket for the boys' games with the sled. They spent hours outdoors any day it was possible, thus keeping from under Hannah's feet for long stretches, and coming in so tired from all the fresh air and exercise they were only too glad to go to bed early with no more than token protest.

Evenings passed much as they had before, with Hannah sewing or reading and Will smoking his pipe while he worked with rope, leather or an odd bit of wood before departing for bunkhouse or herd. Sometimes he wondered that they could be so casual, so ordinary. He was grateful. Without this semblance of normality, their situation would have been unendurable.

He no longer allowed himself even a passing thought of Eve without stomping down on it hard. She was over, done with, out of his life forever, he told himself. As he should have months ago, he realized. Each day he set himself anew the task of uprooting her from his heart, of scattering his memories to the four winds, flinging them like ashes, far and hard so they might never take seed again.

One evening when they were sitting, Will at the table repairing a gap in his boot and Hannah in her rocker, head bent over a book, he asked what she was reading.

She held it up. "It's by Miss Bronte. *Wuthering Heights*. Becky loaned it to me at Christmas. I haven't gotten very far," she confessed.

"Don't know why not. Nothin' to do all day except cook and clean and take care of four active boys. Why, you should have all the time in the world."

Her eyes sparked in a rare lighting, but she said gravely enough, "You're right. I'm just lazy, I guess."

"Why don't you read some to me? The way you've been lost in it, it must be pretty good."

Startled, but pleased, she said impishly, "Why, Will, I didn't know you had a fondness for books."

For an instant he was back in his mother's room at the boarding house and her voice, coming to him over the years, was like a remembered fragrance. "Never give up reading, Will," she was saying to the fidgety boy seated by her knee. "Even if it's only a few pages at a time, what you read can never be taken from you. It'll be yours to keep forever." The image faded and he was once more in the warm, lighted kitchen of more than half a lifetime later.

He pulled the leather strip though a fresh-punched hole. "Don't get much opportunity to read," he said briefly, "but that don't mean I don't like it."

Her eyes lingered on him for a second before dropping to the book. "Might as well start at the beginning. It won't make much sense otherwise." In her low voice she began: " 'I have just returned from a visit to my landlord — the solitary neighbour that I shall be troubled with ...' "

Will listened intently until she reached the end of the

chapter. When she laid the book aside, he protested. "You ain't goin' to quit now, are you?"

Again that lighting of her eyes, although she said solemnly enough, "If I keep reading, Isaac'll outgrow this new shirt before I ever get it finished."

"Why don't I read while you sew? Unless you want me to sew his shirt and you read."

She eyed the newly patched boot and handed him the book.

Nearly every evening thereafter, one or the other read. They became so engrossed in the problems of Cathy and Heathcliff, they tended to forget, for this space of time, their own. When they finally came to the end, both felt a little lost. Until he said, off-hand, "Got somethin' to do outside. I'll be right back." He put on his hat and coat and was gone with the words.

He pushed through the slushy yard and entered the dismal chill of the bunkhouse. Pausing only long enough to light the Angle lamp, he knelt beside his bunk and pulled out his warbag. Casting aside boots, socks and his Sunday tie, he finally unearthed the bulky bundle in the bottom. Pulling it out, he unwrapped the oilskin covering, assuring himself the contents had not been damaged by mice or weather. Replacing the wrapping, ignoring the mess he had made, he blew out the lamp and returned to the house.

Hannah, assuming she knew the nature of his errand, started to politely disregard his return, but her casualness became questioning as, without stopping to take off his coat or hat, he crossed to her and pushed the package into her lap. "Go on, open it." He turned to pull off his coat.

"Books, Will!" she cried in delight. "Shakespeare!

Wherever did you get them?"

"They were my Ma's. She read 'em all, I don't know how many times. She could quote passages a mile long out of all of 'em. Said anybody knew Shakespeare and the Bible could hold his own with the best of 'em." Then, as though he owed further explanation, he added, "They're just sittin' out there gettin' weathered. Might as well put 'em to some use."

She touched them as one handles a treasure, smoothing the covers, running her fingertips over the gold lettering. The glow in her eyes when she raised her head pleased him absurdly.

"Well, why don't you start one?" he suggested gruffly to hide his emotion. "They won't read themselves."

She turned the pages, coming to *Julius Caesar*.

January had come in cold and snowy and dreary. February blew in cold and wet and dreary. Will, spending long hours with the herd in storms that were half rain, half snow, time after time came in drenched to the skin. Hannah marveled that he never caught a chill, but he turned her concern aside casually. "I'm too ornery," he'd tell her.

Toward the middle of the month the weather moderated so much it was as if spring had come early. Days of sunshine tempted Hannah to an early spring housecleaning even though it was increasingly difficult for her to move easily. Her time was very near now, and Will warned her sternly each time before he left for his own duties that she was not to overdo. She promised dutifully, but if he came in unexpectedly he was likely to find her scrubbing the floor or as once, washing the walls.

"Hannah!"

She had been so intent on her work she hadn't heard his approach. She started and whirled, almost dumping her pan of dirty suds on his head. "Will, you scared me half to death!" Her exasperation matched his. "I didn't hear you come in. Next time give me some warning, for heaven's sake!"

Ignoring her scolding, he took the offending pan of water and helped her down from the chair. "You promised!" he reminded her indignantly.

"Will Braden!" She shook her head impatiently. "I feel fine. The work won't wait for me to sit around getting fat as a cow and lazy, as well. Besides, it's not as if I'm not experienced in my 'present occupation.' I've been through it four times before and ought to have enough sense to know how careful I should be."

Temporarily outgunned, he subsided, but took to riding in as frequently as he could to check on her, always with some excuse so that she saw through him, and for the first time in weeks, really laughed.

Late one such sunlit afternoon he rode in earlier than usual, although he wasn't prepared to admit to Hannah it was to make sure she was all right. Even if she had been through this "present occupation" four times before and felt herself a top hand at it, he had never been ramrod to such a situation. It made him nervous each time he rode off and left her. What if she commenced having it when he was gone and couldn't go for help? On the other hand, what if the little critter decided to come when he was there? He couldn't rightly figure which way was more nerve-wracking to think about.

So he continued to make frequent checks on her, and she continued to tease him about being a mother hen with one chick. But it brought amusement to her green eyes so long sober, and he reckoned it was worth it, even if he couldn't personally see the humor.

Pulling into the yard this early evening, he caught sight of a horse and buggy tied near the back door. Uneasiness nudged him. He didn't recognize the rig right away, but since the weather had cleared and the roads dried a little, various of Hannah's friends had come calling. Most had come simply to visit, knowing how difficult it was for her to get out. A few came bright-eyed with curiosity. As Hannah had pointed out to Will, there was nothing like a juicy bit of gossip to prove who one's friends were. She had tried to make light of it, but finding out the truth about some of her "friends" cut deeply.

As Will dismounted, he heard voices, but the words didn't register until he pushed open the door.

"... you really ought to get your laundry in off the line before it picks up damp, Hannah. After all, you don't want to be putting cold, wet diapers on all those poor little bottoms if you can help ..." The voice broke off and three pairs of eyes regarded Will in sudden total silence.

Hannah, heavy now, but as ever graceful, rose from her rocker to stand beside him. "Will, you know Pearl Gilby and Miss Mabel."

Yes, Will knew them — the cause of Reverend Wardley's disastrous visit last fall. Hadn't they done enough harm that they had to come back for more? It was tongues such as theirs that kept scandal burning even when there was nothing to fuel it. *As there was nothing now*, he reminded himself roughly. If he watched his words carefully enough, maybe — just maybe — it would be all right. If there was anything they didn't need it was another scathing visit from the good Reverend.

With effort, Will greeted them politely, if coolly, before turning back to Hannah. "You all right?"

"I'm fine. I'm glad you're home," she said simply, which admission told him for certain she was upset. She realized, too.

She went on hastily, "They stopped by for a visit and were reminding me to bring in Micah's diapers from the line. I just haven't had a chance to do it, yet." She touched her hands to her aching back, realized what she was doing, and quickly straightened.

Pearl, ignoring the weariness in Hannah's voice, smoothed her gloves and settled in deeper for a cozy chat. "You really shouldn't leave them out there much longer, dear," she said reprovingly. "The night damp will get to them before you know it, and then you'll have to wash them all over again. By the way, there's something sticky on your floor, dear. Right over there. I noticed it as I was walking in. My foot almost came out of my shoe when I stepped there. I can't imagine what it might be." Her tone indicated that she imagined only too clearly what it probably was. "You really should clean it up before someone falls."

Hannah had a swift mental picture of herself kneeling on all fours, her stomach brushing the floor as she scrubbed up the sticky spot while Pearl and Mabel in their best black dresses and best black hats daintily sipped their tea and gave advice on how to do the job properly. Tactfully ignoring their neighborly suggestion, Hannah held up an ill-sewed, small garment for Will's inspection. "They brought me some baby clothes."

Will murmured, he hoped, an appropriate response, totally out of his depth in these feminine waters.

"Yes," Pearl said graciously, "we knew you'd be needing some new outfits. Your other baby clothing must certainly be worn out after four times around. Knowing what an expense it can be when one already has several other children, Mabel and I got some of the other ladies in town together, and we bought material and made you these." She gestured to the rather pathetic little pile. "The other ladies helped, of course, but Mabel and I did most of the work," she admitted modestly. "Since we haven't seen you at church these last several weeks, Hannah, we thought we'd just drop in and see how you're doing and give you these, poor dear."

Whether it was the pitying tone, the implied charity or the "poor dear," Will wouldn't have laid bets, but Hannah's chin rose perceptibly. He said hastily, "Hannah is doin' just fine, as you c'n see. We haven't been to church f'r a while because the roads have been so bad. We didn't think the joltin' would be a good idea right now, but we're sure the good Lord understands." He smiled genially.

"My goodness, Hannah, Will certainly does look out for you. The way he protects you, a body would almost think he was your husband and the baby's father instead of Luke." Pearl laughed archly.

Hannah, having managed to remain mute up to this point, finally broke in. "Mrs. Gilby," she said, still pleasantly — and only Will saw her fists clench — "marriage vows don't make a man a husband, and the act of conceiving a child doesn't make a man a father. That part's easy, or so I've been told. The second part — to be a husband or a father — is a whole lot harder. Only time, love and caring can make that happen."

Both women drew horrified breaths at this bluntness. Pearl was the first to recover. "Come, Mabel, we must be going," she said stiffly. Gathering gloves and reticule, she detoured widely around Will as though he had the hydrophobia and might bite her. Mabel followed in her mother's wake, eyeing him as if he were an unknown specimen of snake, surely poisonous.

"Thank you for the baby clothes," Hannah called as they stomped out.

Pearl paused by her buggy, foot up on the step. "You poor dear," she said clearly and hoisted herself into the rig. "Come, Mabel," she added tartly.

Mabel's glance at Will and Hannah, standing at the top of the steps, was filled with burning curiosity and malicious amusement. She had no time for more — she had to scramble into the buggy as Pearl started it with a jolt. And they were off under full wind.

"To gossip," Hannah said bleakly. "Oh, Will!" She turned blindly, and he reached out and drew her into his arms. She buried her head against his shoulder as he gently smoothed her hair.

"Now, honey," he said stoutly, "you were magnificent! You ain't goin' to let 'em skunk you after the way you spoke up. You can't."

She buried her face deeper into his shoulder. "I kind of lost my temper," she confessed. "Reverend Wardley'll probably burn up his buggy wheels getting here."

"Prob'ly," Will agreed, "but I don't see much point in worryin' 'bout it till he gets here."

She raised her head and drew a deep breath. "You're right. We can't let them get the better of us now, can we?"

"You better believe not! After all, I'm your 'protector,' remember?" he said in his best save-her-from-all-evil voice.

She laughed, shakily. "That's right. Mrs. Gilby's own words." But she shivered as she looked off where the buggy had disappeared, and her fingers moved instinctively to her stomach as if to protect the child from all the cruelty and ignorance an uncaring world was already heaping on it.

That evening as Jeremy helped Will milk, he asked hesitantly, "Mr. Braden, is Ma goin' to die?"

Startled, Will glanced at the worried little face and back to the milk bucket. "No, son," he said as calmly as he could. "Why do you ask?"

The child searched Will's face. "Ma's gettin' awful fat, and when Eddie King's Ma got fat like that, she died. I don't want my Ma to die!" His voice rose in terror.

Will pushed quickly away from Daisy. "Jeremy, come here." He reached out his arms and the child stumbled into them. Will held him close while shuddering sobs racked the small body. Then he backed him up, perching the boy on his knee so they could look directly at each other.

"Jeremy, listen to me. Your Ma is not goin' to die. She's goin' to have a baby and very soon now. Did you know that?" A cautious shake of the tousled head.

"Well, she is. That means you'll have another brother or maybe even a little sister before much longer."

Jeremy thought about that. "But how come she ain't goin' to die like Eddie's Ma?"

Will took a steadying breath. "Jeremy, son, women don't die just because they have babies. Once in a long, long time, like Eddie's Ma, yes, they do. But not all the time or very often. If they all did, no one would have a Ma. But you've got one, and so do the rest of your friends."

"Do you have a Ma, Mr. Braden?"

Will spoke calmly, steadily. "No, my Ma died a few years ago. But not f'r years and years after I was born."

"You mean she got old and died like Jackie Slade's dog?"

Was 43 old? Yes, from the viewpoint of 6 years, he supposed it was ancient as Noah.

"Yes, Jeremy, she got old and died."

"Do you miss her a lot?"

His throat tightened. "Yes, son, I miss her a lot."

"I'd sure miss Ma if she died," he said simply.

"Yes," Will agreed, "you would. But she's not goin' to so you don't have to worry anymore. We'll take good care of her, you and me, and she'll be just fine. But if we don't get this milkin' done and into the house f'r her to strain, she's liable to skin both of us alive!"

Jeremy squealed in playful terror. Will set him down and resumed milking. The little boy chatted a mile a minute all the way to the house, his fears apparently set at rest. But at

the first opportunity that evening, Will drew Hannah aside.
"I think it's time you had a talk with Jeremy."

Startled, she glanced over to her oldest son, playing happily on the floor with the other boys. "Will, what's wrong?"

"Nothin' to fret 'bout. It's just that your son's growin' up. He got a few facts twisted 'bout your ..." he hesitated "... present occupation." She blushed but he plowed on. "He asked me and I think he's straightened out now, but it seems like it'd be a good idea f'r you to talk to him, too." He explained about Eddie King's mother.

"Poor Jeremy. He must have been so worried. He never said a word to me, but I noticed he's been looking at me kind of funny. I just didn't stop to think." She bit her lip. "Thank you, Will, for talking to him."

He waved her gratitude aside. "No problem. I figure if a young'n is old enough to ask the question, he's old enough to get a straight answer." He grinned. "Comes down to it, I had the easy part. You're the one's goin' to have to explain the rest of it to him. I don't envy you."

She blushed again but managed a small laugh. "Thanks so much. I don't envy me, either!"

Her talk with Jeremy was obviously successful, for the child showed no more fears for her safety. Instead, he chatted freely about the coming brother or sister. "It better be a brother. We don't need no girl sisters 'round here!" He showed a marked interest in the activities of the rooster and hens wandering around the yard and even treated Will to a lecture on the subject the next evening when they were milling.

Will listened seriously, and when Jeremy had finished,

said gravely, "That's right, son. You've got straight facts, now. That means your Ma knows you're growin' up and that's pretty special. Your Ma's pretty special, too. You know that?"

Jeremy nodded. "She's the best Ma in the whole world," he burst out, "and I bet she's smarter than anybody else in the whole world, too. Except maybe you," he added generously.

Will, reporting this conversation to Hannah, had to smother a smile.

"He's really taken hold of his lesson with enthusiasm, hasn't he?" she asked wryly. "I know most other parents don't hold with telling the blunt truth like that, but I just couldn't lie to him. I want him to be able to trust me — he needs to know that he can, no matter what. I just hope he calms down about it pretty soon."

"I'm sure he will. It's just that it's all new to him. But let's hope he settles down before he decides to pass on his new-found information to someone like Pearl Gilby."

"Good Lord," she breathed. It was the first time he had ever heard her use such an expression.

Fourteen

Reverend Wardley didn't, after all, burn up his buggy wheels coming to see Hannah and Will. Sure as they were that Pearl Gilby had hastened to report the newest of the "scandal," they fully expected him to show up in all his indignation. They didn't know why he failed to appear, but they were grateful.

After relenting with those few blessed days of sunshine, Nature took hold once more in a last frenzy of winter and sent — not snow — but rain. Day after day it either drizzled or poured, but for the rest of that month all the sunshine they saw could have been cupped in the palm of one hand.

It made all their tempers short — the constant wetness, the chill that seemed to seep into their very bones. Hannah, weary enough now in her last days, coping with the headache of never being able to get anything completely dried out, stepping around, over, and on the boys reluctantly confined to the house, thought those days of sunshine must have been a dream.

On the evening of February 25, Will sat at the table watching as she moved slowly, setting her bread dough. She seemed so tired and listless. He worried she had overdone that day, but as always she insisted she was fine. "I'll just be glad when it's over," she admitted. "Only a few more days to go!"

He, too, would be glad when it was over. The strain was making him old before his time, he was sure. He had had an idea for quite a while, but had hesitated to broach it. With sudden decision he cleared his throat.

"Hannah." She turned questioningly. "I've been thinkin' it'd be a good idea if I bunked here on the floor these next few nights." She started to speak, but he went on hurriedly. "What are you goin' to do if you need help in the middle of the night? If I was here in the kitchen all you'd have to do is whoop — or cuss. It'd be a lot easier that way." He trailed to a stop as her hands stilled on the dough.

"If you don't mind, it would take a care off me," she said quietly. "I was wondering how I'd manage. I could send Jeremy after you, but ..."

"I don't mind a bit," he assured her.

"The floor's pretty hard."

He grinned. "I've slept between so many hard spots and rocks this floor'll feel like a feather!"

In the morning she laughed at his worry. "I told you it wasn't time yet," she teased. "A woman knows, believe me."

All that day — it was Sunday — she sang at her various tasks:

Wait till the darkness is over,
wait till the tempest is done;
hope for the sunshine tomorrow,
after the shower is gone.

"I just feel good," she told Will lightly. She did look much better, he saw with relief. Well, maybe all she had needed was a good night's sleep. How was he supposed to know about these things?

"You worry too much," she insisted. Yet even as she made light of his concern, she marveled that he should take on so about her. *Not even with Jeremy had Luke* ... She stopped herself sharply. But the wonder of it remained.

Rain fell in a cold drizzle most of the day, and with dark came the first thunder mutterings.

"I wish you didn't have to go out in this lightning," she said anxiously as he shrugged into his coat.

" 'You worry too much,' " he mimicked wickedly.

She wrinkled her nose at him. "Just what I need, a dose of my own medicine!"

He grinned, but only for a moment. "I'm not wild 'bout goin' either, but I don't have no choice. Weather change like this, there's a good chance they'll cut out. I'll be back soon as I c'n, I promise." He touched her cheek and was gone into the night.

Outside, he turned to look back for a long moment at the closed door and the lampglow warm in the window, before he pulled his hatbrim down and plunged into the increasing murk.

Arriving out at the herd, he found the animals were, indeed, jittery with instinct of the coming storm. The far-off thunder rumblings, the wind gusting past their ears, the increasing heaviness of the drizzle descending upon them —

any one of these annoyances alone could spark a stampede. Combined, it was practically a notarized guarantee. Jason, Matt, Aaron and Dan had all gathered, and they briefly discussed the positions they would take. During the following long, dreary, wet hours, they rimmed the bunch time and again, singing softly to keep them from spooking.

Over and over, Will, riding drag, hunched in his slicker, trying vainly to keep the wind from blowing those icy trickles down the back of his neck, gave forth unmusically but determinedly:

> *The years creep slowly by, Lorena;*
> *   the snow is on the grass again.*
> *The sun's low down the sky, Lorena;*
> *   the frost gleams where the flowers have been ...*

Off to the east, carried by the wind, Will could hear snatches of strains nearly as unmelodious as his own:

> *As the blackbird in the spring, beneath the willow tree,*
> *Sat and pip'd I heard him sing, singing "Aura Lee."*

That was Aaron, partnering him, plodding through his particular tune. Ahead, they knew, Matt and Dan at swing and Jason at point were offering the herd choice samples of musical effort. The bawdy words didn't carry clearly to the rear, but the general idea did.

Will wondered, fleetingly, that the critters didn't cut and run just from the ear-jarring rendering of the cowhands' verses. They didn't, though. Contrarily enough, the tunes seemed to ease their anxieties and keep them from stampeding. He'd always known cow-critters hadn't much sense. He grinned. If this didn't prove it, he for sure didn't know of anything that would.

There was, however, another very good reason for each man to sing, however unskillfully. The songs soothed the cattle, true, but the men's voices, carrying across rain and dark in a favored melody, identified not only the singer but his position in relation to the cattle. In the blind panic of a total stampede, a man could be cut to ribbons easy as not, and his singing served to let the other hands know he was riding, unhurt, with the herd.

So they circled and sang, and circled again. Thunder growled distant faint. They circled and sang. Lightning flickered fitfully and the herd shifted uneasily, heads tossing, nostrils snuffling out the far-off storm.

They circled. And sang and circled again until a blinding streak of lightning splashed the world crimson.

Until an explosion of thunder cracked the world to shreds.

And the herd was gone.

There one second, the next headed hell-bent for Texas, with the men and horses trying furiously to keep pace, to get ahead, to turn them.

As his night horse, Sunshine, pounded across the plains in the rain, darkness and howling wind — cutting, dodging, turning before his rider could signal the need, Will hunkered in the saddle, urging him on, wondering with a strange flash of memory, whether it had been this way with his own father.

A hundred months have passed, Lorena,

since last I held that hand in mine ...

Had Caleb Braden on that last, wild ride felt this fierceness, this exultation of pitting his strength against the force of Nature — knowing that it was — one way or another — a battle to the end?

And what we might have been, Lorena,
had but our loving prospered well!

Had Caleb Braden, plunging over that cliff on another night of wild storm with lightning blinding his eyes and thunder deafening his ears and wind and rain in a dance gone mad — had he gone singing to his death?

The hopes that could not last, Lorena,
they lived, but only lived to cheat.

Had he, in those final, desperate moments, glimpsing that cliff gaping ahead of him, knowing what was coming, thought of his wife and son and what he had left behind for them?

"For if we try we may forget,"
were words of thine long years ago.

Had he, in that last, long, plunging moment that became forever, known regret?

A duty stern and piercing broke
the tie which linked my soul with thee.

Day Star Rising

HAD HE??

The question lashed Will's soul even as the rain lashed his body and Sunshine's hooves pounded and the herd, flashing by, roaring along, was only a blur. He wondered if this would, indeed, be the end and felt piercing regret that it might be so when there was so much of life yet to be lived.

HANNAH! Hannah ...

But never after was he to know whether that wild yell flung from his mouth to be borne away by the uncaring wind or whether it was only the anguished, protesting cry of his heart.

For finally, finally, the herd began to turn, to slow. To stop, heads hanging, chests heaving and tongues lolling. They had turned, and there had been no cliff, no horse and rider plunging, screaming, to be trampled into eternity. No grief-stricken woman. No yearling-sized boy left forced to grow up too soon.

It matters little now, Lorena,
the past is in the eternal past.

Jason and Dan had turned them. Dan, risking everything when he had no stake in this herd, beyond his friendship with Matt ...

There is a future, oh, thank God!
Of life this is so small a part;
'tis dust to dust beneath the sod,
but up there, up there, 'tis heart to heart.

Not until long after midnight, the storm died away to the

south and the cattle finally settled down. When Will at last rode into the house yard, he was dog-tired, drenched to the skin, and wanting nothing so much as a cup of scalding coffee and a change of dry clothes. He tended his mount, rubbed him down and turned him into the corral — all in a blur of exhaustion — before he turned to the bunkhouse to see to his own wet self.

The lamp Hannah always set out when he worked late glowed its warm welcome at the window as, afterward, he trudged up the back steps. Weary and sodden, he closed the door behind him and paused. The kitchen was neat and still. He crossed to the stove, reaching eagerly for the coffeepot waiting on top. Empty. Only a few muddy swallows sulked in the bottom.

Half-asleep on his feet, he started to fill the pot with still-warm water from the reservoir. *It wasn't like Hannah not to have plenty of hot ...* He halted in mid-reach as, finally, realization slammed him with a hard fist. Thumping the pot down, he hurried across the too-quiet kitchen to Hannah's door. Hand on knob, he hesitated as he heard a low moan. Waiting no longer, he pushed open the panel — to Hannah's quick, harsh breathing. Her lamp had burned out, but the glow from the kitchen gave enough light for him to grope his way to the bed. She was lying rigid, eyes tightly shut.

"Hannah?"

She lurched and her eyes flew open. "Will! I didn't hear you come home. I'm so glad you're back." A whisper, it carried volumes of relief.

He swallowed hard. "Hannah, are you ..."

"Yes, I'm afraid I am."

In the first shock of the moment, he froze. "You're sure?" he asked needlessly, hoping she'd change her mind. But as a contraction gripped her, he knew there was no doubt. "I'll get the lamp," he told her hastily when it had eased. "Be right back."

Dashing to the kitchen he grabbed the lamp off the windowsill, and rushed back to the bedroom, only to find her in the grip of another spasm. He set the lamp on the dresser, and feeling helpless as a calf under a branding iron, turned back to her. "Would it help to hold on to me?" he asked, floundering.

For answer she seized his hands and hung on as though to a lifeline. As the contraction eased, she caught her breath, trying to smile up at him. He reached a shaking hand to smooth the damp hair back from her forehead.

"You all right?" He tried to ask calmly, telling himself it was no time for panic, but almost immediately she stiffened again. This time it lasted longer and her grip on his hands was more crushing.

When it was over she tried to laugh, but it was a weak effort. "They're coming closer. And harder," she admitted.

"I'll go f'r help," he blurted. "I'll be back soon as I c'n." Thought of physical action brought him overwhelming relief.

But already she was lost in another pain. When she could speak, she said firmly, "Will, there isn't time. Don't leave me. Please!"

"But Hannah ..." His panic-stricken protest was cut off by yet another spasm. He did the only thing he could at the moment — took hold of her hands while she clutched his hard.

When she relaxed, he spoke again in a rush to get the

words in before she should be seized by another contraction. "Hannah, I got to go f'r help! You have to hang on until I c'n get someone." She was shaking her head, but he rushed on, frantically. "I don't know anythin' 'bout babies droppin'! Calves and colts, sure, but not ..." But again she was past listening to his plea.

"Will, you've got to," she begged when she could get her breath. "There isn't anyone else! I've got everything all ready." She indicated the chair beside the bed. He saw now, neatly arranged on it, all the necessities for ushering her child into the world. *All the necessities except one — someone who knows what he is doing.*

"But ..."

"Will, I ... think he's ... coming!"

Hope fled, wailing. Despair entered, tripping over its own big feet. And the god of fate sat hunched, laughing fit to kill.

"Will!"

Gritting his teeth, he flung back the covers. One hasty glance informed him she was, indeed, right in her thinking. "God help us," he breathed. For sure as grass was green, Fate knew as much what to do about it as Will.

Suddenly there was no time either for panic or for uncertainty. Murmuring words of comfort and encouragement, such as he had a thousand times to heifers and mares — But this was Hannah! "You're doin' fine. It's almost over, honey." Praying to God he wouldn't do something stupid to hurt her more than she was already hurting.

With a choked half-cry, half-laugh, she suddenly went limp.

And abruptly, his hands were full of a slippery, unbelievably tiny bit of humanity.

"You did it, Hannah!" It, too, was half-laugh, half-cry. "You did it, sweetheart," he said softly, staring awed at the squirming mite in his hands.

She was trying to rise up, straining to see. "Is he all right, Will? Make him cry. You have to hold him up and spank him!"

It seemed cruel to Will, considering what the little critter had just been through, but Hannah had been right about everything so far. Gingerly, afraid of dropping the wet little thing, he held it head down. But before he could deliver a reluctant slap, an indignant squall echoed through the room.

And now Hannah was laughing again, as much at Will's dumfounded expression as at the baby's angry scream.

"Is he all right, Will? Let me see him, please!"

"Just hold on a minute, little Mama." He tied the cord, cut it — at least he knew to do that much — saying as he did so, "Seems to have the necessary number of arms and legs — and lung power! Can't stop now to count the fingers and toes. You'll have to do that." Grabbing a piece of toweling, he wrapped the baby in it, moved to Hannah's side and carefully handed the bundle into her outstretched arms.

"Will," she breathed. "Isn't he beautiful?" She cradled the mite close to her side.

"Beautiful," he confirmed, kneeling to her level. But his eyes were on the mother rather than the baby.

"He's so tiny. All the other boys were so husky. You don't think there's anything wrong, do you?" Her voice caught in panic.

" 'Course not," he said soothingly. "It's just you've got a little filly, there. Sorry to disappoint you."

"He's a girl?" Hannah could only stare at Will.

He grinned. "Now that's one thing I am sure of!"

Her eyes dropped to the now-quiet baby already nuzzling blindly for her breast, and such a look of wonder filled her face that his own vision blurred. He reached out a big finger to touch one dainty fist curled under the tiny chin. Stumbling to his feet he said gruffly, "I better get some water to give this little lady a bath. I'll be right back."

But he paused, gazing down at Hannah for a long moment. Suddenly bending, he brushed a kiss against her hair before he hurried out. Her eyes filled as she watched him go, and protectively, she drew the baby closer to her side, resting her cheek lightly against the tiny head.

When Will returned with a pan of warm water, they were both sleeping. As he stood gazing down at them, it hit him full-force. *God Almighty! I delivered Hannah's baby!* The sudden awe-filled realization made him so weak-kneed he had to sit down before he fell. He slumped, dazed, for several moments until further realization edged in around his shock. The baby still needed cleaning up, and there was no one except him to do it.

Steeled by bare necessity, he reached for her. At his touch, Hannah's eyes opened and she blinked at him, puzzled, before she remembered. "I'm just goin' to spruce her up a bit," he said to her unspoken question and she let him take the child.

Following her directions, clumsily, but still more easily than he would have dared hope for hands big as his, he bathed the baby, wrapped her in a soft blanket, and returned her to Hannah's waiting arms. Then he hesitated, but only for a moment. "Hannah," he said gently, matter-of-factly, "it'll be a while before Becky c'n get here. You must be pretty uncomfortable. I helped my Ma out, when she was so sick. If you want, I c'n fix you up, too."

She looked up at him as he waited for her to make the decision. There was no laughter now, but there was no embarrassment either. Only quiet concern for her welfare. "Why, I don't mind your helping me if you don't mind," she said as quietly.

He smiled, then. "Glad to be of service, ma'am."

When he had bathed her and settled her into the clean bed, she sighed. "It feels much better," she admitted with a smile, holding out her hand to him. He clasped it warmly in both of his. "Thank you. With all my heart."

A big lump came to his throat, but he smiled. Such a tender, gentle smile that her eyes filled again. "Aw, shucks. Weren't nothin' to it. You did all the work. But I think," he said wryly, "I'd better stick with calves and colts. They're more my line!"

He touched a curl bright as a copper penny. "Have you thought of a name f'r her?"

"I guess 'Adam' wouldn't fit too well."

He shook his head. "She don't look much like an 'Adam'," he admitted.

"What was your Ma's name, Will?"

"Phebe. Why?" Then it dawned on him.

"Phebe. Phebe Anne," she said softly. "It has a nice sound, doesn't it?"

To his horror, the lump returned to his throat, so big he couldn't swallow. "It's a fine name," he managed huskily.

225

"Ma would be mighty proud." He stumbled to his feet. "I guess I better go get Becky and the doc if you'll be all right f'r a while."

In the doorway he turned. "Named f'r two of the three finest — and bravest — women I've known." He rushed out the door.

Becky was horrified when she found Hannah had had her baby before the doctor could get there. "The poor thing! She's been through so much, and now this!" She was lamenting even as she hurried to get ready to go back with Will.

"Now hold on, Becky. She's just fine. No need to go gettin' all upset."

"A lot you know about it, Will Braden! Honestly, if you men had to have the babies once in a while, you'd appreciate a little more what it's like!"

Will stood in the doorway, hands jammed into his coat pockets. "I didn't say it was easy f'r her," he said stiffly. "I just said it's over now and she's not all upset, so there's no need f'r you to be."

She only gave him a withering look and slapped on her bonnet. "I'm ready." Her voice would have chilled spring water.

Jason had volunteered to ride for the doctor, so after a hasty kiss to Becky, he pounded off toward town as she and Will turned their horses back toward the Crescent C.

She maintained a stubborn silence during the entire ride, and Will, after one glance at her grim expression, held silent, too. They swung down near the back steps. Becky grabbed the bundle she had brought and dashed into Hannah's bedroom. Will, following behind, paused in the doorway, leaning against the jamb as she bent over the bed. "Hannah, I'm here ..." She stopped dumfounded as Hannah beamed up at her.

"Hello, Becky. See your niece? Isn't she beautiful?"

Becky stared from the baby to Hannah.

"What's wrong?" Hannah asked anxiously, her smile fading.

Will, seeing that, decided enough was enough. He stepped into the room, but before he could say anything, Becky burst out, "The baby's cleaned up, and you're all neat, Hannah, looking as if you hadn't a care in the world. What's going on? You didn't ... you couldn't have ... by yourself ..." She sputtered to a stop.

"No, I didn't," Hannah admitted. "But Will did. Didn't he tell you he helped me? And just as gentle and caring as any woman could have."

Becky gaped up at Will. "You didn't tell me, Will Braden! You let me think ..."

"I tried to tell you," he pointed out, "but you didn't give me much of a chance."

"I — " Becky turned scarlet. "I didn't, I guess. I'm sorry. Truly. My tongue does get the best of me sometimes. Too often, Jason says."

Will relaxed. "F'rget it. Don't really matter long as Hannah and the baby are all right."

"They look just fine to me. Now you scat on out of here." She tried to shoo him toward the door, but he bent over Hannah first.

"You take care of this little lady, now." He smiled into her eyes, touched the baby's cheek lightly, and retreated.

Becky, open-mouthed, watched him go. "Who would have believed it!"

"I would," Hannah said quietly.

Will paced restlessly outside the bedroom door until he heard the boys stirring. In relief at having something to do, he went in to supervise their dressing, then back out to the kitchen to see about finding some breakfast. Morning chores were waiting, but he felt a curious reluctance to be away from the house even for as short a time and for as short a distance as it was to the barn.

The boys piled out of the bedroom eager for breakfast, but stopped short when they saw Will at the stove instead of their mother.

"Where's Ma?" Jeremy asked for all of them.

Will decided it would be all right to tell the news instead of waiting for them to hear it from Hannah. He gathered the boys around him, hunkering down to their level. Only Isaac pulled away and Will let him be. "Your Ma's in bed."

"Is she sick?" from Sam.

Will smiled into the anxious little face. "No, not sick. You've got a little sister."

Jeremy's eyes widened. "Ma had her baby!" he shouted.

Will hushed him hastily. "Not so loud. Your Ma and your new sister need to rest. They're really tired."

Jeremy immediately lowered his voice importantly. "C'n we go see her?"

"Pretty soon. Your Aunt Becky's in with her right now."

As Will stood, he felt a tug at his hand. He looked down into Sam's worried face. "When do we have to send her back?"

Bewildered, Will shook his head at the little boy. "What are you talkin' 'bout, Sam? Send who back?"

"The baby," Sam gulped, close to tears.

Once more Will hunkered to the child's level. "Where did you get that idea?"

"From Jeremy. He said if it was a girl sister, we'd have to send it back. I don't want you to send her back. I want to keep her here!"

Torn between laughter and a sudden lump in his throat, Will reached out and tousled Sam's already rumpled hair. Before he could say anything, however, Jeremy spoke up. "Oh, Sam," he said learnedly, "we ain't goin' to send her back. It don't work that way." Then he looked anxiously up at Will. "I didn't mean it, Mr. Braden. Honest. I was just teasin'. We c'n keep her, even if she is a girl!"

Will put an arm around each of them. "I'm glad you feel that way, Jeremy. And that you want to keep her here, Sam, because you'll both be able to teach her 'bout things you already know how to do. That's a very important and special job that only big brothers get to do."

"We'll teach her," Sam burst out. "She c'n even play with our sled!" he said generously, then looked anxiously at Jeremy. "Can't she?" he amended cautiously.

Jeremy thought about it for a moment. "Sure. We'll teach her how to jump off and make a snow angel when she lands."

Will hastily pushed aside the vivid mental picture of Hannah's reaction to these enthusiastic plans. "I c'n see you're goin' to be the best big brothers there ever was. She's a mighty lucky little sister. Ain't that right, Micah?"

The child had been standing, open-mouthed, not under-standing any of this discussion, but as Will spoke his name, he grinned and toddled forward for his share of the hugs being exchanged. Only Isaac held aloof. When Will tried to put his arm around his small shoulders, the child jerked away.

The boys were almost through breakfast when Jason and the doctor arrived. Doc Fergus went immediately into the bedroom and shut the door, leaving Will and Jason to wait once more. Jason ate, but Will had a strange lack of appetite. When the boys had finished and been sent outside to play, for lack of anything better to do with his hands, Will began to wash the dishes. Jason eyed him curiously and cleared his throat. "Don't know how you did it, Will," he said admiringly. "I'd of been scared out of my socks, f'r sure!"

"Oh, I wasn't scared," he said off-hand.

Jason stared in stunned disbelief.

"I was petrified," Will said simply.

Jason grinned sympathetically. Without a word he picked up a dishtowel and began to dry.

Strain as Will might to make out the activities going on behind the closed bedroom door, he could hear only a mur-mur of voices and occasional footsteps. More murmuring. More footsteps. The dishes finished, Will began once more to pace restlessly. Jason tried to distract him with casual conversation, but it was no use.

He knew, now. *Something had gone wrong. I did something wrong. Why else could Doc possibly be taking so ...*

The door opened and the doctor, followed by Becky, came out. His expression was unreadable, as usual. Becky wouldn't look at Will, but slipped over and buried her face against Jason's shirt front. He put his arms around her in wordless comfort — of what?

Will chilled to the pit of his stomach.

"That coffee smells good," Doc said. "I sure could use a cup. Jason, here, rousted me out before I got a chance to have any this morning."

Will poured him one, numbly. "How is she?" he finally burst out.

Doc eyed the contents of his cup. "She — Hannah — has some lacerations, but not bad. Considering everything, she came through it pretty well, and so did the child. But I wouldn't recommend doing it this way next time." His glare switched from the coffee to Will. "I paid good money, spent a lot of time in medical school. First baby I ever delivered I was scared spitless. And I had someone standing at my shoulder, telling me what to do. I hope you're not going to make a practice of this."

Will felt such an enormous thrust of relief that his knees went water-weak. "I already told Hannah from now on it's calves and colts only," he said limply. "But she ... they're really all right?"

Doc's grimace was, for him, an earsplitting grin. "Really. She'd like to see the boys."

Still dazed, Will called them in.

Jeremy took Micah's hand, and trailed by Isaac and Sam, tiptoed solemnly into the bedroom. Will glimpsed Hannah reaching to them and heard the sudden rush of feet across the floor.

He turned back. Becky, still shame-faced, reached out her

hand to him. "Will, I'm really sorry I was so ..." she began, but he waved her words aside.

"You were worried 'bout her. You didn't know." Jason and the doctor were regarding him curiously. He gave a general, silly grin. "Guess I'll get to the chores," he said to no one in particular. As he descended the steps they were still standing, watching him go.

Fifteen

The first nights after Phebe's birth, Will bunked on the kitchen floor, to be within call if Hannah or the boys needed help. Becky, Catty or Eve came early each morning to take charge of the house and children. Walking in and finding him scrubbing the boys or cooking breakfast, they laughed at him and asked if he didn't want to give up ranching immediately and hire out to them instead as a housemaid.

He was genuinely glad to see Becky and Cat come. They had always been friendly toward one another, and although they teased him now about his "domesticity," it was all in fun and he took it as such. Outwardly, their attitude toward him was the same as ever — friendly, accepting, comfortable. Inwardly, however, he sensed a surprised, newfound respect for him that secretly made him chuckle.

When Eve stopped by, however, he could not be so casual. Her own pregnancy was visible, which didn't make matters any easier, but he hadn't spent all those hours since Christmas Day uprooting her from his life to go back on his resolution now. So, polite but distant, he usually managed to escape quickly to the herd, staying away until it was time for her to go home. He realized she was no more comfortable in his presence than he was in hers. In some strange way, this knowledge eased his own discomfort. After all, it had been her choice.

Hannah protested he was spending too much time away from the herd, but he told her not to fret. The others were covering for him, and Jason had assured him there was no problem.

Becky confirmed this when Hannah confided her concern. "Jared and Reuben are filling in, but he's doing his fair share, Jason says. If he says so, you can believe it. So you're not to worry. Just enjoy your rest. It'll be soon enough you'll have to be up and at it again," she warned, "so take advantage!"

"You've all been so good to me. It's such a luxury not to have to worry about anything while I'm lying here. But I'm getting spoiled. I think Will'd even feed Phebe if he could!"

Becky became very busy folding the diapers she had washed that afternoon. "I've been wanting to tell you how bad I feel not being here to help that night. It must have been awful."

"Wasn't much fun," Hannah admitted, "but not so bad as all that."

"But when I think how embarrassing it must have been for you with just Will here ..."

"Actually, there wasn't time to be embarrassed. It all happened too fast." Hannah reached to touch the capable hand that had stilled on a diaper. "Please don't feel bad. It's over now, so promise me you won't think about it any more."

Becky took a deep breath. Obviously unwilling to risk upsetting Hannah further, she laughed. "If I don't quit folding this same diaper, I'll have it worn out before Phebe has a chance to!" Putting it aside she said lightly, "I'll go check on the children." In the doorway she paused. "He's really special, Hannah. But then so are you." She ducked out before Hannah could answer.

When Hannah was up and about again, life took on a new richness, a new contentment. Spring had come in those first days after Phebe's birth and everywhere the promise of life was being fulfilled.

On a bright noonday as Will rode into the yard, he glimpsed Hannah heading toward the corner of the house. He watched, puzzled, but when she reached to examine a branch of the lilac bush, he understood.

"It's in bud," she said joyfully as he joined her. "It's come through the winter."

"Did you doubt it would?"

"That's just it," she said softly, "even when everything seemed so hopelessly cold and dreary, the promise was there. Now it's being fulfilled."

He remembered what she'd said about the lilac and God being there in the dark times as well as the bright. "Do you think it's a good-luck sign? We could sure use ..."

The rattle of an approaching horse and buggy interrupted him. Turning, they caught sight of Reverend Wardley pulling his mare to a halt. "Oh, no," Hannah breathed. Will just groaned.

Then, together, they said it. "Chin up." They started to

laugh but quickly stifled it. No use adding to their already long list of "sins" by showing unseemly hilarity.

Wardley, catching sight of them, hesitated in the act of clambering down from his buggy. But only briefly. He stepped to the ground and straightened his coat. "Hannah. Will."

"Reverend Wardley," Hannah returned levelly. She paused perceptibly. "Won't you come in? I have coffee on."

"Thank you. It sounds good," he said stiffly in the face of her coolness.

The boys were at the table, eating their noon meal. They eyed the minister in solemn silence as he greeted them heartily.

Jeremy answered politely as he had been taught, but the others stared, tongue-tied.

"Isaac, I think your hair gets redder every time I see you," Wardley said jovially. "And Micah, here, isn't far behind."

Micah ducked his head bashfully, but Isaac's brows drew together in a scowl. Young as he was, he had already learned to resent teasing remarks about his red head.

Hannah saw it coming, wished for one tempting instant — and regretfully squashed the thought. Before Isaac could get it out, she put in hastily, "Finish eating, boys." She set a cup of coffee in front of the minister. "Would you like some vegetable soup, Reverend?"

Distracted from Isaac's glower, Wardley shook his head. "Thank you, no. Just the coffee." He glanced at the boys, once again eating busily and paying no attention to the adults. "I'd like to talk to both of you," he said finally.

Hannah and Will exchanged a swift glance. Wardley saw and smiled a little. "Not like the other time, I assure you."

Another glance between Will and Hannah before she sat at the table. Will remained standing behind her chair, his hands resting on the back. As during that other talk, they waited for Wardley to speak first.

He cleared his throat. "I've come to apologize. To both of you. I've done you a great wrong and I know it. I am sorry."

Hannah caught her breath, and Will's hands tightened on the back of the chair. Wardley plunged on. "I knew better, that day I was here. The accusations I made were most unfair. I have no excuse except to say I was caught between two choices. And I chose wrong. Pearl Gilby had come to me with the full story of talking to you in town. When she told me all the details, it was easier to believe her than it would have been to fight her. You know how she can be."

"We know," Will said grimly.

Wardley had the grace to redden. "You surely do. I was having problems of my own right then, and more to get rid of her than anything else, I agreed to talk to you. That was all I intended to do, but it got out of hand. When you made that remark, Will, about preaching a sermon on not judging others, you couldn't know I'd just received word from my superior that he felt my preaching was lacking in forcefulness. When you told me what you did, I took it as a personal insult. Which was ridiculous. But, well, that was it. I just plain lost my temper, and I made you both suffer for it. I am sorry."

Hannah had sat frozen through this explanation. Now, wordlessly, she looked up at Will. He put his hand on her shoulder and pressed hard. "We appreciate your bein' honest with us, Reverend. It does put a whole different light on the matter. It did hurt. More than you'll ever know."

Wardley reddened again but went on determinedly. "I also want to tell you I admire your courage in coming to church after that. I'm not so sure I could have done it."

"It wasn't easy," Hannah said softly, "for it did hurt. So terribly much."

"Even the strongest faith can tremble when great wrong is done the heart. But you obviously didn't lose your trust in God. I admire you for that, too."

"Why should we have lost trust in Him?" she asked, surprised. "God was never against us. We always knew that. We had no reason to turn against Him and every reason to turn to Him."

Wardley looked long at them, first Hannah, then Will. "I'm glad," he said simply. He fiddled with his coffee cup and avoided looking at either of them. "I have something else to say." Will's hand tightened on Hannah's shoulder.

"Pearl Gilby came to me a few weeks ago with a most dramatic account of her last visit to you. All about how defensive you were when she made a few 'perfectly innocent' remarks. Her words. She tried to convince me it was obvious that you, Will, were the father of Hannah's child. According to her, that was the only possible explanation for your 'crude behavior and remarks.' Again, her words."

Will looked straight at Wardley. "What did you tell her?"

Wardley looked straight back. "I told her I didn't believe a word of it, and that if she didn't do something about curbing her gossiping tongue, the church would have to take action against her. She stomped out and I ..." He broke off, shocked. Hannah's shoulders were shaking and Will, beet red, was quite frankly strangling on his laughter.

Bewildered, he stared as Hannah covered her mouth with her hand and squeaked, "Reverend Wardley, I'm so sorry, but ..." It was no use. Words failed her and she laughed until the tears came.

Will, in even worse shape, tried, too. "Reverend, if you only knew ..." He couldn't get any further, either.

Finally Hannah wiped her eyes. "Reverend Wardley, you haven't met Phebe. Would you like to see her?"

The abrupt turn of the conversation alarmed Wardley even more, but he managed to answer with magnificent composure, "Why certainly." As calmly as though Will and Hannah hadn't gone totally insane before his eyes.

"I should have come sooner," he said to Will as Hannah fled to the bedroom. "I know that, but, again, my pride ..." He broke off as Hannah came back carrying a blanket-wrapped bundle.

Her eyes were twinkling with unholy merriment but she said solemnly enough, "This is Phebe," and laid the baby in his arms. He — veteran of many a christening — took her expertly and Hannah casually tucked the blanket away from the tiny face, letting her hand linger a moment against Phebe's hair.

Wardley stared, then raised startled eyes to Will and Hannah, who were again doing their best — and failing — to contain their mirth. In total silence he eyed Isaac's blazing head, Micah's carroty curls, and Phebe's copper-bright ones.

"Luke's brand," he breathed. "Proof to one and all if ever ..." He choked and turned a deep, painful red.

"I guess Pearl Gilby can't count very well," Hannah said innocently.

The four boys had stopped eating earlier to watch curiously Will and Hannah's unusual display of hilarity. Now they stared, awed, as their dignified minister laughed so hard the tears streamed down his cheeks and he had to clutch his aching sides. Nor did they understand when he managed to gasp something that sounded strangely like, "Let Pearl Gilby put that on her needles and knit it!"

The evening of Reverend Wardley's visit was a merry one, for in their mutual release of tension, the relief went quite to their heads. In a most unprecedented manner Hannah and Will laughed and joked and sang silly songs:

> *The fox went out on a chilly night,*
> > *prayed for the moon to give him light*
> > *for he'd many a mile to go that night.*

> *He ran till he found a big, big pen*
> > *where the ducks and the geese were put therein.*
> *"Tonight two of you will grease my chin ...*
> > *before I leave this town-o."*

They felt that springtime had, indeed, come into their lives.

The little boys joined in, only Isaac rigidly sat back and refused to be a part of the fun. If he was trying to dampen their high spirits, he failed utterly, for nothing could quench their joy in this day.

They could not, however, forever evade the fact of Isaac's hostility. Since the baby's arrival he had been more aloof than ever, standing off when his brothers admired or talked to their new sister, totally refusing to have anything to do with her. "She stinks," was his comment the one time he bent over her cradle.

"Well, let's see what we can do about that." Hannah lifted her up. "Do you want to be my helper?" But Isaac had already run outside.

Just when Hannah first felt fear, she couldn't have said, but once she acknowledged her concern, she knew it had been there, growing stronger, for days. Did Will see what she did? Suddenly she felt an overwhelming need to discuss it with him, if only to have him tell her she was being silly.

She brought up the subject a few evenings after Reverend Wardley's apology visit. They had been sitting on the steps watching the boys play in the last of the sunset light. Phebe slept in her cradle behind them in the kitchen. Will, smoking his pipe, lounged bonelessly against the railing while Hannah darned Sam's sock. The shouts of the boys playing hide-and-seek drifted now close, now distant.

"Will?"

"Hmmm?" he said around his pipe.

"Will, I'd like to talk to you."

At the sober note in her voice, he removed the pipe and turned to look up at her.

"It's Isaac. Will, I'm getting worried," she burst out. "Since Phebe came, he's been more distant than ever. He won't talk to her or hold her like the other boys. If he does anything, he just glares. Especially when I'm holding her. I've tried to spend time with him but he just pulls away, won't have anything to do with me." Her voice broke.

"I've noticed, Hannah. And I'm concerned, too. I don't know how to reach him, either. God knows, we've both tried."

"I'm so afraid." Their eyes met.

"Of what, Hannah?" he asked slowly as a finger of ice touched his heart.

"That Isaac's going to do something terrible. To Phebe."

How could Will convince Hannah she was wrong about Isaac? Especially when he was not at all sure himself. They even talked to Doc Fergus, who knew how to listen when the occasion demanded it, but he could offer little assurance.

"He's a mighty troubled little boy, and he's got a lot of hostility built up in him. He probably doesn't even understand it all. We doctors can do so much with the body when it's sick, but when the mind is hurting, we're horribly limited. Maybe someday we'll know more what to do." He regarded them gravely. "And 'someday' is no comfort to you at all."

All they could do was keep a close watch, never for a minute leaving him alone with Phebe. But for the rest of his childhood? It was a chilling thought.

"Maybe he'll outgrow it. Maybe something will snap him out of it," Doc had said. In the meantime they watched and prayed for both children.

In the end, however, it was not to Phebe that the "something" happened, but to Jeremy.

It began innocently enough.

In those first, warm days of spring after the long, bone-chilling cold of winter, they spent as much time outside in the sunshine as possible. Will had changed the boys' Christmas sled to covered wagon, and they spent hours playing soldiers and Indians. They even constructed a crude fort at the side of the house where many a fierce battle raged with such realistic screeching and groaning that at times Hannah was hard put to convince herself that they were truly only playing.

On a Sunday of blue skies and gentle breezes, with trees and bushes swelling into bud, Will decided it was time to check Eagle's shoes. Jeremy, his faithful little shadow, wanted to know if he could help.

Will assured him that by all means he could and together they approached Eagle, dozing in the corral. The little boy scrambled up the railing. "He sure is a nice horse." He reached to pat the velvet muzzle.

"He is," Will agreed, smiling.

"I wish I had a horse of my own," Jeremy said wistfully.

"I'm sure you will before very long. You're gettin' to be a mighty big boy."

"When did you get your own horse, Mr. Braden?"

Will thought back. "When I wasn't much older'n you, I guess. I knew how to ride, of course, but my Pa said a horse was a big responsibility and a man had to be trusted to take care of him proper, not just ride him f'r fun."

Jeremy sighed. "My Pa never even let me ride. He said I'd just fall off and get hurt."

With effort, Will held back an unsuitable response. Luke again. How many bitter seeds had he sown?

"Well, son," he said carefully, "your Pa was right 'bout

fallin' off. But that's the only way to learn. You have to get right back on and try again."

"But don't it hurt?"

"Sometimes. But if you let yourself go limp with the fall, it doesn't hurt that much."

"Have you ever fallen off, Mr. Braden?"

"Many times, son."

"I like it when you call me 'son'," Jeremy said shyly. The bright little face so trustingly upturned was, in that moment, frozen into a fragment of time that would haunt Will forever.

Unknowing, he grinned back.

"Mr. Braden, is my Pa ever goin' to come home?"

The unexpectedness of the question rocked Will. So seldom did Jeremy mention his father's leaving or return any more. He answered carefully. "I don't know, son. I just don't know."

Jeremy ducked his head. "I wish you were my Pa. Is that bad?"

Will cupped the sturdy chin in his hand. "I don't know whether it's bad or not, Jeremy," he said slowly. "But I do know I wish you were my son."

Such a light burst over the serious little face that Will felt a lump come to his throat. Hastily he rumpled the child's hair. "Let's get these shoes checked. Then after we're all done, maybe you c'n ride him to test them out."

"I c'n?" Awe struggled comically with seriousness. "I'd be real re-respos—"

"Responsible," Will supplied.

"I sure would!" Awe won over seriousness as he gave a

great shout of joy.

Working quickly but carefully, "You c'n ruin a horse f'r-ever if you don't shoe him right," Will reminded the child, and Jeremy nodded solemnly.

Finally they led Eagle, newly shod, into the area in front of the barn. Remembering his promise, Will saddled him and set the boy up on the broad back, instructing him how to grasp the reins and to use his knees and heels to guide. Excited beyond measure, Jeremy did his best to follow directions.

Will walked beside him for a few minutes until he figured the child felt secure enough. Then he told him, "You sit tight. I'm goin' to his head and lead him by the bridle. Think you c'n manage the reins?"

Jeremy's face screwed into intense concentration. "I c'n. I know." Hannah was just coming down the back steps. "Look, there's Ma." She caught sight of her son sitting so tall and straight — and high up — on Eagle. If her heart quailed, she hid it admirably, waved and started over toward them.

"All right, I'm goin' up to his head now. Remember, hold the reins easy but firm and use your knees." Will stepped from Jeremy's side and reached for the bridle. In that split second when he didn't have hold and the boy was totally on his own, a large rock hurtling from around the corner of the barn slammed into Eagle's flank.

The horse lurched in pain and surprise. Will grabbed for the bridle, but Jeremy, having neither balance nor skill to hang on, shot over the side. His cry of terror snapped off as he hit the ground with a sickening thud.

But Hannah's scream seemed to echo on and on.

Day Star Rising

In that first, frozen second in crazy, unreal flicks, Will saw the small, crumpled body lying so still in the settling dirt; Hannah, hand pressed to mouth as though it could choke back that wild scream; and clearly — too clearly — Isaac hunched by the corner of the barn, staring in horror.

Sixteen

Will grabbed Eagle's bridle to pull him away before his hooves could strike Jeremy. He didn't stop to calm the animal, but threw the reins down to ground tie him before dropping to his knees beside the child.

Hannah flung herself down on Jeremy's other side, reaching for him.

"No, don't touch him!" Will yelled. She froze as if he had slapped her. Jeremy had fallen face up, his neck bent at an angle, and a smear of dirt smudged one cheek from which all the color had drained.

Will bent, put his ear to the child's shirt. "He's alive. His heart's beatin'." Hannah stared at him, her eyes enormous. He grabbed her arms and shook her. "Do you hear me, Hannah? He is alive." Her face crumpled and she went so white he thought she was going to faint.

She gasped, "His neck ..."

"It could be broken. That's why we don't dare move him. Fetch a blanket to cover him. Soon as you get back, I'll ride f'r the doc." She was on her feet and running toward the house before he had finished speaking.

His heart twisted into a knot of pain that spread through him as he gazed down at the small white face with its dirt smudge and its freckles and its total stillness. He reached out, very gently touching the rumpled hair. His vision blurred. He thrust an impatient fist across his eyes as Hannah, skirts flying, came back with a blanket. Together they settled it carefully over the still form, and then Will jerked to his feet.

He grabbed Eagle's reins. "I'll be back just as soon as I c'n."

"Will!" She stumbled to her feet, reaching blindly for him. He caught her, held her hard against him. "Be brave. Don't give up hope." He released her, swung into saddle and was gone in a pound of hooves.

He rode hell-bent for Jason's, pulling up in the yard so abruptly that dirt showered. "Becky," he bellowed without dismounting. "Becky!"

She jerked the door open. "Will, what's the ..."

"Jeremy's hurt. Go stay with Hannah while I get the doctor." Pausing only long enough to make certain she understood, he wheeled Eagle and tore off toward town.

That ride through the sun-drenched, springtime-green countryside was, to Will, a horror directly out of his worst nightmare. No matter that Eagle's hooves were flying in an all-out run. No matter that his flanks heaved and foam slapped back onto Will. No burst of speed was fast enough to outrun his tortured thoughts. Jeremy's face — and Hannah's — over and over. At first clear and separate, then merged into a sickening whirl.

He thundered into town, scattering the people unlucky

enough to be in his way on that mad dash to the doctor's office. He jerked Eagle to a skidding halt in front of the small building. "Doc!" And yet again, "Doc!" *If Fergus wasn't in his office ...*

Doc swung the door open. "What's ... Will Braden! What's happened?"

"It's Jeremy. He fell off my horse. I think his neck's broke."

"My God." For the first time in Will's memory, the doctor blanched. Then steeled, his usual professional self. "Did you move him?"

"No, we ..."

"How was he breathing when you left? Did he seem to be getting enough air?"

"He seemed to. He ..."

"I'll get my bag and be right behind you." As Will wheeled Eagle, slamming him into a hard run down the dusty street, Fergus was already ducking back into his office.

That ride back to the Crescent C was, in its own way, even more horrible than the trip in had been. For now that help was on the way, a new, even more dreadful cold gripped Will. *What if we're too late? What if Jeremy is already ... No! He's still alive! He has to be.* But Jeremy had trusted him. And so had Hannah. His stomach roiled as nausea swept him at memory of that total trust.

He thudded into the yard at a dead run, saw Jeremy still lying where he had fallen. Hannah and Becky, sitting close beside him, had already started to rise at the sound of Will's approach. Hannah had been nursing the baby; now she thrust Phebe into Becky's arms, and heedless of the infant's protesting squalls, ran to meet Will even as he leaped to the ground. Her dress and apron were dirt smeared from kneeling in the dusty yard. Her usually neat hair was breeze-whipped around her face. He caught her hard by the arms.

"Is he ...?" He couldn't say it.

"He's still breathing just like he was. But he hasn't moved — not once." Her voice choked off.

"Doc's on his way. Remember — chin up."

Over her shoulder he saw they had brought another blanket from the house. Jared and Reuben were holding it over Jeremy's face to protect his eyes from the bright light. Catty and Eve were watching over the other children, who were huddled in a group like shy prairie creatures afraid to come too close to danger.

As he dropped Eagle's reins, Jason, followed by Aaron and Matt, hurried over to him. "I'll take him and fix him up," Jason said.

He scarcely heard as he pushed past to kneel beside Jeremy. He put his hand to the child's forehead and glanced over at Hannah, kneeling at his other side.

"He's getting warm. That means fever." She pressed her hand hard to her mouth.

"Doc's comin'," he assured her again. "He'll be here any minute and he'll take care of him."

As if in answer to the words, Doc's rig rattled into the yard. Aaron appeared from the barn to grab the reins as Fergus climbed down with his bag and dropped beside the boy. Will, making room, knelt beside Hannah on the other side, putting his arm around her in silent support. He felt her trembling and his grip tightened.

Doc began his first, hasty examination. He checked eyes and ears and nose, listened to the heartbeat. "Has he had any bleeding at all?"

Wordlessly, Hannah shook her head.

The doctor's skillful fingers gently probed the bent neck. Under Will's arm, Hannah went rigid.

Fergus carefully straightened Jeremy's neck. Looking to her, he said, "It's not broken."

Hannah didn't cry out, but for the second time that day she went so white Will was certain she was going to faint. She swayed against him, but even as his arm tightly gripped her, she caught herself. "You're sure?"

"I'm sure," he said gently. "But I think he's got a bad bruise at the back of his neck, where the skull meets the spinal cord. I want to get him to the house. We'll have to carry him very carefully. Catty, Eve, go ahead of us and get his bed ready. No pillow," he called, for they were already running toward the house.

Doc gestured to Jason, Aaron and Matt, who were hesitating a short distance aside as if, like the children, they feared to get too close. "Listen carefully. It's very important that we carry him without jarring his neck. Will, you put your hands under his head and neck like this. Jason, you and I will support his upper body here. Aaron and Matt, hold the lower, like so."

Awkward, scared of hurting Jeremy further, they took up their positions. "Now, we all lift together, smoothly, when I say. Remember, even and together. Ready — lift."

At the word they rose as one body, bringing Jeremy with them. "Good. Now, in step, to the house."

Slowly, carefully, Hannah close beside and Becky behind with Phebe, who was still mouthing disapproval over the interruption to her dinner, they made their way across the yard, up the steps and into the bedroom where Cat and Eve waited. Gently, without jerking, they laid Jeremy on his bed.

"That's fine," Doc assured them. "Now if you'll just step into the kitchen, I'll give him a more thorough examination." Shuffling, relieved, the men backed out.

Becky turned to Eve and Cat. "We'd better round up a few youngsters. No telling where they've got to by now," she said, drawing them with her into the kitchen.

Doc glanced at Hannah, still standing beside Jeremy's bed, and at Will, who stood firmly beside her. "You all right, Hannah?"

Hands gripped tightly in front of her, she nodded. "I'm fine."

Doc permitted himself a reassuring smile. "Good." From him, it was high praise. "I want you to wait outside with the others," he said gently. As she started to shake her head, he said firmly, "I can make a better examination. It's for Jeremy's good, Hannah."

Will put his arm about her. "Come on. Doc's right."

She let Will lead her away, but the look in her eyes seared even the doctor's crusty heart.

In the kitchen, Hannah finished nursing Phebe while they waited and prayed. No one said a word aloud — what could they say? — except, when necessary, to one of the children. After she had tucked Phebe into her cradle, Hannah sat at the table, head bowed into her hands. Will stood by the window, staring out at nothing, but seeing Jeremy as he had been in those last, happy minutes. The others sat or paced the floor restlessly while the Seth Thomas clock ticked on and on.

Finally, the bedroom door opened and Doc faced them. Hannah rose, slowly. It was in minutes like this the doctor wondered why he hadn't followed in his father's footsteps and taken up farming.

"How is he?"

Doc put his hand on her shoulder and looked directly into her eyes. "I'm going to speak straight truth because I know you, of all people, can handle it. His neck is not broken. He does have a bruise at the base of his skull and a fever. Whether it bruised the spinal cord, I don't know. But it's vital not to take a chance."

"When will we know?"

Where does she get her strength? he wondered. "When he regains consciousness and starts moving. Right now I get no reflex responses from him. But with rest and care, the bruise will have a chance to heal."

"What if it doesn't heal?" Hannah's voice was only a breath.

"If it doesn't," Doc said, "he'll be permanently paralyzed."

Days of hope blurred into nights of tortured uncertainty.

Hannah, white with anguish, refused to leave her son's side even to rest. She fed Phebe when they laid the child in her arms, scarcely aware she was doing so. Will, in his turn, would not leave Hannah. But what words of comfort could he give her when his own heart was so racked?

No matter that Isaac had thrown the rock. It was Will who had encouraged Jeremy, had put him on the horse. It was Will Jeremy had trusted. Each time his thoughts circled back on that one bitter truth: Jeremy — and Hannah — had trusted him. And he had failed them.

But how could he even begin to explain this to Hannah, distraught with grief as she was? She was barely hanging on to self-control now. Only by sheer force of will had she not broken completely before this. No, he could not add his guilt to her burden. So, together, they stayed. And watched, and waited, and prayed for some sign of response from the once-sturdy body that with the passing hours seemed to grow more frail, to melt away under their very eyes.

Not stopping once to think that, in actuality, Will had no right to be there, that this burden of responsibility he had assumed for his own shoulders belonged, in fact, to another man who knew little of responsibility — and cared less.

So it was that early morning hour Becky approached Hannah, sitting beside the bed, her son's limp hand clasped in hers. "Why don't you come rest?" she suggested gently.

Hannah merely shook her head.

"But you're overtired, you're wearing yourself out."

"I'm not leaving him."

"Hannah." Becky reached to put her arm about the rigid shoulders.

"No!" Hannah flung the comforting arm violently aside. "I'm not going to leave him, and you can't make me," she hissed. "So you might as well save your breath!"

"But ..."

"No!" The single word was all the more terrible because

she had screamed it, yet it had come out a bare whisper. Dismissing Becky's presence, she turned back to Jeremy.

Such a blast of fury from mild Hannah left Becky with her mouth hanging open. Glancing at Will, she signaled urgently that she wanted to talk to him. He had been standing by the window, sunk in his own bitter thoughts, when Hannah's outburst roused him.

Becky drew him over to the door and whispered to him. "You sure?" he asked anxiously.

She nodded. "Talk to her, Will. You can make her understand."

His mouth twisted at such supreme confidence in his abilities. He'd faced Hannah's wrath before, without overwhelming success.

When he bent over her, she said flatly, "I'm not going to leave him. Don't even try to make me."

"Hannah, honey, listen to me. You aren't gettin' enough rest and you aren't eatin' right." She drew breath for a scalding answer but he plunged on, not giving her a chance to override him. "If it was just you, it'd be one thing, but there's Phebe, too."

"You're not going to ..." She froze in mid-fury. "Phebe? What ..."

"Your milk, honey. It's not agreein' with her while you're so upset. You don't want her sick, too."

"Will," she said, horrified. "Is she all right? Is she ..."

"Now calm down. Becky says she's still doin' fine, but not as good as she would if you'd take it a little easier."

"Let me see her! Where is she?"

"I'll get her." Becky placed the baby in Hannah's arms.

"See, she's fine, but just not eating as much as she should."

Hannah gazed down at the tiny face. For the first time since the whole terrible ordeal had begun, tears came to her eyes. Biting her lip, she blinked them away. "I'll rest."

Becky took Phebe, and Will led Hannah over to the other bed. "Just right here, honey, where you'll be close. I'll keep watch and let you know the second anythin' happens." He drew the cover over her.

"Promise?"

"I'll be right here, watchin'."

"I know that. But you'll tell me if anything happens, even if I'm asleep?"

"I promise."

She gave a shuddering sigh, closed her eyes and slept.

He brushed her hair with his lips. Straightening, he returned to Jeremy's side to take up his vigil.

As it happened, there was no need to rouse Hannah when a turning came. She had awakened and taken her place beside Jeremy once more. It was she, watching so yearningly, who saw first. "Will, look!"

But Will had seen, too, the faintest movement of Jeremy's head to the side and the flash of pain that registered on his face. Frozen, they watched as his lips parted in a soundless cry.

Will twisted to his feet, leaping for the door. "Doc," he hollered, "get in here!"

Doc Fergus, snatching a cup of coffee at the table,

almost dropped his cup. He hurried into the bedroom and saw Hannah, tears on her cheeks, staring at her son. His first instinct was that the boy had died, but one swift glance assured him it was not so. He bent over the child.

Jeremy stirred again, restlessly. Doc pulled back the covers and felt the small hands and feet. As he ran his finger over the palms and soles of each one, Jeremy flexed.

Doc looked at Hannah, wide-eyed, scarcely daring to breathe — and Will not daring to hope.

"He's not paralyzed."

A soul-deep sigh escaped from Hannah as Will closed his eyes against a wash of relief so intense it made the room spin.

Before they could do more than grasp the wonder of the doctor's words, he spoke again, gently but implacably. "Hannah, he's not out of the woods yet. He's still a very sick little boy. We've got to get that fever down."

She nodded. Some of the light went out of her eyes. "But he moved." Nothing could take away her joy in that. Nor did the doctor wish to, for it was a knowledge of prayer fulfilled, something to cling to in the dark hours that followed as Jeremy's fever soared.

Doc Fergus was neither godless nor heartless. He had simply seen too much pain and too much death in his three decades of practice. He had seen relatives pray with quiet desperation over a loved one — as Hannah Clayton was praying now — and the patient had died. He had seen others, just as sick but with no one to pray over them, get well. The reverse had been true, too, he had to admit. But what was it that made some get well while others, not half as sick, had turned over and died? He was no philosopher, and he had no answer, but he was not about to deny Hannah the comfort of her prayers. Secretly, he was surprised the boy had survived this long — it had certainly been against all the odds. Privately, he was sure Jeremy could not live much longer. His still-mounting temperature would, literally, burn his brain up. In which case death could only be a welcome release.

But it wasn't up to him and he would fight to the last ditch, until the decision was taken irrevocably out of his hands. As he bent over the bed, he wondered how many times he had seen the look of death written plain across suffering faces. It was stamped clearly on young Jeremy Clayton's features right now.

Bringing ice from town, they packed it around the small body in a desperate attempt to cool him down. Where he had been so still before, now he tossed restlessly, sometimes crying out — the sounds coming only faintly through his fever-dried lips. Most of the time it was, "Ma!" scared and pleading.

Each time, Hannah would bend close and say in a firm, clear voice, "I'm here, Jeremy. I'm right here."

But once it was not "Ma" that he uttered so brokenly, but "Pa." It was clear, though low, no mistaking it.

Startled, Hannah looked down at her son. There was no way she could answer for Luke, so carelessly free and far away. She bent over him. "Pa's not here, son, but I am."

"Pa," he muttered beseechingly. "Pa!"

She looked helplessly up at Will. "How can we make him understand?"

"We can't. But we can't let him fret, either." He bent over the boy, took the hand Hannah wasn't already holding and gripped it in his. "I'm here, son," he said clearly.

"Pa!" A kind of light settled over the little face as he sighed and slept.

Will waited to make sure Jeremy would not waken before he unclasped the thin hand from his and laid it gently on the cover. Turning to the window, he stared outside for a long time. When he returned to the bedside, Hannah reached with her free hand to touch his.

"Thank you, Will. See, he's still quiet."

"It was no lie, but true enough," he said gruffly. "I reckon you know that."

She bowed her head. "I know."

Seventeen

More days of hope when Jeremy's fever eased a bit and he even seemed to gain, although he was still unconscious. More nights of anguish as his fever took hold again, and they had to watch helplessly as the bit of progress he had made ebbed away. Although Doc Fergus had not put his medical conclusion into words, Hannah, with growing terror, knew what he was thinking. She, too, had seen the look of death before. It had been on the faces of her mother, and her father, and her little brother before they had died. It was on Jeremy's face now.

Prayer. Every thought, every movement, every breath a plea for her child as though by sheer force she could hold Death back, keep the greedy hands away from him as she would have protected him from any other evil seeking to hurt him.

Was this, then, how her own mother had felt, watching Jonah die? He, too, had been just 6 years old.

Was this, too, how another mother had felt as she watched her Son die on a cross? Had she stood and watched Him, and remembered? How, in a burst of proud helpfulness, He had painted the side of the house with mud? Had He, in shy triumph, borne home to her a bouquet of weeds and wildflowers clenched in His hot little fist, picked "Just for you, Mama."?

She had thought she could not be more torn than she already was by Jeremy. But when they brought Phebe to her and she plainly saw her daughter's fragility, she knew. Then, she knew. But how could she choose one child over the other? If she for an instant lessened that total force of concentration she was keeping for Jeremy, he might slip away. Yet, if she neglected Phebe, the baby would surely sicken. What if she chose Phebe and Jeremy died? What if she chose Jeremy and they both died?

And Jacob their father said unto them,
me have ye bereaved of my children:
Joseph is not, and Simeon is not,
and ye will take Benjamin away:
all these things are against me.

What if she chose Jeremy and they both died?
The words, wrenched from her soul, were a bare whisper. "I'll rest."

Just before dawn the doctor bent over Jeremy and — for the thousandth time? — checked his forehead. He frowned, checked it again, listened to his breathing and felt for the pulse. Hannah, terror written plain upon her, watched wordlessly while Will gripped her hand in silent support.

"Tell us, Doc," he said roughly.

Doc glanced at them and back down at Jeremy as if to confirm his findings. He looked up and a tremendous grin split his haggard features. "The fever's turned! He's sleeping natural."

Hannah stood rigid, her face stark white, her eyes enormous. "Did you hear me, Hannah? He's going to be all right!"

She had heard. As if with no more strength left to hold herself up, she sank to her knees, covered her face with her hands and began to cry. Will bent down beside her, put his hands over hers. Raising her head, she saw that his cheeks, too, were tear-wet. In wonder, she reached a finger to touch that dampness. Trying and failing to speak, he simply drew her close as she buried her face against his hard-thumping heart and cried and cried. While the doctor, with suspiciously moist eyes, kept saying gruffly, "He'll do. He'll do."

Oh, the rejoicing that morning as the spring breezes blew in fresh and sweet, dispelling the last dark shadow from the farthest corner. The lightness and the laughter where for such a dreadful space of time had been deepest fear.

When Hannah and Will left the bedroom, they found the entire family grouped in the kitchen. Waiting, fearing to learn the worst, for they had heard only Hannah's wild weeping, not the reason for it, and they could only conclude that Death had won his grim game at last. One look at Hannah's face was enough, however, for them to know the truth.

Becky, Eve and Catty all hugged Hannah as joyously as though Jeremy were one of their own children. Aaron and Jason pounded Will on the back in their relief. Matt had been standing to the side but now he came forward, his hand out. Will hesitated, finally stuck out his hand, and they shook, briefly.

Will jammed his hands into his pockets, but before he

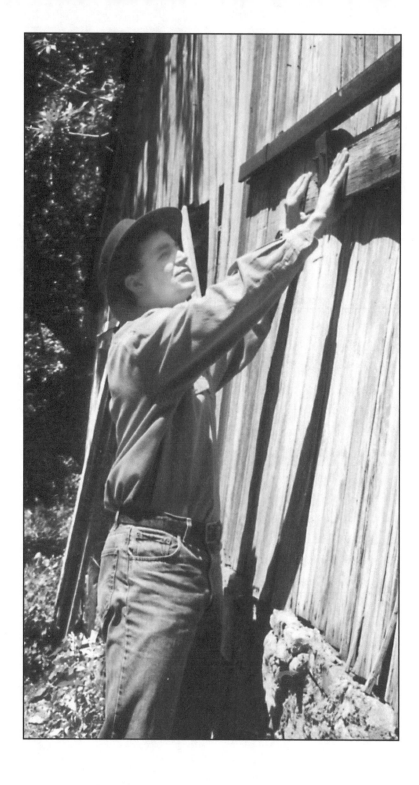

could think of anything to say, Jason laughed. "Women! Just look at 'em! Cryin' when they're supposed to be happy. Will any of you fellas ever be able to figure 'em out?"

If Jason noticed that each man's eyes, as well as his own, were also damp, he grandly ignored the fact.

"Ma?" At the small, hesitant voice from Hannah's bedroom door, Becky, Cat and Hannah — all mothers — turned automatically without knowing which, or whose, child called. Sam, holding Micah's fist in his, stood uncertainly.

With a glad cry, Hannah reached out and the boys stumbled into her arms. Isaac had been trailing behind them and Hannah reached to hug him, too, but he evaded her grasp and ran out the door. She started after him, but Will said quickly, "I'll go."

At the bottom of the steps he hesitated. He remembered the boys' "fort" at the side of the house. On the chance, he turned that direction. "Isaac?" No answer. He wedged head and shoulders through the crawl space that served as door, but stuck there. The little boy was huddled in the farthest corner. "Isaac, come on out."

No answer.

"If you don't come out, I'm comin' in after you. If I do that, you won't have much of a fort left." The flatness of his voice left no doubt he meant every word. Slowly, reluctantly, Isaac crept out.

Will grabbed him by the shoulder. "Now, young man, you and me are goin' to have a talk." He tried to squirm away, but Will tightened his hold. "Don't try to get away again. Because if you do," he said pleasantly, "I'm going to spank you like you've never been spanked before. Do you understand?"

267

Isaac looked up into the stern face, decided the man towering so tall and grim above him meant every word, and nodded sullenly.

"Good. Now we got that straight, let's sit down and talk." He pushed the boy down and sat beside him, back to the house wall. "F'r starters, you threw that rock, didn't you?"

All Isaac's defiance suddenly collapsed. "Is he dead?"

Will started. He hadn't reckoned on the child's full realization of the terrible gravity of Jeremy's illness, but looking into that terrified, small face he knew Isaac did understand, at least in part.

"No," he said more gently, "Jeremy isn't dead. He's goin' to be all right."

The relief that came over Isaac's face was pitiful. He burst into tears, and Will hesitated only an instant before he took the boy onto his lap, holding him close while he cried it out. The tension the child had been under must have been unbearable, he realized now.

Finally, the wild tears quieted to sobbing hiccups and Will set him back on the ground. "Now," he said firmly, "we are goin' to talk." A hiccup from Isaac. "You threw that rock, didn't you?"

Fear came to the boy's eyes again, and he ducked his head.

"Isaac, I want the truth."

A barely perceptible nod.

"Why?"

A long hesitation. Will put his hand under the boy's chin. "You must of had a reason."

He glared at Will. " 'Cause you was lettin' him ride your

horse, and you didn't let me ride. You always do things with him and never with me!"

Will managed to hide his astonishment. "But you never wanted to do anythin' with us. Whenever I asked you, you always ran away."

" 'Cause Jeremy and the others was always there, too. You never wanted to do nothin' with just me like you always did with him."

Will stared at him, knowing with a thrust of guilt the boy was right. He had favored Jeremy, totally without realizing. "I'm sorry," he said slowly, "you're right. I wasn't bein' fair to you. But just because I was wrong didn't give you the right to throw that rock and hurt your brother. That's called takin' your temper out on somebody else and it's just as wrong as ... as lyin' or stealin' because it c'n do such terrible harm. You found that out, didn't you?"

Isaac, head down, nodded slowly. "I'm sorry," he muttered.

"Takes a man to admit he's wrong." Will stuck out his hand. "I'm proud, son, you could do it."

Isaac eyed his out-thrust hand in amazement. "You called me 'son', just like you do Jeremy!" He put his small hand in the man's big one and shook it solemnly. The mixture of little-boy incredulity and grown-man importance on his face could have been comical. But Will had never felt less like laughing.

"Now we got that straightened out, there's still somethin' else." Isaac looked wary. "I'm talkin' 'bout the way you've been treatin' your Ma. You haven't been very nice to her, you know."

The light faded from the boy's eyes and guilt returned.

"You been, well, pushin' your Ma away, and she hasn't

been ignorin' you. She's tried to spend time with just you, and you wouldn't let her. That hurt her an awful lot, just like it hurt you when I paid so much attention to Jeremy."

Isaac squirmed, ducking his head again.

"She's a very special Ma, you know. She tries so hard to do things f'r you, and it hurts her somethin' fierce when you act mean in return."

"I didn't mean to hurt her," Isaac burst out. "Pa went away and didn't take me ..." He stopped, fumbling to explain something he couldn't even fully grasp.

"Your Pa went away, and your Ma was still here so you took your temper out on her."

Isaac stared, still not understanding.

"The thing is, son," he said patiently, "you can't take your feelin's f'r one person out on another. If your Ma was mad at Micah and spanked you, that wouldn't be fair, would it?"

A vigorous shake of the head. That he understood.

"It's the same with your mad f'r your Pa. It's not fair to take it out on your Ma."

Isaac thought that one over. "I was pretty mean, wasn't I?" he said slowly.

"Yes, you were."

"I'm sorry."

"Why don't you tell your Ma? I know she'd be glad to hear."

He looked doubtful. "Maybe she don't like me no more."

Will stood and held out his hand. "Your Ma's pretty understandin'. Why don't we go see?"

The child slipped his hand into Will's big one. As they rounded the corner of the house, Will saw Jason and the others harnessing up, getting ready to leave. But at the moment, he didn't dare stop to talk. In the kitchen, Hannah was sitting in her rocker, head bowed into her hands.

Isaac looked questioningly at Will, who nodded and gave him a little push. The child walked slowly over to stand in front of Hannah. "Ma?"

She raised her head unbelievingly. "Isaac." She held out her arms. He was into them like a rocket. Over his head she saw Will, who grinned foolishly, winked, and backed hastily out the door.

Outside, he caught up with Jason as he was lifting Patience into the wagon box. Words could never say it. He just gripped Jason's hand, hard. Jason clasped him by the shoulder in equally wordless understanding.

Becky, from the high seat, said briskly, "You make sure Hannah gets some rest. Hear me?"

"Yes, ma'am," he said obediently as Jason climbed up.

"And get some yourself!" she called back as the wagon rattled out of the yard.

He waved, in acknowledgment to her and farewell to the others already pulling out. As he returned to the house, Hannah's singing drifted to him:

Wait till the darkness is over.
Wait till the tempest is gone.
Hope for the sunshine tomorrow ...

She broke off as he stepped into the kitchen and surveyed the peaceful confusion. Sam and Micah were in their chairs, waiting for breakfast, jabbering nonsense to each other only they could understand and giggling wildly. Isaac was setting the table. Hannah turned from the stove where she was frying sausages and hotcakes.

"You should be lyin' down," he protested.

"But I feel fine. I just want to enjoy being a normal family again," she said softly.

"Becky made me promise to see that you rest," he said sternly to hide his own unwonted emotion.

"I will. In a little while."

"I'll hold you to that. She'd skin me if I didn't!"

When they were seated, Hannah reached for her Bible. " 'Sing unto the Lord and give thanks ... weeping may endure for a night, but joy cometh in the morning ...' "

After they finished eating, Will cleared his throat. "Isaac, how would you like to take the other boys out to play? You'll have to keep a careful eye on 'em. I want to talk to your Ma."

Bursting with importance, Isaac washed the syrup off his brothers' well-supplied faces and hands. They thought it a fine game and resisted, giggling, but at last he had them reasonably well unstuck. Dragging Micah from his chair, he shepherded them out the door.

Hannah started to stack the used plates, but Will put his hand over hers. "I do want to talk to you."

She put the plates down, sank into her chair and regarded him questioningly.

"Did Isaac tell you 'bout our talk?"

She smiled. "He said he was sorry he was so mean, that he threw the rock because he was mad at you. But he won't ever again because 'you can't be mad at one person and mean to another.' That's 'not fair.' That was about it."

"I just didn't realize I was payin' more attention to Jeremy separately than to Isaac. So the blame really falls on me," he admitted ruefully.

"He also said you called him 'Son. Just like Jeremy.' "

"It just seemed to come natural. Same as it does with Jeremy. Do you mind?"

Her eyes met his and she shook her head slowly.

After a long moment, he said gruffly, "Guess I've been treatin' him like one of the littler boys, and he's ready to be treated like an older one. I keep f'rgettin' he's 5, not that far behind Jeremy."

"I'm guilty, too. "I've always given Jeremy more responsibility because he's the oldest. I dare say it's more than time Isaac took a share."

"Hannah," he hesitated. "Maybe I'm pokin' my nose in again, but I think you're right. And what better time to start than now? Isaac's been punished f'r sure these last days, not knowin' whether he'd killed his brother. But he shouldn't be able to get by on just that."

"What do you have in mind?"

As ever, he was awkward at discussing emotions. "He was jealous because I spent so much time with Jeremy."

She waited.

"Doc says Jeremy'll have to stay in bed a couple of weeks. If Isaac takes over all Jeremy's chores as well as his own, plus a few others we c'n come up with, he might just learn a lesson besides what he's already found out."

"You mean ..."

"I mean work his little tail off. He wants to do things with us. Well, we'll be right alongside him. He'll find out it's not all fun and games takin' on an adult's work."

She bit her lip. "I don't know. It just doesn't seem fair."

"Oh, well, never mind then." He went on quickly. "It was just an idea."

"I didn't mean that," she broke in. "I meant fair to you. I think it's a fine idea, but to expect you to do so much ..."

"Wouldn't volunteer if I didn't want to," he said gruffly. "But I do want to. I kind of owe it to him, seems like."

She smiled at that. "You don't. But I understand what you mean. If we can just keep Isaac cooperating!"

When they told him of the plan, he was highly enthusiastic. But as the first day dragged on and he found that stock tending and barn cleaning were work, and often unpleasant at that, his exuberance waned. He passed from enthusiasm to rebellion to tears.

Will worked beside him that first morning, explaining and demonstrating much as he had with Jeremy. He found the boy quick enough about things he liked to do, such as pitching hay to Daisy, but when it came time to rake out her stall, he dragged his feet. He quit dawdling only after Will spoke sharply, and even then his willingness was in noticeably short supply.

Will, ignoring his sulking, went whistling to tend the team. He had noticed a weak spot in Rusty's harness, but with Jeremy's illness it had gone unmended. Aaron, Jason and Matt had done the Crescent C chores along with their own these last days, but there were several odd jobs such as this one that had to be caught up on.

As he stood examining the harness strap, Isaac, who had trailed after him, spoke up. "I know how to fix that."

Will glanced at him and smiled tolerantly. "We better mend it before it snaps completely," he explained. But Isaac had run out of the barn.

"Isaac, come back here! You're not goin' to skin out of helpin' that easy," Will finished — to himself, for the boy had cut around the corner.

Will started after him in grim determination. He had disappeared from sight and Will paused. *Probably hiding, the little ...*

He called out. No answer. Grim determination was swiftly becoming outright anger. *When I catch up to him that boy will learn a lesson for sure!*

Figuring he had probably retreated to his fort, Will headed that way, but as he was passing the tack room, he heard a scrabbling inside. He shoved wide the partly open door, letting it crash back against the wall. "Here you ..." he began furiously, and stalled in confusion.

Isaac had jumped at the banging of the door. Now he shrank back from the man's obvious anger.

"What do you have there?" Will demanded.

Isaac brought his hands slowly from behind his back. "I was just gettin' the tools f'r you." And he held out the cutters and riveter.

Will stared from the tools to the child's eyes, which were wide with uncertainty, and felt like wilting into the floor. "How do you know which ones to use?" he finally managed weakly.

"My Pa showed me." Then, with a kind of defiant bravado, "Me and him took care of all the horses!"

Will had to hide a smile at the childish boast. But even as he took the tools, which were, indeed, the correct ones for that particular job, he realized Isaac might not be stretching the truth all that much. The one detail about ranching Luke had taken to was horses. Neglect the rest of the chores as he might, as he had from the condition of the place when Will had come, his horses had seen the best of care. The animals weren't the finest because he couldn't afford that kind of price, but since he had put so little money into other parts of the ranch, he had extra to put into his horseflesh. And they were good.

Hannah had mentioned that Isaac had spent a lot of time with Luke. Will was ready to bet most of that time had been around the horses. He couldn't doubt Isaac had picked up a lot of knowledge. He was only surprised Luke had taken the time and patience to teach him, and that he had remembered after all these months.

Remember he did, however, as he explained in detail to Will how to mend the harness. After they finished, Isaac even put the tools away without being told. When Will praised him for this, he said simply, "Pa says if you don't put 'em away, you won't have 'em next time you need to fix somethin'."

Will agreed he was right, thinking with sour amusement it was too bad Luke hadn't extended this philosophy to other aspects of his daily life.

After they had caught up on a few more of the outside chores, Will sent Isaac in to help Hannah. Although he knew he could have done no differently, he felt he had been neglecting his share of tending the herd these past days and nights. His not being there had put extra burden on the others and he well knew it, even though no one else had said a word. But that was the way of the Clayton family, he thought with admiration — and a sudden stab of jealousy. They always closed ranks to take care of their own. And he, who had no family, could never know the feeling of being part of such a one. Thus his thoughts ran as he rode out to the herd that fine morning — a day on which it was, truly, good to be alive.

With spring roundup coming on, the next days were busy ones, and Will had to be away with the cattle for odd periods of time. Before leaving, he pointed out specific chores he expected Isaac to do while he was gone. On his return he held an accounting. The first time this happened, Isaac went wailing to his mother. He never did so again for he found, to his dismay, that Hannah was even stricter than Will. He quickly learned it was far easier to do as he was told than to face the consequences of disobedience. Folding clothes, drying dishes and weeding a section of the new garden plot were all included in his education.

His resentment and foot-dragging didn't evaporate magically overnight, but at the end of the two weeks, a thoroughly chastened little boy stood looking up at Will.

"Do you think you learned anythin', son?"

Isaac nodded solemnly.

Will hunkered down to the child's level. "What?"

"You and Ma work awful hard."

"That's right. If it's honest work, no matter how hard it is, a man need never be ashamed of it. Did you learn anythin' else?"

This time Isaac's nod was vigorous. "Hard work sure makes you hungry!"

Will laughed. "That it does, son." He held out his hand. "Let's go see if your Ma has supper ready."

With shy eagerness, Isaac slipped his hand into Will's and they started for the house.

Will told Hannah about it later that evening. She was sitting in her rocker, cuddling Phebe to sleep, and he was at the table carving on a bit of wood.

"It did him a world of good, didn't it? But I don't think I could have stuck it out by myself, even though I knew it was necessary."

"Yes, you could of," he said with quiet assurance.

"You have a lot more confidence in me than I do. Especially after that first night when he fell asleep at the table with his face in his plate!" She was laughing, but close to tears, too.

"That was rough, wasn't it?" His own smile was twisted. "But I don't really have more confidence in you. I've just got a better view of you than you have."

She blushed. Seeing her discomfort, he said gravely, " 'Bout Jeremy, I've been huntin' the words to tell you how deep-down sorry I am 'bout gettin' him hurt that way."

"It wasn't your fault," she said, astonished. "It happened. I know you didn't let it happen deliberately. When Jeremy was so sick, I was thinking a lot of mixed-up things. The oddest thoughts kept jumping into my head, but blaming you wasn't one of them. You were right there hurting with me, and I knew that. It was, I think, the only thing that made it bearable at all. You do believe me, don't you?"

Their eyes met for a long moment and an enormous weight lifted from his heart. "Because you say so, I believe you," he said simply.

Jeremy awoke, pitifully pale and weak but ravenously hungry. The fever had sapped his strength to such an extent that the first few days he slept a lot and was content to lie quietly.

During these days visitors appeared once more at the kitchen door, bringing good wishes for Jeremy's recovery and fresh-baked bread, cake or soup. Not once was mention made of "scandal" or anything relating to it. Pearl Gilby didn't come, but Reverend Wardley did. He had stopped by frequently while Jeremy lay so sick, but he had neither preached nor mouthed empty phrases. Rather he sat quietly, saying little, his silent presence, indeed, the greatest comfort he could have given.

Now he took Hannah's hands in his. "The ways of God are mysterious, indeed," he said gently. "For some reason He has seen fit to put more burden on your shoulders than He does most. He must love you very much."

"It has been a long winter," she said quietly. "I'm so glad spring has come at last."

When Wardley looked totally confused, she did her best to explain. "It's just that it seems like so much bad has happened, it's easy to overlook that we've been deeply blessed, too. I try to think of the good, not just the bad, but it isn't always easy."

"Of course it isn't. You must have asked many times 'Why me?' Perhaps you're not meant to know. Not yet, anyway." He smiled at her in comradeship born of bitter trial. "I can only repeat what Will pointed out so forcibly once. And I quote: 'You're one hell of a lady, Hannah Clayton.' "

A few days after the Reverend's visit, Will was striding

down the back steps when Eve drove up. He hesitated, not wanting to make a scene, but refusing to turn tail and run either.

She saw him standing irresolute, and she paused, drawing her shawl more closely around her thickening figure before she climbed out of the buggy. "Will," she said briefly as she passed him on her way up the steps.

As she did so, something in him snapped. He was sick of all the dodging and discomfort and evasion. They would have to settle it eventually. Now was as good a time as any.

So deciding, he reached out a hand to stop her. She looked startled, for he had kept a strict distance from her ever since Christmas Day. Before she could question or draw back, he said firmly, "I want to talk to you."

He saw wariness flash in her eyes and smiled thinly. "Eve, we have to talk. I've got somethin' to say. I want you to listen, and then neither one of us ever has to bring it up again. Will you agree to that?"

"I ... guess so." Obviously, she wasn't overly enthusiastic about the idea.

"I've done a lot of thinkin' 'bout us." Leaning against the porch railing, he crossed his arms and stared past her. "When you told me it was over, I should of accepted your word f'r it. But my heart just couldn't let you go. Then after our talk at Christmas, I tried hatin' you. That didn't work, either." His voice softened. "I just couldn't hate you no matter how hard I tried."

He glanced at her, standing so stiffly, but she said nothing, just waited for him to go on. "F'rgettin' hasn't worked," he said briskly. "Hatin' hasn't, neither. You're a mighty persistent little critter."

"Will ..."

He plunged on, determined. "I don't want to spend the rest of my life avoidin' you whenever possible and bein' uncomfortable when it ain't possible. I don't think you want that, either. So I want to tell you, here and now, that it really is over. You'll always have a place in my heart. I can't deny that. But it's a happy place, not a hurtin' one. I hope someday you'll be able to feel the same 'bout me."

He uncrossed his arms and straightened away from the porch rail. "That's about it."

She studied his face a long moment, warily, as if judging whether he truly meant it. "Will," her relief was unmistakable, "thank you for telling me. I want us to be friends. I never meant to hurt you." She glanced at the kitchen door and smiled.

"I told you Christmas I hoped someday you could find the happiness that I have. I still hope that. With all my heart." She reached her hand to him. "Friends?"

He hesitated only a second before clasping her hand in a warm grip. "Friends," he agreed quietly. He watched her continue up the steps into the kitchen, stood a long moment looking at the closed door before he jammed his hands into his pockets and walked away from her ... forever.

Eighteen

Springtime came with warm breezes blowing and new life stirring, the promise of Nature's fulfillment on every side. Jeremy, thin and shaky, was out of bed now, allowed to sit on the back steps and soak up the day's healing sunshine. Was there any greater joy to be found this side of heaven?

Yet, even as he walked through these glorious days, Will knew a deepening unease. Here, centered in one space, was all the joy and contentment a man could possibly ask of life: four sons; a small daughter who could turn a man's heart to water with just one glance of her wide blue eyes; work so soul-satisfying he could conceive of no other; and the heart and center of all — a warm-hearted, generous woman who could make life what it was meant to be. No more coldness, no more heart-hurt, no more loneliness.

And he had no claim, none at all, to any of it.

Thou shalt betroth a wife,
and another man shall lie with her;
thou shalt build an house, and thou
shalt not dwell therein;

thou shalt plant a vineyard,
and shalt not gather the grapes thereof. ...

Thy sons and thy daughters shall be given
unto another people, and thine eyes shall
look, and fail with longing for them all
the day long; and there shall be no
might in thine hand. ...

"... no might in thine hand ..." he whispered. That was what cut the ground from under a man's feet, turning the warm green of springtime to ash-dust in his mouth. The seeds of discontent sowed so long ago while Luke was still a child, nurtured by all the helpless frustration of those who loved him, watered by the tears of mother and wife, had produced a bitter crop.

But only now was that crop truly being harvested, and the yield was a poisoned one, indeed. So many lives damaged, destroyed because of the one: Anne and Ben dead so untimely, so senselessly; Hannah and her five children forced to pay the price of Luke's folly; and Will, himself, who in picking up the pieces of his own life and the lives of Hannah and her children, had found in the fragments a more perfect whole than he had ever dreamed possible. Now, once more because of Luke, the whole would be shattered into pieces too tiny to ever be mended.

Why? Why should it be so? Why should Luke, the cause of so much suffering, escape with so little retribution? For if there was one thing certain in all this pain, it was that Luke — the careless, the wild, the thoughtless — was not aware, much less concerned with, the trail of wreckage he had left strewn behind.

Useless to argue that, had Luke not left, Will would never have been thrown in with Hannah, would never have come to know the joy of her love, the contentment of being part of a family. It was much too late for that. How had it happened? For sure the last thought in his mind that warm August evening had been a relationship between Hannah and himself. She had voiced his own feelings with total accuracy when she had called him a "hired hand" that first night. But Fate, cleverly weaving innocent circumstances into a sturdy net, had enmeshed them both.

What could — or should — either of them have done differently? Useless now to ask or even wonder. He didn't need Christmas Night to know her feelings were as his. A look, a word, a gesture — a thousand small truths she wasn't even aware of — spoke their own story. But it was a story that could have only one end. He had loved Eve, and lost her. Was he now to lose Hannah, too? *You can't lose something you never had*, he told himself bitterly. And knew it wasn't true.

But what was the answer? As long as Luke lived, Hannah would be tied by her marriage vows to him. And if he died? If he died, she would still be bound because, in all probability, she would never even find out.

Where was he? What was he doing? What were his feelings about the family he had left behind? Only to the last question could Will frame an undoubtedly accurate answer.

Just when the idea crept in, became part of his consciousness, he couldn't have said. Perhaps it had been deep within him all these last months and he only now dared acknowledge it. But the more he considered, now he had actually given words to it, the more it was the only answer.

He put it to Hannah that evening.

She had been setting pancake batter and had suggested he read aloud. When he didn't answer right away, she turned to see him sitting at the table watching her intently, but with something questioning, too.

"Will, what is it?"

He regarded her, still with that searching expression, then drew a deep breath. "Hannah." As always, when he needed words the most, they stuck in his throat. But he had to make her see.

She turned back to her batter. "Something's bothering you. You know I'll help if I can."

There was no way except to bring it out straight. "I've been doin' a lot of thinkin' 'bout us."

Her hands stilled over the bowl at that, but she said nothing, just waited for him to go on.

"Hannah, we both know how it is between us. There's things I want to say to you, but neither of us has the right. Either f'r me to put my feelin's into words or f'r you to listen."

She turned at that but still just stood silent.

"We got us a mighty peculiar situation here, you'll have to admit." His gesture took in the whole room. "We're a family — you and the young ones and me. We're a family. But no one else sees it that way — or ever will. That's not what I want. Do you understand what I'm sayin' — what I would say if I could?"

"Yes," she whispered, her eyes on his. Thus she made

her own declaration and suddenly there was no going back, ever. "It can never be any more than we have right now. And that's not what I want, either. But what are we going to do?" Only with great effort she kept her voice steady.

He studied his hands. "There's one thing I c'n do."

He heard her intake of breath and looked up. She wet her lips as though to speak, but the silence stretched between them. "You're going to find Luke," she said finally. It was statement, not question.

"Yes," he said, as simply. "I am goin' to find him. And I'm goin' to face him down." Suddenly all his anxious milling ceased. It had only needed to be put aloud into words, this one thing out of them all he could say to her.

She made no outcry, either of protest or of pleading, but she went as white as on the day of Jeremy's accident. He knew full-well the awful burden he was putting on her. That was why he had made it statement, not question. For how could he ever ask her to choose between him — and all the love he had to give her — and the life of the father of her children? For deepest instinct told him it could end no other way.

Much as he could, he had eased the pain of decision by taking the choice from her hands, putting it squarely on his own shoulders. It would be a personal thing between Luke and himself. Whatever the outcome, she need never feel guilt or shame. It was, right now, all he could give her of love.

She was gripping the handle of her stirring spoon so tightly her knuckles were white. "When will you go?"

He shifted in his chair and tried to make his voice casual. "As f'r that, I c'n hardly just go ridin' off like I hadn't a care in the world. But I don't feel it's anyone's business except ours. So, if it's all right with you, I'll discuss it with Jason. Just him, nobody else. He'll keep his mouth shut. As a matter of fact, I think I'll go put it to him now, while it's all fresh in my mind what I want to say."

He stood and reached for his hat when he wanted so much to reach for her, to feel the comfort of her in his arms. He turned at the door. "I'll be back quick as I c'n." He hurried out, leaving her standing. As his hoofbeats thrummed into silence, she moved around the table to the chair where he had been sitting and pressed her hands against the back as though it were Will himself she was touching. Slowly sinking down, she covered her face with her hands as though so doing could hide her terrible fear.

"Will, come on in. I've just been goin' over the books." Jason, surprised at his appearance this late hour, covered it well.

"I know it's late, but this ain't a social call. Evenin', Becky," Will added.

"Would you like some coffee?" When he refused, just stood, Becky gathered up her sewing. "Patience hasn't been feeling well. I'll go check on her." She laid her hand a moment on Jason's arm before she disappeared through a nearby doorway.

Jason poured himself a cup. "Sure you won't have one?"

"No, thanks. I want to talk to you. 'Bout Luke."

Jason jumped, sloshing coffee over the side of his cup. "Luke," his voice was peculiarly flat, "what 'bout him?"

"I'm goin' to find him."

Jason stared. "Just like that. You're goin' to find him. I was of the opinion he don't want to be found."

"I have to try," Will said grimly.

"You better sit, and tell me what's goin' on."

How to explain in a few simple words? "It's Hannah. And me. I want to marry her."

Jason strangled on his swig of coffee. "Marry her? Hannah? But ..."

"But she's already married. To Luke. If you call that a marriage. He ran off and left her, Jason. A low-down, mean trick if there ever was one. Is her whole life supposed to stop because he did that? One thing 'bout Luke, you c'n be sure his life hasn't stopped because of the little matter of a wife and five young ones."

Jason cut in. "I ain't arguin' the right or wrong of either of 'em, Will. I can't agree with you more that he did her dirt — did all of us — but that don't change the fact they are married, fair and legal. Which don't leave her much room to marry you."

"There'd be room if I found Luke," Will said quietly.

Jason's eyes narrowed. "Just what are you sayin'?"

"We don't even know whether he's alive or dead. Somebody could of stove his head in months ago, and how would we know? If anythin's sure, he's not carryin' a callin' card with his name and address."

"He might be dead, true. And he might be very much alive. What then? You bust his head in, you think Hannah'll be able to live with that?"

That flatly, Jason stated Will's worst fear, the one that

turned him sick. If it came down to it, what would — could — he do? He shoved back his chair and began to pace violently.

"I don't know."

The words hung in the air. "But I have to try. We can't go on like this."

Jason nodded, slowly. "He's my brother, but God help me, I can't blame you. Luke cut himself off from all of us the day he rode out of here. Maybe a lot longer ago than that. Maybe Hannah should of known better'n to get tied up with him. But God, she sure never deserved what he's dealt her." He eyed Will.

"You figure you and her could make a go of marryin', do you?"

"We do. If we could have the chance."

"Five young'ns. You'd be takin' on a ready-made family, f'r sure."

"I feel like they're my own already," Will said gruffly. "Fact is, they are — in my heart. Seems to me that's what counts, not just makin' 'em," he finished roughly.

"The one thing Luke did with any regularity," Jason agreed brusquely. "How you plannin' on goin' 'bout findin' him?"

"That note he left. Said he was trailin' after the gang that raided your folks. That'd be up near Red Canyon. Way I see it, Luke'd head that way just as a goal. Then after he got there, he wouldn't be in no hurry to leave. That'd take ambition, and Luke was hidin' behind the door when that got passed out."

Jason smiled sourly. "Not only behind the door. He was in the wrong room. What'll you do if you run across him?"

Will stopped pacing to face his friend squarely. "I don't

know. All I'm certain of is, one way or another, he's goin' to answer f'r what he's done."

Jason eyed him, knowing with deep sureness that he meant every word. "I'll help all I c'n. You'll need an excuse f'r leavin' since, I assume, you're not plannin' on announcin' this to the world?"

"We weren't. Just you, me and Hannah know."

"Best that way, near as I c'n see. I was figurin' on takin' a jaunt up north to look at a blooded bull I been hearin' 'bout. Busy as we are, I haven't felt right 'bout leavin' just now. But I would like someone with a good eye to give me his opinion on that bull, see if we ought to consider his like f'r our own herd. What do you say to your goin' and checkin' him out f'r me? Jared and Reuben could take over the heavy chores f'r Hannah while you're gone."

Will stared at Jason. "Be a shame not to take a look at him. I'll be glad to ride up there f'r you."

Jason clapped him on the shoulder. "Good. Prob'ly be best if you got an early start. You'll have a ways to go."

"You're prob'ly right. No tellin' how long the whole trip will take."

"Just check him out good. Don't decide nothin' hasty."

Will reached for his hat. "I'll sure use care. There's too much at stake not to."

Jason followed him out onto the porch. "Will."

When Will turned at the bottom of the steps, Jason continued gruffly. "I always thought Hannah was on the receivin' end of a pretty raw deal. Looks like now, maybe, she's got the chance f'r a good hand at last. She deserves it if anybody does. You take care she don't get cheated out of it. You hear?"

Will grinned. "I hear. Thanks, Jason."

Jason gave him a half salute and watched him ride off into the night, not knowing whether he would ever see him again.

Luke. Always Luke.

Will didn't go back to the house upon his return. He needed time to think, to plan his actions so he could tell them to Hannah with calm decisiveness. Even more so, now that he had declared himself to her, he was not at all sure he could face her with the impersonal ease of the last months. But it had to be that way, for both their sakes, until this trip and its unknown results were a thing of the past. They could not go back to their former casualness, but they must use care not to bring themselves greater future anguish. And he was not at all sure he was that strong.

Resentment had raised its wall between them, initially. After it had crumbled, a barrier compounded of Luke, Eve and mutual respect had kept them impersonal. In these latter months, a natural reticence because of her pregnancy had served its purpose. *Except for Christmas Night* ... but he twisted away from that thought and its still-accompanying pain.

Now there were no barriers, no walls, no reticence to keep them apart. Except what was within themselves. They were young, and warm-blooded, and they had found a love that could endure.

And after tonight they might never be together again.

Will flung to his feet, so torn he was scarcely aware of what he was doing. He jerked the bunkhouse door open.

With clouds blanketing the stars and quarter moon, the world was dark, except for Hannah's lamp glowing warm in the kitchen window. He stared at the yellow square. A long time he stood in the doorway, hands jammed into his pockets, and watched that rich gleam. Finally, slowly, he stepped back inside and shut the door.

Lighting his lamp with an unsteady hand, he searched for pen and paper. He found a pen and ink on a shelf, but the only paper he could come up with was that in which Hannah had wrapped his shirt at Christmas. He tore off a sizable piece and sat down at the table.

Dear Hannah,

Talked to Jason tonight, and he wants me to ride up north to check out a blooded bull, to see if we should consider one like him for our own herd.

I decided I better get an early start — it'll be a long ride. Anything comes up while I'm gone, just let Jason know. He'll send Jared and Reuben over to help with the heavy chores, so don't you go trying to do them all yourself, hear? I don't know when I'll be back, but just as soon as I can, I promise. In the meantime, chin up.

Until I can be with you again,
Will

He stared at what he had written, knew it said nothing of what he really wanted to tell her. Would she understand? She was Hannah, and he felt reassured.

Folding the note, he jammed a few necessities into his

warbag. Picking up his Colt, he regarded it a long moment before he buckled it on. As he left the bunkhouse, for the first time the total enormity of his intentions hit him like a sledgehammer. He tightened his jaw. He would do what he must — take the consequences and let God judge the rest.

As he stepped quietly into the silent kitchen, however, some of his iron resolve melted. How long, if ever, before he would once more stand in this small room that contained all of home a man could ask?

Turning the lamp low, he stood a long time absorbing the warmth and goodness of the room. Hannah's chair where she had sat so many evenings these last months, reading or sewing. Her knitting lay neatly on the table beside her chair, the box he had carved positioned carefully to the side. The corner where the Christmas tree they had decorated together had stood. The romps with the boys and the high, childish laughter that seemed to linger. The pain of that darker hour when he had, all unwittingly, walked in on her bath. Christmas Night when, with a few words, she had showed him what it is to truly love and to give ...

Compelled by a need he couldn't put into words, he crossed to the boys' doorway and pushed the panel open. Shielding the lamp with his hand, he paused beside the beds, gazing at each sleeping face: Jeremy, still pale but rapidly returning to health, a good, decent boy — Hannah's son through and through; Isaac, arms and legs sprawled, restless even in sleep — Luke's son to be sure, but Hannah's, too; Sam and Micah, small boys growing so fast. What would their futures be? And would he, Will, have a part in shaping them? *In my heart, always, no matter what* ... He wished he could see

Phebe — his "little lady" — but knew the thought was futile.

He set the lamp on the kitchen table, propping the note against it where Hannah would be sure to see it. As he was bending to blow out the light, her bedroom door flew open. She stood framed in the lamp glow, staring at him bewildered. She had pulled a shawl around her, but her black hair, loosed from its customary knot at the nape of her neck, flowed over her shoulders in gleaming contrast to the white of her nightgown. In that first, startled glance, he saw her bare toes sticking out below the ruffled hem.

"Will! I was waiting. You didn't come ..." She caught sight of the paper propped against the lamp, and her words trailed off. She stared from it to him, unbelieving. As one caught in a nightmare she walked slowly forward, reached to take it.

"Hannah, I ..." But words failed him, too, at the utter pain on her face as she read. When she raised her head, the look of betrayal in her eyes seared him.

"Hannah ..."

She was shaking her head from side to side like some hurt animal. "You were going to leave a note and just ride off in the middle of the night. Like Luke ..." It was a cry of anguish.

"No!" he said fiercely. "No! Not like Luke!" One long step and he seized her by the shoulders, pulling her roughly against him. He felt the wild beating of her heart against his.

His desire for her, too-long denied, seemed all but consuming him. She, glorifying in the solid, unyielding strength of the chest against which she had laid her head those brief, blissful times of his comforting her during these past months — perception rushed through her in one blinding ache of longing, of knowing how it could be.

Suddenly all her resistance collapsed, and as on Christmas Night, she clung to him while he held her as if never to let go. They could have their forever on this one night because this night might be the only forever they would be given.

Nothing to stop them except what was good and decent within themselves.

Finally, slowly, he released her. Drawing a long, shuddering breath, he looked deep into her eyes. The hurt was gone. In its place was joyous wonder.

Just before she buried her face against his shoulder, he heard, "No, not like Luke. Never!"

He pressed his cheek to her hair, gently stroked the gleaming black waves while with his other arm he continued to hold her tightly. "Hannah," he murmured, finally. "I never meant it that way, I swear to God. I never even thought ..."

She raised her head. "I know, but just for a second it all came back. It was happening all over again. And it hurt so."

Her words choked off as once more he held her fiercely. "I'd never in this world hurt you deliberately. You have to know that! Don't even think such a thing, ever again. You hear me?"

She nestled her head against his shoulder with a little sigh of contentment that told of trust so complete he had to swallow hard before he dared speak. "That's better," he said sternly.

Finally, reluctantly, he put her from him. "I got to get goin'."

"Are you hungry?" she asked suddenly.

"As a woodpecker with a busted beak," he confessed. "I didn't eat all that much supper."

"Well, good heavens! Get the fire going. I'll see what I can whip up."

Louise Lenahan Wallace

What she "whipped up" was coffee, sausage and eggs, and a mountain of hotcakes so high the stack quivered. But he came remarkably close to demolishing it. While he was thus occupied, she busied herself packing a bundle for him to take.

When he finally pushed back his plate, she laid the bag beside it. He looked at it questioningly and she said casually, "Just coffee and bread, and some cookies and such."

"But Hannah, I'm so stuffed I couldn't eat another bite!"

She stared at him in amazement. "Not now! To take with you." Only when she saw his broad grin she realized he had been joking. "You ..." But she couldn't help smiling her pleasure at his teasing, even if it was at her expense. It was so good to share a joke, to know she wouldn't be ridiculed.

Thus, they were both smiling when he stood, and the scraping back of his chair was like a bitter wind rustling through the warmth of that room.

He saw her eyes darken and said quickly, "I already looked in on the boys. But I'd sure like to see Phebe f'r just a second, if you don't mind."

In answer, she lifted the lamp, leading the way into the bedroom. He knelt beside the cradle and reached a big hand to ever so gently cup the fuzzy red-gold curls. He silently touched the tiny fist tucked under tiny chin. Rising abruptly, he muttered, "Don't want to wake her," and backed hurriedly out to the kitchen.

Picking up the sack of food and his hat, he said as matter-of-factly as he could, "You take care, Hannah. Get Jason if anythin' comes up. And I don't want you doin' any heavy chores. Tell the boys goodbye f'r me," he dug into his pocket, "and give this to Isaac to keep f'r me till I get back.

Tell him I expect him to take good care of it."

He opened his fist over her hand to lay his battered pocketknife on her palm. "Tell him my Pa gave it to me and it's mighty important to me. Maybe that'll help convince him I'm not runnin' out on him after he's finally decided to trust me."

She just looked up at him, wordlessly.

"Hannah." He put his free arm around her, pulling her tight against him. He kissed her, and it was a kiss for all the yesterdays they had shared, for all the tomorrows they could not share — a kiss to bind them into eternity.

Then she was reaching up to press her hand against his cheek and saying softly, "God go with you. Come back safe to us." Putting, at last, her heart into words.

He touched her hair, one last gesture, and putting her from him, strode into the night.

Nineteen

After Eagle's hoofbeats had died away, Hannah stood long at the west window, staring into the yard now patchwork-patterned in starlight and shadow. Fear clutched at her heart and choked her throat. She had never before known such anguish. *Will ... if he shouldn't come back ...*

But she didn't dare think that way of what he was doing and why. To put it into words, even in her own heart, was to give complete sway to the terror already all but consuming her.

"Luke ..." His name in her mouth brought a bitter taste. *Why?* she cried in silent torment. *Luke — why?*

Her thoughts slipped back to that night in late May when Luke, without telling her, had ridden off to town. He had returned very late and very drunk and flat broke. Hearing from the bedroom his shambling entrance into the kitchen, she had gone out to try to get him to bed before he could wake the boys with his thumping and cursing.

As she paused in the doorway, clutching her shawl over her nightgown, her hair in its thick braid over her shoulder, his eyes had fallen on her. "Han-nuh." He stumbled, striking his hip against the sharp corner of the table. Loosing another curse, he had peered at her through eyes that refused to focus.

She saw, then, that he was in much worse shape than he had been any of the other times, and she felt a stab of fear. Hiding it as best she could, she said steadily, "There's coffee on. I'll get you a cup."

"No." His head swung from side to side like an irritated buffalo's. "Don't need no cof-fee."

She made no answer, and irritation had become swift anger. "Don' look at me accusin' like that! I ain't drunk. Leastways not's drunk as I'd like t' be."

Still she had made no answer, and he roared, "I said don' look a' me like that!"

Then she moved. "The boys ..."

"The boys be damned! I'm sick o' always bein' quiet 'cause I 'might wake the boys,' " he mimicked sarcastically. "Mebbe they should see me ... see wha' happens to a man when his ... lovin' wife holds 'im back from doin' anythin' tha' makes him feel ... like a man. Well, you ain' goin' t'hold me back ... tonight!"

He lunged toward her and she tried to dodge, but the wall behind and the rocker to the side trapped her. He grabbed her arm in a savage grip, twisting her around to face him.

"Don' try t' get away from me!"

The total fury on his face chilled her, and she tried to draw back, but his grip tightened so that she cried out in pain in spite of herself. "Luke, you're hurting me!"

"I tol' you not to do that," he gritted. "Suppos'd to obey me — my ever-lovin' wife. Wife. Hell!" He spat past her so that, involuntarily, she dodged again. And again he jerked her back to him.

"Luke, no ..." She struggled wildly, futilely in his iron grip.

He had laughed cruelly. "At least you're showin' a little life. Tha's more'n you ... done f'r a long time!"

As his slobbering mouth and his stinking breath and his muttered obscenities engulfed her, she had drawn upon her only defense, shrunk into herself, lying totally motionless, willing her mind to believe that what was happening was to a body other than her own.

She marveled now that something so sweet as Phebe could come out of such a loathsome moment.

By the night of the raid on Ben and Anne she had begun to suspect that she was once again pregnant. By the time of Matt and Eve's wedding she had been certain. But remembering Luke's furious denunciation of Micah, his scathing insistence she was trying to keep him from getting anywhere by tying him down with a "bunch of snotty-nosed brats," she had hid her bitter knowledge and her morning sickness from him.

It hadn't been difficult.

Then she had awakened on Eve and Matt's marriage morning to find Luke gone and only that note to let her know it was all her fault and none his. Without choice, she had taken her sons and gone to the wedding, holding her head high through it all.

But all her bitter humiliation and the explanations she had had to make had drained something — some sense of decency, of self-respect — from her soul, so that, Christmas Night, she had had to overcome her instinctive terror, remembering how it had been with Luke. But, faced with Will's greater anguish, her own fear had been of strangely little importance. Even his refusal of her had been reassuring, in its own way. She remembered her words spoken such a short while ago in this room: "No, not like Luke. Never!" And knew them for truth, forever.

" 'Cowards die many times before their deaths; the valiant never taste of death but once.' " The words as Will had read them aloud one night echoed eerily in that silent room and Hannah remembered thinking, even then, *How unaware he is he has just described himself and Luke*. Suddenly all her hard-bought strength drained away and she leaned forward, bowing her head against the night-cold window. She clenched her fists against the glass in silent despair and felt a hard lump in her right hand.

She opened her palm — to Will's pocketknife. She had totally forgotten it these last minutes, and she stared, dazed. " 'To keep f'r me till I get back.' "

He will come back! He will. How could she ever convince Isaac if she didn't believe it herself, with all her heart? Total trust ... Did she really place so little value on all he had given her of love these past months? Shame flooded her.

Slowly, slowly she drew a deep breath. Her chin lifted, perceptibly.

As happens with most worry, Will's fretting over Isaac proved groundless. When the boys came bouncing out of their bedroom, eager for breakfast, it was Jeremy who asked where Will was.

Bracing herself, she explained casually that he had to go on a trip up north.

"I hope he comes back by tonight," Isaac said. "We're goin' to have a wrestlin' contest!" The little boy, once so aloof, was now a devoted participant of these evening romps. "He's goin' to show us how to arm wrestle!"

Hannah drew a deep breath and put her hand on Isaac's shoulder. "He won't be back by tonight. His trip will take longer than that."

Her heart sank as the bright eagerness faded from the small face. "But he promised!"

"Son, this is something he couldn't help. He had to go. But he'll be back just as soon as he can, and then I'm sure he'll wrestle with you." Isaac turned slowly away, shoulders drooping. "I want you to listen to me and try to understand." She reached out, turning him gently but firmly, and the look on his face pierced her heart. But she said steadily, "Isaac, Mr. Braden has never lied to you, has he?" A reluctant shake of the head. "And I've never lied to you, either, have I?" Again the slow denial.

She knelt to his level and gazed into the unhappy eyes. "I'm not lying to you now, either," she said clearly. "Mr. Braden will do his very best to come back as soon as he can. He couldn't promise more than that, just that he'd try. Do you understand?"

Slowly he nodded, his eyes so sad that her heart ached for him. She wanted to hug him but knew that if she became anything other than matter-of-fact, she would break down. So she smiled and brushed a lock of flame-bright, unruly hair back from his forehead.

"He did leave something for you, though." Reaching into her apron pocket, she drew out the knife. "He wanted you to keep this until he gets back." She clasped the knife in her own fingers for another precious moment before she laid it gently on the boy's palm. "Do you think you can do that for him?"

Isaac stared in awe at the battered object.

"His Pa gave it to him when he was about your size and it's very important to him. Do you think you can keep it carefully, not lose it?"

He raised shining eyes to hers, all disappointment gone. "I sure c'n, Ma!"

"Now part of having it means being very careful. It'll cut you, same as any other knife, if you get careless."

"I'll take care, Ma. I promise!"

"Into your pocket with it, then, and get washed for breakfast."

With an ear-stretching grin, he scurried off.

Only then did she see Jeremy, head drooping, start to trail after him.

"Jeremy."

He turned, eyes on the floor. "Yes, Ma?"

"Do you understand why he gave Isaac the knife instead of you?" Still kneeling, she was at his level as he shook his head dejectedly.

"He gave it to Isaac because he thought Isaac needed something to be able to hold on to, to be able to see to remind him that he, Mr. Braden, will do his best to come back just as soon as possible.

"But you, son, he thought you're old enough to understand that he'll do his best, that you wouldn't need something — like a knife — to know that." She put her hand under his chin to tilt the small face up. "It means he's treating you like a grown-up and trusting you to act like one. That's something very special, son. More special, really, than a knife."

His eyes were wide and serious. "Did he give you somethin' to keep, Ma?"

Remembering the tenderness of Will's final kiss, the strength of his arms holding her, she had to swallow hard. "No, son, only his promise he'd do his best to come back soon, same as he gave you."

Silently, gravely, Jeremy studied her face. Finally, "I hope he comes back real quick, don't you?"

All her iron resolve melted, and she couldn't answer.

Suddenly Jeremy flung his arms about her neck in a strangling hug. "Don't worry, Ma. I'll take care of you till he comes back, I promise!"

"Oh, Jeremy." She blinked hard. "I know you will, son." She hugged him to her a moment more, drew a deep breath, and stood him back. She cupped his cheek for just a second with her hand and smiled. "Now you better get washed up for breakfast before the other fellows eat it all!" She gave him a gentle swat on his backside. He scampered, giggling, to the washbasin.

During the next days, Hannah was kept so busy she had no time to sit and brood. Chores around the ranch — for Jared and Reuben couldn't be there to do everything — in addition to her regular duties of laundry, cooking and cleaning, and all the other tasks necessary to caring for five small children would not wait while she sat with hands folded, fretting.

But every waking moment of each hour, her heart cried out to Will. Each breath she drew was a prayer for his safety. Any unexpected sound from outside took her, trembling, to the door. Each horse and buggy driven by friends stopping to visit was the potential bearer of the news that would be her own death knell.

In the darkest night hours, lying wide-eyed, she remembered how it had been these last precious months. With deepest gratitude she thanked God for sending Will to her so that, for a short space of time they had had so much. Because she always circled back to her final, inescapable truth: One man had given love, but one had given life. One would live and one die. It could end no other way.

And yet — she knew. Even if Luke should survive and Will die, her heart would ever belong to Will, whether in this life or in eternity. Nothing, certainly not Luke's physical presence would — or could — ever change that. But, in the next moment, tears streaming down her cheeks, she pleaded frantically with God not to let that be all they should ever have.

So the long days and the longer nights passed in work and worry, and bitter fear and bargaining, and deepest prayer and pleading. The lilac — always before its message had sustained her in her most despairing times. But never, even in her most desperate moments with Luke had she known darkness such as this.

Because, in spite of everything, Luke was still the father of her children — a fact hard dismissed. But Will — Will was her love.

On a soft, blue-and-green morning a few days after Will's departure, Hannah, drying the breakfast dishes, heard a buggy stop outside. Through the curtain she saw Becky step to the ground and turn to lift Patience down.

Plate and towel still in hand, Hannah hurried to the door. "Becky, come on in!" Her heart caught at sight of the solemn expression on her sister-in-law's face. "There's not trouble?" She clutched the plate.

"No," Becky said quickly, reassuringly. She tried to laugh. "I know this is a terrible hour to come, but I do so want to talk to you."

Hannah gave Patience a warm hug. "Honey, the boys are playing with their wagon. Why don't you go join them?"

The little girl looked dubious, but her mother motioned her to obey. "Yes, ma'am. I sure hope they don't scalp me this time!" She trudged down the steps and around the corner of the house.

The two women exchanged what-will-they-think-of-next expressions that quickly sobered. Hannah led the way into the kitchen. "Have a seat, Becky. If you don't mind, I'll just finish up these dishes."

Becky picked up a towel. "Let me help. I always talk better when I'm busy." At Hannah's questioning look she tried to laugh. "I guess I'm being a nosy sister-in-law again, but I just can't help it."

"What is it?" In spite of herself, Hannah's voice sharpened with fear. *Will* ...

"Don't look like that!" Becky blurted. "I just wanted to talk to you about what's going on. With Will."

"Have you heard anything?"

"No, nothing. That's what I mean. Something's going on but Jason flat-out refuses to tell me what. It's not like him to keep things from me. I've tried not to pry, but I can tell he's really worried about something. And it's been since Will came by the other night, late. The next morning Jason said Will was going up north.

" 'To look at a blooded bull,' he said. But leaving you like this — and with spring roundup coming on? Hannah, what's happening? You haven't slept for a week from the look of you. Jason's grouchy as a bear with a sore paw. I don't want to interfere, but I do want to help, if I can." Her voice choked off.

"Jason didn't tell you anything?"

Becky pressed her hand to her mouth and shook her head.

"We didn't mean for you not to know! When we said just Jason, Will and me, we didn't mean Jason wasn't to tell you. "I'm so sorry! I never thought ..."

"What is it, Hannah?"

"Will's gone to find Luke."

Becky dropped the pan lid she was drying, the crash of it ringing through the room as she stared, speechless for once.

"We want to be married," Hannah said softly, "but we can't as long as Luke ..." It was her turn to stumble to a halt.

"You and Will married? Hannah, that's wonderful!" Becky burst out, stopped, stricken.

Hannah saw her dismay and the light faded from her own eyes. "But we can't until we know — about Luke. Whether he's ... " She swallowed. "So Will's gone to find out, one way or the other." She suddenly cried, "Becky, I'm so scared!"

Thrusting the towel aside, Becky moved to comfort her as best she could. Finally, sitting at the table, Hannah explained haltingly how it had all come about and her terrible fear for what might be the consequences.

Becky listened, saying little — which was just short of heroic for her — until Hannah had talked herself out, the best thing either of them could have done.

There was so pitifully little Becky could say in the way of solace, but her warm understanding served better than a dictionary full of words.

When at last she rose to leave, she said quietly, "I told you before, I thought he was special. I pray with all my heart it does work out for you."

Hannah hugged her in wordless gratitude.

On Sunday morning Hannah hitched up the wagon. Settling Sam and Micah in back with a word of caution to Isaac to watch them, she put Phebe's basket on the floor up front, with Jeremy on the high seat to keep an eye on her. Climbing up beside her oldest son, she shook out the lines. She had taken extra care to ensure that the children were scrubbed and shining — she could only pray they would stay that way until after church.

She had also taken special pains with her own preparations, although it was hard to put into words that the reason was any other than to look nice for Sunday services. Standing in front of her mirror that morning, she had eyed the lines of the plain, dark gray dress and the contrasting white of her scared face. She had stared at that — to her, dismal — reflection and something stirred deep within her. Reaching to put on her bonnet, her hands hovered.

Face drained of color except for green eyes wide from misery. Black hair pulled into customary severe knot at the nape of her neck. She stared. White face, black hair, green eyes stared back. Prim. Proper. And woebegone. The image her mirror had given so many times that she had stopped seeing it — When? She couldn't answer.

The beginnings of disgust had stirred again, stronger. In sudden decision she had dropped the bonnet and reached to the coil of hair at her neck.

Now, high up on the wagon seat, she glanced at her — for the moment — neatly dressed children, and her hand lifted, self-consciously, to touch the braids wound about her head. Even though her bonnet covered them most decorously, she felt an uplifting of her spirits, a surge of confidence she badly needed.

Strange how something so simple as a hair-style change could alter one's outlook. But was it really so odd? For the first time she put into words the depths to which she had changed. She was not the innocent young girl Luke had married. Neither was she the embittered wife he had walked out on. Nor yet was she the anguished woman Will had bid goodbye to that dark night. She was none of them — yet she was all. How could that be?

Whatever she now was, whatever all the past harshness had molded her into, she could only pray that it was to the good, for there was no going back, ever.

She knew it was taking all her courage to make this trip,

to face her neighbors and friends as casually as though the world weren't shivering on its foundations. She reminded herself sternly that only she, Jason and Becky, and Will knew the truth. However, remembering the past months, it was soul-shriveling to even think of facing the town again.

But out of these changes, out of the person she had become and the one she hoped to be, she knew she must. How could she fear something so simple as facing a few questioning glances when Will was gambling his very life for their love? He was willing to risk everything for her; this gesture, however small, was at least something she could do in return.

She pulled up in front of the church, and carrying Phebe, Isaac in charge of Sam and Jeremy holding Micah's hand, she ushered her brood up the steps. But the only pew with enough room was up near the front. So, drawing on all her courage, she shepherded the children up the aisle, keeping her eyes on the goal of empty space. Not until they were seated and she had assured herself the boys would behave, did she look up. She almost choked.

Pearl Gilby, with Mabel alongside, was sitting directly in front of her. Hannah stared, dismayed. *Of all the seats in the church she could have picked!* Suddenly she felt a hysterical impulse to laugh. Her entrance, with the five children, had not been exactly noiseless. As they had proceeded up the aisle, heads had turned — most smiling in welcome, a few curious.

She realized now that neither Pearl nor Mabel had turned and that the back of Pearl's neck was beet red. Abruptly, all Hannah's fears of this day fled. She knew, with sweet sureness, that she had triumphed.

> *... he will not be slack*
> *to him that hateth him,*
> *he will repay him to his face ...*

As Reverend Wardley announced from the pulpit that the opening hymn would be *Amazing Grace*, Hannah caught Jason's and Becky's smiles from across the way as if they understood her victory.

> *Amazing Grace, how sweet the sound*
> *that saved a wretch like me.*

> *I once was lost but now am found,*
> *was blind but now I see.*

> *'Tis Grace has brought me safe thus far*
> *and Grace will lead me home.*

At the close of services, Reverend Wardley stood beside his pulpit once more. "Some of our congregation could not be with us today. Homer York, who fell from his barn loft and broke his leg this last Friday — our sympathy to you, Homer; Lettie Kilian, who, just this morning gave birth to a beautiful baby girl — congratulations, Lettie and Evan; and Will Braden, who was called on business up north — may you have a safe trip, Will."

Hannah started and he smiled her way. "Let us offer our prayers for all of them that they may soon rejoin our services."

Hannah glanced over at Becky and Jason and saw they

were as surprised as she. She could do nothing except hold her head up during the singing of the final hymn, but as she made her slow way with the children back down the aisle, she realized what Reverend Wardley had really done.

He had brought Will's absence into the open, giving it church approval, thereby cutting off at bedrock any possibility of reverberations. Apparently, however, no one intended to make any, certainly not Pearl or Mabel, who stamped out of the church past Hannah without a word or look. Pearl's face was the approximate shade of a ripe plum, and Mabel's color was not far behind.

"Hannah, I do so hope Will is able to complete his business soon — and successfully."

Turning to the voice at her elbow, she searched Reverend Wardley's eyes. How much did he know — or guess? "Thank you, Reverend. I hope so, too."

His gaze was very direct as he patted her arm. "God, and our prayers, go with him — and with you, too, Hannah."

"Thank you." He turned to speak to Jason. He knew. She was sure of it. Somehow, he knew where Will had gone, and why. But he could not tell her what, at this moment, she so ached to know.

Where are you now, Will? What's happening to you?

Twenty

Aside from heading the general direction reason told him Luke had gone, Will made no other plan except to act just as footloose and irresponsible as he was certain the other man had, and see where it led.

According to the note Luke left Hannah the night he took off, he had intended to find the men responsible for the night raid on the Arrow A — that raid leading to the deaths of Anne and Ben Clayton. The meager clues they gathered after the murders all pointed to the probability that the raiders had come from the Red Canyon area in the northern part of the Territory, countryside as lawless as it was rugged. Red Canyon itself had become a refuge for such outcasts because it was a natural stronghold, easily guarded by a few determined gunmen. Thus Will angled north and west.

A number of towns and ranches dotted the Laramie Plains, but common sense said Luke would get farther afield from home and family. If he were to slip successfully into anonymity he must be a safe distance away. So after only casual inquiry, Will pushed on.

As he drifted northward, the character of the countryside

changed: The heavily timbered Medicine Bow Range
loomed to the west and the Black Hills to the east — the local
sources of railroad ties, telegraph, corral and fence poles. He
passed the deposit owned by the Wyoming Marble Company,
said to be 80 feet wide, traced for 10 miles on its surface and
prospected to a depth of 100 feet without reaching bottom.
Farther along, there was a vast wasteland, rough and broken,
with rocks, hills and mountains on either side — so different
from the grassy plains he was accustomed to. His cattleman's
eye noted thinning of the grass except along creeks and
streams. Sagebrush and greasewood edged in; the country
became more rolling.

He splashed through, left behind the Little Laramie
River, Rock Creek, the Medicine Bow.

He passed the all-but-obliterated remains of old Fort
Casper. The garrison, named for a young cavalryman killed
in an Indian skirmish, had been burned to the ground after
the Army abandoned it.

Now towns and ranches thinned out, even as the grass
had thinned out earlier. But as he had been doing all these
travel-tedious days, every place Will encountered, by accident or by previous information, every face he chanced upon
he put his questions: Had anyone seen a tall man? Fiery red
hair, blazing beard. Hang-dog look.

No.

He found, unfortunately, that some generous souls, not
possessing the facts he wanted, obliged by making them up.
One lead he had, of a man fitting Luke's description "like a
reflection in glass," sent him on a three-day chase through
rocky, water-scarce country, only to find his quarry following

a plow while house, outbuildings, wife and brood of skinny youngsters gave ample evidence the fellow had been in this area considerably longer than Luke had been missing.

That was the devil of it. He had to follow every lead, no matter how slight or far-fetched — or how far it took him out of his way. Because just as sure as snakes slithered, some path, sometime, would take him to Luke. There was no guarantee at all that it wouldn't be the least likely, most totally unexpected one.

Thus, by discouraging, disappointing degrees, he came at last to Red Canyon.

Four small towns dotted this region within a radius of approximately a hundred miles. Instinct told him he would either find Luke in one of these towns or he wouldn't find him at all. He would have to be systematic, he realized — go from one to the next until he had covered them all.

He quickly learned, however, that besides being systematic, he had to be just plain careful. A lawless element ruled up here away from the restraints of more civilized ideals, and he fast found that asking questions of the wrong man — any man for that matter — could bring trouble down on his own head. Lawless as the place might seem to an outsider, a peculiar code of honor existed among its population, and they viewed with deepest suspicion the stranger asking questions about another man. He speedily adopted a tough attitude and learned, if necessary, to back words with fists.

He had always considered he knew himself fairly well. With shock he learned how easily he discarded the veneer of civilization to become as those around him. At times, in near panic, he wondered whether, when it was over, he would be able to return to being that other self with whom he had lived for nearly 27 years and who now seemed the most remote of strangers.

If he could so simply slip into a way of living he had never before even considered, how much easier it must have been for Luke, so careless about responsibilities — about life itself. Only two things kept him from losing all touch with that former Will. One was Hannah, his remembrance of her goodness and trust and warmth. The other, curiously enough, was Phebe. Phebe as he had last seen her in her cradle — hand tucked under chin, deep in the sleep of the totally innocent. Hannah's love and Phebe's innocence! Two realities he could keep in front of him in a world rapidly becoming unreal.

A thousand variations of the same question — a thousand answers that all boiled down to one dead end: No one had seen a tall man with carroty-colored hair and a curly beard. But in return Will had to fend off — without seeming to — questions concerning his interest in this other man. When put to it, he answered that he had a message to deliver — a personal one. He figured if word got back to Luke, it'd make him curious without alarming him to the point where he'd skip the country. If a description of Will accompanied the message, well, he wasn't overly worried about that either. How could Luke recognize him by word of mouth when he no longer even recognized himself when he looked directly into a mirror?

Days and nights slipped behind him with each passing town. He lost track of time, knowing only that it was running out. If he didn't find Luke soon ...

He rode into Sunset late one afternoon. Preoccupied as he was, he still felt a sting of curiosity about the individual who had christened it. Some homesick miner with unsuspected poetry in his soul, riding in at dusk and glimpsing the splashes of crimson and gold that even now were staining the rocky, mine-scarred slopes? Or a woman fresh from the East, trying to give the stark and unfamiliar a touch of home and beauty?

He guided Eagle up the town's main street into the bustling activity of freighters cursing their mule teams and miners returning from the hills, eager to spend their day's hard-earned pokes in one of the several saloons beginning to show lighted windows. No one paid him the slightest attention as he halted Eagle in front of the livery stable. A blocky man with the muscles of a blacksmith and eyes the color of the Emerald Isle took charge of the chestnut, promising to give him an extra measure of grain.

Will strode along the boardwalk, aware of the pulsing activity around him, but mostly just letting it wash over him without conscious thought. Pushing open the door to the sheriff's office, he blinked in the cool dimness before catching sight of the man just bending to put a match to the lamp on a battered, paper-crowded desk. Smoking matchstick falling from his fingers, in the same motion the fellow whirled, hand dropping to the Remington at his hip.

Will raised his hands carefully away from his own holstered Colt. "Easy, mister. I don't want no trouble. I've just come f'r some information."

Hand still on gun butt, the man studied him warily. "What information?"

In the lamplight, Will took in the eyes sunken with weariness, the general unkempt appearance — and the star twinkling on the rumpled vest. He also noted, in spite of the obvious exhaustion, a determined steeliness in the lawman's eyes. Will opened his mouth with the intention of delivering the same evasive speech he had prattled in each of the three previous towns. What he heard himself saying was, "I'm Will Braden, from down Laramie way. I've come lookin' f'r a man, name of Luke Clayton. It's possible he's in your town." Will had no time, then, to wonder why he had blurted those words after all his personal sermonizing on caution.

The sheriff, hand still hovering near his gun, with unconcealed bluntness studied him from the crown of his dusty hat to the toes of his battered boots. "Any reason I should believe you?" He asked without hostility, but with an unnerving directness.

"Not one that I c'n think of," Will returned, "except that it's the truth."

The lawman's gaze swept him once more, hat to boots, then, reaching his decision, he nodded slightly and stuck out his hand. "Jesse Wolcott, sheriff of this garden-spot of beauty." The glint in his eye became, for just an instant of time, a gleam that could have been a twinkle. Will shook the outstretched hand and Wolcott turned to the stove. "Coffee?" He poured two cups, handing one to Will. "Spoon always stands up in it this time of day, but it keeps me goin'." He gestured to a chair and settled heavily into his own.

Will took a taste of the coffee that was everything the lawman had promised. "Why do you do it, Sheriff?"

Wolcott took a sip of his own brew, shuddered, and ran his hands through his already disheveled hair. Straightening, he eyed Will squarely. "It's my town," he said with such quiet finality that no further question was possible or necessary.

Will thought of the lawmen he had known through the years, good, dedicated men for the most part, working for scanty wages to bring decency and civilization to townspeople who showed little appreciation for the effort made, but who were quick to complain loudly if successful results were not swiftly achieved. Lawmen such as the one before him, who too often ended up in an early grave. And who was there who would remember them?

Will took a deep breath. "Like I said, I'm lookin' f'r Luke Clayton. Stands tall as me, has red hair and a curly beard."

Wolcott studied him. "Why you lookin' f'r him?"

As briefly as he could, Will explained about the raid on Anne and Ben, and Luke's hasty departure. He saw no need to explain about Hannah and himself, although he suspected the weary lawman before him would sympathize, especially if he knew Luke. "He left a lot of unfinished business behind him — a wife and five young ones, f'r starters. They can't get on with their lives until they know what he's doin' with his." The sheriff said nothing, but eyed Will with a sudden keenness that made Will shift his feet in spite of himself. "The rest of his family — his brother and sister — they're left wonderin', too," he added doggedly.

"And you — not even a member of the family — got elected to chase all the way up here after him? Why didn't one of them come?" The question was not abrupt, but it was direct.

Once more in his life, Will found himself struggling to put elusive emotion into common words. "Ben and Anne — their family — they're all as close to me as my own folks."

And then he found the words. "What Luke did to them, he did to me," he said simply.

The sheriff pondered. The silence stretched. Will became aware of a clock ticking somewhere behind him.

"What will you do if you find him?" Wolcott asked finally.

Will stared at him as Jason's words came back, mocking him eerily. *Seems to me Luke don't want to be found.* Only memory of Hannah, smiling up at that other Will in that other world, gave him the strength to answer the sheriff honestly, as he had answered Jason. "I don't know. I just know I have to find him. Then I'll take it from there. Try to get him to go home, I guess," he finished heavily, and wondered whether, if the time came, he could actually carry out such a noble plan.

Wolcott picked up a pencil and began twiddling it between his fingers. "I have trouble a plenty in my town," he finally said slowly. "I sure don't need to go diggin' up more. Or have other folks dig it f'r me." He sighed. "This 'Luke' character. You say he has red hair and a curly beard?"

Will tensed. "You know him? He's here?"

The sheriff shook his head. "Might not be the same. Fella come to town last fall. Tall as you. Red hair. No beard. Mouthy cuss. His favorite brag seemed to be that he was 'second to no man.' "

"Is he in town now?" Will asked with deadly quiet.

"He got himself a job at Dill Blaine's livery. Doin' up the horses. Didn't look like he'd be much of a one f'r the short haul, let alone the long one, and Dill wasn't real enthusiastic, but he kept insistin' he knew horses. Wouldn't give up till Dill took him on, mostly with the thought of firin' him as soon as he could. Surprised the spit out of Dill, I'll tell you. Dill says he knows horses like most men only wish they did. The only brag I know of that he's made good on. But Dill says it's worth it to keep him on. He sleeps in the loft when he ain't pesterin' 'em over at the Gold Nugget. You might say takin' care of horses is his moonlightin' job. Drinkin' and poker appear to be his real callin'," he said dryly.

Will leaned forward. "Sure sounds like him, even without the beard. Luke could charm a horse into a tree if he took a mind to." Everything in him was yelling to hurry, but the sheriff was hesitating perceptibly. "Might as well tell me the rest. What's he done? Rearranged someone's teeth? That's Luke's style, all over."

The sheriff leaned back in his chair. "I'll give it to you straight, just like you asked f'r. Not just 'someone.' You said he's a family man, but there's a gal over at the Nugget. Goes by the name of Jewel. If it's her true name, it's the second fancy thing 'bout her. F'r some reason, her and this fella've taken a shine to each other. Neither one'd be to my taste, but they say there's someone f'r everyone." The sheriff shrugged and shook his head. "What does concern me is he slaps her 'round right regular, but I can't get her to press charges so I c'n toss him in jail. Each time, she just says, 'Oh, he was a little drunk. It won't happen again.' But it always does. Can't rightly figure a woman not married to him puttin' up with it, but then I've never been a great one f'r figurin' women, anyhow."

Will stared at the sheriff, but his thoughts were backtrailing the years. *Had Luke* ... And he knew, with sudden sickness, that Luke had. Hannah had never so much as hinted at it during her time with Luke — or in the last months Will had been there — but a thousand unspoken clues, unheeded at the time, now shouted the truth so that he felt a surge of nausea and a burning shame along with a rage so violent that it shook him to the core. *How could he not have known?*

He realized Wolcott was getting to his feet. "Got to make the rounds. I'm late already. You comin'? I c'n take you by the livery and the saloon on my way."

Will, still light-headed with anger, stood. "Sheriff," he said tightly, "all this time you ain't called him by name. Why not?"

Wolcott, reaching for his hat, paused. "It appears ever'thin' fits, but one. He ain't goin' by 'Luke'."

Will's voice sounded far away, even to himself. "What is he goin' by?"

Wolcott held Will's rigid gaze. "He's goin' by 'Ben Clayton'."

The first few stops they made on the lawman's rounds were lost on Will as he tried to make sense of all Wolcott had revealed. Still fighting down anger so intense it blurred his vision — he would have his reckoning with Luke over Hannah — he concentrated doggedly on Luke's choice of a name. If that wasn't just like him, to take a clean, respected name and claim it for his own! As if so doing would somehow brighten his own soiled reputation ... Will doubted, now, that anything else Luke could stoop to do would surprise him. What would Ben say at knowledge of this latest betrayal by his son? And Anne ... ?

He was jolted out of his dismal thoughts by Wolcott's voice. "Here's the livery." They had halted in front of the stable where Will had earlier left Eagle. "Ben — Luke — he's prob'ly not here. He heads f'r the Nugget every night right at sundown. Or before." He stuck his head inside the doorway. "Hey, Dill! You here?"

From deep within the building an Irish voice boomed out, "Step in and see what's come my way, Sheriff!"

As they entered the dusky interior, the good smells of horse, leather and hay teased Will's nose and he wondered, fleetingly, if life would ever again offer him the everyday gift of stepping into a barn and feeling its comfort as he pursued his round of daily work.

The barrel-chested man who had taken Will's horse earlier motioned them forward. "Come see. But be easy now. He's spirited, this one is. Just got him today," he added proudly.

"Lord A'mighty, he's a beauty," Wolcott breathed. "Where'd you find him?"

Will, in silence, let the words flow past him as he gazed at the stallion before him. Muscles rippled beneath the gleaming black coat as the thoroughbred arched his neck at their approach. Seventeen hands high and every inch an aristocrat. He whickered as Will put out a slow hand for him to whiff. "Ain't another like him in the whole Territory, I'll wager," he offered, finally. The horse let him stroke the velvet muzzle, but pulled away from further caress. "You sellin' him?"

Dill Blaine laughed. "Not this one. Not yet. Annual county race is comin' up in two weeks. I just might have a chance this year."

"More'n a chance, I'd say," Will returned. With difficulty, he dragged himself back to the present and its burdens. "I got unfinished business," he reminded Wolcott.

The lawman, too, returned reluctantly to duty. "That's right," he sighed. "Dill, you seen Ben Clayton?"

Even aware as he was, the name jolted Will. The liveryman shook his head. "He left here same time as always. Headed f'r the saloon, I reckon. I heard tell he's been beatin' up on that gal of his again, that she's sportin' another black eye."

"Dill," the sheriff cut in hastily, "this is Will Braden, knows Ben's kin."

Dill shifted his feet apologetically. "Sorry, mister, if he's one of your'n. I didn't mean nothin'."

Will shook his head. "Luke's the one should be apologizin'. And I've put off gettin' to him long enough. You comin', Sheriff?"

Blaine looked confused and grabbed the sheriff's arm as he went past. " 'Luke'? I thought ..."

Wolcott pulled away. "I'll explain later. Right now, I got to keep an eye on this fella and make sure he's not spellin' big trouble. He's got a burr under his saddle, f'r sure." He hurried after Will, who was already on his way out the door. Catching up to him, he spoke sharply. "Now look here, mister. You got good reasons f'r what you're thinkin'. I ain't denyin' that. But I can't let you take the law into your own hands. This is my town. I'm paid to keep order in it, and that's what I aim to do. Don't start what can't be finished," he warned grimly, for Will had not paused or even glanced at the sheriff.

"Seems to me Luke started it a long time ago, and it's

way past time f'r someone to end it. Looks like I've drawn the short straw on this one."

Wolcott shook his head. "But you can't just bust in without a plan and without support."

Will stopped, then, and faced the sheriff, who smiled grimly. "Just remember, I've had time to get to know him, too. Even if not as long as you. Some folks don't take much learnin', just a whole lot of caution."

"It still has to be my mix, not yours," Will said slowly.

"Don't sound unreasonable, long as you don't start nothin'. Fact is, I'm obliged to arrest the first one to make trouble. As my Pa was fond of sayin', 'Don't throw the first punch, but be blasted sure you throw the last.' " He chuckled. "A smart man, my Pa. I'll be waitin' outside where Ben — Luke — can't see me. No use makin' your straw any shorter than it already is."

They halted outside the saloon doors that were standing open to the spring evening. Wolcott positioned himself to the side, where he could see and hear, but be unnoticed. Will, with a peculiar feeling in the pit of his stomach, now that the moment had actually come, stepped inside the Gold Nugget. The room was crowded, but he had no trouble spotting and hearing Luke straight off. He was busy haranguing the bartender over the skimpiness of the just-poured drink in front of him. The bartender was ignoring him, but the young woman at his side was trying to get him to sit at the nearest table. Will studied her curiously. She was short, blond, and verging on plumpness — in sharp contrast to Hannah's tall slenderness and gleaming black hair. Her voice was high-pitched in her anxiety to pull Luke away from impending trouble. Only when she turned and Will glimpsed her full-face, he saw the dark puffiness of her left eye. The here-now lightness in the pit of his stomach jelled into a sudden, cold lump of rage. Taking a fierce grip on his temper, reminding himself he had come too far to risk everything by a foolish display of anger, he stepped forward.

"Luke."

At sound of his name, Luke whirled, at the same time grabbing the woman so that she was placed between him and potential danger. As he recognized Will, the astonishment on his face would have been comical if Will wasn't already busy being disgusted at Luke's callous use of the woman as protection. *Some things never change.*

The blond, in her turn, was displaying justifiable confusion and fear. "Ben — what — ?"

"Shut up," he snarled, still keeping her positioned between Will and himself. He grinned wolfishly. "Well, well, if it ain't Will Braden! Is this a social call? Should I get out the cups and tea?"

"This is no social call, Luke. I think you know right well why I'm here." His glance flitted to the woman, now staring with her mouth open unbecomingly. "We need to talk private, Luke."

Luke chuckled and released his grip on the woman's arm. "Naw. This here's Jewel. Lives up to her name, she does. We're fine friends, ain't we, honey? Anythin' ol' Will's got to say, you c'n hear. 'Cept I don't think he's got nothin' to say to me worth hearin'."

Jewel closed her mouth enough to sputter, "But Ben, what's he talking about? Who's Luke?"

330

"Shut up!" he snarled again, and she subsided.

Will had been taking all this in, even as a thousand thoughts tangled in his mind. Hannah — but he mustn't think of her now and the pain this knowledge would cost her ... "I got plenty to say, and you're goin' to hear it, Luke."

With a smirk, Luke raised his shot glass of whiskey, saluted Will, and downed the contents. "This might be kind of interestin' after all. Go ahead, Will. Tell me what you think I should hear." He settled a hip on the table behind him and waited.

Will glanced once more at Jewel — it was Luke's choice. "You hurt a lot of people, leavin' like you did. Hannah, the boys ..."

"Hannah!" Luke spat the word. "What did she ever do f'r me except cause trouble whinin' and havin' all those brats of hers? Makin' me look bad in front of my folks so they'd blame me f'r ever'thin' when it was always her fault. Don't tell me 'bout Hannah!"

Jewel tried once more. "Who's Hannah? What brats? Ben ..." She got no further, for Luke stood and in the same motion backhanded her across the mouth.

"I said shut up!" he roared. The force of the blow knocked her backward even as a bright red stain smeared her lips.

Will sprang. Without conscious thought he leaped forward, grabbed Luke by the arm, spun him around, and smashed him in the mouth. It was Luke's turn to reel backward as bright red smeared his mouth. He crashed into the table, taking a chair with him as he plunged. Will, fists clenched, stood above him. "That one was f'r Hannah. Now come on, you coward. Get up and fight. You won't do it with someone who'll hit back, will you? Yellow!" he hissed. "Yellow clear through! Why I even bothered ..." He shook his head and glanced at Jewel, who was slumped by the bar, staring at him dazedly. "Can't say I much admire your taste in friends, ma'am." He turned on his heel and strode from the room.

As he reached the doorway, a roar from behind warned him. He had no time, however, to turn or step aside before Luke launched himself in a tackle that caught Will at the knees and barreled them both out the doorway onto the sidewalk. Twisting, Will managed to break Luke's hold, but before he could gain his feet, Luke was upon him again. Excessive drink and lack of hard work had softened Luke, but he was powered by such rage that Will had to use every ounce of energy in his own lean-muscled body just to keep on even terms with him. He managed to bring his knee up, just as Luke charged again. Pure satisfaction shot through him at the resulting on-target contact he made with Luke's groin. *That one's f'r Hannah, too*, he gloated as the bull-bellow of fury Luke emitted paled his other efforts into insignificance.

How long the fight might have gone on, Will never knew, for a sudden crack above his head deafened him momentarily. His next awareness was Sheriff Wolcott, Remington in hand and obviously ready to use it, hauling Luke back off him.

"On your feet, Ben — Luke — whichever you be. This is one night you will spend in jail!"

Luke fisted blood away from his mouth. "He started it! He attacked me inside the saloon!"

"And did he steal your candy, too? All I know is you was doin' the tacklin' when you both come flyin' out the door.

Did anyone see it any different?" He looked around at the figures who had gathered to watch the show. A muttering and shaking of heads answered him. Will glanced over to the lighted doorway. Jewel was standing there. She caught his eye, holding it a long moment before she fingered her swollen mouth, turned, and with bowed shoulders entered the saloon.

Will felt a strong hand grasp his arm as he tried to rise. "Sure now, and you do pack a punch," Dill Blaine was chuckling above him. "Glad not to be on the receivin' end of it, I'll tell you! Here, c'n you make it?" he asked anxiously as Will swayed. "We'll get you over to the livery and fixed up right smart." Will hesitated and Blaine chuckled again. "It's a privilege, man, to be assistin' the one who finally gave that black-hearted devil his comeuppance."

Wolcott, with Luke firmly in tow, paused beside Will. "Pa'd be proud, seein' his advice taken so good. Stop over at the office when you're repaired," he added, giving Luke a no-nonsense shove toward the jail.

Once Blaine got Will back to the livery, he took him to his office, brought water and a rag to blot the cuts on Will's face. "Don't look bad at all, under all the blood. You'll have a bruise or two, I'm bettin', or Kathleen ain't an Irish lass. One thing's sure, you won't be near as sore right now as Ben — Luke." He roared with laughter. "The look on his face! That'll pleasure my dreams f'r a long time to come!" He stood off and admired his ministrations. "You'll do, my friend. And now f'r the medicinal part of the treatment." He reached into a drawer and drew out a bottle. "Irish, of course. Only the finest f'r a fine occasion like this!"

In spite of the liveryman's praise, Will felt a deepening depression. Satisfactory as the physical contact had been in avenging Hannah, what had Will really accomplished? Only alienating Luke past any hope of reasoning with him.

Finally escaping Blaine's good-natured congratulations, Will stepped outside. The town was quiet, the sheriff's office showing one of the few lights now burning. Instead of heading that direction, however, Will turned east, away from the center of town. He wandered aimlessly for a time, past the hotel and the hardware and the general store where the freight wagons, their goods unloaded, had gone on to their next stop. And what would he do? Where — what — was his next stop?

For certain he had failed Hannah.

Whatever future they may have had — no matter how brightly it had gleamed — was now quenched under the bushel of Luke's existence.

What did you expect? he asked himself bitterly. *To find Luke conveniently dead so you and Hannah could live happily ever after? A child's tale — and you're not a child, even though you act foolish as one sometimes.*

He stopped to stare up at the night sky, recalling the evening he had left the Crescent C to begin this wild-goose chase. He had watched the light in Hannah's window shine brightly — a gleaming future beckoning them on. He remembered her willingness to give herself to him so they might have one moment of all their lives to remember — and his refusal in the certainty that the future held more for them than one stolen night ... More fool he!

He began wandering again, and slowly the bitter truth began taunting in his heart. He ignored it at first, but the

334

knowledge became more insistent. "I can't!" he gritted to the uncaring stars. "She'd be better off without him than with him!"

That's not for you to decide, the heart-voice said coldly. *That's her decision. You've made enough wrong choices to last a lifetime. How about letting her decide what's right for her? She at least deserves the right to make her own choice without more interference from you.*

"But ..."

What's the matter? the voice jeered. *Don't you trust her enough not to make a wrong decision?*

"I trust her to do what she feels is right." Will bowed his head. "That's why I'm so afraid."

Twenty-one

The sheriff's office showed a dim lamp-glow, but Will knew if he put off speaking to Luke now, he wouldn't find the courage to do it later. Only memory of Hannah, as he had held her in his arms that last night, kept him from turning away right then.

Wolcott looked up as Will opened the door. "Well, thought maybe you'd done your bit f'r justice and departed town." He motioned Will to take the same chair he had occupied earlier. "Coffee?" He waved the pot. "Spoon don't just stick up in it this time of night. It plain melts." At Will's refusal, he poured himself a cup, took a slug and grimaced. "Knew you f'r a smart man the first time you walked through that door." He dropped into his own chair. "We got to do some figurin'. You aimin' to press charges against our leadin' citizen, here?" He indicated Luke, snoring soggily in the cell beyond.

Will shook his head. "I threw the first punch, Sheriff."

"Not accordin' to my eye witnesses. Can't find one to say it was you first. Can't find one who saw anythin' except he backhanded the gal across the mouth. Me — I didn't see nothin'. I was behind the door and you two come flyin' out and he's got you in a full tackle. Like my Pa said 'bout first and last punches, he also give me some right good advice on takin' information and runnin' with it when you know you're right." He eyed Will. "I c'n do this job without you. It's just that your cooperation'd make things a sure-fire lot easier."

Will pushed back his chair. "You're goin' to have to go it without me, Sheriff. I've already done more'n my share of damage. What I want now is to talk to Luke one more time."

"But you tried talkin'. He didn't listen, in case you didn't notice."

"I noticed. But I still have to try one more time to convince him."

"Convince him of what, f'r God's sake?"

Will's mouth went dry. "To go home to his wife and five young ones, and try to make it work."

The sheriff refused to unlock the cell door and let Will in with Luke. "Any convincin' you c'n do c'n be done from this side of the bars. I still think you're plain loco."

Will was too busy agreeing with him to answer. He waited while Wolcott stood at the bars and yelled through Luke's drunken sleep. "Hey, Clayton, wake up! You got a visitor."

Luke stirred, mumbled, and yanked the blanket over his head.

"Clayton, up and at 'em. You got company!"

Luke threw off the blanket and peered blearily at the sheriff before his eyes fell on Will. The change in him happened so fast it was uncanny. One moment he was sitting on the side of the bunk, holding his head. The next instant he was gripping the bars of the cell as though it were Will's neck he was squeezing. The utter hatred on his face caused Will to step back involuntarily. "That's right," Luke snarled. "You keep your distance from me, you lousy, no-good son of a ..."

"There'll be none of that!" the sheriff cut in. "Will's here to talk to you sensible. I suggest you listen, less'n you want your mouth rearranged some more." He dropped his hand to his gun butt.

Luke gave him his best glare, but in the end turned back to Will. "What's the matter, Will? Too scared to fight your own battles, now that I licked you? And I did lick you! I'm surprised you ain't hightailed it clean back to Laramie by now."

Will took a deep breath — and a sharp grip on his temper. "I came to talk to you one more time 'bout you goin' back to the ranch — back to Hannah."

Luke started laughing so hard he swayed and would have lost his balance had he not backed up to the bunk and fallen onto it.

Will stared at him a long moment before he turned, and without a word or look for the sheriff, walked out of the office, that maniacal laughter following him down the street. What to do, where to turn? He lifted his hands curiously. They held steady in front of him without the faintest trace of a quiver. But neither was there any feeling in them. It was like times he had cut himself. He could see the slice, watch the blood ooze out and feel nothing — no pain of any kind. Before it would strike with full-fledged savagery.

Louise Lenahan Wallace

How long he wandered, he did not know. It didn't matter. He had a vague feeling it ought to matter. He couldn't have told why.

So much later that night it was actually early morning, he found himself lying in the hay of Blaine's loft. How had he gotten there? He had no memory of it. That didn't matter, either.

A sudden commotion in the stable area below reached his ears. "Braden! Will Braden, you still up there?" He recognized Blaine's voice, heard the urgency in it, and thought he should respond. Before he could make up his mind, Blaine's stricken face appeared at the top of the ladder. "Thank God you're here! I was out ridin' the stallion when the sheriff sent me lookin' f'r you. He wants you to ride out of town, now! Federal marshal's bringin' in some prisoners. He needs to use our jail, which means there ain't no room f'r Ben in it. Sheriff's lettin' him go. He wanted you warned first, so you c'n get out of town. Ben sees you, there'll be blood spilled f'r sure. Sheriff ain't so concerned 'bout Ben's, but he is kinda partial to you keepin' yours inside where it belongs. The marshal's due any minute. You gotta come now!" Even as he was speaking, Blaine was tugging Will toward the loft edge. The liveryman tumbled him down the ladder, almost pitching him on his head in the process. With practiced movements Blaine saddled Eagle and led him to the doorway. "Here you are, son. Now get aboard. And ride!" He flung the reins at Will.

Will realized, vaguely, that this man had been a friend to him and was still helping him. He put out his hand. "Thanks f'r all you've done. You're ever down Laramie way, look me up." He spied the black stallion standing saddled where Dill had tied him to the corral gate in his haste to find Will. Will strolled over and stroked the velvet muzzle. "Say, Blaine, you ever want to sell him ..."

"Oh, dear Lord!"

Blaine's horrified exclamation broke off Will's aimless attempt at politeness. "Jesse let him go. He's headin' this way. You best ride, mister!" Once more he flung Eagle's reins at Will.

It was a futile gesture. Luke had spied Will standing at the corral gate, and charging him at a dead run, was upon him before Will could react. "No way in Hell!" Luke yelled. "This is one thing you ain't gettin'!" Shoving Will aside, Luke snatched the stallion's reins, flung himself into the saddle, and dug his heels into the glossy black flanks. For one endless instant, nothing happened. Until the stallion reared, pawing the clouds with his hooves. With a long-drawn scream, the horse came to earth and was gone like dynamite exploding. Luke, living up to his claim to fame as "the best rider this side of Hell," managed to stay in the saddle for about twenty-five yards before the animal gave a wicked sunfish twist that lifted all four of his feet off the ground. Luke, still groggy with drink, never had a chance. He flew up, out, and over the enraged animal, landing directly beneath the flailing front hooves. The stallion screamed again and shot on down the street, scattering early rising citizens like chaff, leaving a huddled bundle lying horribly still in the settling dust.

In that instant, the long-delayed pain struck Will — a giant fist clutching and squeezing his insides — spawning the sensation that the motions of his body were not his own.

Running to Luke on booted feet that seemed nailed to the ground. Reaching him. Kneeling in the dirt where he lay sprawled on his side, eyes half-open. Thinking at first he was already dead. Turning Luke onto his back. Raising his head. Touching Luke's skull. His hand coming away sticky-dark.

"Luke," he said fiercely, "c'n you hear me?" In the growing dawn light, Luke's eyes stared from his gray-bleached face. When Will shook him, the eyes dragged wide, peered up at him. His lips parted, but not in the spasm of pain Will expected. Unbelieving he listened to Luke chuckle.

"Will. No way ... you gonna have a better horse ... than me. I won't be ... second to no ... man!" The old boast was a weak cry. "Guess I'm done. Hell of a time ... while it lasted."

There's no remorse in him, Will thought dismally. *Would even death have no effect on him?*

"Luke, you hurt a lot of people, leavin' like you did. Hannah — "

"Hannah." His voice was a thread. "Never gave me ... chance ... to prove I was ... man. Held me back ... whatever I wanted ... to do." His voice strengthened in a sudden rush of anger. "Her fault ... all ... her fault."

"Don't blame Hannah," Will said coldly. He would not let Luke go to his grave heaping all the guilt on her.

But Luke's mind, fading, had switched directions. "Four boys. Showed her ... I was man ... in one way. Best way. Especially when I ... knew she hated it."

Do you hit a dyin' man? Will wondered bleakly. *No, not even Luke.*

"There's another baby, a girl this time." With supreme effort, Will kept his voice steady.

Day Star Rising

Luke's eyes, dulling, stared up at Will. "Girl? You and Hannah?" Again that horrible chuckle, but this time abruptly stilled as his head fell back, his eyes staring at nothing.

Will, stomach churning, lowered him to the ground. Swallowing hard, he fought back the urge to throw up.

Unrepentant even in death, blaming Hannah to the bitter end, accusing her with his last breath of being unfaithful — yes, that was Luke — the way he had ever been. Why should a little matter like death change him?

Will looked up — straight at Jewel. He had not even realized she was there. Her eyes held his for a long moment before she slowly bowed her head over Luke's body.

Will put his hand up, felt the stickiness of blood already drying, stared at it numbly. Luke's blood — on his hands. *No!* he told himself violently. And felt a sudden great weight drop from his soul. His search was over. He could face Hannah with a clear heart.

He could go home. *Home — to Hannah.* It was his one lucid thought as he stepped away from Luke's body.

"Will." The word cut across his awareness, sharp as a knife slash. Sheriff Wolcott was blocking his path, his way home to Hannah. "Will, come to the office with me. Right now." His voice brooked no argument, although it seemed to come from a distance. Strange, when the man was standing directly in front of him.

But he was the sheriff. *The sheriff must be obeyed.* Will dragged that thought up from somewhere. Obediently, but awkwardly because his legs suddenly seemed unable to bear his weight, he followed the sheriff through the crowd of curious, silent — curiously silent? — citizens. A man with a

343

black bag hurried past them, followed by a fellow in a tall hat and black suit. They knelt, conferring over the body where Jewel still huddled in the dusty street.

Once inside the office, Wolcott pushed Will into the chair he had previously occupied and handed him a cup of coffee. "Drink." Again Will obeyed because it was easier than making his own brain function enough to make a decision.

The coffee was scalding, thick, and liberally laced with whiskey. The thought poked up its head that, with all this coffin varnish being pushed into him, he'd be as soused as Luke before he was done. *Luke* ... Will thrust the thought away. Slowly, awareness sank in of the other occupant of the office — a burly man wearing the star of a federal marshal. The two badges conferred while Will drank the rest of the coffee.

"Will, you hearin' me?" He looked up to Sheriff Wolcott's anxious face.

"I'm hearin' you."

"Will, we need you to tell us just what happened out there. Take your time, but fill us in on ever'thin' you c'n think of."

Will almost chuckled at the sheriff's choice of words. Think? Fortunately — or unfortunately — the whiskey-laced coffee had done its work and a semblance of reality was returning. In clipped sentences, Will related the facts.

"That's it? He charged you, grabbed the horse and took off? You didn't do nothin' to him first?"

Will shook his head. The badges conferred some more, and Wolcott said decisively, "That's it, then. Your story and Dill Blaine's agree. The whole thing was unprovoked on your part. The horse was just too full of vinegar. An accident, plain and simple."

Something clicked in Will's reviving brain. "C'n we get a paper sayin' that he died accidental?"

Wolcott picked up his pen. "I'll write one out right now. Hodges, here, and me c'n both sign it. That should be official enough f'r anyone." As the pen scratched on paper, Will knew one more item remained undone. Did he want to do it? In total honesty, no. The images of Hannah and five small faces floated to him. Would he do it? Yes.

As if in confirmation of Will's decision, the office door opened and the black-suited figure who had been hurrying to Luke's side earlier strode in. He gazed at the solemn faces and said quietly, "Jesse, I need to know what to do with the body. You have any instructions?"

Wolcott gestured to Will. "This here's Will Braden. He's the one to speak f'r the next-of-kin, not me. Will, this is Ingram, owns the local funeral parlor."

Will rose, awkwardly. The undertaker extended his hand. "I'm sorry to intrude, but I do need to know your wishes."

Will shook his head. "You're not intrudin'. I appreciate you takin' care of what needs to be done." Before his resolve wavered, he dug into his jeans pocket. His ten dollar lucky gold piece lay cool on his palm as he summoned to mind his father, bearded and barrel-chested, ever the dreamer, pressing the gleaming coin into his son's hand just before he rode away on that long-gone spring day. He thought of his mother, paying for her husband's dreams with her own brand of quiet courage. He, Will, who was both of them, now faced his own truth: For every dream the price must be paid. By someone. He, too, had dreamed. And now the cost was before him.

Louise Lenahan Wallace

He laid the coin on the sheriff's desk. "See to it he has a Christian burial, Sheriff." He turned to go. Wolcott pressed the paper into his hand. Without reading it, Will stuck it in the pocket that had held the gold piece. Nodding to Ingram, he descended the steps into the morning sunshine. Dill Blaine was waiting with Eagle. Will took the proffered reins and swung into saddle. Without glancing back, he guided the chestnut out of town at a fast walk.

Epilogue

Will arrived back at the ranch on a late afternoon. He felt so incredibly old and weary it was hard to believe he had been gone only six weeks. Six weeks that had changed his life forever. After leaving Sunset he had ridden long and far. But he had discovered, as on the day of Eve's wedding, that he couldn't outrun himself or change what he had left behind. Hannah's husband was dead because of him.

He had deliberately gone searching for Luke. Well, he had found him. And the consequences were now burned into his soul, forever.

A stop in a town whose name and description would ever be a blank. A scalding bath as though he could scrub his spirit clean of the lingering sense of guilt; a shave and haircut to restore him to his rightful place in society, and the first of the shell of horror began to crumble. He could, after all, only try to make peace with his own heart, not take Luke's sins upon himself as well.

He scarcely knew what he was going to say to Hannah. How do you tell a woman whose husband had died violently that his last words were a sneer on her fidelity, his last breath a chuckle at the thought?

As he sat, now, watching the scene before him, he just didn't know what he was going to tell her. How much his the right to protect? How much hers the right to know? What would such knowledge do to five innocent children?

Hannah and the four boys were in the garden. A basket in the shade of a cottonwood indicated Phebe, too, was nearby. Isaac was energetically pulling weeds alongside Jeremy, but Sam and Micah were teasing him, tickling the back of his neck with a long, feathery weed.

Even at that distance, his bellow came clearly to Will. "Cut that out! I'm tryin' to work!"

As he watched, for the first time in days a faint trace of a grin eased the harshness from Will's face. Memory stirred of that evening so many months ago when he had first come to this ranch. "We've both gotten a lot older since then, Isaac," he muttered.

Dismounting, leading Eagle, he started slowly down the slope. Jeremy, strong and brown and well again, caught sight of him and let out a whoop. "Mr. Braden, Mr. Braden!" He hurtled himself into Will's arms. The other boys, seeing, came at a run.

Isaac threw his arms around Will's legs. "I knew you'd come back. I knew you would!" He dug into his pocket. "See, I kept it f'r you. Just like I promised Ma." He laid the pocketknife on Will's palm. The little boys, straggling up, clung to Will in sheer exuberance of spirits. They didn't totally understand why he had reappeared so suddenly, but they entered gladly into the spirit of the moment anyway.

Over their heads Will saw Hannah, the spring breeze

tugging at her yellow skirt, come slowly up, to stop before she reached him. He stared, puzzled, before he realized she had changed her hairstyle. The knot at the nape of her neck was gone. Her hair was now coiled in two thick braids at the back of her head — a gleaming black coronet that softened her features and brought back youthfulness to a face grown too soon old. After a startled second he realized he liked it very much.

Her eyes held relief, but terrible questioning, too. She had lost weight from an already slender frame, and he knew he could only guess at what she had endured these past weeks — just as she would never fully comprehend all he had undergone.

Gently putting the boys aside, he suggested they finish their work, then they would be able to play. Obediently, they scurried off. Wordlessly, then, he faced her. And he still didn't know how to tell her.

"Luke ..."

Slowly he shook his head. "He's dead, Hannah."

She must have known already, but the words were still a shock. She stared at him, her eyes enormous. "Did you ..."

"No, I didn't."

She stared at him another long moment before her face crumpled and she turned away, shoulders bowed.

He could not comfort her. She had a right to her pain that he could not intrude upon.

But neither could he bear to see her hurting. He took a step toward her and put a hand on her shoulder. "Hannah."

She turned and he saw her deep torment. "I hated him. And now he's dead. I've wondered so many times how it would feel to have someone stand in front of me and say those words: 'He's dead.' And now you have and I don't know what I feel." Her voice broke but she rushed on. "I hated him. I suppose I should feel shame for that, but I just can't. I did love him, once. I couldn't be married to him for seven years and have five children with him and not love him. It just hurts so to know what we might have had. We just missed, somehow."

What might have been ... How well Will understood.

She began to cry, deep wracking sobs. He drew her into his arms, cradling her head against his shoulder.

At last her breaths eased. She raised her head and wiped at her cheeks with the backs of her hands. "I'm sorry."

He pushed his neckerchief into her hands. "Prob'ly even dirtier and smellier than before, but it'll do the job. Don't be sorry. Reckon you had a right to do that. You've had an awful load to carry."

"Will, what happened with Luke?"

At the wariness in his eyes, she stiffened and drew back. "Tell me. You must. I have to know."

Drawing a deep breath, looking straight into her eyes he told, as simply and briefly as he could, about finding Luke. But not about Jewel. What would have been the use of that except to add more hurt? Besides, Hannah was no fool.

She listened without flinching as he described how Luke had looked and acted. He was the one who faltered, then, hunting the words that would hurt her the least.

She was pale, her hands clasping the neckerchief tightly, "Go on."

So he told her, as gently as he could, about Luke's pushing

him aside to ride the stallion and about there being nothing anyone could do when he lost control of the animal. About reaching him in the few moments before he died.

"Did he say anything?"

"Somethin' 'bout the boys and you. He was mutterin' mostly, and it didn't make much sense." The truth, total and complete. What Luke had actually said had made no sense at all to Will.

She drew a shuddering breath. "And that was all?"

Speaking slowly, he simply, clearly told her his knowledge that if he hadn't persisted like he had in his efforts to force Luke to return to the ranch after his initial refusal, Luke would still be alive.

In total silence, she listened. He faltered to a stop. The silence stretched. In that unbroken stillness, the crackle of paper was loud as he pressed the sheet into her hands. "It gives the date he died 'of a fall from a wild horse.' But — now you know why." *The price must be paid* ... sometimes with interest ... by giving her a chance to make her own decision based on full knowledge of the facts. But would stamping the debt "Paid in Full" also stamp out any hope of a future for them? Would he take back those words if he could? Frantic, futile questions, now ...

She looked long at the paper before she raised her head, and his heart twisted wickedly at the undisguised pain in her eyes. "If it's any help," he said desperately, "I told them to give him a Christian burial. They said they would."

"A Christian burial? After all he ..." Her words faded into nothing and she stared beyond Will's shoulder into a past he could not see.

"Hannah." The desperation in his voice brought her once more to awareness of his presence.

"I can't! I just can't forgive and forget that easily! You don't know how he used to — what he used to do to me — and then laugh and laugh because he was stronger."

As her voice choked off, all his resolve crumbled. "Hannah," he said brokenly, "I'm sorry. I didn't know until this trip. But I know now. I found out when he was doin' some of his fancy braggin'. I swear to God I wanted to kill him with my bare hands."

Wordlessly, she stared at the naked hatred on his face as he rushed on. "And I shouldn't have expected you could just toss it out the door like yesterday's dishwater. I thought, maybe, it would give us a chance — you, me, the young ones — if we set it straight as we could with him and I could show you how it'd never be that way with you and me." He pushed out the final, bleak words. "I'll go now."

He turned away. From her. From their future. From their lives ...

"Will!" The anguish in her voice was the utterance of the raw pain in his own heart.

Even as he turned, he felt her hand on his arm, twisting him back around to her.

"No, Will! It wasn't your fault! But if my not forgiving him means losing you — You can't ... I can't ... I won't let you go. Not like this!" She flung herself into his arms, burying her face against his chest.

As her full meaning enveloped him, a sudden lump closed his throat. He swallowed hard. But before he could push any words out, they found a much more efficient means of communication. She raised her head even as he lowered his mouth to hers. As their lips met, all doubt, all fear melted into knowledge that this was good, and right, and forever. Finally, with a wordless murmur of rapture, she nestled her head on his shoulder. His arms encircled her tightly, even as his own heart echoed her sigh of joy.

He pressed his cheek against her gleaming hair. "A man could get mighty spoiled, a homecoming like this," he said gruffly. "Do you intend to repeat this very often?"

She tucked her face closer into his neck. "Only as often as you come home," she confessed. "Can you forgive me?"

He put her from him just enough that he could look into her eyes. "I'm the one who needs your forgiveness, not the other way 'round. The way he was, I should of realized how he was treatin' you."

"Will, no! We both have to put it into the past, and know that it is in the past. Forever." She paused. "You look so weary. This trip was so hard for you." She gently touched his cheek.

"I'm all right, now I'm back here with you. But after all that's happened, maybe it's not best f'r you right now. Maybe you need some time. I don't want to be unfair."

"Will, I told you I loved Luke. I did. When we were first married, at least. I tried so hard to be a good wife to him. But he turned against me. With everything else, he walked out on me — left me, left the boys without giving a thought about how we'd get along. For me, I think he really died that day. I can't spend the rest of my life or let my children spend theirs suffering for what he did. He left us to make our lives, and that's just what we're going to do. And I'm not going to feel guilty about it!" She stopped, out of breath.

His arms tightened about her. "You are quite a woman, Hannah Clayton."

She smiled wistfully. "Not really. I just wish I was." She hesitated. "What about you and Eve?"

"Me and Eve?"

"I know she was very special to you."

He was silent for a long minute. How to explain? "Yes," he said finally, "she was. But what we had — it's over. It was over a long time ago. I just wouldn't admit it. And I was wrong. I'm not sorry I loved her. Because what she and I had makes what you and I have now just that much better. C'n you understand?"

She searched his face and saw written plainly there all the love and tenderness he had to give her. "Yes, I can understand. And accept that. It's the same with Luke and me. Not the same love. But richer and stronger because of it." She tried to smile. "I used to be so jealous of Eve. She had so much, it seemed to me, and I had ..." Her voice trailed off.

Seeing his amazement, she laughed ruefully.

"I never knew," he murmured. "I never realized. But, believe me, you don't have to be, ever again." His eyes reflected all the love she felt in her own heart.

"Because you say so, I believe you." As she raised her head to meet his kiss, a jubilant cry lifted behind them. Startled, they turned to see Jeremy standing near the corner of the house.

"Ma, Mr. Braden, look!" Clear and joyous, his call floated to them. Swiveling to the direction he was pointing they saw, beyond doubt, that springtime had come at last.

Sometime, silently and unheeded these past dreary days, the lilac had burst into glorious bloom.

About the Author

Biography

In her hometown of Port Angeles, Wash., Louise Lenahan Wallace is a former editor of *Footnotes*, her state square dance magazine.

Day Star Rising is the sequel to *The Longing of the Day,* also available from the GRIT Fireside Library. Her other publishing credits include two stories in GRIT, *Eight Letters* (July 14, 1996) and *The Ten-Cent Christmas*

Louise Lenahan Wallace

(Dec. 26, 1999); and one in *Chicken Soup for the Single's Soul*. Louise earned a bachelor's degree from Western Washington University in 1992.

Publishers acknowledgment

Published by Ogden Publications
1503 SW 42nd St., Topeka, Kansas 66609

Edited by Angela Moerlien, lead editor, and Andrew Perkins,
associate editor. Cover design by Diane Rader

Photography by Angela Moerlien. Cover's flowers and
sun from *GRIT* Photo Library. Gold Liberty
dollars by Larry Tekamp, Dayton, Ohio

Publishing Credit:

Lines from *Wuthering Heights*, by Emily Bronte, public domain, Random
House, Inc.